Mermaids of Eriana Kwai
Book One

ICE MASSACRE

Rogue Cannon Publishing
Canada

First published in Canada in 2014
Rogue Cannon Publishing, Abbotsford, BC

tianawarner.com

Praise for Ice Massacre

★ "... thought provoking and intelligent ... fresh and thoroughly entertaining ... Warner does a fantastic job creating a tight plot and masterfully creates a sense of atmosphere through subtle yet potent descriptions ... Ice Massacre is a truly exceptional book."

— *Foreword* Clarion Reviews, 5-star review

★ "Fascinating, unique, scary and written with a beautiful economy of words..."

— 23rd Annual Writer's Digest Self-Published Book Awards

Winner: 2016 Best Indie Book Award, Young Adult
First Place Winner: Dante Rossetti Awards 2014
Foreword 10 Best Indie YA novels of 2014
Foreword Reviews' 2014 INDIEFAB Book of the Year Finalist

Dedications

To Dad, whose knowledge about obscure geography and weather and hunting weapons proved to be not so useless, after all.

To Mom, for so many positive words of encouragement I actually don't know what to do with all of them.

To Steph, my #1 source of feedback and the Lucy to my Ethel.

My deepest, most heartfelt gratitude to all the wonderful people in my life who've supported my lofty ambition.

The young man aimed his crossbow at the water, ready to fire a bolt of solid iron at the first glimpse of flesh beneath the surface.

"Sir," he said, "shouldn't we have seen one by now?"

The captain turned his back to the salty wind, jaw tight. "They know we're here."

"So what are they doing?"

He followed the captain's gaze. Blackness merged with the empty grey horizon in every direction. A long silence passed, filled only by gentle swells lapping against the ship.

The captain drew his own crossbow.

"Forming a plan."

All twenty men aboard the ship readied their weapons, reacting in a chain until the last man at the stern took steady aim at the waves.

"Make ready your iron, men," shouted the captain. "We have ripples approaching off the port side."

A handful of places in the water puckered, as if something lingered just below the surface. The sea was too black to tell.

Then it happened. Fifty, maybe sixty sea demons burst from the water and slammed against the ship. The men wasted no time. They reacted with trained speed and agility as the demons thrust stones and jagged shells into the wood, both to break holes in the ship and to scale the sides. The men picked them off with bolts of iron and watched them fall one by one back into the sea.

But they were outnumbered. Soon the demons were upon the ship, pulling themselves across the deck with bony arms.

The young man had already shot a dozen and the water reddened with each passing second.

Slow scraping sounds threatened him from behind. He whirled around, crossbow ready. Burning eyes met his, and sharp teeth, bared to rip into his flesh. He gripped the trigger, felt the bow tighten—

And the demon was gone. The young man stared into the wide gaze of a girl his own age. With a startled cry, he jerked his aim so the bolt barely missed her.

She held a black shell in her hand, sharp at the edges and ready to use as a club. But she didn't raise it. She just looked at him.

He lowered his crossbow.

Her blonde hair fell heavily over her shoulders, dripping beads of water down her naked chest and stomach, pooling where her torso joined her tail.

He blinked, but made no other motion—*where her torso joined her tail.* Scales faded into flesh like some sort of beautiful, green and tan sunset.

She pulled herself closer.

"Stay back," said the young man, unsure what prompted him to hesitate.

He looked into her eyes—emeralds surrounded by pearl white—where moments ago they had burned red. Her sharp teeth had retracted behind rosy lips. The seaweed-coloured flesh of her upper body was now olive and raised with goose bumps from the icy wind.

"*Hanu aii,*" she whispered. *Do not fear.* She spoke his language.

He loosened his grip on the crossbow, studying her. She lifted a frail arm and pushed the hair from her eyes, then motioned him forwards.

His pulse quickened as he stared at the beautiful girl.

"*Hanu aii,*" she said again, her voice resonating sweetly, as if she sang without singing.

Suddenly, he was kneeling in front of her, level with her luminous eyes. The sounds around him faded but for the soft purr in the base of her throat.

She reached up and held an icy hand to his cheek, not for a moment breaking eye contact. The hand slid behind his head and pulled his face towards hers, slowly but firmly. He inhaled her sweet breath.

"No!"

He flinched. He turned to see the captain racing towards them, aiming his crossbow at the maiden.

The young man grasped the scene around him. The ship was empty. A few stray weapons and barrels bobbed serenely in the water. Blood soaked the deck in places, and even the main mast had a splatter across the bottom.

The captain fired wide. Before he could reload and aim again, the sea demon put a hand on the young man's chin and pulled his gaze back to hers.

Her eyes blazed red. Her skin rippled into the rotten colour of seaweed. Her ears grew pointed and long like sprouting coral. She opened her mouth to reveal a row of deadly teeth.

The young man screamed.

The demon pulled him against her with more strength than three men combined, and they dove headfirst off the side of the ship.

They disappeared into the blood-red water.

CHAPTER ONE

Tomorrow

A mermaid hunter must be aggressive, bold, and, more importantly, nimble on her feet—because her feet are the only advantage she has over a mermaid.

That, and her iron crossbow.

"Again," I said, wiping an arm across my sweaty forehead. I cranked the lever, dropped an iron bolt against the shaft, and hitched the crossbow up to my shoulder with practiced speed.

Annith braced herself against her knees, her frizzy hair plastered to her face. "Can we catch our breath for a second?"

I gritted my teeth. No, we could not catch our breath. Not when at this time the next day I could be taking my last one, sprawled on the red-stained deck of our ship and watching a demon eat my insides.

Annith must have read my expression, because she straightened up for another round.

Five years had passed since my training began. Along with nineteen other girls, they'd pulled me from my education before I had a chance to go to high school. I spent every day of those five years—days that should've consisted of math, science, and literature—learning to sail, survive, and murder.

For those five years, we'd mourned our losses as twenty men were sent out each spring and never came back. Now it was my turn. And things were going to be different.

It was our final day of the training program and I ran drills with Annith on The Enticer, a warship that'd been rotting in the forest for longer than anyone could remember. It was the most famous landmark on the island, if you could call any part of Eriana Kwai famous. Whoever built it put painstaking effort into the carvings on the helm, and it had obviously been a beautiful ship in its time. When the Massacres had begun nearly thirty years ago, they'd patched up the decaying parts and used the ship as a place dubbed the Safe Training Base.

Only fifth-year warriors, those who were eighteen, got to use The Enticer. The younger years trained on the rest of the old campground, which had been built around the landmark ship. Cabins had been converted to classrooms for first aid, survival skills, and sailing and combat theory. The dining hall had been cleared for hand-to-hand combat. A glade once used for campfires and games had been systematically destroyed for fitness drills. The archery pit proved convenient for dagger and crossbow practice. The pool was meant for swimming lessons, though that was optimistic, since if anyone was in the water she was probably about to become lunch.

Annith hurled beanbags at me as I shot the mermaid-shaped slats of wood erected across the deck. I hit five in the heart and dodged just as many beanbags when Anyo, the training master, called my name.

"Your report card, Meela."

I heard Annith's sigh of relief.

"You're totally ready," she said between breaths. "Don't tire yourself out before tomorrow."

My strained nerves wouldn't let me agree as we hopped off the deck—a short drop to the spongy forest floor. I shook loose my sweaty ponytail, attempting to comb out the chocolate-brown mats before piling it back atop my head.

Anyo handed us each a flimsy piece of paper. The first year we'd gotten them, I thought they must have been a sick joke. How could they give us report cards? Wasn't it enough to send us out to sea, knowing that if we failed to learn, we would fail to survive?

I skimmed the page. I'd achieved an *A* in nearly everything. My only *B* was in First Aid. *B*, for *Barely Ready*. Every time we talked about lacerations or broken bones, the thought of so much blood made me squeamish and light-headed.

"We'll make a good team," said Annith, peering at my report card. "I got an *A* in First Aid, but only a *C* in Rigging."

C, for *Clinging to Survival.*

I glanced at the bottom of my card and saw an *A+* next to Rigging. What did that tell me? I could work the ship, but so help me if I sliced myself open in the process.

A loud voice cut across the glade. "I got a hundred percent in Combat!"

I had no doubt Dani spoke extra loudly to ensure everyone heard. She flipped her sleek mane of hair over her shoulder and stood taller, as if ready to pose for a photo of her shining moment.

"Paper proof that you're terrifying with sharp objects," I said under my breath.

Annith turned away from Dani. "I'm so not surprised she got that mark. I hated being her partner. I thought she was going to finish me off for real."

"Bet she would've if Anyo wasn't watching."

"What'd you get, Meela?" yelled Dani, fixing me with narrowed eyes. "For your parents' sake, I hope you at least passed everything. I'd hate for them to lose another one."

I shot her a glare. "Eat—"

"Meela!" said Annith. "Ignore her."

"Does she not realise I'm holding a crossbow?" I looked down and noticed my knuckles had tightened over the grip.

Dani set her pouty lips, looking satisfied. She turned back to Shaena, Texas, and Akirra—the handful of toadies she liked to call friends—and gushed about how she couldn't wait to apply combat to 'real prey'.

Texas—nicknamed because her father tended the island cattle, and she was the only girl on the island who could rope a cow from the back of a horse—asked Dani if she'd practiced with the iron daggers.

"You have to stab forwards like this," said Dani loudly, jabbing towards Shaena's stomach. "My father taught me this years ago. He says if you can get it right into their gut ..." She mimicked gripping the invisible dagger in Shaena's stomach with two fists. ". . . and twist it, it'll split them right open."

She rotated her hands as though grinding an actual dagger through bone, her teeth gritted. Annith and I exchanged looks of repulsion as Shaena tried the same thing on Texas.

"All right, girls," said Anyo, breaking up the invisible carnage. "Line up for your badges."

I was about to hang up my training crossbow for the last time when something caught my eye. A fat rabbit emerged from the bushes, sniffing the ground.

"Move," I whispered to Annith.

She obeyed.

I notched a bolt and raised the crossbow. The bow steadied as I exhaled. I squeezed the trigger slightly, but not enough to plunge the iron bolt into the rabbit's furry ribcage.

Turn it off, I ordered myself, just as the training master had been telling me since I was thirteen.

I imagined black tar melting over my heart to seal in any emotion.

Jaw clenched, I pulled the trigger. The rabbit didn't have time to spring forwards before it fell over dead, a bolt thick as its front leg buried in its side.

Lowering my crossbow, I turned to Annith and smiled. "Dinner."

"Well done, Meela!" said Anyo, no doubt delighted with the girl who couldn't so much as squish a spider five years prior.

Eyrin, a frail girl who hadn't said more than a few words in all the years I'd known her, was standing in front of Anyo and looked like she couldn't decide whether to be appalled or impressed by my kill.

The correct response would have been to feel excited and inspired. Turning my face away from the group, I picked the rabbit up by its back feet. I couldn't look directly at it. The black tar over my heart started to drip away.

"Does your family need some?" I said to Annith, holding up the rabbit.

"No. My father caught a deer like, three days ago, so we're good for a while."

"Oh," I said, impressed and slightly jealous. I much preferred deer meat to rabbit.

I hung my crossbow on the rack, hovering for a moment. I wondered how the brand new weapons would feel in comparison. I wondered, too, how it would feel to battle on the wooden slats of a new ship, rather than on the familiar but uneven model beached on the ancient forest floor.

We lined up to get our badges.

"I've never had this much confidence in a group of warriors," said the training master. "I thank the gods every day for the privilege of training you."

I knew the committee wanted to sack him after the strategy he'd tried a few years prior. But his stubbornness was the reason he survived his own Massacre, and he refused to back down.

"As women, you have an edge the opposition won't expect," he said. "Without the power of allure, a mermaid's prowess is limited to her skill in combat. And from what you've shown me, your skill falls nothing short of remarkable."

"Do you think they'll send their men when they realise we're girls?" said Annith.

Texas scoffed. "Obviously not. Demons don't train their men for battle."

Anyo nodded. "As far as we know, that's correct. Mermen don't possess the same allure—or the drive to hunt."

"They're like lions," said Shaena. "The girls do all the work. All the guys do is eat and make babies."

A wave of laughter passed over us.

Anyo flushed. "Right. Well, review your notes tonight before you go to sleep. Throw a knife against a target to make sure your motor skills are sharp. Don't forget to wear your badge tomorrow over your uniform. And eat a big breakfast."

"Then it's time to spill some mermaid guts!" said Shaena.

I took a deep breath, my nerves and excitement in a full-blown fistfight in my stomach. I wanted to believe this Massacre would be different. Maybe twenty skinny teenage girls did stand a better chance than the men we'd sent out every year in recent history.

I scanned the warriors around me, the girls who'd become my family over the last five years. We were as ready as we'd ever be.

Maybe because of us, Eriana Kwai would finally taste freedom again. We'd be able to go fishing, maybe even catch enough to export some for a profit, like we did before I'd been born. We'd be a self-sufficient nation again, not a pathetic mass of rock relying on the dry and canned donations of the few Canadians and Americans who remembered we existed.

First in line, Dani pinned her badge to her jacket before whirling around to beam at Texas. She glanced down at the rabbit in my fist and wrinkled her nose. I expected a snarky comment, but she said nothing. I wondered what her family would be eating for dinner that night.

The training master presented me with a copper badge. I studied the handcrafted engraving of the northern saw-whet owl. My people had put so much time, effort, and faith into me. Too much. My throat tightened, like the butterflies in my stomach had tried to fly out and gotten lodged.

Anyo's hand squeezed my shoulder and I lifted my gaze. His dark eyes were serious, and the lines on his face stood out in the dim light peeking through the trees. It made him look wise, and tough. Up close, I could follow the line on his scalp and ear where a mermaid had once torn his skin clean off.

"Remember to turn off your emotions and you'll be unbeatable," he said, voice low for my ears only. "I shouldn't say this, but your skill surpasses your brother's. Nilus would have been proud."

The mention of Nilus—and the idea of someone being proud of me—made my stomach clench with guilt.

I managed a stiff nod. I waited for Annith to get her badge, and when she met up with me, nerves had turned her face a little green.

"I'd better get this rabbit home for dinner," I said, then added hesitantly, "See you tomorrow."

She looked afraid to open her mouth in case she vomited.

As I traipsed home, I thought of the Massacre in light of the privilege it brought and tried to suppress the feelings gnawing at my insides. I'd been given an opportunity to honour my family and my people, to slaughter the demons that took the lives of so many innocent men. I would get to bury iron bolts in their hearts like I did the rabbit dangling from my fist—only the demons, at least, deserved it.

"I'm sorry," I whispered to the rabbit, still not looking at it.

The dirt road led to a dead end where my driveway sat. The house, modest compared to the greatness of the surrounding trees, greeted me with a soft blow of smoke from the chimney. My parents and I lived safely inland. All the beachfront homes had been abandoned after the mermaids came in from the Atlantic. In our mossy glade, the giant cedars rarely let the sunlight warm us. Sunlight wasn't common, anyway, on Eriana Kwai, because the clouds always ran into the Queen Charlotte Mountains and emptied their rain on us.

I hesitated with one foot on the front step. *Gaawhist*, read the sign on the door. *Home, sweet home.* I turned and went around to the backyard, as though I could pause time if I moved slowly enough.

At the edge of the cliff, I flopped onto the grass and looked down the rocky slope to the beach. Two orcas glistened in the distance, and beyond that, the small protrusion of Haida Gwaii.

We were alone on Eriana Kwai. Few people came, few people left, and in my whole life, few ships had dared to cross this far north in the Pacific Ocean.

Watching a pair of seagulls float below, I felt nostalgic for the beach. I curled my toes. I wanted to feel the pebbles beneath them instead of the insoles of hard leather boots. I wanted to feel the crusty salt in my hair, and even the slimy seaweed as it wrapped around my legs. Something about those sensations was simple, and it calmed me.

Footsteps rustled behind me.

I pressed my face into the grass. *Not now.*

I didn't turn, but seconds later, Tanuu flattened out next to me. From the corner of my eye, I saw him fold his arms and prop himself up so he could stare at the side of my face.

Reluctantly, I turned to him. The whites of his eyes popped against his dark skin and hair.

"It sure came up fast," he said softly.

"No. I've been waiting for this since I was ten."

And I don't feel any better about going.

He must have misinterpreted the bitterness in my voice, because he said, "I know you'll return home. You're trained for this. You can kill a crow before I'd even be able to aim. I've seen it."

I rested my chin on my arms and gazed at the darkening horizon.

"Look," said Tanuu. "I'm not happy about you going. It should be me, and Haden, and all the other guys graduating next month. If the training program hadn't made the change, I'd be the one going on the Massacre."

He was right. If I weren't going, it'd be him, and I knew I had a much better chance of surviving than he did. I pressed my lips together in an almost-smile.

"Here," he said.

A clover was pinned between his fingers, and he held it out to me. I looked from the clover to his dark eyes, then took it. It had four leaves.

"Make a wish."

I twirled it between my fingers. Wishing on the outcome of the Massacre would only jinx it.

"Meela," he said in a low voice, as if trying to make himself sound romantic. "I want you to know I'll be waiting right here when you get back."

I sighed. "Where else would you be? Swimming to the mainland?"

"You know what I mean."

"Not really." I supposed I knew what he meant, but I thought he was being stupid.

"I'll never be with another girl."

I kept staring at the clover, wishing he would stop talking.

He placed his hand over mine and whispered, "I love you."

I leapt up, as if I'd been stung by a wasp. "You *what?*"

"Don't act oblivious." He stood and took my hand again. "You know I love you. I think you love me, too, if you'd just admit it."

I shook my head and stepped towards my house, breaking my hand from his grasp. "No you don't, Tanuu. Don't say that."

He stepped forwards, but I backed away again.

"Meela, you don't have to worry with me. I have a house, a job, even a savings account—you and I, we could have a family together."

"Stop!" I turned away from him, and for a second I wished I was still holding a crossbow.

He did stop, and after a moment I turned to him again. He had his hands in his pockets. His eyebrows were pulled down so his face took on the helpless innocence of a big-eyed, baby seal.

I opened my mouth, but any words I might have said got stuck, so I closed it again.

"You should just leave," I said, finally. "I'll see you tomorrow at the Departure Ceremony."

He nodded, a pitifully romantic expression still stuck to his face. "See you then."

He walked away without glancing back. The second he rounded the house, I faced the water again.

I knew he loved me. When I stopped denying it, all the signs were there. There was nothing wrong with Tanuu. He was smart, and attractive, and probably right that I wouldn't have to worry if I wanted to have a family with him. The proper thing would have been to love him back.

I looked at the four-leaf clover still pinched between my fingers and bit my lip. According to Annith, being in love was something you "just knew", because your heart felt swollen and you never stopped thinking about him and you wondered how you were ever happy before.

Well, my heart felt no fatter than usual, and I found it a bit too easy to stop thinking about Tanuu. I loved him as a friend, but I "just knew" I didn't love him the same way he loved me.

I held my palm flat, watching the clover's frail leaves shudder in the breeze.

Darkness was falling. The water below had blackened, and the first star of the night twinkled above the horizon.

"I wish Eriana Kwai will be free again," I said.

I took a deep breath and blew. The clover lifted from my hand and floated gently off the cliff, beginning its descent to the ocean. The wind carried it away, and I watched it rise and drop smoothly until the sky engulfed it. I wondered, fleetingly, if it would finish its journey in the water or if it would find its way back to land.

When I finally walked into the house, my mother threw her arms around me so abruptly I wondered if she'd been waiting on the other side of the door. She smelled like maple and bannock. We held on for longer than usual, and when she pulled away, her eyes were glassy and pink around the edges. I dropped my gaze when I felt mine start to look the same. I was glad my father wasn't home yet.

"I'm so proud of you," she said. Yet her eyes spoke differently. *After tomorrow, I might never see you again.*

"Do you need help making dinner?" My voice was weak.

She shook her head, taking the rabbit from me. "I'll fix this up and it'll be ready in no time. Why don't you go change?"

She turned to the sink. The bones in her shoulders stuck out beneath her worn blouse, and her spine and ribs had been distinct beneath my arms when I hugged her.

For her, I was glad I'd killed that rabbit.

I couldn't wait to slaughter the demons who'd made my mother look like this.

"Mama?"

"Hm?"

I hesitated, wondering if I should forget it. But this was my last chance to release what had been curdling inside me for so long.

"I shouldn't be going on the Massacre," I said.

My mother dropped the half-skinned rabbit in the sink. A second passed, but she didn't look at me.

"You don't think it right to send women," she said finally, picking up the rabbit to continue her work.

"No. That's not what I mean," I said. My tone was angry. I took a breath. "The Massacre is the highest honour for our people. Everyone says so: Papa, the training master, the survivors. I don't deserve that honour. Not after . . . after . . ."

My voice broke. I hadn't brought it up in years.

She faced me. "Every warrior of Eriana Kwai deserves that honour."

"I'm not a warrior," I said. "I'm trained to be one, but I don't feel like one."

"Meela, I've known since you were a child that you were born with the blood of a warrior. Our people are blessed to have a woman as brave as you fighting for our freedom."

"You mean the people I betrayed?" The words were sour on my tongue.

A crease appeared between her eyebrows. "You made a mistake as a child, but it was out of honesty and compassion. You risked everything to defend what you thought was right. That is the mark of bravery."

I felt my face contort. How could she use the word 'mistake' so casually?

"Nilus would have been pr—"

"No," I said. "Everyone keeps saying that, and it's not true. Nilus would not be proud of me."

Her eyes widened. "Honey . . ."

Words flooded out before I could stop them. "What if it's my fault he's dead? What if *she's* the reason so many warriors have disappeared in the last few years?"

My mother stared at me for a long time. My words hung over us, and I had to bite my lip to keep a hard face. Then she placed her hands on my shoulders and looked at me with a determination I'd never seen in her before.

"Meela, the training master told me your skill with a crossbow is as great as your father's."

"So what?"

"That type of skill is not learned. It's gifted. You were born a warrior. The gods have given you the opportunity to amend your mistakes."

Vengeance seemed to bleed into me through the hands squeezing my shoulders.

"Embrace your destiny," she said. "Avenge your brother's death."

My breath caught in my chest. She was right. This was my fate. I was a warrior of Eriana Kwai, and my purpose was to fight this battle.

My people had put their faith in me. This was my chance to pay them back—to make up for my mistakes.

The success of my Massacre would determine whether the people of Eriana Kwai would suffer or prosper. For them—and for Nilus—I would get revenge. I would make the demons regret the day they invaded the Pacific Ocean.

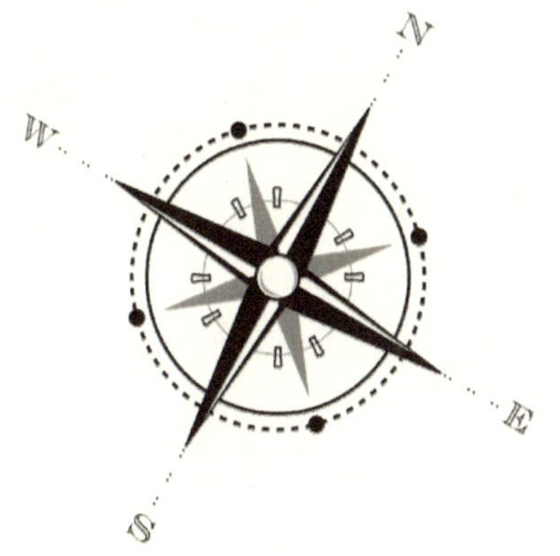

Eight Years Earlier

CHAPTER TWO

Secret Meetings

Soft ripples spread out from where the mermaid's head submerged. Her coppery blonde hair revealed her position, but only just. If I hadn't seen her a moment ago, I would've mistaken it for a clump of seaweed floating in the murky waters.

Slowly, I pulled myself from the bush and crept down to the beach, crouching low into the grey sand and rocks. Black clouds masked the sun's rays, making it easier for me to blend with my surroundings.

A mermaid hunter must be stealthy, nimble.

With a quiet lapping sound, her hair disappeared. I paused, balancing on two stones with my bare feet.

Steps away from where she'd been, another ripple, this time brushing the line between the sand and water.

I held my breath and focused. The water was shallow in the tide pool. Up to my waist, maybe. That was no reason to assume I was at an advantage.

The rocks under my feet didn't budge as I stepped closer. After months of practice, I could move with the fluid silence of a puma.

Her forehead emerged. Her blue eyes glimmered like sapphires, inhumanly large and adapted for catching prey in the black waters.

My stealth was futile. She looked right at me.

With a war cry, I pounced. I landed on top of her with a great splash, soaking myself and the surrounding rocks.

She twisted beneath me and wriggled from my grasp with ease. I was left on my hands and knees at the edge of the shallow pool for only a moment, and then a pair of arms grabbed me around the middle and rolled me back onto land.

She pinned me on my back with her icy hands.

"Surrender, weakling!"

I thrashed beneath her arms, trying to free myself even a sliver so I could push her off me. "Not fair, Lysi! You're stronger than me."

She sat on my stomach and crossed her arms. Her tail waved in the pool, creating its own tide. "My brother says mermaids are stronger than humans."

Grunting, I rolled onto my stomach and forced Lysi to slide onto the wet rocks.

"I know that."

She smiled wryly and smoothed her knotted, seaweed-laced hair. "I bet I'm already stronger than your papa."

I jumped back into a crouch. "A ten year old? Fat chance, slowpoke!"

I soared through the air and knocked her backwards. We splashed into the water in a fit of giggles, scrambling to pin one another down.

"I—made you—something," she said amidst our scrapping.

Pinned beneath her again, I spared a minute to catch my breath. "What is it?"

Lysi pushed herself off me and reached to the bottom of the tide pool.

Before she could even tell me what it was, I knew it was the most beautiful thing I'd ever seen. She must have read my expression, because her face broke into an enormous smile.

"It's meant for wearing around your neck. It protects you from the wrath of the sea god, or something. Also, it's pretty."

"A necklace," I said, awed.

"Necklace." She said the word to herself a few times, adding more of my language to her vocabulary. She had a funny accent when she talked, but I didn't mind because her voice carried in a way that made everything like a song.

I took it gently. It was a string of seashells, beaded along a twisted rope of seaweed in the most beautiful array of colours I'd ever seen—pastel blues and greens and violets, all glistening in the dim light.

"It took me months to find all the colours. I made two." She pulled another from beneath the water and slipped it over her seaweed-logged hair. "Now we can wear them and think of each other."

I dropped mine over my head, hoping the necklace looked half as pretty on me as it did on her.

"Thanks, Lysi," I said, rolling a soft shell in my palm.

She beamed at me with her even, white teeth, and the whole sky behind her seemed to brighten.

"What are the fish like underwater? Are they as pretty as the shells?"

I gazed into the tide pool by Lysi's tail, where an abandoned starfish clung to a rock beneath the surface.

"I wish you could see them all," she said. "By my house there's this rock—no, not a rock—I don't know how you say it in Eriana. It's all sorts of colours and fish live in it and even the rock is alive. I like to float and watch it sometimes."

"I think you're talking about coral," I said, still inspecting the shells around my neck.

"Coral. Coral. Coral," she repeated, turning the word into a melody.

Goosebumps rippled over my body and I hugged my knees, envying the way Lysi never got cold.

"I want to see fish and coral up close. One day."

I gazed out at the waves. The sea was calm, and not far from us, a pair of seagulls floated on their bellies.

Lysi stiffened and her deep blue eyes widened. "Maybe you can."

"I can what?"

"See underneath the ocean."

My eyes widened, too. "How?"

"You can become a mermaid with me."

I gaped at her for a second, then giggled and lay down on the pebbled beach, looking up at the cloudy sky. Warm, fat drops of rain splashed my face. "That'd be fun."

"You could live with me. We can be sisters!"

"Could I meet all your cousins?"

She nodded. "There's a way to do it. I've seen it."

My breath caught in my chest. "You've seen a human turn into a mermaid?"

"Well, I know mermen who used to be humans. I'll ask my brother how they did it. He'll tell me."

"If I was a mermaid, I could meet your brother," I said. She talked about him often, and it always made me miss my own big brother.

Lysi smiled. "You'd like him. I think he's like Nilus used to be."

"How Nilus *is*, not how he *used to* be," I said, careful to correct her. "He could still come home."

Lysi took my hand, her cold skin leeching what warmth was left in mine. "Of course he'll come home."

He would. I'd given him my onyx ring for good luck before he left on his Massacre. It was the same one he'd given me when he came back from training one day, claiming to have found it in a tree trunk. I was sure he had actually bought it from a store—but he and I liked to believe in magic sometimes.

"Meela!"

I let go of Lysi's hand and jumped up, looking over my shoulder towards home. Not far from here, Mama's voice carried on the wind.

I turned to say goodbye to Lysi, but she was already gone. Ripples spread out from the point where she'd plunged back into the ocean. The rain swelled, making the rings fade and gentle droplets slide down my nose. I huffed in defeat as I stuffed my gumboots in my backpack.

Slinging my bag over my shoulder, I cut through the bush so it would look like I came from the road. I was old enough, now, to realise that pushing through the thorns of the blackberry vines was better than Mama and Papa knowing I was at the beach.

Smoke puffed gently from the chimney, and I picked up a run, excited to be near a warm fire.

The sticky front door popped open only once I'd leaned into it with all my weight.

"You're like a rogue cat out there, honey," said Mama. "Always sneaking around . . . I never know where you are."

"Oh, Mama. Where am I going to run off to?"

A strange smell met my nose, like a kind of vegetable soup. Mama looked up as I entered the kitchen and her eyes fell to the string of shells hanging around my neck. She dropped the soup ladle on the counter. "Where did you get that?"

I looked around her to the steaming pot on the stove. "What's for dinner?"

"Stinging nettle soup. Where did you get that necklace, Meela?"

I cupped a shell and rubbed the soft underside, wondering if I should've tried to hide the necklace. "I found it."

She wiped her hands on her dress and marched over to me. "Meela, you know you can't go to the beach. I forbid you from going outside on your own if you're—"

"I didn't find it on the beach. It was lying in the rocks, by the grass. Don't worry."

She sighed and held one of the shells in her hand, turning it over. "It is beautiful. Make sure you hide it. Don't let your papa see it."

I smiled and hugged her, burying myself in her soft belly that she thought unattractive, but that I thought was perfect for hugging. She felt so warm compared to Lysi. "I won't."

Mama hugged me back, then held me at arm's length, looking down at my feet. "Honestly, child, they invented shoes for a reason. Go clean up and then come eat."

Before I'd made it two steps, she added, "And brush your hair. It looks like a seagull could lay eggs in it."

I pushed a matted lock away from my face, wishing my hair was shiny like Lysi's, which was always pretty, even with seaweed stuck in it.

Running my fingers through my hair to untangle it, I ducked through the beaded curtains hanging across my bedroom door. Mama never liked them because they got in her way when she was trying to clean up, but the sea-blue beads made me feel like I lived in a grotto. I decorated the rest of my room to match, tying green ribbon in places and pretending it was seaweed. I never told Mama or Papa why, of course—they wouldn't welcome such fantasies.

I tucked the necklace safely in the bottom of my closet, which had more clothes on the floor than on hangers.

"Don't tell anyone," I said to Charlotte, who watched me from the window. She stayed there, motionless and non-judgmental as always.

Charlotte hadn't been a particularly welcome guest, but my window was a great spot for catching flies, so I let her stay and build her web. I didn't want her to go hungry because of me. That was several weeks ago. When she didn't leave, I'd picked her name out of an American story Mama once read to me. I liked that story because it made me think about friendship and loyalty, and how anyone can be friends—even if one of you likes to kill and eat bugs.

I watched her bob idly in the wind for a moment before realising I was hungry enough to eat stinging nettle.

The front door creaked. Papa was home. I rushed to scrub my feet clean in the tub and dried them by shuffling across the bathroom rug.

Papa was grumbling when I entered the kitchen, his wide back to me as he stood over Mama. He'd brought the smell of petroleum and wood shavings into the house with him, masking the warm smell of soup and bannock.

". . . bad feeling in my bones about this one," he said. I pulled a chair from the table and he turned, squinting down at me. "Nice of you to join us, Metlaa Gaela."

I sat down quietly. Papa almost always called me by my full name. He and Mama had named me after the earth and a sort of matronly figure, a choice I always thought was terrible. I liked the sea better than the earth and I sooner would've taken care of a snail than a baby.

"How was your day, Papa?" I said, not looking up from my hands.

"No action down at the shop," he said grumpily. "Nobody's got a penny to spend."

I didn't know what to say, so I kept my eyes on my hands and nodded in an understanding sort of way.

Mama shuffled over with our largest bowl full of steaming soup and set it down in front of Papa.

"A man does miss having fish," said Papa, frowning at the bowl.

"I know, dear." Mama looked at the side of his dark face with concern.

"I'll have milk with it."

Mama hurried to the fridge to pour him a glass. Papa guzzled it and handed it back to her for a refill. I watched him take another sip, then put it down and start on his soup. Mama brought me a much smaller bowl and a glass of water.

"Did you finish your homework?" said Papa, raising his bushy eyebrows at my full backpack by the door.

I swirled my spoon around my bowl. "Not yet."

"Why not?"

I lifted one shoulder.

He looked pointedly at the old handmade clock on the wall. "It's five o'clock. You should've done it straight after school. I won't have a lazy—"

"I was at Annith's house," I said quietly, still swirling my spoon.

"Eh?"

Mama cut in as she sat down with us. "She was at a friend's house, dear."

It was partly true. I was there for a whole hour after school before I'd gone to see Lysi.

"On a weeknight?" said Papa, sounding angry.

"She's only ten years old. They don't have much homework at that age."

"Then give her chores, Hana. She's growing up to be lazy."

Mama said nothing, but I knew she didn't think I was lazy. I always helped her when she asked.

Papa returned to his soup and I glanced at Mama. She pressed her lips together in a shadow of a reassuring smile, which made me feel better.

I lifted my spoon to my lips and slurped tentatively, expecting something grassy and bitter. But the soup was bursting with flavour, and I smiled at Mama, once again amazed at her ability to turn weeds and scraps into something tasty.

"It's delicious!" I said, and lifted the bowl so I could drink it more quickly.

"It'd be better with some meat in it," said Papa.

Mama made an indiscernible noise, maybe in agreement or pity, and we spent the rest of the meal in silence. I listened to the loudly ticking clock, then to a sudden downpour of rain against the kitchen window, then again to the ticking clock. I thought of the necklace sitting in my closet, colourful and shimmering. Annith would think it was pretty, too. I'd have to sneak it to school and show her.

"We heard some good news today," said Mama, setting down her spoon in her empty bowl.

I looked up. "About the Massacre?"

She nodded. "It's rumoured that the lighthouse reported a sighting."

"Nilus' ship?"

She placed her hand over mine. "No, honey. This year's."

"Oh."

She glanced at Papa, but he didn't lift his eyes from his bowl.

My gaze darted from one to the other. "Well, it's still a good thing, isn't it?"

"Of course. Elaila will be happy to see her husband again."

Elaila was our neighbour. She'd married her boyfriend at seventeen, just before he left on the Massacre.

Papa put down his spoon.

"If they'd had any success, we'd know," he said. "We wouldn't have so many mermaid sightings because the vermin would all be dead."

Mama stared back pointedly, whispering, "Not in front of . . ."

She nodded towards me.

I frowned. "I can handle it. You don't think the sailors are gonna make it, do you?"

Neither of them said anything, but Papa raised his eyebrows at Mama.

I looked down at my empty bowl. Why did we have a Massacre every spring when they weren't working? Every year, we grew shorter on fish to trade with the mainland, which meant no supplies coming into our port. Every year, we had to harbour more fishing boats because it was only a matter of time before the mermaids decided they'd had enough and another boat was lost to the bottom of the Gulf of Alaska. Every year, it kept getting worse, and even though we tried to fix it, all we had to show were more boys lost at sea.

"Whether or not they come back," said Papa, "they're heroes to this island. Eriana Kwai only chooses the most able-bodied boys to go on Massacres, and I don't doubt for a moment they battled for our freedom with all their hearts and souls."

"So listen for the Homecoming bell tomorrow, Meela," said Mama.

I prodded at the dregs in my bowl. "I know."

The Massacre was the only time we were allowed near the water—to watch the warriors depart on the first of May, and if we were lucky, to watch them return some weeks later when they'd driven away the sea demons. When the ship was about to dock, the boy on lookout rang a big rusty bell and everyone went to see it arrive.

Two years before, my brother had been sent out on a ship with nineteen other boys. The Homecoming bell had not rung in three years.

CHAPTER THREE

Deep Waters

"Unbelievable! Where'd you get it? Did you make it? How many shells are on it? Oh my gosh, is that seaweed? Do your mama and papa know you have it? Are you allowed to keep it?"

Annith was beside herself when I pulled out the shell necklace at recess. She was my best friend next to Lysi—although she thought she was my only best friend because she didn't know about Lysi.

"I found it on—near the beach," I said, slipping it around my neck. "There are twelve shells on it and, yes, my mama knows, and she thinks it's pretty."

Annith's mouth gaped open, stretching her long face and making her look comical. She was sweet and freckled, but always wore her sister's hand-me-down dresses, giving her a distinctly frail appearance.

She reached out and touched one of the shells. I let her gawk.

"Maybe a mermaid did it," she whispered.

"Maybe." I forced myself not to agree with too much excitement.

She leaned in, hazel eyes wide, and dropped her voice even lower. "D'you think mermaids wear jewellery, too?"

Before I could answer, we were interrupted by a loud, disapproving voice. "What *is* that?"

We turned and looked up into the thin, pointed face of Dani, who put her hands on her hips when we didn't answer at once. She glared at us with slitted eyes. Dani had to be the nastiest person I knew, ever since the day I'd met her in kindergarten, when she slammed the classroom door on my fingers and laughed when I started crying.

Her eyes bore in the direction of my necklace, wide and malicious. "Did your brother mail that to you from the bottom of the ocean?"

I zipped my jacket up over the necklace, protecting it from her glare. "Watch what you say about my brother."

She laughed, dismissing my threat.

"I mean it!" I said, my face heating up. "Or someone will have to mail *you* home from the bottom of the ocean!"

Annith gasped. "Meela!"

Dani straightened, her face souring.

"You shouldn't have shells," she said. "Unless you're trying to show the whole island you're siding with flesh-eaters."

"Are you calling her a traitor?" said Annith.

Dani ignored her. "They're a bad omen and you know it. Get rid of them, or else—"

"Or else?" I said. "What are you going to do about it?"

She dropped her arms, fists clenched. Annith stepped between us, looking wary. "Maybe we should all—"

"Stay out of this, Bucktooth."

I pushed my way around Annith, a little too forcefully in my anger. "Don't talk to my friend like that!"

Annith turned and pushed me back with two hands before I could do anything. "Let's just go."

She took my hand and led us away. I looked over my shoulder, where Dani was already striding back to her friends, three boys who always fought over who would be her partner in gym class. They lingered a small distance away, avoiding our exchange.

"You have to ignore her," said Annith, bringing my attention back. "You always let her make you so angry."

"She needs to mind her own business."

"I know."

I huffed. "It's a wonder she has any friends at all. I don't know how those boys can stand to hang around a porcupine like her."

"Boys don't care if a girl's mean, as long as she's pretty."

I watched the way the boys looked at Dani, with her extra long legs and extra wavy hair and extra plump lips, and I decided Annith was right.

We trudged through the muddy field until we reached Eriana Trench, and Annith deemed it safe to let go of my hand.

Our field had the most giant puddle in the entire island, so big that none of us knew how deep it was in the middle. Years ago, some older kids had named it Eriana Trench. If anyone was ever brave enough to try and get to the middle—usually on a dare—he would only get up to his waist before a teacher would come over and get us all in trouble. Most kids played there at recess and lunch, battling paper boats and seeing whose could stay afloat the longest. I imagined the trench floor to be a graveyard of paper shipwrecks.

"Maybe you should keep the shells a secret," said Annith. "Dani won't be the only one who thinks—"

"Man overboard!" I said, pointing into the Trench.

Annith looked, but I knew she didn't see it.

"A bumblebee," I said. "It's drowning."

I stood at the edge of the puddle and watched it thrash in the water.

"Let's save it," I said, scouring the ground for something useful.

Annith just watched me in silence.

"My big sister says we have a famine coming," she said eventually.

I peeled a soggy maple leaf off the ground and cupped it in my hand. "That's stupid."

"Is not. She says it isn't safe enough to go fishing anymore. Even if we did go fishing, the mermaids have eaten all the seafood."

"That's why we're getting food from the mainland," I said, tossing aside the maple leaf and picking up a muddy stick.

"But the mermaids are attacking the ships that bring the food over."

I stretched as far as I could with the stick, but I still couldn't reach. I waded further into the Trench until the water touched the tops of my gumboots.

"Regardless," I said, trying to sound like a grown-up, "I do not agree with the Massacres and I think they should stop immediately."

"Why?"

The icy water sloshed heavily inside my boots, threatening to suck them off my feet.

"Just because the mermaids are eating a bit of our fish doesn't mean we need to kill them all."

"They started killing us first! Besides, they totally don't belong in the Pacific. My mama calls them an *invasive species*, and says they're the worst problem—"

"We saved him!"

The bee clung to the end of the stick, and I held him high above the water as I trudged back to shore.

Annith sighed, offering me a hand when she saw me struggle against my water-filled boots. When I got to land, I sat to take them off.

Footsteps approached behind us and a boy's voice spoke up. "Whatcha doing?"

I looked up to see Tanuu and four of his friends staring at me.

"Nothing," I said, dumping the water from my boots. "What are you doing?"

Tanuu squinted at the bumblebee on the ground. Behind me, Annith was as mute as she always was around boys.

"Whatcha saving a bee for? He'll just sting you, soon as he gets his breath back."

"Bumblebees don't sting," I said, jumping to my feet and preparing to defend the bee from the underside of a boot. One of the boys scanned my muddy clothes and smirked. I crossed my arms.

"Do, too," said Tanuu.

"Not this one. He knows I saved him."

Tanuu looked at me, then at the ground, then scooped the bee up with cupped hands. "Better get him to a dry place, then."

Tanuu moved the bee into a clump of bush where nobody would step on it, and I pressed my lips together to keep from smiling. Maybe he wasn't as bad as other boys.

"Wanna play Demon Tag at lunch?" he said.

I glanced back at Annith and saw her peering shyly at one of Tanuu's friends, Haden. I rolled my eyes. "Sure. We'll play with you."

Tanuu flashed his stark white teeth at me. I looked down.

"See you at lunch," I said, and turned back to the puddle as if very busy cleaning the mud from my hands.

From the corner of my eye, I saw Annith give a small wave to Haden, and then she squatted next to me.

"Oh my gosh, he's so cute," she said in the same tone the older girls used when they gushed about boys.

"You wouldn't know a cute boy from a toad."

"Do, too. His cheekbones just make me melt."

I pictured her melting into the puddle at our feet and giggled. "That doesn't even make sense. You've been listening to your sister too much."

The bell rang, signalling the end of recess, and Annith stood and smoothed her oversized dress.

"Well, I think you should go out with Tanuu. He's totally cute and he's always talking to you."

I made a face. "I think I would rather go out with a toad."

I kept my eye on Dani the whole day, ready to pounce if she stepped anywhere near my backpack in the cubby room. But she stayed put. With Miss Paige watching, she was a lamb. Grown-ups always thought she was "such a delightful girl," and I hated her even more for it.

Annith was right. All the boys might have liked Dani, but she didn't have many friends. The thought satisfied me in a vengeful sort of way that probably should've made me feel guilty. Whenever Dani did make a friend, only a month or so would pass before I would see the other girl crying by herself at recess. One time, that girl was Annith. In grade one, Dani picked her as her new best friend and they spent every day together for a week. It was when I found Annith crying in the cubby room that she and I became best friends. Real best friends.

The school bell sounded, and the class hesitated before standing. My own problems dropped like stones. The Homecoming bell never rang today. Miss Paige bowed her head, maybe owing the sailors a moment of silence before we were dismissed.

"There's still the evening," Annith whispered to me, sounding forcibly hopeful.

But the whole way back down the dirt road, through the bush and across the beach to my meeting place with Lysi, the Homecoming bell still didn't ring.

Lysi jumped on me as usual, but I wasn't paying attention and didn't even see her.

I laughed and pushed her off me, but she seemed to sense something wasn't right. She studied my face with her thin eyebrows knitted together.

"The bell didn't ring today," I said.

She continued to stare at me in confusion. I realised I hadn't known her long enough for her to understand what that meant. "Our sailors were supposed to come back from . . . um . . ."

I couldn't finish the sentence without looking down. She knew about the Massacre, anyway. I fixed my eyes on the dark rocks beneath my legs, wet from where we'd splashed them and continuing to dampen in the mist.

"Oh," she said after a moment. "Well, I hope they come back. For your sake."

I looked up at her and smiled a little.

She didn't smile back. "They've killed our troops. A lot of mermaids haven't returned."

"When did the last ones get sent out?" I said, wondering if the ship got attacked since the lighthouse sighting yesterday.

She shrugged. "A few days ago. The attacks start once a ship gets close to the army base, near Utopia. Then they go out in hordes until . . . well . . ."

I bit my lip, imagining swarms of mermaid warriors attacking our ships. A few minutes passed where neither of us said anything, and the sharp, cold rocks pressed into the backs of my legs.

I took my gumboots off and dipped my bare feet in the tide pool, wanting to bury my toes in the rough sand.

"Lysi?" I said, breaking what looked like a serious thought process. Her hard expression softened a little when our eyes met. "Why are mermaids even here? Why didn't you all stay in the Atlantic?"

Her mouth fell open, and I quickly added, "Not that I don't want you here! I'm happy you're here. I'm just curious."

"Well," she said, rolling onto her stomach in the lukewarm tide pool, "my parents came over when the Ice Channel melted."

"I knew that already. We call it the Northwest Passage. But why didn't they stay in the Atlantic?"

"My mama and papa said Adaro didn't like the way the Atlantic Queen was ruling. So he came to the Pacific to make Utopia."

"Adaro is your king?"

"Yes."

"What happened? Did he get a divorce from the Queen?"

"No. Adaro was never King before. I don't know who he was before he came here."

"So now that he's made Utopia, why doesn't he stop attacking sailors?"

She grimaced, but didn't answer.

"He should know my people are going hungry because—"

"Well, humans have land to live on."

She pushed her jaw forwards, and I thought she looked a little angry. I averted my eyes to a piece of seaweed lodged in her coppery blonde hair.

Part of me knew that was true, but part of me was appalled that she didn't care about my people being attacked.

"We need to eat fish, too," she said.

"Isn't there enough to share?"

She dropped her gaze, looking uncomfortable.

I stared at her lashes. She waved her tail up and down, making ripples that dampened the rocks on the other side of the tide pool.

"You would also get in big trouble if someone found out we were friends, wouldn't you?" I said quietly.

Her eyebrows pulled down and her shoulders slumped, but then she threw herself at me in an icy-cold hug that smelled like brine.

"All the kings and Massacres in the world couldn't make me stop being friends with you, Mee."

I giggled and squeezed her back.

She pulled away and smoothed my hair down affectionately. "One day there won't be any Massacres."

The thought lifted my spirits, until I remembered Homecoming. Mama would need my company. I stuffed my gumboots in my backpack. "I better go help make dinner."

"Wait." Her icy fingers clamped around my wrist.

"Ouch!" I said before I could stop myself, and she let go quickly.

I rubbed my wrist, surprised at her strength.

Lysi picked up a rock. "I just wanted to show you . . ."

She stacked a few rocks on top of each other. "This will help us visit. I'll make a pile of rocks when the tide is up, and when the tide is down and you see it, you'll know I'm close."

I returned her smile, and with it a promise that this was our special secret.

We said goodbye and I traipsed back to the road, shivering against the biting wind. I'd never thought so much about merpeople before, and I started wondering about other things I'd never thought to ask Lysi. Were there countries beneath the water? How long had merpeople lived in the Atlantic? How did they cross the Northwest Passage when the water was so cold?

Mama was quiet when I got home, and I put on my best cheerful face as I helped her make rice and cabbage for dinner. But the Homecoming bell still didn't ring, and Mama's face wilted, and she moved slower and slower. And I remembered the time my brother didn't come back.

"You said Nilus would still come home one day, right?" I said. "Maybe this is it. Maybe this year's sailors found him while they were on the Massacre."

I thought the hope of seeing her son again would make her happier, but she said nothing. I wondered if that was the wrong thing to say.

The front door banged open and I screamed, dropping the lid for the pot of rice. Papa stormed across the kitchen, heading straight for me. I jumped off my chair and backed away from his dark eyes.

"Where is it, Metlaa Gaela?"

"Papa?" I tried to look innocent—but I already knew. My insides clenched painfully.

"You know what I'm talking about." His voice boomed through our small house. "Bring it to me or I will turn your room inside out and dig it up myself."

How did he know? Who told him?

My eyes burned as I put my head down and went to my room. Papa followed me, giving me no privacy as I opened my closet, reached for the back corner, and dug up the shoebox I'd hid so carefully. I pulled out the necklace and turned to him.

His face was purple. His calloused, dirt-creased hand trembled as he took it from me. Mama stood behind him, and she nodded to me solemnly.

"Do you have any idea how you've shamed this family?" Papa's voice was so angry it made my lips quiver.

"The sea is our enemy. It's an inferno, not a pretty pool of water we cherish and make jewellery from."

My eyes sprung with tears. I wanted desperately to tell him he was wrong, that the ocean was not an inferno, that it was the most beautiful place, filled with coral and orcas and friendship. But I'd learned long ago never to talk back to Papa.

"The entire Pacific Ocean has been infested with sea demons since I was a boy, and our people have suffered because of it." He shook the necklace in his fist as he talked, and the delicate seaweed began to fray. "Don't you wonder why we need to import food from the mainland? Don't you wonder why this island is slipping into poverty? Sea demons! Mermaids! They steal our food, sink our ships, murder our children!"

I closed my eyes, wishing he would be swept away by the hollow wind blowing at my window. Nothing he could say would change what I knew about Lysi.

"You put yourself in serious danger by going near the beach, Metlaa Gaela. One swipe by a mermaid and you'll be gone forever. They'll feed on your skin and bones like a wolf on a rabbit."

"That's not true! They're not all evil," I shouted, the words bursting from my mouth.

His eyes widened, and his face grew an even deeper shade of purple.

"You don't know what I've seen." He whispered, probably because if he spoke any louder it would erupt from his mouth in a roar that would be heard across the island. "Do not forget about my Massacre. I won't let you take that pride away from this family."

The door slammed, leaving me alone in my room.

His Massacre. I lost count of how many times he'd bragged about it. The year he was chosen, the sailors killed more mermaids than ever.

"Five hundred and four kills," he always said. "The vermin stopped coming after two weeks! There hasn't been another Massacre like it."

How could he think mermaids were demons? How could Lysi be a killer? I didn't believe it.

"I hate you," I mumbled.

I swiped the tears from my cheeks and flopped on my bed. I wanted to shout after him that he couldn't take away my things. That necklace was mine.

How did he find out about it? Did someone see me with it? Or did Annith tell someone? She would never. We'd kept each other's secrets for years, and I'd never known Annith to be a snitch.

The only other person who saw the necklace was Dani.

I sat up. Dani. It had to be her. She was jealous the moment she saw it. She probably ran straight home and told her papa, who told mine. The two of them did work together at the woodshop, after all.

Everything made sense. That was why she stayed so quiet for the rest of the day: she had planned to tell her papa, knowing I would get in trouble for it later.

I looked out the window where the sky was darkening and the trees began to look grey, and I swore I would get her back for it.

CHAPTER FOUR

Shipped Home

The day I met Lysi was the third time I'd ventured to the edge of the beach without permission. For the third time, I felt peaceful as I listened to the splashing waves, delighted as I watched the seagulls float on their bellies, exhilarated as the pebbles massaged the soles of my feet.

It happened nearly a year ago. I had gone there to look for my brother. Maybe I would find him swimming to shore or docking a makeshift raft, and he would come running to me with his beard scruffy and his pants torn at the knees, and he would tell me he missed me and he was glad to be home after being lost for so long.

I'd spotted a body lying at the edge of the water, half submerged, waves crashing over it. A cluster of seagulls watched curiously from the surrounding boulders as the figure rocked back and forth.

I hesitated for only a moment before sprinting down to the water. Was it Nilus?

The skin glistened white against the dark rocks—much too fair, after all. What if it was another sailor, stolen by the sea from somebody else's family?

As I approached, forced to move slowly over the jagged stones on my bare feet, I could make out the limp body as that of a girl—a young one, maybe my age. Thick locks of coppery blonde hair fell across her shoulders and tangled around her neck like a noose. It was laced with seaweed and looked like it hadn't been brushed in months, and although darkened by water, I could tell it would be a most beautiful shade of gold when dry.

I only knew a handful of families with skin so pale. Had I found a castaway from the mainland?

"Hey," I said softly. She didn't stir. A thick rope was wrapped around her; some was draped across the sand and I couldn't tell how much was still in the water.

The pungent smell of the ocean met my nose—salt and seaweed and water as old as the earth itself—but I didn't know anymore if I smelt the ocean or a dead body. How long had this girl been here? I shivered, only partly because of the breeze coming off the water.

When I stepped sideways to try and see her face, my throat tightened. I instinctively stepped back. Where the girl's legs should have been was a long tail, greenish-brown in colour and scaly, like a salmon. I studied the tail, but I had to look away when my breathing grew panicked.

She was the myth I'd heard about. Her kind was the reason my brother went out to sea in the first place, to never come back. A sea demon.

As I watched her body rock in the waves, I suddenly didn't understand why my people wanted to kill the sea demons. Why would a grown man kill a little girl, even if she was only half of a little girl?

Her face was so smooth and gentle that I found myself touching my own nose and cheekbones and eyebrows, wishing I were that pretty.

I studied the rope around her small body. A fishing net. The mesh entangled her so tight, it left red lines on her ivory skin. I reached down and touched her. Her skin was icy, not a degree different from the water.

Hands trembling, I was about to pronounce her dead when her stomach moved. She was breathing.

"Hey," I said, excitement in my voice. "You're alive. Wake up."

I rubbed her arm, trying uselessly to warm her up.

Her eyes opened and she looked right at me. Her irises were sapphire blue, brighter than any I'd seen on a human.

I knew right then we would be friends forever.

"I'll help you," I said, though I knew she couldn't understand.

I pulled her gently from the water, not sure if mermaids could drown. I ran back to the house as fast as I could to get a knife.

Taking extra care not to pull too hard or catch her with the blade, I cut the net away. She stared, wide-eyed, like she wasn't sure if I was trying to help or hurt her. When I finished, she kept her gaze on me until I set down the knife and smiled.

She sought out my hand and pressed her palm against mine, stretching her fingers skywards. When I stretched my own fingers and she saw the way our hands lined up, brown skin against white, she returned a hesitant smile. She closed her fingers around my hand as though in way of thanks, then dove back into the water with grace I'd never seen. She left me staring after her with a strange, exciting mix of awe and fear bubbling in my chest.

We'd both returned to that spot the next night. Since then, we came back to see each other nearly every day, and, over time, I taught her to speak Eriana. We knew our friendship would go severely punished—but not for a second did that stop us.

I didn't realise I'd fallen asleep when an annoying and repetitive sound woke me up. My hands reached groggily for my pillow. I threw it over my head to try and smother myself in silence.

My door burst open. I flung my pillow off and bolted upright, my heart jumping into action.

"Meela, get up."

It was Mama.

"What?" My own voice boomed in my ears.

"The bell. Homecoming."

My feet hit the cold floor. Blood rushed to my head, making me dizzy. The bell. The sailors. They'd made it.

I pulled my favourite sweater from my closet. Once belonging to Nilus, it was four sizes too big and worn thin with age. I threw it on, following the sound of Mama crashing around in the entrance. Papa already waited there, wearing clean jeans and a button-down shirt, watching Mama pull gumboots over her bare feet.

When he saw me, he said, "Let's go," and opened the door to lead us through the mist. It clung to my face and bare feet like a damp cloth, and I was glad the rest of me was warmly bundled.

I instinctively looked in the direction of the ocean as we walked, but of course I couldn't see it through the trees and the darkness.

Nobody said anything as we followed the main road to the docks. I wanted to ask questions, but something told me it was not the time. The bell grew louder, its slow gongs reminding me of an old and broken clock ringing long past twelve.

When we rounded the bend out of the forest, the docks and the black water came into view beneath a floodlight. Knots of families already filled the edge of the dim halo of light, and hundreds more still approached. The spectators always stood on a hill that dropped down to the water, so even kids could see over the heads of the adults in front of us. Part of me wished I couldn't see at all.

The large brass bell clanged loudly now. A boy I didn't recognise rang it with both hands. He looked frail and tired, even from afar.

The black water stretched outwards until it blended with the horizon, leaving the world in front of us desolate— if not for the soft, lonely glow in the distance. Something was definitely coming. The light flashed in a rhythm set by Eriana Kwai: one, two, one-two-three; one, two, one-two-three. It was our ship.

Everyone stayed cautiously away from the water's edge. I thought we could get closer for a better view, but when I looked up at Mama, her face was crinkled. Papa's was hard as stone. Neither of them looked at me. I supposed Mama and Papa did know some of the boys who were sent away, even if I didn't.

So I turned back to the sea and watched the light grow larger. *One, two, one-two-three.*

And the bell continued to toll. *Gong, gong, gong.*

My feet grew numb and I began to shiver, so I curled my toes in and out over the sharp bits of gravel to try and warm them. I glanced behind me. Probably a couple thousand of us were huddled together—about half the island—and more gathered in the shadows. Nobody spoke.

"All hands," someone yelled, startling me. I snapped my head forwards and watched five men stomp onto the docks, ready to help tie the ship.

The crowd seemed to hold its breath, and I wondered if they thought mermaids would attack the men on the dock. I looked up at Mama again, but her expression hadn't changed.

The ship drifted in slowly to avoid snagging its bottom on the shallow rocks. It scraped along anyway, but a bit of rocks against the bottom was nothing compared to what it had faced over the last month. The decayed mainsail fluttered, wind hissing through gashes taller than me. Patches on the mast and railing looked darker than others. Craters. Every wave seemed about to sink the fragile ship.

None of it mattered now. The few Massacre ships that made it back got retired.

I knew a ship would normally be anchored a safe distance away, and a smaller boat would be used to bring the sailors to shore, but someone must have decided there was greater danger in putting sailors in a tiny unprotected boat by themselves.

So we waited as the boat groaned its way to the dock. I strained my eyes, but couldn't see any people aboard.

The crowd was quiet as mice. The only sound came from the waves lapping against the dock and the ship. Where were the sailors? Shouldn't they all have been leaning against the railing, waving to their loved ones and shouting?

A soft mumble, like a swarm of bees, passed over the crowd. I wasn't alone in thinking something was wrong.

One of the men on the dock split the air with a shout, startling me again. I clutched Mama's nightgown—a childish action, but I didn't care. She wrapped a comforting arm around my shoulders. The man was only announcing that the ship was safely tied to the dock. The sailors were free to disembark.

The ship rocked on the waves for a moment longer, bouncing off the dock, and then a figure appeared at the end of the gangplank.

He stared out at all of us. I didn't recognise him in the darkness. All the men we sent out only one month ago were thick, strong men. This one stooped as he walked, and his clothes hung from his bony arms and shoulders like dead leaves.

One of the men on the dock rushed to help. The frail man clung to him, and the dark figures shuffled down the gangplank together. When they reached the land, the sailor straightened, eyeing the crowd. He trembled under the yellow halo of the floodlight.

I stood on my toes to see his face, unsure whether I should clap or cry for him, or just stay quiet. The choice was made for me in the long silence that followed. I grew more uncomfortable with each passing second.

Someone pushed past us, breaking Mama and I apart. A woman in her nightgown and a man's lumberjack coat fought her way to the front.

"Hassun!"

The crowd turned to look.

Someone else pushed out of the crowd on the other side—a teenager, a girl of about eighteen.

The two figures met the sailor in a teary hug. I dropped my gaze, feeling like an intruder on a private family moment.

"Oh, dear," said Mama, covering her mouth.

I looked up at her. "Is he the only—"

She put her hand on my hair and told me to "shh."

I remembered Mama talking about Elaila.

The murmuring crowd became louder. I could hear people crying. Not far from us, a grown man started to wail. The anguished sound made me feel like my insides were sinking into the rocks at my feet.

Papa turned and pushed his way out of the crowd.

A gust of wind cut through the people surrounding us, blowing my hair across my face and making hollow sounds against the old boathouse. Mama looked as cold as I felt.

"Can we go?" I whispered.

She turned away, keeping a warm arm around my shoulders. I watched my feet as we left, not wanting to see the faces of all the grieving people.

"Poor Elaila," said Mama. Her voice was thick. "What evil, to be widowed at her age."

We walked home in silence. I couldn't think of anything to say. When we opened our front door, Papa stood in the kitchen, staring out the window into pitch-blackness.

"I don't want to sleep," I said. "Can we stay up and have tea?"

"Go to bed, Metlaa Gaela," said Papa, not turning away from the window. He sounded tired, but his tone dared me to argue.

I turned and marched to my room, slamming my door loudly enough to make sure they heard it.

The colour of the sky told me the sun was about to rise, and I rolled over to face my window. I'd hoped to watch Charlotte build a new web, like I sometimes had the privilege of seeing when I lay awake at night, but she wasn't there.

What happened to the other sailors?

"Don't think about it," I said aloud, and rubbed my hands along my sheets, focusing on the texture against my palms. That was what Mama told me to do if I started thinking scary thoughts when trying to fall asleep. Distract my senses.

But Papa's angry voice echoed in my head, and when I closed my eyes, I saw his fist clenched around my fragile necklace. More than anything, I wanted it back. I wanted to hold the shells and feel their ribbed texture against my palms. I wanted to sleep with it beneath my pillow, close to me like I used to do with Lucky Ducky—my stuffed duck— before she got too frayed to sleep in my bed.

How could Papa take it away from me? He never let me have anything fun. He probably threw it away without bothering to notice how pretty it was. And now I would never see it again.

It wasn't up to him to decide who I was allowed to be friends with. I was ten years old already, and I could be friends with whomever I wanted.

My anger at Papa thickened the longer I lay there, until I brooded about him for so long I was sick of thinking about him.

This was all Dani's fault. If she hadn't blabbed to her papa for the sake of making me miserable, I would be hugging my necklace right now instead of my cold bed sheet. Someone needed to teach her a lesson about meddling in other people's business. I couldn't let her win.

A knock sounded at my door.

"Time to get ready for school," said Mama.

I sat up and looked out the window. The sky was blue already, and I hadn't gotten a moment of sleep. I pulled on a pair of brown pants from the floor of my closet, ripped a t-shirt from its hanger without looking at which one it was, and marched out of my room.

I didn't want to lay eyes on Papa, so I bolted out the door with my backpack before Mama had the chance to tell me to put my gumboots on. I stomped there in bare feet and messy hair, planning how I would confront Dani.

"I think you should learn to keep your mouth shut," I said, practicing.

No, too wimpy. I tried more of a threatening approach.

"You'd better watch who you tattle on, Dani."

Still not tough enough.

Arms crossed, I waited in the schoolyard, rehearsing different threats in my head that ranged from "keep your pointy nose out of my business," to "do it again and I'll push you in the Eriana Trench."

When Dani arrived, looking smug with her hair clean and glossy, she saw my expression and balked.

"What do you want?" she said, when I kept glaring at her.

"Who did you tell?" To my satisfaction, my voice sounded even more low and challenging than when I'd practiced.

She narrowed her eyes but didn't say anything.

"Who did you tell about my necklace?" I said, louder.

"I didn't tell anyone!"

"Liar!"

She huffed. "It's an ugly piece of junk and it just reminds us of our curse. You can't wear it."

"Well, I'm not wearing it, am I? You know why?"

"Did you give it back to a slimy sea rat?"

"No! I'm not wearing it because you're a snitch!"

She stepped closer so she was looking down on me. "Well, you're a traitor. You're a traitor just like your brother. I heard he didn't want to go on the Massacre. I bet he went willingly into the ocean with a sea dem—"

Abandoning restraint, I slammed the heels of my hands into her shoulders. She gasped, stumbling back.

"I told you," I said, yelling now, "don't talk about my brother!"

She made to shove me in the shoulders, but I clamped onto her wrists.

"I hear mermen are hideous," she said, lip curling. "So your brother will fit right in. I bet they made him king."

She yanked her wrists away from my hands, but I dug my nails into her skin.

Dani shrieked. Her eyes filled with rage. Then her hands were attacking my face, clawing and scratching and grabbing for my hair. I closed my eyes instinctively as her nails dragged across my cheeks and lunged at her with all my strength. We toppled to the ground and I landed on top of her, flailing my arms and making contact with her neck and shoulders and head. She kicked upwards and we fell sideways. Then she was on top of me, and we still flailed, both of us screaming, no longer forming proper words. When our skin became too slippery with mud, we grabbed each other's hair.

I opened my eyes. Her face was covered in mud, her teeth clenched in fury. She pulled my head down by a fistful of hair, bending my neck painfully. I roared, letting loose another blow to her neck.

"*Meela!*"

I didn't look up to see who was yelling at me, but seconds later, a hand wrapped around my upper arm and hauled me to my feet.

My other fist was still swinging, but a second hand grabbed that one and whipped me around. I found myself staring into the bulging eyes of Miss Paige.

"Go to Principal Ray's office," she said, and she looked so angry, I thought her eyes might pop out of her head.

"But she—" I immediately shut up when her expression darkened further.

She let me go and pointed in the direction of the school. I shot one last glare at Dani and was pleased to see her covered in mud. Her normally thick, shiny hair was flat and damp, and she tried to wipe mud off her face with the back of her even-muddier hand.

I stomped to the school, rubbing my hands on my pants, uselessly trying to clean them off. The best I could do was push the hair from my eyes and wipe the snot from my nose. I must have looked as sorry as a stray dog. My bare feet made sticky sounds on the floor of the empty hallway.

I passed empty classrooms and tried not to let the other teachers see me. The artwork on the walls of the hallway mocked me—glued pieces of braided grass and flowers that reminded me of seaweed, and drawings of friends smiling together in a sunny field. I even saw a few hopeful paintings of a docking ship, and complete families holding hands as someone's older brother returned from the Massacre.

My stomach knotted as Principal Ray's office drew near. By the time I reached the door in my ever-slowing pace, Miss Paige was only seconds behind me. The principal's eyes swept over me, then over Miss Paige's serious expression. His rosy cheeks drained of colour, like I'd just brought a thunderstorm to his perfect day. Miss Paige walked past me and shut the two of them in a small adjoining room.

I sat on the Bad Kid Chair at the far corner of the office—a ratty kitchen stool I'd seen two or three times before. Grey and torn, with an odour like mildew, it possibly hadn't been replaced since the beginning of time.

By the time Principal Ray and Miss Paige came out, I was shivering from the wet mud.

They didn't even ask me what happened. The principal just rubbed a hand over his bald head, scanning me up and down once more.

"Go home, Metlaa Gaela," he said. "You're suspended. I'm calling your parents so they know you're coming."

CHAPTER FIVE

Consequences

Their faces told me it would be stupid to speak, so I rose without a word, feeling like my brain was sloshing in the same gritty water dripping from my hair. I took my backpack from Miss Paige and let myself out of Principal Ray's office. My feet seemed to move without my control, taking me across the schoolyard, past Eriana Trench, and back to the road. I didn't make eye contact with anybody I passed, but I felt gazes on me in my mud-covered state.

The rain started, but I was already wet and I decided it would be good if some mud washed off my skin before I walked in the door. Coming home early was embarrassing enough; I didn't need to look like I'd spent the morning making mud pies.

It occurred to me that once I made it home, I wouldn't be allowed out again for a long time. I turned off the road and traipsed through the woods, stopping at the edge of the beach.

A small rock tower waited for me at the shoreline. I hesitated. I couldn't help but feel like Papa and the missing sailors and Nilus had all put their arms across my path, stopping me from going further.

The rain soaked my hair until I felt like I'd just taken a bath. I pushed forwards. I picked up the rock at the top of the pile and threw it as far as I could into the water.

The sound of the rain drowned out any noise it made when it landed. But she would hear it under the water.

Sure enough, a blonde head poked out of the waves some ways away. It sank back down, and seconds later, she was right at the shoreline. She eyed me, plainly wondering why I'd come so early.

"What's wrong?"

I plopped down on the wet, jagged rocks, and my tears started flowing.

"Oh, Mee, don't cry," she said, pulling herself from the water.

Her arms wrapped around me in a hug. Her skin was cold as always, but her embrace was soothing, so I buried my face in her hair that smelled of seawater.

She patted my hair and said nothing until I was able to stop long enough to explain.

"Papa took away the necklace."

I couldn't look at her when I said it.

She was quiet, but after a moment, she hugged me tighter.

"Don't let that old man get to you. He probably wanted to keep the shells for himself."

I shook my head, spraying water from my hair. "He hates the sea. He always says—"

I couldn't bring myself to tell her how much he hated mermaids, how my parents would lock me in the house forever if they knew where I ran off to all the time.

Lysi pulled back, looking at my puffy eyes. "I can make you another one, Mee. Please don't cry because of that. The ocean is full of shells. I'll make you an even nicer one. You can hide this one so your papa won't find it."

I smiled a little and wiped my eyes, rubbing dirt and sand across my face.

Lysi laughed. "You can be so messy."

She wiped the dirt from my face with a clean hand.

"You're not much better," I said, my voice thick, and I pulled a wad of seaweed from her coppery hair. I tried to smile, but it faded right away. "Now I can't even go back to school. I got in a fight. I bet Papa's going to keep me in the house 'til I'm eighteen."

"No, he won't," said Lysi, though she sounded unconvinced.

We sat in silence for a long time, and I watched the waves smash into each other and break into a white, frothy spray. I couldn't stop thinking about having to face Papa. But what could I do? Stay out here forever? Live in a hut by the sea and never go home? The idea was tempting.

"No sense in getting sad about it," said Lysi, and I realised she'd been watching me intently. She reached over and tickled me until I was forced to start giggling.

"That's better," she said.

I wiped the last of my tears, still laughing. She always had a way of making me feel better.

"Want to see something neat?"

I nodded.

She sat up and smoothed her hair, reminding me of a much older girl fussing over herself in the mirror. I sat taller as well, trying to copy the way she positioned her shoulders.

"You ready?" she said.

"Ready."

Lysi closed her eyes meditatively, and for a minute I considered sneaking around and scaring her from behind. But then she snapped them open, and I gasped. The soft whites of her eyes and deep blue irises had been replaced with a fiery shade of red.

Her teeth were clenched in concentration while I sat frozen, staring with a mixture of fear and curiosity.

"How do you do that?" I whispered, and the sound of my voice was enough to break her concentration so her eyes faded back to normal.

"It only happens when I feel really angry," she said.

"What'd you do to make yourself angry?"

She smiled and took a lock of her hair in her hand, twirling it around her finger. "Just now, I imagined your papa taking away your necklace."

I dropped my eyes, feeling my insides deflate again.

"Other times, I imagine fighting off someone who comes to take you away from me."

"Like a kidnapper?"

She slapped her hands on the ground and pulled herself towards me with her small, frail arms. She made her eyes red again as she said, "Like a big, scary, flesh-eating—"

"Stop!"

She stopped, letting her eyes drain back to normal.

"You're scaring me," I whispered.

"If you were a mermaid, you would be able to do that too."

I thought of myself with big, fiery red eyes and smiled, feeling devilish. "It'd be fun to scare people who make me angry."

I thought of Papa, and how scared he would have been if my eyes turned red when he tried to take my necklace away.

"More of me will change as I become a grown-up," she said, "like my skin and my teeth—and my fingers, I think."

I scanned from her hair down to her greenish-brown tail. "All the time? Or just when you're mad?"

"When I'm mad."

I looked at my hands, wondering how fingers might change in an instant.

"I know how you could do that too, Mee. If you want."

I snapped my head up. "You mean you know the way to make me a mermaid?"

She smiled coyly. "Maybe."

"Tell me!"

She swirled her hands in the water for barely three seconds before the secret became too much.

"Okay, I'll tell you." She leaned in and cupped a hand around my ear so she could whisper, as though protecting the secret from eavesdroppers. "My brother says a mermaid *kiss* will turn a human."

I gasped. "A kiss!"

She giggled and fell backwards into the water, splashing me. When she emerged, she had stopped giggling and was looking at me curiously. "It won't work until I'm a grown-up. I'll know because my skin and my fingers and my teeth will all change, not just my eyes."

I felt a stab of disappointment. The ocean would have been my perfect escape. I was suspended from school; Papa was sure to yell at me and make me cry when he got home from work; Dani would be impossible to face once she found out I got suspended. I would gladly abandon life above water, especially to be with Lysi.

"Well, I feel like a grown-up," I said hesitantly. "Do you feel like a grown-up?"

She thought for a moment. "Yes, I think I do."

I thought of Mama, who I might miss if I couldn't see her every day. I might miss Annith, a little. But I definitely wouldn't miss Papa.

Lysi pulled herself up on land again. "Should we try it?"

She slid closer and I suddenly felt nervous. I'd never kissed anyone before, unless I counted one time when Tanuu ran up and kissed me on the lips before I could push him away. I remembered finding him later and rubbing mud in his face in revenge.

I looked again at the frothing waves and tried to imagine what it must be like to live underneath them.

"Do you want to?" she said. I felt her studying the side of my face.

I took a breath. The thought came to me that it'd be much easier to find my brother if I was a mermaid.

"Yes."

"All right."

She was right next to me now.

I faced her and tried to smooth my sopping wet hair. She leaned in, until our noses almost touched.

"Close your eyes," she said.

I did. I pushed my lips out, not sure what to do but trying to copy the way older kids kissed.

It was over quickly. Her lips touched mine and then she pulled away. There wasn't even a kissing sound like the older kids made.

I opened my eyes.

"How do I know it worked?"

Lysi frowned. "Do you feel different?"

I touched my lips. "My lips are tingly."

I ran my hands over my arms and legs. They felt the same.

"Try putting your legs together, so it's easier for them to turn into a tail."

I did so.

Lysi shook her head. "I don't think it worked. We'll have to wait until we're grown-ups. I bet turning someone into a mermaid has to do with my teeth growing in."

I glowered at my stupid human legs, tears burning my eyes again. Dodging my punishment was not in the forecast for me that day.

Suddenly, something whistled past us behind Lysi. We both jumped and Lysi spun around, making an odd hissing noise. I grabbed her wrist and peered behind her. The top of a bolt protruded from the rocky sand.

We stared at each other, our eyes wide. Lysi's mouth hung open. She had jumped between me and the water— and I was sure a second bolt would've followed if I wasn't in the way. I looked behind us. A dark figure stood between the trees, aiming a crossbow.

Papa.

I leapt to my feet, shrieking. "No!"

Lysi flattened herself into the rocks as another bolt shot wide of her, burying into the sloppy shoreline.

"Papa, stop!" I put a hand out. My fear was only heightened by the panic in my own voice.

His shout boomed across the beach as he aimed again. "Move aside, Metlaa Gaela!"

I turned back to Lysi, who was still flat against the rocks, her eyes wide and terrified. "Lysi, get away!"

My heart gave a painful jolt when she looked at me with such terror in her pretty blue eyes.

"Get away!" I said again, and I stepped in front of her so it'd be harder for Papa to aim.

He roared. "Meela, move!"

I glanced back to make sure Lysi made it into the falling tide.

Her eyes locked on mine, and they burst red. She opened her mouth—and I must have imagined the sudden sharpness of her teeth, the way the smooth ivory of her skin seemed to rot away. She screeched, and the sound rippled down my core like ice.

I screamed and stepped back. My foot caught on a rock and I fell. Papa had a careful aim, and he shot around me. The bolt whizzed over my head and splashed into the water.

Lysi screamed.

I scrambled to my feet. "No—Lysi!"

Her tail flipped up, but then she was gone. Blood stained the water.

I ran into the waves, my feet clumsy, and soon found myself paddling helplessly in the shallow water.

"Lysi!"

My feet kicked against the pulling tide, and my pants clung heavily to my legs.

I screamed for her again, paddling outwards. What happened to her? Did she sink? Or was she swimming away? My foot cracked against a rock beneath the water, but the pain was nothing beneath the echo of her scream.

The waves crashed around me. Already, the blood-red water dispersed, leaving only black in its place.

"Meela, get out of there!" Papa's voice was closer now, down on the beach.

I couldn't control my sobs as I tried to find Lysi, to see if she was all right or if she was hurt and needed help.

A hand gripped my upper arm. I strained against it, but Papa was too strong. He pulled me from the water and dragged me to shore, and all the while I kicked against him. I screamed at the pain in my arm from his grip, and in my knees and feet from the rocks, and in my eyes from the stinging saltwater, and most of all in my heart as I remembered the paralyzed fear on Lysi's face.

We stomped through the bush and onto the dirt road. Papa kept a firm grip on my arm that burned every time I stumbled. My cries of pain did nothing to make him ease up.

Before we got to the front door, he let me go and faced me, dark eyes bulging.

"Were you trying to get yourself chewed on like scrap meat?" he yelled. I instinctively stepped back from his booming voice. "I can't even begin to imagine what you were doing down there!"

"We live on an island," I yelled back. "You can't expect me to stay away from the sea my whole life!"

He clenched and unclenched his fists like he was struggling to relieve tension. "Were you trying to make friends with that demon?"

I didn't know what to say. Should I tell him the truth and make him angrier? Or should I lie and betray my friendship with Lysi? What would he think I was doing, if not making friends with her? Would he think Lysi was trying to kidnap me?

My silence stretched for too long, and Papa's lined face turned purple.

The door opened and Mama's jaw dropped. She looked from me to Papa, who faced each other on the front porch, Papa's eyes bulging, tears on my cheeks, clothes soggy, hair dripping.

"What's happened?"

Papa pointed at me with a shaking fist. "Your daughter was at the beach, getting cozy with a sea demon."

Mama's face turned to horror and then to sadness. Tears sprung to my eyes. What kind of daughter was I, causing this look on her face?

Papa turned to me again. "This is the most foolish, selfish thing you have ever done. Think of what your mother and I would have to go through, losing our only remaining child."

"You wouldn't have lost me!"

"Do you understand what you were willingly sitting next to?"

"She's my friend!"

I didn't know which was worse: Papa's stunned silence, which stretched for so long I thought it might never end, or the yell that followed, which must have been heard across the island.

"*They feed on human flesh*, Meela! You think that's the mark of a friend?"

"They're not all bad, Papa," I shouted.

He took a breath and covered his eyes. When he looked at me again, he didn't blink, like he really wanted me to understand. "All those sailors—every one of them that was supposed to come back yesterday—do you know what happened to them? Do you know what happened to your brother?"

"Kasai, dear," said Mama softly, but her voice sounded like a warning.

"No," said Papa, snapping. "She's ten years old! I was already a man when I was ten—a hunter."

I stared at Mama, unsettled by the way her eyes had widened.

"Meela," said Mama, speaking before Papa could go on. "You remember what we told you when your brother didn't come back from the Massacre? That his ship would still return one day?"

I didn't respond, but she continued anyway.

"Honey, we didn't want to scare you."

Numbness grew in my fingers, working its way upwards.

"Your brother was murdered," said Papa. "All of them were. The entire ship was murdered and fed upon by merm—"

"*No!*" I clapped my hands over my ears, not wanting to hear the rest. Mermaids had not killed my brother. Mermaids did not eat him. It wasn't possible.

The whole world seemed to stop. Why had Mama and Papa let me believe he could still be alive? Did they think I was too fragile to know?

My arms and legs and lips felt numb, like the blood rushed away from them. He wasn't lost. He was dead. But somehow I knew that. Deep down, I always knew my brother was dead. The mermaids really had killed him.

I just never wanted to believe Lysi's kind was responsible for my family's pain.

Mama's arms wrapped around me, pulling me into the house.

Lysi would never kill and eat a human. She was good. Mermaids had to be good.

But I remembered what she'd shown me this afternoon, the way her eyes became so inhuman.

Something must have changed on my face, because Mama said softly, "It's only a matter of time until her instincts take over, honey. We're looking out for you."

My eyes burned. I couldn't stop the tears from escaping. My voice came out high-pitched and unconvincing. "Our friendship is stronger than her instincts."

Mama opened her mouth, but Papa spoke first. "A demon's allure only mimics true feelings. Your friendship was a fake attraction, the same one that ends in the death of sailors everywhere."

"It isn't fake," I yelled, but my heart thudded against my ribcage, hammering doubt into my bones. "She wanted to be my friend. If it was all phony we wouldn't have been so . . . so . . ."

So what? Strongly connected? Loyal to each other? What could I possibly try to explain that couldn't be faked?

"They sent her to trick you into false companionship. It was a test of her abilities."

Mama put a hand out to Papa, but he continued.

"You were a game to her. It's happened before, to—"

"Please, Kasai!" said Mama, and Papa stopped.

"Calm down," she said to me. My breath escaped in quick sobs, and I sounded like Mama did when she was having an asthma attack.

She reached for my cheek with a soothing look on her face, but I turned and ran down the hallway, a lump in my throat so thick I thought I might choke on it.

I dove onto my bed and buried my face in the quilt, trying to calm my panicked breathing.

"It wasn't fake," I screamed into the blankets, but I didn't know anymore if I was defending Lysi or trying to reassure myself that Mama and Papa were wrong.

Even if she was growing up and had instincts that made her eyes go red ... even if she did have the urge to murder ... she would never hurt me.

But even as I thought that, betrayal pulsed through my veins like ice, and I wondered what it meant to have a real friend. How did I know any of my friendships were real, if not Lysi's?

I knew mermaids lured men, of course. Lysi and I had talked about it. But even if I was lured—whatever that really meant—who was to say our friendship wasn't real?

I spent the afternoon curled under my blankets, watching the broken spider web in my window. I wished Charlotte would come back so I could look at something more interesting than the fluttering strings of silk.

Sometime after I'd listened to the low murmurings of conversation and clanking of dishes as Mama and Papa ate dinner, Mama knocked on my door and let herself in.

"Can we talk, honey?"

I said nothing, considering whether or not I should pretend to be asleep. But my eyes betrayed me and opened to look at her.

"Was that mermaid being nice to you?" said Mama. She tucked a lock of my frizzy, salt-crusted hair behind my ear. Her hand was warm and smelled like dish soap.

I hesitated, then nodded once.

"You know she was pretending to be nice so she could lure you into the water."

"That's not true."

"How do you know?"

"She's my friend. Her name is Lysithea. And if she was going to lure me into the water, she would have done it already."

"How long has she been your friend?"

I lied a little. "A few weeks."

Mama sighed. A familiar crease appeared on her forehead and her mouth tightened around the edges.

"Mermaids are not people, honey. You must understand that."

"I do, but—"

"They're closer to monsters than to humans."

"You haven't met one, so you don't know."

"I don't have to meet one to know. How can a creature that feeds on human flesh be good?"

I didn't answer, unable to believe Lysi could feed on humans.

"When the mermaid grows up, she'll have an instinct to kill you." She shook her head gravely. "I only hope your papa was able to get her before she swam away."

"But Mama, she's my best friend!"

"Don't be ridiculous. You can't be friends with something you can't communicate with."

"She speaks our language! I taught her."

Mama froze, staring down at me, her eyes huge. I pulled my blanket up past my nose.

"You taught her to speak Eriana?"

I gave a nearly indistinguishable nod.

She put her head in her hands. "Oh, Meela. Do you know how dangerous this is? The mermaid could use our language to lure someone into the water by pretending she's a human."

"Lysi would never hurt—"

"Please understand me. That mermaid was never your friend. She was using you. Probably to learn to speak Eriana."

I sat up. "You're wrong."

"If she taught it to other sea demons, they'll all have a severely dangerous method of luring our sailors."

"But other mermaids already know bits of our language. They pick up words from the ships."

"Ships they're invading and killing!"

I crossed my arms and looked out the window.

Some moments passed, during which I hoped Mama would just leave, before she said, "Did she pick up our language easily?"

I kept my eyes on the tree outside the window. "Yes."

"What kinds of words did you teach her?"

I might have been mistaken, but I thought Mama sounded interested.

"Lots of words," I said, my nose in the air. "We had lovely conversations."

"What about her language? Did she teach you to speak it?"

"No."

"Why not?"

"People can't make the sounds. It's like those clicking noises dolphins make."

She was quiet again, and then said, "She gave you the shell necklace, didn't she?"

This time, the silence stretched for so long that Mama stood to leave.

"You're to stay in your room, Meela. I'll bring you dinner, and once you've eaten I want you to brush your teeth and go straight to sleep."

Her footsteps crossed my room. The door opened and closed. She left me to sit by myself in a hollow, pressing silence.

CHAPTER SIX

The Ravages

My suspension carried me to the end of the school year, and I spent only seconds thinking my summer vacation had started early. I missed Track and Field Day, which was always the best day of school. The last day of class was always fun, too, because after cleaning the classroom we spent the rest of the day playing.

Instead, I spent the entire time grounded. When Papa was home, I had to stay in my room. Mama at least let me out, even if it was to do chores.

Part of me wanted to sneak away for a short time when Mama ran errands. Whenever I thought about Lysi, I felt desperate, because I didn't know if she'd tried to come back, or if she'd been hurt, or . . . I couldn't think about it. Not knowing if she was all right was tormenting.

But another part of me didn't want to go back to the beach. When I thought about our friendship, my stomach gave a strange twist.

On the last day of school, I was helping Mama pull weeds in the backyard when someone knocked on our door.

I crossed through the house and opened it to find Annith's long, freckled face smiling at me. I jumped forwards and hugged her, making a point of being silent so Mama wouldn't hear us and make her leave.

Annith held out a big orange bag. "Your stuff from your desk."

"Thanks," I whispered.

"Gosh, you look miserable."

I pulled off my gardening gloves and wiped an arm across my clammy forehead, pushing strands of frizzy hair out of my eyes. "What's happened at school?"

"Nothing really," she whispered, pushing her sleeves up her bony arms. "Everyone heard about you being suspended, but nobody saw what happened. So Dani told everyone you went crazy and tried to sock some little kid for no reason, and Dani was like, the big hero who pulled you away, and you punched her in the middle of your rage."

I gaped at her. "*What?* She said that?"

She flipped her long hair over her shoulder and scoffed. "She's unbelievable. Now everyone's saying you had to get sent to the mainland for two weeks to go to a correctional school or something."

"I didn't—you don't believe—I wouldn't—that horrible—"

"I know," said Annith, reaching out to pat my arm. "Don't worry, I don't think you tried to beat up a little kid."

"Everyone else does!" I said, my voice high.

"Not everyone. Most kids know Dani lies a lot, so they don't really believe her."

I didn't know what to say. My guts twisted in anger. I wanted to push Dani into the mud all over again.

"Meela?" Mama's voice rang through the open back door. "Who is it?"

"I want to know why you got in that fight though," said Annith quickly. "What happened?"

I looked past her at the road, then back to her curious eyes. I spoke to one of the freckles on her right cheek. "It was the shell necklace. She tattled on me."

Annith gasped, looking infuriated. "So you're grounded for two weeks because of a necklace?"

I lifted one shoulder. Annith and I always shared secrets, but the fact that I'd been going to the beach to talk to Lysi was one secret I never shared with anybody except Charlotte.

"Meela?" Mama's voice drew nearer. I could hear her footsteps.

I jumped back from Annith and closed my hand on the orange bag.

"Well, thanks for bringing this, Annith," I said loudly, then turned to see Mama stop in the doorway.

"Hi, ma'am," said Annith, staring at her own gumboots.

"Annith was just bringing me my stuff," I said cheerfully.

"That was nice of you, honey," said Mama. "Thank you."

She said it in a final way that did not invite Annith to stay over and play.

Annith met my eyes and I grimaced apologetically.

I stuffed the bag in my closet and left it to fester until September, then went back to the yard to continue helping Mama. Most days, I felt lucky when my chores were outside. Today, however, I did not feel lucky to be in the yard. It was gloomy and misty out, and my hair kept sticking to my face. The inside of my gardening gloves had grown wet long ago, and my jeans were soaked through at the knees and ankles.

"Can I go inside and watch TV now?" I asked for the hundredth time after another hour of pulling weeds. I hadn't given up on asking since I first got suspended, figuring she must let me watch something if I proved to be too annoying.

In addition to the Eriana Kwai news station, we got a handful of channels from British Columbia, which meant I could watch some of the English television shows. TV was the only reason I liked learning English in school.

"Of course not." She stood, looking as sticky and as cold as I felt, and peeled off her gardening gloves. "Stay out here and finish weeding. I'm going out for groceries."

I glowered at the dirt beneath my gloved hands. She was just making an excuse to go indoors and be warm and dry.

"It'll take me hours to finish this by myself," I said in a whiny voice. It was true—the weeds Mama made me pull were Ravendust bushes, a stubborn plant that grew all over Eriana Kwai and had deep, thick roots that clung to the ground. Mama hated them around the garden because its leaves were black as tar, and she said it made the whole garden dreary.

Not long after our old, rusty car sputtered out of the driveway, I decided cutting the weeds would be faster than pulling them. I'd make double-time without Mama there to make me dig the roots all the way out.

Mama and Papa always told me not to go into the shed because I could get hurt from Papa's sharp tools, but I was ten now, and I would be careful.

I opened the shed door to the sound of tiny claws scuttling out of sight. I squinted into the blackness, hunting for Mama's pruning shears. Nothing but shadows met my eyes, so I slipped inside and felt along the wall for a light switch. The shed stunk like gasoline and mildew.

My toes bumped into tools, and I stepped carefully over them. Still, I found no switch—though my fingers did break through a thick cobweb. I leapt back with a small scream.

"*Gross,*" I whispered, wiping my hand on my pants.

After a minute spent squinting at the shadows around me, shivering, I had the revelation that the light must have been above my head.

My waving hand caught the chain and pulled. The light clicked on.

My eyes fell immediately on the back wall. Above the lawn mower, hanging all by itself in the centre, was a black crossbow. Beside it sat three rusted coffee cans overflowing with bolts. Two were sealed in place by a blanket of cobwebs. One was recently disturbed.

Papa's Massacre weapons.

I couldn't stop myself from walking over. I pulled a plastic bin out from under the shelf and stood on top of it, bringing my eyes level with the crossbow.

This bow shot Lysi. Before that, it must have killed hundreds of mermaids.

Mouth dry, I closed my fingers around the nearest bolt. The cobweb crackled as I removed it from the shelf. The ammo sat heavy in my palm—solid iron, longer than my hand and wide as my thumb. I placed it back and reached for the crossbow. My arms shook, straining to support the huge weapon as I took it from the wall. The handle was cold—and also made of iron. I wondered why they didn't make the whole thing out of wood, which would've been lighter.

Beneath my feet, the bin creaked suddenly, and I screamed as it snapped under my weight. The crossbow fell from my hands and hit the lawn mower with a crack.

My feet landed on a stack of books inside the bin. Heart jumping, I leapt out and stared down at the fallen weapon. Nothing was broken, except for the bin.

I breathed deeply to calm myself, glancing over my shoulder impulsively. My eyes fell onto a pair of pruning shears hanging near the door.

Remembering I was supposed to be gardening, I snatched up the shears. I turned off the light and backed out of the shed, leaving the crossbow on the ground. I felt silly, but my pulse raced and I didn't want to be near those cold, dark weapons.

I wished I'd never gone into the shed. The sight of the crossbow and bolts only made my chest tighten. My eyes blurred with tears, which I blinked back as I chopped the Ravendust weeds with vigour.

I finished quickly and went to watch TV, knowing it would be a while until Mama came home.

TV did nothing to lighten my mood. I watched SpongeBob and Plankton sing about friendship, and when that was over and Carly and Sam started celebrating their best friend anniversary, I changed the channel.

I was about to change it again, not caring to watch the news, when I noticed the scene in the background: it was the beach, not far from where Lysi and I met every day. Annith's mama was Eriana Kwai's news anchor, and she spoke very seriously into the camera.

"You can see behind me the devastation caused by the demons. The origin of this boat is yet unknown, but it raises questions about the state of fishing in other countries. It seems the demons are doing everything in their power to clear these waters."

I stood and moved closer to the television, as though that would help me see behind her more clearly. An empty fishing boat had washed ashore; it was tipped on its side, exposing its barnacled hull to the sky. The fishing nets were torn in dozens of places, strewn across the rocks. The sight of the upturned boat made my stomach queasy, and I tried not to think about what happened to the fishermen who were aboard.

The camera turned towards the sea. I watched the rocks and the waves go by, feeling wistful.

Then something on the beach made my heart jump. Was it—it couldn't be—was I imagining it?

I put my hands on the sides of the television as if to push myself through the screen.

The story switched to an interview with the old man who owned the grocery store.

"No!" I said, pushing my face closer still. "Go back!"

"Ordinarily, the price of fish in a shortage would skyrocket," said the old man, "but I'm afraid I can't even say that. The price of fish hasn't moved, because there simply isn't any fish. Our seafood deli is bare. Our main export has stagnated. The price of goods is through the roof and will continue to escalate until we find relief from the mainland."

They never did go back to filming the beach. I backed up and sat on the couch, staring at the television blankly.

I was sure of what I'd seen on the beach: a rock tower stacked against the shoreline, subtle, but definitely there. Lysi had been there, and I had never shown up to meet her.

She was alive!

My heart leapt, anxiety and excitement gurgling in my stomach.

When did she expect me? Did she still expect me at all? She could have abandoned the tower days ago. Or maybe she left it up for a reason.

She must have thought I was horrible, not showing up to meet her after what Papa did. She must have thought I didn't care whether she was alive or dead.

I glanced desperately towards the front door. She needed to know I was sorry, and that I never wanted Papa to hurt her.

The only problem was that I was still grounded. Going anywhere would be impossible, never mind the beach.

The trouble I would be in . . .

I wandered to my room and leaned on the windowsill, hoping to spot Charlotte. Her web was gone, blown away by wind and rain.

I stared, instead, into the empty woods until the front door opened and Mama called my name.

"Help me unload these," she said, passing me one of two bags of groceries. "Then we're going to Elaila's to give her this pound cake in condolence."

I placed the milk and butter in the fridge, recalling the news coverage and wondering how much all of this cost, and if it put Mama and Papa's bank account under stress.

Mama set the pound cake on the counter. I gazed at it with a watering mouth. "Can't we keep it for us?"

She smiled down at me. "I'll get a treat for us next time, all right?"

It took only a minute to unload the groceries, and then Mama made me carry the pound cake to Elaila's house.

"Did you finish the garden?" she said as we crossed the dead-end dirt road.

"Yes."

"After this, you can help me cook dinner, and then I won't make you do any more chores today."

I sighed gratefully.

Elaila opened the door wearing a hole-filled nightgown that was frayed in more places than not. Her hair was piled on top of her head in the remains of a ponytail, greasy locks falling loose on all sides.

"Hi, honey," said Mama. "Is this a bad time?"

Elaila shook her head. Her normally youthful face was swollen and blotchy, and her red nose made her look like she was suffering from a cold.

"Come in," she said thickly.

"We brought you a cake," said Mama, pushing me forwards.

I handed the cake to Elaila and tried to smile. She took it and beckoned us inside without looking at me.

"That's nice," she said. "Should I make tea and . . . and . . . ? Here, let me get some plates."

"No, that's all right," said Mama. "We won't stay long."

Elaila set the cake on top of a pile of unopened mail and flyers on the counter, then turned to face us with swollen eyes.

"Look at me," she said, sounding disgusted. "I'm a widow to an unfaithful *jerk*."

"Now, honey," said Mama, stepping over a pile of coats and shoes and guiding her to the kitchen table by her shoulders.

"I haven't slept since the Homecoming. It's bad enough losing a husband, but . . ." She lifted a hand to her mouth, and when no more words came, she waved it dismissively.

I cleared dirty clothes off a kitchen chair for her while Mama rubbed her back. "You have every right to grieve, Elaila."

"I'd be proud of him if I found out he went down fighting," she said, collapsing into the chair I pushed behind her. "But by the sounds of it, he went down . . . *smooching!*"

"I was quite surprised," said Mama overtop her sobs.

I stood rooted behind them, dumbfounded. Did Elaila think her husband dove willingly into the ocean with a mermaid? Did she think he betrayed their marriage that easily?

She went on, her voice growing steadily higher. "Thirteen years old, we started going out. I never thought he'd betray me."

"He didn't betray you, Elaila," I said, unable to keep quiet any longer.

Mama and Elaila turned to me with wide eyes.

"I know Sam loved you. He would never betray you."

Elaila gazed out the window with a trembling lip. "That's a sweet thought, Meela."

"He did love you," I said. "Their allure is more complicated than that. Mermaids can hypnotise even the most loyal men, if they want to."

"Hypnotise?" said Mama.

"Yes." I stepped closer. "Men don't stand a chance against mermaids. They fall under a trance."

Elaila raised her eyebrows at me. "What makes you think . . ."

She and Mama made the briefest eye contact, but then Mama stood and put an arm around me. "Now, Meela, that's enough. Elaila doesn't need you intruding on her personal life."

"But—"

"Thank you for inviting us inside," she said to Elaila, who stared at us in wordless confusion. At least her tears had dried up.

Elaila saw us out the door, and Mama waited until we reached the end of the driveway before saying anything.

"What do you think you're doing, making up stories like that?" she whispered, grabbing me by the elbow as we walked. "You'll terrify people to death if you start talking about mermaids that way. As if you know them—as if they're people!"

"But she needs to know—"

She jerked my elbow. "Stop it, Meela!"

I looked at her in alarm. Her eyes were wide and her breathing shallow, as if she was about to have an asthma attack.

"Sorry," I whispered.

She let go and her expression softened. "You can't say things about mermaids that other people don't know. They'll wonder where you got it from."

"I didn't mean . . . I'm sorry," I said weakly. I didn't want to disappoint Mama any more than I already had.

A voice broke through the clearing. "Hana!"

Tanuu's mama was running towards us, Tanuu trailing shortly behind.

She stopped abruptly when she saw me and put a hand to her chest. "Oh, thank heavens, Meela."

Tanuu stopped, too, and his expression changed from strained to shocked to relieved.

Mama turned to face them. "What is it?"

They strode closer. Sweat glistened on their faces.

"A demon," said Tanuu's mama between strained breaths. "A demon just snatched a child off the beach."

Mama swayed, and my hands flew towards her as though to hold her upright.

"Gone completely?" said Mama.

Tanuu's mama nodded, her mouth tightening.

"A friend of my pop's seen it happen," said Tanuu after a moment, when no one else was able to speak. "He thought the girl on the beach was Meela. Must've looked just like her."

His eyes flicked over me. I felt strangely blank.

"Who was it, then?" I said.

Tanuu's brow pinched and he shrugged.

"I'm just glad you're all right," said his mama, and suddenly she had her arms around my head and my face pressed into her chest. I had to turn my head so I could breathe.

When she let me go, Mama still looked like she was about to fall over.

"Let's go inside and make you some tea," I said, and this time it was me grabbing Mama by the elbow.

She looked down at me as if coming out of a trance and opened her mouth. No sound came out at first, but then she managed, "Yes. Yes, let's do that." She looked at Tanuu and his mama. "Won't you come inside with us?"

Tanuu's mama must have also thought Mama was going to faint, because she said, "Yes, that'd be a good idea."

I led the way inside, dreading spending time alone with Tanuu while our mamas drank tea. Annith and I usually pretended we were deer living in the woods, or witches brewing potions inside a hollow stump, or giants and all the pinecones were tiny horses we kept as pets. Tanuu wouldn't like those games. He would think I was a baby, or stupid, or boring.

To my horror, Mama put a hand to my cheek when I sat her down at the kitchen table and said, "Why don't you two run off and play while us mothers have a minute to chat?"

I hoped Mama would read my expression, but she either ignored it or didn't see it, because she forced a tight-lipped smile and patted me on the bum to push me away.

Tanuu and I walked outside in silence.

"Well, what do you want to do?" I said.

He crossed his arms and shrugged, taking in the patch of grass we called a backyard. Suddenly, he seemed a lot more timid than when we were at school.

"We could . . ." I began, but then didn't know what to suggest, so I trailed off and turned my gaze towards the ocean.

"That a cliff?" said Tanuu. He was looking at the ocean as well.

"Not a big one."

We walked over and I pushed a few branches of Ravendust out of the way so we could peer at the rocky beach below.

"If you lay down, you can get closer to the edge without your knees wobbling."

We did so, and slithered up to the edge so our faces and arms were suspended in the air, far above the rocks. The waves crashed against the shoreline and the seagulls cried.

"I'm happy it wasn't you."

I stared at him. "What wasn't me?"

"The girl that got . . . the mermaid. I'm happy it wasn't you."

"Oh," I said. "Well—me too."

I noticed how close together we were and my face grew hot. But I didn't shuffle away because I thought that would be even more embarrassing.

"I wonder who it was," I said, turning back to the sea.

He didn't say anything. I tried to think of a girl I knew who looked just like me, but plenty of girls on the island might look like me from afar.

We would find out who it was soon enough, and I shuddered to think one of my schoolmates was gone forever.

"Heard you're grounded," said Tanuu after a while.

I didn't look at him. "So?"

"Is it true?"

"Where'd you hear that?"

"From Haden, who heard it from Annith."

I sighed. "Yeah."

"Maybe I shouldn't say this, but Dani deserved it. Getting socked in the face. Whatever you was arguing about. She's not very nice."

I gawked at him, but his earnest expression made me laugh.

"I thought all boys liked her," I said.

He made a face. "Not me. Not any of my friends."

We made eye contact, and I turned to the water again. I still felt his dark brown eyes on the side of my face.

"Four-leaf clover," I said, and plucked it from the grass.

"Is not. That's just three leaves and one of 'em ripped."

"No, it's real!" I held it up to his face so he could see it more closely.

He studied it for a minute, then seemed to deem it real. "Better make a wish, then."

I twirled it between my fingers, thinking of Lysi.

Tannu cleared his throat after a moment, and he hesitated so much before speaking that it made me look at him sharply.

"I was thinking . . . If you weren't grounded, I was gonna see if . . ."

He stopped, like his throat had sealed up. My heart jumped, because I thought I knew what he was going to ask me.

Tanuu's throat came unstuck abruptly, and his words flooded out. "I was gonna see if you wanna go to the movies."

My stomach flipped over. He'd said exactly what I was afraid of.

"Oh," I said, because that was the only word that would come out.

He seemed to be waiting for me to say more, but after a minute, he said, "You're grounded though. So, I guess it don't matter."

"Right."

"But would you go with me? If you weren't?"

I buried my face in my arms. "I don't want to be your girlfriend, Tanuu."

"Why not?" His voice changed from smooth to whiny.

"Because we're only ten!"

"So? I think you're pretty! I like you!"

My face burned even hotter and I sat up to put distance between us.

The front door popped open behind us.

"Tanuu," shouted his mama, "let's go."

Tanuu stood. He looked down at me, smiling despite the cold rejection. "Maybe you can come over one day this summer. Even if it's not a date."

"Maybe," I said, averting my eyes from his snowy-white teeth. As we walked to the house, I supposed it was nice to have company after being grounded for so long—but I didn't admit this to him.

He stopped before we reached the door. "What'd you wish for? On the clover?"

I looked down. "I can't tell you. Wishes are supposed to be a secret."

He scrutinised me for a moment, then seemed to realise I wasn't going to tell him and kept walking.

"Stay away from the ocean," he said, smiling grimly over his shoulder. "Don't want you going missing for real."

I nodded once.

He and his mama walked down my driveway and back onto the dirt road, leaving me to wonder why so many people thought they could tell me what to do.

CHAPTER SEVEN

Midnight Encounter

I couldn't close my eyes as I lay in bed that night. My foot wouldn't stop moving, like I was tapping my toe on my blankets.

How many days ago had Lysi made the rock tower? Was it only yesterday? Was she waiting for me now? What if this was the day she had given up waiting for me? She could be on the beach this second, knocking down the rocks. I might never see her again, and she'd swim away thinking I didn't care whether or not she was alive. She wouldn't know how sorry I was for what Papa did.

I sat up. Then I thought of Papa in the next room, sure to waken at the slightest sound.

So I flopped back down and rolled on my side.

What, then? Would I let Mama and Papa ruin my friendship with Lysi? Would I just accept never seeing her again? If I didn't go out to see her tonight, I would be as good as giving up. This would be the first day of the rest of my life: a life without Lysi.

I sat up again. That was not an option. We were supposed to be friends forever. I couldn't abandon the chance to fix everything Papa had broken. The thought was unbearable.

What about Mama? I couldn't disappoint her again—but would I be disappointing her if she never found out?

I slipped out of bed before I could change my mind. I would get a flashlight and my coat, and I'd be back before anyone knew I left.

My door opened without a squeak. I dropped to my stomach and slithered under the beaded curtains, careful not to touch them.

Mama and Papa slept with their door open, so I made sure to move on tiptoe, keeping close to the wall where the floor didn't creak so loudly.

Papa must have had a flashlight somewhere—but I refused to go back into the shed. There had to be one inside the house.

I crept to the rolltop desk in the corner of the living room. It was littered with stray items: measuring tape, stapler, lighter, playing cards, broken pencils.

The drawer was tough to open. I pulled hard, realising it was a stupid idea when it clattered off its slides. I let go and dove to the floor behind the desk.

I clapped my hands over my mouth, listening, but the only sound that followed was the ticking clock on the wall. Mama and Papa hadn't stirred.

Still, I waited, crouched on the floor and listening. After what felt like forever, I stood and gripped the drawer handle again, gently this time. It stayed jammed. I struggled with it only briefly before deciding it wasn't worth risking the noise.

Defeated, I glanced around for another option. My eyes landed on a cast iron lantern by the fireplace. A candle was inside, still waxy enough to get me to the beach and back. I pocketed the lighter on the desk.

Lantern in hand, I tiptoed to the front entrance to get my coat, then back to my bedroom where I could slip out the window.

Not so much as a snore came from Mama and Papa's room at the end of the hall, and I didn't know if that meant they were quietly asleep, or awake and listening.

I slithered back under my beaded curtains, the lantern cradled inside my jacket so it wouldn't scrape the floor, and softly shut the door.

My window opened soundlessly. I tossed the lantern into the soggy leaves, where it hit the ground with a clang. Then I hoisted myself over the ledge.

Summer might have been coming, but the temperature on Eriana Kwai was steadily cool year-round. I was glad I had my jacket. I zipped it up to my chin as I crept around the side of the house opposite Mama and Papa's bedroom window. Only once I reached the road did I light the lantern.

The walk felt longer than usual. The only sounds were a faint buzz of insects, the occasional hoot of an owl, and my bare feet patting against the hard dirt. I couldn't help feeling like the animals of the night were watching me as I followed the empty road. I stayed in the middle, somehow feeling safer there—like the animals were less likely to jump out at me if I walked far enough away from the forest's edge.

Eventually, I reached the point when I could no longer avoid going into the woods, and stopped. I glanced into the misty darkness on either side of me. After a moment's hesitation, I took a breath, switched hands on the lantern to give my left arm a rest, and stepped inside.

The blackness overwhelmed me, even with the glow of the lantern. I hastened forwards, stumbling over tree roots. My coat kept snagging on long-fingered branches. I didn't care; I was just glad to be wearing it. Already, my teeth chattered—although I didn't know if that was from the cold.

The whispering surf grew louder with every step, and knowing it was close kept me pushing forwards. By the time I emerged on the rocky beach, I trembled all over, and the skeletal sight of the overturned fishing boat tipped me over the edge of panic.

"Lysi?"

It was too soon for her to hear—she would be at the shoreline, not up in the dry rocks—but I needed to hear a voice, even if it was my own.

Only sloshing waves met my ears.

I gave the fishing boat a wide berth, trying to ignore its ghostly presence. Its black shadow and spider-web fishing nets made the beach seem haunted.

"Lysi, are you here?"

Something sat by the water, perched on a rock. I stopped and held the lantern higher to make sure I wasn't imagining it. The figure sat gracefully upright and statuesque. I wondered whether it really was Lysi and not just a curvy piece of driftwood, but then the end of a tail flipped up, and she lifted a hand and beckoned me over.

My face broke into a grin. I ran towards her, jumping carefully through the rocks, the lantern clanging loudly.

"I didn't know if you'd be here," I said, breathless. "I only saw your rock tower a few hours ago."

I held the lantern between our faces so Lysi and I could see each other properly.

Only I didn't see Lysi. I saw a stranger—maybe in her mid-twenties, beautiful and porcelain, with waist-length black hair and a long, slender tail.

"Hello, Meela," she said, and her pointed teeth glinted in the lantern's light.

I knew from her eyes that she wasn't smiling at me—she was baring her teeth.

"I feared we'd waited too long," she said in a rolling accent, thicker than Lysi's. "But Lysithea was right. You would still return."

I stepped back, feeling like my stomach was pushing its way up my throat.

I'd never seen another mermaid except Lysi. Lysi was just a girl, like me—a friend, one who had a tail instead of legs. But something about this mermaid was so inhuman, like she was too perfect, each of her features exaggerated beyond real beauty. Something sinister lived beneath her porcelain flesh.

"I should give Lysi credit for doing a convincing job," she said. "Or maybe you're just naïve enough to believe a human and a mermaid could actually be friends."

What did she mean, Lysi doing a convincing job? My mind worked in slow motion. I was too seized by fear at the sight of this mermaid to form words.

Her upper lip curled, and her eyes changed. A familiar shade of red seeped through them like they were filling with blood, hiding her pupils and any fleck of white.

Something instinctive exploded inside me, yelling at me to run away and preserve my life. This mermaid was about to kill me. She was about to eat me.

"I'm so happy I finally get to see you in the flesh," she said, reminding me of a purring cat. Her lips retracted from the row of pointed teeth. "Lysithea might not have been strong enough to take you . . . but she said you were easy to fool."

I screamed, abandoning any attempt at staying unnoticed. Blindingly fast, the mermaid's hand shot out and seized my ankle. Her long fingers were colder than ice. I tried to step back but her grip was like stone, and I fell hard on my side. My hand shot out to brace my fall and skidded painfully off a rock. The lantern crashed to the ground and the flame died.

The darkness spun, dizzying me as I rolled onto my stomach. A musical sound met my ears, rolling like laughter. Lysi's laughter.

I scrambled across the rocks, kicking as hard as I could, but she still held my ankle.

"How should we do this?" said the mermaid, her tone suggesting we were about to play a game. "Would you rather be drowned, or strangled?"

She slid off her boulder behind me. My foot made contact with her face, but it was like kicking a tree trunk. She grabbed for my other ankle and caught the leg of my pants.

"Maybe suffocating isn't your style," she said. "I don't mind. You'll taste better if your heart is still beating."

She pulled me towards her. I screamed too much to speak. The mermaid's strength was impossible, even stronger than Papa had been when he hauled me away from Lysi.

My body bumped across the slimy rocks; any stones I tried to grip came loose, but I turned and hurled them at her head. They bounced off her with a dull crack. Her hands stayed clamped on my legs. She didn't even flinch—I might as well have been throwing sponges.

"You don't need to draw this out," she said, her voice now rough and angry.

One of my flailing hands brushed the lantern; I stuffed my fingers through the sides and swung it around with all the strength I had. It smashed into her cheek with another dull crack.

This time, she screamed.

She released my ankles, hands flying to her face where the lantern had struck. I kicked away and crawled over the rocks, ignoring the pain of my knees against the stones.

Her voice exploded with fury. "What is that?"

A hand closed around my ankle again. I screeched and whirled around, striking another blow with the lantern.

She screamed again and fell back.

I gaped at the lantern. Why did this work, but not the rocks?

An odd sizzling sound met my ears, like meat on a grill.

I raised my eyes to the mermaid, unblinking. The sound was coming from her.

Was it the fire from the lantern? I looked down. No, the flame had been extinguished.

The mermaid coughed, as though choking on something. Her red eyes glistened as she locked me into her gaze. She hesitated.

Suddenly I remembered Papa's weapons hanging in the shed, how the bolts and crossbow had felt in my hands. Cold, black iron.

I stared at the lantern clutched in my fists. Of course—iron!

Without a second thought, I lunged at the mermaid and pushed the lantern hard against her skin. She screamed even louder. Her sharp teeth glinted in the moonlight.

Her hands found their way around my neck. "Get off me!"

But it was working. The sizzling grew louder, and I fought against the urge to let go of my weapon and try to pry her hands away from my throat. I couldn't breathe—my face felt ready to pop—but I kept the lantern pushed against her skin.

I could see her face blister and darken. The iron burned her wherever it touched. My head felt light, like I was going to lose consciousness. Her strength was overwhelming. I wondered whether she was going to squeeze my head right off.

I told myself to keep pressing the iron against her face, but the feeling in my hands grew distant. My mouth opened and closed like a dying fish. But I still heard the sizzling sound her flesh made. I couldn't see anymore. Her face must have been blistered, searing . . .

With a cry that echoed through the trees behind us, the mermaid let go of my throat and threw me backwards. All at once, I gasped for breath, hit the rocks with a crack at the back of my skull, and fumbled for a grip on the lantern as my hands bashed against a sharp stone. My vision clouded with spots. I must have been on the threshold of passing out.

My stomach churned as the smell hit my nose, like a mixture of smoke and seaweed and rotting fish. I gave a great, choking sob. My throat still felt like it was being crushed in her stony hands.

Abruptly, the mermaid's shrieking stopped. I sat up, still gasping and dizzy, and swung the lantern in front of me.

She vanished. I couldn't see anything, but in the ringing silence, I assumed she'd jumped back in the water.

I stumbled to my feet and sprinted back to the trees. I dropped the lantern in the woods, the muscles in my fingers unable to hold on anymore.

I didn't stop running, even when I tripped over roots and my breath came out in wheezes and my lungs begged me to stop. I kept running as fast as I could, all the way through the trees and down the dead-end dirt road.

When I reached my yard, I only slowed a little to pull my jacket over my nose and mouth, hoping it would muffle my gasping.

My limbs trembled violently but, somehow, I managed to climb back through my window. I peeled off all my clothes and stuffed them into the gap between my bed and the wall so I could deal with them in the morning. Naked, I jumped under my quilt and pulled it over my head, sealing myself in its cocoon.

For a moment, I stared into the total blackness. And then I started sobbing. I couldn't stop myself. Pain filled me, from the top of my head to the soles of my feet, and my throat hurt so badly, I kept gagging, even though those icy fingers had long since released me.

Lysi had set me up. That mermaid was supposed to finish me off. The thought was more agonizing than the physical pain throbbing all over my body. Like a needle run through my ribs and into my heart, it brought more pain than anything Mama or Papa had told me about mermaids.

She said you were easy to fool.

Mama and Papa were right. Lysi was supposed to kill me in the end. She'd only been my friend so she could lure me in.

It made sense, when I finally accepted it. Her instincts weren't to befriend me—they were to trick my emotions so I'd go with her into the water. That was what sea demons did.

I eased over beneath my blankets, sweating and shivering. Though my eyes were shut tight and the quilt enclosed over my head like a den, I knew the sun would be rising soon. Somewhere very, very far away, a bird chirped joyfully.

I considered that Lysi perhaps didn't know about the other mermaid waiting there. But that didn't make sense. What about the rock tower? The mermaid wouldn't have known to set it up, and she wouldn't have known when and where to wait unless Lysi had told her everything.

Besides, that mermaid had spoken in perfect Eriana. Lysi did teach it to others, after all. Did the mermaids use it to lure sailors? Our sailors?

She said you were easy to fool.

I shuddered convulsively and curled my knees even tighter to my chest. My tear ducts felt dry, eyes swollen shut.

The mermaid's words were ingrained in me, and I would never forget them. I could never forget the words of Lysi's betrayal.

CHAPTER EIGHT

Changing Tactics

I awoke to the sound of unfamiliar voices in the kitchen, and lay there for a moment, listening. I could only recognise Mama, Papa, and Elaila.

A sharp pain in my hands came to my attention, which was relieved when I unclenched my fists. I looked at my palms and saw deep, bloody trenches.

Aching all over, I rolled out of bed and put on my bathrobe. Smudges of dirt and blood covered my sheets, and I tried to wipe them off without success. I pulled my quilt up, hoping Mama wouldn't notice. I wondered how hard it would be to use the washing machine. I'd have to stuff my sheets in next time Mama was out.

Voices still mumbled in the kitchen. I opened the door and padded down the hall to eavesdrop. The smell of freshly cooked rice met my nose, and I supposed Mama had served it for breakfast since that was all we had. Or maybe it was already lunch.

"How long are we going to keep this up?" said Mama. "Until the last of our men have been slain and we doom the Kwai to extinction?"

I leaned against the wall, listening.

"The Massacres are doing nothing to help us," said Elaila. "They aren't worth our losses."

"What do you suggest?" said a man whose voice I didn't recognise. "We let the demons take over the ocean and eat all our fish? We leave future generations to die?"

"We get off this island!"

"How?" said the man. "The demons will swarm the boat carrying our women and children. Besides, this is the most dangerous infestation the Pacific Ocean has ever seen. We need to eradicate the demons before they spread along the whole North American coast."

"Maybe if the problem spreads," said Elaila, her voice heated, "we'll finally get some outside help."

"If you want to abandon our island, go! I'm sure you can find a Canadian helicopter to come get you. But Eriana Kwai is my home, and I won't give it up to the demons."

I crouched and risked poking my head around the corner so I could see them with one eye.

Around the kitchen table sat Mama, Papa, Elaila, two men with their backs to me who I couldn't recognise, and the training master for the Massacres. I knew the training master by his scalp, which Nilus said he kept bald because a mermaid once swiped the hair and skin clean off the left side. I thought he'd probably told the truth, because the man's ear looked mangled, like the mermaid had almost taken that too.

"Relax, please, everybody," said the training master, his voice calm. "We have a new system in place."

"The next guaranteed plan, I'm sure?" said Elaila, still sounding angry.

"We are teaching our men to fight blindfolded. This way, they won't be tempted by the demons' beauty."

In the seconds of silence that followed, what I could see of Mama's expression became livid.

"So," she said, sitting up taller, "you're going to send them out with a blindfold and an iron machete and tell them *good luck?*"

"Our current training program has been preparing them for five years. They live and breathe combat. These warriors are invincible."

Papa spoke up. "This won't work."

The table fell silent, and the training master considered him seriously. Papa continued.

"Everything about the demons is alluring, not just their appearance. Their sound, their smell—even a blind sailor is at risk."

"True," said the training master, "but sight is the dominant source of the allure."

"Won't work," said Papa.

"What do you recommend we do, then?" said Elaila.

Papa's eyes dropped to the table, where his knuckles had been rapping a quick rhythm like they usually did when he thought hard about something.

One of the other men—the only one who hadn't made a sound yet—spoke up before Papa could say anything more. "Send women."

His voice was so low, a few seconds of silence passed before anyone seemed to process what he'd said.

Women? I thought. *What women?*

The training master raised his eyebrows. Mama's face turned frantically between the man and the training master.

"We can't turn our maidens into warriors," she said, sounding breathless.

"Why not?" said the man. "We can train them to fight just as we do with our boys. The demons won't tempt them, and the advantage is ours with our more developed weapons."

"That's absurd," said Papa. "We can't send young girls on a mission like this. It'd destroy them, physically and mentally. Have you forgotten what it's like out there?"

"Kasai," said the training master. "Girls are just as capable on the battlefield. You have a bias because of your daughter, but if you look at—"

Papa's chair screeched against the floor as he jumped to his feet. "Bias? I'm not the only one with a daughter at this table!"

I automatically clenched my fists when Papa's anger flared, and pain shot through my palms. Mama stood and placed a hand on his shoulder, shushing him.

The training master stood, too. "Let's calm down, everybody. Sit down."

Papa sat down stiffly, and Mama and the training master followed.

"The suggestion is a valid one," said the training master. He paused, staring at each face in turn. "I think this could be our solution."

"A little girl is not the way to get rid of the demons," said Papa.

"We'll first try the method we've been focusing on," said the training master. "Battling sightless. If our sailors don't return . . ." He dropped his eyes, rubbing his scalp. "Well, then we know it's time for a different approach."

Mama spoke up. "Who is going to volunteer their daughters? Tell me that. Who will—"

"The choice is not that of the child's parents. We'll select the strongest for training at age thirteen, like we do the boys. By the time they're eighteen, they'll be expert warriors."

"And you're prepared to lose your own daughter," said Elaila, in a tone more accusing than questioning.

"Adette is only six," said the training master. "I'd wager our girls will eradicate the demons by the time she's old enough to enter training. If not, Adette will go as a duty to her people. If we've trained them properly, I won't be losing her."

"Dani will go, too."

It was the man who'd made the suggestion. I studied him closely—a thick man with no neck, and hands made for working with oysters. The side of his face I could see when he turned to the training master was hard as stone, and his cold eyes looked permanently narrowed in scrutiny.

So this was Dani's papa. I'd heard about him a few times from my own papa, how he used to be in charge of all the fishing boats, but now worked at the woodshop, and how he always bossed others around even though he had no authority, and how Papa would've fired him for being so defiant if he didn't need him for heavy lifting.

"See?" said the training master, clasping his hands. "Already we have cooperation from parents. How old is your daughter? Ten? By the time the bill is passed she'll be the perfect age to start training. She and her friends—Meela and the rest of them—will train together and become skilled warriors."

The shock of hearing my name nearly made me fall forwards out of my hiding place. I pulled back and stared at the wall, seized by terror. I wasn't allowed near the beach my whole life because of mermaids . . . and now my people were talking about sending me out on a flimsy ship in the mermaid-infested waters?

No. Mama and Papa would never send me into training. My brother could do it because he was tough and strong. I could never be a killer.

I unfroze my spine and leaned around the corner. Papa had stood again.

"I won't have this," he said. "This is my house! I have seniority on this committee! I won't let us make such an extreme—"

"Eriana Kwai values our warriors above all," said the training master, even louder. "Becoming a warrior grants the individual and his family eternal honour."

"*I know what*—"

"That said, Kasai, we will let the whole committee decide if we want to privilege our women with the same honour. Tonight we'll make the proposal. This decision is not solely yours to make."

Papa's chest swelled, but he only shook his head and mumbled, "They won't agree. This won't pass. You'll see."

Mama's face looked as I felt—like someone had hit her on top of the head.

Elaila looked sickened. "We're talking about sending girls *like me*! I'm eighteen! I could never . . . I mean, just the thought of having to shoot one of those crossbows . . ."

"Dani will be ready for warrior training by the time she's thirteen. I will personally make sure of it," said Dani's papa.

In the stiff silence that followed, I hid behind the corner again. This couldn't happen. Eriana Kwai would never train girls like me to be warriors. It was barbaric.

I heard chairs push back, and I hurried to my room on tiptoe.

Was the island becoming desperate? Would our attempts at controlling the sea demons really come to this?

Footsteps crunched away from the house, but the door didn't close yet.

Dani's papa's voice, low and growling, carried down the hall. "Think of this as a lesson. Maybe once your daughter faces a few sea rats, she'll see the real dangers of the ocean. She'll stop thinking—"

"If you value lessons so highly," said Papa, "I can teach you one now about meddling in my family's business."

Of all the times Papa had been angry with me, his voice had never sounded that cold and severe.

"You can't deny it'll show her why you insist she stays away from the beach."

"Get out of my house, Mujihi!"

The door slammed.

I did understand the dangers! I wanted to shout it down the hall at that awful man. More than ever, I understood how dangerous mermaids were. I shook my arms to try and loosen my aching muscles, pacing the length of my bedroom.

Mama's panicked whisper carried down the hall.

"She might not get drafted, Kasai."

"Of course she'll be drafted!" said Papa. "She's tall and healthy. She's got fire in her. She's everything they're looking for in a warrior."

"But the other girls . . ."

"I've seen the other girls her age. If anyone's not going to get chosen, it'll be that scrawny friend of hers with the buckteeth."

There was a moment of total silence.

"What should we do?" whispered Mama.

"We hope it doesn't come to this. And if it does, we won't be cowards. We'll send our daughter proudly so she can honour her people."

Mama fell quiet. I thought she might have been crying.

"Maybe Mujihi's right," said Papa, his voice so low I could barely hear it. "Maybe this really is the only way."

Mama still said nothing. Seconds ticked by, and I leaned against my door, realising how hard I was breathing.

The island couldn't agree to training girls as warriors. How long had we been training boys to fight? Twenty years? Sending boys was based on tradition. Nobody would agree to change that now—would they? But these last few years had failed miserably, leaving the island worse off than ever. Maybe the rest of the island would think it time for drastic measures.

Something caught my eye in my dresser mirror.

I lunged towards it, yanking my bathrobe away from my neck.

Black. Long, narrow, finger-sized strips of black on all sides of my neck. If my purpled knees and heels of my hands weren't enough, the bruises where the mermaid had tried to strangle me jumped out like I'd smeared my skin with a Ravendust bush.

"No," I whispered, poking at the tender spots.

I dove for my closet and threw my clothes around, hunting for anything that would come up to my chin. I landed on a wrinkled, faded turtleneck and a zip-up sweater. Would Mama be suspicious if I wore these old clothes again? Maybe not. She had worse things to worry about.

I zipped my sweater all the way up and studied myself in the mirror. This would have to do. I'd have to wear the same two shirts until the marks faded—and my bruises usually lasted almost two weeks.

My face looked drained in the mirror. I sat on the bed and buried my face in my hands, breathing deeply. They wanted me to fight more mermaids, just like the one who'd done this to me . . . and Nilus had already gone out to fight full-grown mermaids and his battle had ended less fortunately than mine. I couldn't think about it. Trying to get rid of one mermaid was bad enough. Getting rid of all of them seemed impossible.

My insides quivered, but I had no more tears left to cry.

It wouldn't come to this. The boys would come back from the Massacre alive. The mermaids would leave us alone, and our need for Massacres would disappear, and I wouldn't have to face more of those awful monsters.

Time passed and my bruises faded, though Mama did notice my abnormal amount of scrapes and cuts one morning. I told her it was from playing, but she kept looking sideways at me, as if she didn't think I was telling the truth but didn't know how I could possibly be lying.

As the summer wore on, I became less hopeful that our need for Massacres would disappear. In July, grocery store prices climbed so high that Mama suggested selling the car for extra money.

"Who's going to buy that tin can on wheels?" said Papa. "Even if someone did, what'll it buy us? A sack of flour?"

In August, some of the high school kids tried to spend the hottest month of the year like any other teenager in the world: at the beach. A mermaid dragged one of them into the water. Papa went to the funeral.

The first day back to school, the other kids didn't look as healthy as usual. Everybody had a gaunt, sickly look, even the kids who had farmers or hunters for parents. Prices at the grocery store hadn't slowed in their skyward pursuit, and it seemed nobody was any better off than anyone else.

About this time, I knew I'd never hate anyone as much as I hated Lysi. Examining my bony ribs and sunken cheeks in the mirror one morning, I wondered why I ever wanted to be friends with the species causing Eriana Kwai so much suffering.

By December, we ate bannock and cabbage on a daily basis, and Mama's body had shrunk down so that, for the first time ever, I felt her bones when I hugged her.

Tanuu's papa was one of the island's best hunters, and his family invited ours over once a week to share his latest catch. Tanuu always made sure I stuffed my pockets with extra before going home, and I was grateful for it. I decided he wasn't so bad, when he wasn't trying to be a giant show-off. And anyway, his friendship helped me think less about Lysi.

February brought with it a helicopter full of rice and cans from the mainland, but split among the whole island, it only fed us for a few days. A small amount of food was better than no food, though.

"We are aware of your struggles here on Eriana Kwai," said the pilot, speaking in slow, deliberate English. "We are working to form a relief effort for your people."

We had no way to thank him, so we sent him back to Canada with a Ravendust sapling, since the plant was unique to Eriana Kwai. I thought it was lame and embarrassing, but Papa told me the gesture showed gratitude.

Too soon, the last day of April passed, and it went out with pounding wind and sideways sheets of rain. Panic crept up my throat as I wrote the date on my science notes. May 1st. The Massacre was already upon us, and the warriors would depart that afternoon.

Tanuu met Annith and me at the doorway at recess, looking grim.

"What'cha think will happen this year?" he said. "Think they'll finally kill a bunch?"

By that time, the news had spread across the island that the training program had turned out warriors who could fight blindfolded.

"No," I said, watching the rain as we huddled beneath the overhang. "My papa doesn't think this'll work."

Beside us, Annith giggled as Haden tried to show her how high he could jump by taking a running leap and pushing off the wall.

I sighed and looked back at Tanuu.

"What I don't get," I said, "is why the mermaids are being so violent."

"What d'you mean? They're flesh-eating creatures. They hunt humans."

They're not animals, I thought, but I didn't say it aloud.

"I thought they wanted to share the ocean's seafood and living space," I said. "If that's true, they shouldn't be coming onto the land and sinking our boats. Why us? Why not Alaska, or British Columbia?"

"Maybe they just haven't got there yet," said Tanuu, his dark brown eyes narrowing in confusion.

I bit my lip, feeling like we were all missing something. But maybe Lysi's excuse about coming here to build a utopia was another lie. Mermaids were just vicious and dangerous.

"They don't care about us, I guess," I said. I realised I hadn't thought about Lysi at all in weeks.

I felt Tanuu's gaze but didn't look at him.

"Come on," he said, and tousled my hair. "Let's play Demon Tag."

He bolted towards the muddy field. I turned to Annith and Haden, smacked Haden on the arm, and hollered, "You're it!" before sprinting after Tanuu.

School ended early that day. Our parents picked us up and brought us to the Massacre Departure Ceremony.

We shuffled down the road with the stream of families. As Mama and Papa spoke to some other parents, I ran to catch up with Annith and a sporty, ponytailed girl named Fern, who was Annith's neighbour.

"The training master's a pro," said Fern. "He can make anyone a demon-killing machine. Five bucks says those sailors could kick anyone's butt, even blindfolded. Isn't that right, Scarf?"

She pulled her stuffed tabby cat out from her armpit and stared at his beady eyes, as if he'd answer. Annith always said Fern liked to joke around, but I thought she was a little crazy.

"Gosh, they'd better kick butt," said Annith, pushing her straggly hair out of her eyes. "They're toast otherwise."

"They're our last hope," I said, remembering what would happen if the Massacre didn't work this year. My stomach flipped over.

"What d'you mean?" said Fern, pulling Scarf tight to her chest.

"Just . . . things will have to change if they don't come back."

Annith nodded. "We can't keep sending boys out to die."

We stopped as we hit the edge of the crowd, Mama and Papa to my left, Annith, Fern, and their families to my right. In the thick of the arriving masses, we found our places in the middle of the spectators' hill. Everyone chattered in low voices, giving opinions about whether this year would be successful.

Behind me, the dairy farmer and his wife argued in loud whispers.

"Anyo's a crock who should've been replaced years ago. What's he thinking?"

"I think it's a fine idea. The old tactics clearly don't work, and he's always coming up with creative new ways of battling."

"This isn't the time or place for creativity. We need methods that are sure to work."

"Like what? Name one!"

I stood on my toes to look at the docks, and saw the training master wringing his hands.

The murmuring crowd quieted. All eyes turned to the right, where the head of a narrow trail split the dense bush in half. The other end was at a campsite people used to visit back when seaside camping was safe. Since the Massacres began, the warriors marched from that trail and out to the docks every first of May, where we would bid them farewell and good luck.

I counted all twenty men as they emerged from the trail. They walked with broad shoulders, chins level with the ground, and each wore an all-brown uniform designed to repel water on the outside and keep body heat on the inside. Every uniform had a copper badge over the heart: a medal of honour for the warrior's bravery. The medals were once made of silver, but Papa said silver got too expensive. And, rather than engraving the medals with Eriana Kwai's national animal, the sea lion, the northern saw-whet owl had been chosen—an animal of the sky, not the sea. I liked the saw-whet owls—Mama said we had a unique subspecies on Eriana Kwai, making them special to us—but I wished whoever was in charge of the badges would stop being superstitious and just use our real national animal.

Besides, I thought a saw-whet owl gave more cause for superstition than a sea lion. The owls were pretty and graceful and had extra large eyes, and even though they looked innocent, they were predators. They were elusive, and you could miss one if you didn't look closely. They reminded me a lot more of mermaids than a big, chubby old sea lion.

The twenty men lined up on the docks and faced the crowd. I scanned their serious faces. The first warrior in the line continued for a couple of steps before stopping, and stood intentionally separate from the rest.

Something was wrong.

The way the men stared into the crowd gave me chills. They were looking, but they weren't looking. Their eyes seemed blank, their pupils too large and the retinas too dark. The surrounding skin was bright red, irritated. Only the first warrior really looked at us with knowing, seeing eyes.

I realised what had happened seconds after somebody screamed. And then more people screamed, and the dormant volcano surrounding me erupted.

My focus jumped back to the training master, who suddenly had to defend himself from a woman who'd lunged at him from the front of the crowd. A man stepped forwards to pull her off.

"You're a monster!" she yelled, her voice cracking. "Where's your conscience?"

The training master said nothing, watching the man from the crowd pull the woman away. I scanned the faces of the blinded sailors, and not a single one flinched; they remained at attention with their feet firmly planted on the docks.

"Those poor boys!" whispered Mama.

Papa turned to her with small, darkened eyes, then walked away without a word. The crowd let him pass before oozing into the space he left behind.

I leaned against Mama, and she put an arm around my shoulders.

The training master stepped up to the old, brown microphone and flicked a switch on the side. It crackled in the small speaker up front.

"Ladies, gentlemen, people of Eriana Kwai," he said, speaking with his usual fervour. "It's my honour to present you with this year's warriors. These men have toiled and trained for five years, watching others go out to battle and patiently awaiting their turn to prove their strength. We have a new technique in place to guarantee the men the opportunity to slay without interference. These warriors have been trained to fight with one of their senses hindered, and you would be amazed at their ability to sense, react, and ultimately, massacre."

The training master beamed with pride, but to me it looked forced. He was nervous, just like the rest of us. He was thinking about Papa's warning, about how blindness won't help, just like I was.

"And now," he said after stunned silence met his words, "a dance!"

The drums started. Two high school boys beat a solemn rhythm onto the rawhide. A man in his twenties—a past survivor—jumped in front of the drums to dance the warriors off to sea.

I watched his feet jump to the rhythm, his brown and orange and yellow costume swinging hypnotically like an oversized saw-whet owl ready to swoop down on a mouse. Rough lines that reminded me of feathers were painted onto his coat, and the black and yellow circles sewn into his headdress resembled pairs of owl eyes staring wildly around.

As he sang, the training master's daughter, Adette, joined in the dance. She was only seven, though I'd seen her at school. Her hair fell loose, braided with thick blades of grass and waving long past her shoulders. Her skirt was shimmery and brown and drawn tight near the ankles. She was a mermaid.

The two of them danced and sang as the ship drew away, and we continued to watch mutely.

The boy at the helm of the ship—the only one who hadn't been blinded—turned and waved at us, and I was glad I couldn't see his expression from where I stood. I couldn't imagine the terror he must have felt. His eyes were the only set among twenty bodies, and his duty was to stay alive for the sake of the entire crew—even the entire island.

The dance grew more frantic, and we watched the ship wordlessly until it faded behind a veil of fog.

That night, I prayed for the sailors to return, and I wept with the guilt of my selfish motives.

If the sailors didn't return, my training would begin. They would enrol me in the same program as my brother. They would mould my skills and mind into a warrior just like they'd done to him, and my papa, and every one of the strong, tough boys sent out over the years.

If they didn't return, my fate would be sealed. I would have to become a killer of mermaids.

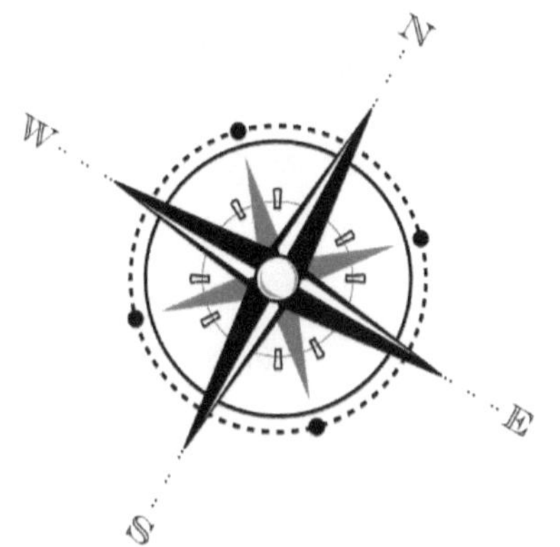

The Massacre

CHAPTER NINE

Bloodhound

I woke from a restless half-sleep long before the sun would rise. Staring wide-eyed at the ceiling with a steadily quickening pulse did nothing to help me fall back asleep, so I sat up.

My room had a bitter chill to it that reminded me it still wasn't summer. I rose and pulled the only outfit from my closet that was still hanging and not tossed to the floor: my Massacre uniform.

They'd been custom-made by the local seamstresses. All earthy tones, all thick to repel the cold, all resistant to water and glued at the seams with a waterproof seal. They were expensive; I had no doubt about that.

I put it on and stood in front of the mirror, hoping to see a fierce warrior and finding a timid, weak-looking teenager instead. I'd gained muscle from all the drills the training master had made us do, but I was still no more than an eighteen-year-old who had yet to grow into her curves.

I studied the copper badge on my chest with mixed feelings. The craftsmanship was so detailed, so impressive up close—but I couldn't help noticing the anger chiselled into the owl's eyes, which in nature were only kind and inquisitive.

Nothing pleasant could come of attempting to eat breakfast, so I sat on my bed, wondering how thirty minutes could have passed already. At this rate, I'd be marching down to the docks before my next breath.

I pulled out one of my binders from training and opened it so I could review some notes before my parents got up.

First Aid

Topic 1: Wounds

Types:

- Laceration – tearing. Caused by conch shells, barnacled rocks

- Puncture – calcified sea spears, blow darts

- Abrasion – surface scraping. Falling on deck or narrow weapon miss

- Ballistic – hit from comrade's iron bolt

- Penetration – stabbing and removal of sea spear

- Contusion – bruising, concussion. Conch shell, rocks, argillite

Treatment:

- Wound infection is common in battle. Cleaning is crucial

- Excessive blood loss weakens the body. Maintaining full strength is vital to survival on the water. Stop blood flow as fast as possible

I snapped the binder shut. I'd accomplished nothing but a cold sweat.

I threw the notes on the floor and curled up under my blankets, trying to stop myself from shivering.

Annith was the best in the class at first aid, and she wouldn't let me bleed to death. As long as she was still alive.

We'd all proven our strengths over the last five years. I just wished I could be good at everything. Having a weakness—any weakness—was not reassuring when leaving for the battleground.

The lines in the ceiling sharpened as the sun brightened behind my curtains. I glanced at the clock, and somehow another thirty minutes had passed. My stomach lurched.

The floorboards in the hall creaked. Someone was awake. I sat up so quickly it was like I'd just woken from a bad dream.

My next breath, my mother was forcing me to eat canned beans for breakfast. The next breath after that, my parents and I were putting on our jackets and boots. The next one, we were walking down the dirt road to the training area.

The universe must have been playing a cruel trick, making time pass so quickly when I wanted only to cherish my last hours at home.

Home. The same place I'd lived every day since I was born. I'd never spent more than a weekend away from it, and even then, I'd only been down the road at Annith's house.

We stopped outside the Safe Training Base, where the warriors always said their goodbyes before their families went to wait by the docks with everyone else.

My mother and father stopped and faced me. I looked between them, not knowing what to say.

Around me, other girls said private, teary goodbyes. Annith hugged her sister while her boyfriend, Rik, stood behind her with a hand on her back. Eyrin stood next to them, hugging her parents and her little brother all at once. There was Nora saying a passionate, lip-locked goodbye to her boyfriend, and Akirra glancing around as though not sure if it was uncool to hug her parents in public. Dani stood beyond that, engaged in what might have been an intense strategic conversation with her father. Arms crossed, he appeared to be the last person in the world to give anyone a hug.

"You've made me proud, Metlaa Gaela," said my father, and his hug took me by surprise.

A second passed before my arms unlocked to hug him back. For the briefest moment, I felt warmth in his arms as they wrapped around me, and then he let go.

I turned reluctantly to my mother, who seemed to tremble from the effort of keeping her face brave for me.

I threw myself against her and hugged her as tightly as I could.

"I love you, Mama," I whispered. Although I was taller than her now, I still felt like a little girl when she held me, and I stooped so I could fit my head under her chin.

"I love you, too," she whispered into my hair.

We held onto each other. She rocked me like she did when I was a child, and neither of us said a word. I blocked out the sounds around me and listened to her heart beating, trying to savour this last moment when I could feel small and helpless under the protection of my mother.

"Time to go, Meela," said Anyo.

Not yet. It was too soon.

"Meela."

"Wait." I wasn't done. I pulled away from my mother and looked around, urgency overcoming me.

"Where's Tanuu?" No sooner had I spoken the words than I spotted him standing some distance away, not talking to anyone but giving me the suspicion that he'd been watching me closely.

I walked over and stopped an arm's length away.

"The Massacre we've all been waiting for," he said, not meeting my eyes. "Make us proud."

I kept staring until he looked at me properly.

"I'm sorry," I said. "I reacted badly. I don't know what—"

He put up his hands. "It's fine. You don't have to say anything. We're only eighteen."

I somehow managed a smile. "Thanks. I . . . I do love you. I just don't know in which way."

He nodded and smiled back, and I stepped forwards to hug him tightly. He smelled warm, earthy, like everything I loved about the island, and I closed my eyes to seal it in my memory. He rested his chin on top of my head and held me securely in his arms, giving me the feeling that nothing could harm me as long as he was there.

But he wouldn't be there. And soon he let me go.

"See you when you get back," he said, and I couldn't help but feel reassured by his confidence that I would, in fact, come back.

Anyo grabbed my arm now, threatening to pull me away if I didn't join the line.

"Bye, Tanuu," I said, my voice frantic.

I searched for my parents in the crowd.

"I love you," I called, and I had to turn away because my mother started sobbing in my father's arms.

I lined up with the girls, front to back. A couple of other girls also had to be dragged into the line—Nora's lips must have been stuck to her boyfriend's, for all it took to peel her away—and after another few moments, we were all ready to go. I couldn't look at anyone else. Many had been crying. I breathed deeply, desperate not to let myself cry, too, because if my mother or Tanuu saw me it would make everything so much worse for them. I had to stay brave for their sake.

Our families started back to the docks to join the crowd, while the girls and I marched forwards through the path in the woods. I could see every dewdrop on the leaves as we strode by, and every particle in the mist curling around the branches. I heard birds singing more clearly than ever, and mud squelching beneath our leather boots, and insects buzzing and even leaves rustling. I inhaled the smell of moss and dirt and tried to commit it to memory before I left it behind. Lifting my face, I let the mist cling to my cheeks, cherishing the clean feeling, soon to be replaced by a sticky, salty spray.

In front of me in her brown uniform, Annith stopped. We'd reached the docks.

A few girls murmured and gasped, and I looked around in alarm before realising they were pointing excitedly at the docks. Floating majestically on the sparkling sea was our brand new ship. My stomach knotted from a wild combination of elation that it was ours, pride that my people had built it for us, awe at the craftsmanship, and fear . . . fear that it was so small against the vast ocean awaiting us.

It was a Mediterranean model, one we'd learned to call a brigantine. The body was wide, flat, and about the length of two orcas from bowsprit to stern. The bottom of the hull would be flecked with iron—just enough to keep the mermaids from smashing holes and sinking us, but not enough to weaken the wooden frame. Two masts thrust high above the water: the fore mast, with three square-rigged sails that reminded me of the mast on a pirate ship; and the main mast, fore-and-aft rigged so the sails ran front-to-back like a schooner's. The saw-whet owl scowled at us from the flag waving at the highest point of the main mast. A few small windows lined the hull, not far off the waterline, presumably to give us a bit of light below deck. The word *Bloodhound* was painted on the side of the ship in elegant cursive.

A fitting name, I thought, for a vessel designed to track down mermaids so we could run them through with weapons.

We faced the crowd. I stared into the anxious, excited, frightened, and stony faces of four thousand people of Eriana Kwai. The reality of the ceremony hung somewhere in the distance, not reaching my consciousness. This was it. This ceremony had happened every year in recent history, and this time, I was among the warriors waiting to set sail.

"Welcome!" said the training master into the ancient microphone. He motioned to us with a sweep of his arm. "It's my honour to present this year's Massacre warriors."

The crowd applauded. A few people whistled.

"The warriors standing beside me are stronger, fiercer, and more determined than any of those we've sent in the past. For five years, not a day has gone by in which they have not worked to better themselves—to train their minds and bodies for the task before them. Today marks the downfall of our curse. We'll live in peace and prosperity once again, all because of the warriors before you: the women of Eriana Kwai."

As he spoke, I looked beside me at the girls who would become my shipmates over the coming weeks—the family I'd grown to know over the last half-decade.

Annith stood to my right. Beside her was a slender girl we called Blacktail, because she was shy and skittish like a deer. I thought she also had enormous ears like a deer, but I never said so. After her stood Sage, Linoya, and Zarra, who I imagined would have been the rebellious kids if we'd gone to high school. Next was Eyrin, stone-faced as always, then Chadri and Nora. Dani, Shaena, Akirra, and Texas closed off the line to my right.

To my left stood the group who liked to play basketball on weekends: Holly, Nati, Kade, Shaani, Blondie, and Fern. We called the one girl Blondie because she was the only one of us with blonde hair—like Nora, Holly, and Shaena, her heritage traced back to the mainland.

At the very end stood Mannoh, our captain. Anyo had chosen her because her father was a former Massacre captain—the same Massacre my father had been on, where they'd killed a record five hundred and four mermaids.

"Before you set sail on your honourable quest," said the training master, "I'd like to present each of you with a parting gift."

He reached into a barrel once used for fish, and revealed a leather tool belt. Two large pouches were stuffed full, their zippers left open so he could flaunt the contents. Four daggers, a multi-tool pocketknife, and a water flask lined the right pouch. A compass hung off the side. The left pouch acted as a quiver, overflowing with iron bolts.

I almost sighed with relief at the sight of the belt. Receiving a parting gift from the island was rare, usually reserved for a group of warriors who might actually stand a chance.

Some other girls whispered excitedly. I wondered how much all twenty belts cost. The entire island must have pooled resources to purchase and make these. Even when parting gifts were awarded—and it had never happened in my lifetime—it was usually something simpler than a full belt of tools and weapons. My father had received a compass alone, which he still kept over top of the fireplace.

Other than my onyx ring, Nilus had never received a parting gift.

Annith caught my eye, smiling through the tears streaking her face.

"And one more thing!" shouted the training master, straining to be heard over the buzzing crowd.

He reached into the barrel and pulled out a bottle of something red. "May you all depart in style!"

He removed the lid with a pop, and the crowd laughed and applauded. It was war paint.

Anyo stopped at each of us in turn, handed us a tool belt, and swiped a thumb of red paint across our cheeks.

By the time he painted the face of the last girl in the line, the crowd grew louder than ever.

I drew a breath, trying to calm the butterflies in my stomach. Maybe the high spirits were a good omen. I let myself fantasize about returning home with a full ship, bringing news of a decimated mermaid population.

"And now, a dance," shouted the training master. "Let the gods watch over your pure souls."

The drums started. The beat grew louder and quicker with every pulse. Time for us to file onto the ship.

Adette jumped in front of the drums as usual, but she wasn't wearing her mermaid costume. She was dressed as a warrior, just like us, with the same uniform and face paint. The difference was in her hair, tied with feathers that fluttered around her shoulders as she danced, and in the feathers that hung from her arms when she raised them. A saw-whet owl, taking off for a hunt.

My chest tightened as I watched her dance, because I knew she had also been put in training. She'd started the year prior, destined to go on the Massacre in just four years' time. If we could slay enough demons, maybe Adette wouldn't have to go.

A young girl I didn't recognise jumped out then, wearing Adette's old mermaid costume. She appeared weak and small next to Adette and all her feathers, and I supposed that was the idea.

I stepped onto the gangplank, averting my eyes from the dance so I could watch my step.

The sensation of the rocking boat was oddly soothing, like being in a massive cradle. Some of the other girls' faces led me to believe they felt otherwise. The training program had warned us about seasickness, and luckily we had plenty of herbs on board to help those who suffered from it.

A chorus of voices erupted in time to the drums, the beat growing louder still, but they didn't sound like a funeral march this time. They sounded strong, and fierce, and above all, hopeful.

I waved to the crowd, fixing my gaze on my family standing to the side, while men untied us from the dock. We drifted away from the land. My parents became smaller, the music dimmer. My chest felt unbearably tight, like someone was squeezing my heart. I turned away. I watched the front of the ship instead, her pointed nose aimed boldly at the horizon.

Once the music and the people of Eriana Kwai faded away, we were left in hollow silence. Surrounded by emptiness, I wondered if this was how all soldiers felt after leaving their people behind.

Shaena positioned herself at the helm—she'd proven to have the best understanding of navigation, so that duty was mainly hers—and the rest of us took turns filing down to the hull to claim our crossbows.

I ran my hand along the grip, raising the weapon to my line of sight. It was sleeker and fit more comfortably on the shoulder than the old training crossbows. The sinew was stiff, sure to fire with more punch than any of us were used to. I slung it across my chest and left it there as we glided smoothly towards the horizon, not a speck of land in sight.

Leaning against the railing, I kept my gaze determinedly forwards, unable to watch the land creep away behind us.

The sea exhilarated me. I became hypnotised by the choppy waves. I watched how the Bloodhound crushed them into a salty spray, remaining steady all the while, unfazed by their size. I watched foam and logs and seagulls float by, and at times thought I could see fish swimming below the surface. The cold wind pushed against me, but I welcomed the goose bumps and pulled back my sleeve to watch them rise up my arm, relishing the sticky mist that clung to my skin.

The salt against my nose and tongue brought tears to my eyes, but in an odd, nostalgic way. It made me feel like a child again—and I turned my head to stop it.

"Meela," said Annith, popping up beside me.

I started, half expecting her to point out a mermaid rippling towards us already. But she had a faint smile on her face.

"Look!"

She held up her hand and showed me the backs of her fingers. I stared stupidly for a minute before realising a small silver band encircled her right ring finger.

I gasped. "Is that from Rik?"

"It's a promise ring," she said breathlessly. "He surprised me with it last night."

I'd never pinned myself as the type of girl who squeals when her best friend tells her about a serious relationship step, but I surprised myself when a high-pitched shriek came from my lips and suddenly we were jumping up and down and hugging each other.

"Let me see!" I grabbed her hand and examined it. It was simple, but very pretty. I wondered how he managed to afford such a luxury.

"He must really love you," I said.

When I looked up, Annith's hazel eyes were glossy and she had a mushy expression on her face.

"I think we'll get married some day," she said, still breathless. "It feels right. Like I've loved him my whole life."

"Annith, I'm so happy for you."

We hugged again. At the same time, I felt a pang of dread in my stomach, because Annith was leaving for an entire month with no guarantee of her survival.

Dani's voice cut through the wind. "You girls want to make yourselves useful?"

We looked up at her. She was poised at the helm next to Shaena, who sang herself a theme song as she steered the ship.

"*A pirate's quest, to slay some pests! We'll sail into the sun!*"

"What do you want us to do, exactly?" I said shortly.

"Swab the deck or something," said Dani. "This isn't a holiday."

"We just left! The deck is brand new!"

"*Yo, ho, we'll find their nest, and run a bolt through each rat's chest!*"

Dani narrowed her eyes. "I'm sure you can find something useful to do, besides stand there like a couple of invalids."

"Drop it, Dani," said Mannoh, stepping between us. "No point in getting all riled up yet. We should explore the ship a bit. Get to know our new home."

Over Mannoh's shoulder, Dani's face puckered, as though Mannoh had just shoved a sack of maggots in her face.

"Yes, *Captain*," she said with an icy sneer.

"*And sail into the sun!*" Shaena sang louder than ever, and she let her ponytail down so her chestnut hair could blow loose in the wind.

I sighed. "I bet Dani's only standing there because she's afraid Shaena will steer us into a rock."

Annith giggled. Mannoh pursed her lips and turned away.

"*We'll head due west, on our pirate's quest! And sail into the sun!*"

Annith and I crossed the main deck, until the wind drowned out Shaena's singing. We watched the passing sea from the bow of the ship.

"Beautiful out here, isn't it?" I said, admiring the way the sun glimmered on the water.

Though Annith's eyes revealed a trace of fear as she scanned the waves, she appeared captivated all the same.

"I'm trying not to think about how far down the water goes underneath us."

I shook my head, not letting the thought enter my mind. "Remember there's even more distance between you and the sky."

"And me and the nearest island, pretty soon."

"Don't think about it. You're part of the sea now."

I wasn't sure where my boldness came from, but somehow I felt like I belonged on the water. I thought maybe it was best not to say that aloud.

I ran my hands along the supple leather of the new belt around my waist.

"Should we check what's inside?" I said, seeing Annith do the same.

We sat on the deck, propped our crossbows against our laps, and pulled out our tools to examine each one. The daggers were beautifully crafted with black handles carved into comfortable grips, the blades shiny enough to reflect my gaze. When turned sideways, the edge all but vanished. One was long, thin, and steel, for cutting up fish. Another was double-edged, its point so sharp I could tell one prick would bring the blood oozing from my finger—perfect for stabbing, but the steel wouldn't kill a mermaid. Another was serrated: for sawing rather than killing. The last was black, heavy, and made of iron. There was no question of its purpose.

I held the compass flat in my palm and watched the arrowhead find its way north. It was elegant and made me feel like a real sailor, but I preferred to get my directions from the rising and setting sun. All we had to do was go west along the edge of the Gulf of Alaska.

I watched the red and white compass needle bob with us as we crested the waves, finding satisfaction in how it always pointed northwards again.

In addition to the pocketknife, daggers, water flask, and compass, I found a vial the size of my index finger, and—of all things—an American brand of lip balm. Annith and I pulled that out at the same time and laughed.

"Watermelon," she said in English, reading the label.

I looked at mine. "Cherry!"

We put them on, savouring the sweet flavours on our lips. I licked it off in a matter of seconds and had to stop myself from licking it directly out of the tube.

"What's in the bottle?" said Annith, holding her vial up to the sunlight. The jet-black contents had the consistency of a moist powder.

"I think it's kohl, for our eyes. To protect them from the sun."

Annith smeared a line across the back of her hand. "Oh my gosh, you're right! Here, close your eyes."

She dipped her little finger, and I held still while she drew a layer around my eyelids. When she pulled back and I opened my eyes, she gasped.

I jumped and put my hands to my face, wondering what went wrong.

"Meela, you look hot!" she said, beaming at me.

I dropped my hands. "Oh. I thought something bad happened."

She laughed and rolled her eyes. "You always assume it's bad if someone stares for too long."

I pulled out one of my daggers and tried to catch my reflection in the steel.

"Do mine!" said Annith, pushing my arm down and forcing the vial into my hands.

I dipped a finger into the damp powder. Annith closed her eyes and I smudged some across her eyelid. My hand wasn't very steady and I drew it on too thick.

"Oops," I said, pausing to fight back a lock of her windblown hair and staining it black in the process. "I'm not very good at this."

"I'm sure you're doing fine," said Annith, keeping her eyes closed. "It's supposed to be thick."

I sighed, dipping my finger back into the vial. "If you say so."

When I was done and she opened her eyes, I grinned. It made me think of the pretty girls I'd seen on TV with shadowy eye makeup. "You look like a movie star. Minus the war paint, of course."

"It looks good, right?" she said, and fixed her hair so it came down in front of her shoulders. "Now too bad there aren't any boys to impress around here."

I laughed. "We'll make sure to wear it when we get home."

Annith smiled, and I realised that somewhere inside me, I must have felt sure we'd make it home.

We fell quiet then. We followed the track of the sun as it made its way across the sky, taking us west towards the Aleutian Arc. Based on stories from Massacre survivors, the demons' nest was somewhere near the volcanic Aleutian islands that curved away from the Gulf of Alaska like a tail. Once there, we'd massacre every demon we could find.

We didn't know exactly where it was, only that it was like a wasps' nest—concealed, alive, and sure to destroy those unfortunate enough to find themselves on top of one.

CHAPTER TEN

Morbles

I'd never considered what it would be like, trapped on a small ship with nineteen teenage girls. The bickering started almost instantaneously, and everyone seemed overly keen to prove how responsible she could be without adult supervision.

Despite the training master's carefully planned schedule, when the time came for dinner, about twelve girls wanted to be first in line to cook. Seven of them crammed into the tiny galley and squabbled about how best to do the venison, and then whether we should have cheese yet or save it, and then, somehow, not a single one of them remembered to check the rice and it ended up burning to the bottom of the pot. Everyone yelled at everyone else.

When Texas finally called us into the galley, it was past eight o'clock and we were all ravenous. They decided to pull out the cheese, after all, presumably because we were so well stocked since Texas' family owned all the cattle. The girls had also made bannock to go with it. It was the best meal I'd had in months.

"Yikes, don't cook everything in our stores before the first week's up," said Linoya, and I groaned as half the girls who'd been in the kitchen yelled, "See? Told you! It's too much!"

The sun was still high after dinner—there was, of course, a reason Eriana Kwai picked May for the Massacres—and we decided to have hot tea on the main deck until bedtime. I was on dish duty with Eyrin and Blacktail. Some kind of wordless understanding passed between the three of us, and we took our time finishing the job. We didn't say much, enjoying the quiet moments spent away from the group.

When we climbed the stairs later, a lot of shouting and arguing was coming from the main deck.

Blacktail, Eyrin, and I exchanged a glance.

"It's gonna be a long few weeks," said Blacktail.

I smirked. She never said much, but when she did, it was always a comment I could appreciate.

Dani, Texas, Shaena, and Akirra stood over the rest of the girls, looking outraged.

"Lighten up," said Zarra, sounding exasperated as she and Texas clung to either end of a box. "We just want to make the first night epic, all right? We're not going to overdo it."

Well-known on Eriana Kwai, the same herbs used to treat seasickness also caused wonderful feelings of relaxation and euphoria when taken in larger doses.

Texas pulled hard. "How can you think about relaxing right now? We should be standing at the railing, ready to shoot a demon in the face!"

"Oh, please," said Linoya, standing up. "We're nowhere near the Arc. In the entire history of the Massacres, no one has ever been attacked on the first night."

"You don't know that!" said Akirra. "You only know about the Massacres that had survivors!"

"We can afford to have fun for—"

"Quit being so *useless*, Linoya," shouted Texas. "All you care about is fun. I don't know why you were even chosen to be here."

Pain flickered across Linoya's face, and she snapped her jaw shut.

"Would you guys cool it?" said Mannoh, stepping between Texas and Linoya. It was a bold move; Texas stood nearly a head taller than Mannoh and looked ready to sock Linoya in the nose. "Texas, just sit with us. You don't have to chew any."

"If the demons come—"

"It won't happen," I said, stopping behind Texas. "Demons don't attack at random. The military command will strategise—wait until we're close enough to their city— before sending troops out in hordes."

They all turned to me. Zarra's mouth opened, but no one made a sound. The training master always talked about the demons like they were a target, a species needing to be hunted, not a human-like army with attack strategies. But maybe it would benefit us to talk about demons that way— even if it did terrify people to death.

"Meela's right," said Mannoh. "All the attack patterns prove the demons are smarter than that. Now let's stop arguing and celebrate our departure."

The captain always had the final word.

While Dani's group sulked away, I poured myself tea from the pot in the middle of the circle and sat by Annith, who nibbled at a palmful of the dried herbs.

Dani made a point of busying herself, clearly trying to prove how productive and valuable she was. She set up a fishing net over the side of the ship, which I had to admit was a good idea. It was never too soon to start supplementing the food in our stores.

"So anyway," said Annith, as if the whole argument had been nothing but a minor sidetrack. "Rik said he knew he wanted to get me this since last year. He wanted me to have it as a promise from him, that he'll be loyal to me while I'm on the Massacre."

"Of course he'll be loyal," said Linoya. "All the hot girls his age are sitting right here!"

We gushed about Annith's promise ring for a while, and then Nora complained about how her boyfriend never gave her anything even though they'd been dating since they were fourteen, and then a few other girls talked about their crushes or potential boyfriends or ex-boyfriends. I mostly stayed quiet, thankful no one pressed me with questions about Tanuu.

The sun dipped below the horizon, and conversations faded as the sky darkened. Linoya jumped to her feet, thrusting a fistful of herbs in the air.

"A toast!"

The rest of us fell silent.

"To our families back home, and our family here on board the Bloodhound. To friendship, love, and the spirit of Eriana. To slaughtering every one of those hell-born sea rats that crosses our path!"

Everyone cheered. Annith and I exchanged a smile, and I raised my mug alongside her clenched fist.

We stayed up until the darkness became absolute and the tea became cold, then trickled to bed a few at a time. Shaena resumed her post at the helm, to be taken over partway through the night by Akirra. Blacktail was still gazing at the horizon when I stood, but she seemed peaceful so I let her be with her thoughts.

A chill crept over me as I scanned the pitch-black water. I crossed my arms and descended to the cabin.

I hung my crossbow by the door alongside everyone else's. Someone had lit a lantern, illuminating the faint images of Sage and Kade as they pulled on their nightgowns, and Nati braiding Fern's hair while Fern squeezed her badly tattered stuffed cat. The other girls already lay in their beds—narrow bunks stacked three-high along the walls.

My bed was second on the right, bottom bunk. One row beyond that, also on the bottom, Dani's dark figure lay curled beneath the blankets. Her ribcage rose and fell with each breath. She might have looked peaceful, for once—if it weren't for the crossbow wrapped in her arms.

Our compasses proved essential by the following afternoon. The rain poured hard, the sky so dense with clouds that we couldn't follow the sun's path. We took turns huddling below deck, having become soaked instantly from rain and ocean spray.

The downpour didn't let up until the following morning, when we awoke to overcast skies and a frost in the air. We all pulled on our thick parkas.

I meditated over the empty waves all morning, dread gnawing at my stomach.

How close were we to the Aleutian Arc? Did the sea demons know we were coming by now?

I turned my back to the water and scrutinised the crew. Annith sat by the cabin door with Fern, but I didn't feel like talking to them. Shaena bounced up and down at the helm, looking inattentive while Texas chattered beside her. Dani checked the foresail and tightened the lines as she saw fit—though I could tell from where I stood that everything was in order. In the centre of the main deck, the normally silent Eyrin was talking to Blondie and a few of her friends. Eyrin held a fistful of iron bolts, tossing them on the deck at varying intervals.

A smile tugged at the corners of my mouth. She'd invented a game. Eager for distraction, I went over to see how it worked.

"She has to stay behind, um . . . behind this line when she throws it," said Eyrin, flush-faced.

They turned when they saw me coming.

"We've called it Morbles," said Holly, "because it's kind of like marbles, only morbid."

She held up an iron bolt, showcasing the deadly piece of ammo against the cloudy sky.

"The objective is, um . . . is to hit the other team's bolts," said Eyrin, tossing one to take her turn, "but . . . but you aren't allowed to step beyond the closest bolt on your own side."

"There has to be a better punishment for missing," said Kade. "Every time you miss, you have to throw the next one from further back."

"How about," said Nati, "every time you miss, you have to throw the next one from a more awkward position?"

She turned around, bent over, and fired the next one through her legs. We erupted in laughter. I joined the game, realising I didn't need to wait until a new game started since there was no apparent structure. Annith and Fern joined us soon after that.

Eventually, we added so many rules that we kept forgetting them, and Holly ended up in a giggling fit over one rule that had her leap-frogging over the other team's bolts. I took a turn lying down and tossing a bolt with my feet, and then Eyrin had to close her eyes while we spun her in a circle for thirty seconds.

Maybe we'd been playing for too long and gotten carried away, because we let Eyrin go with too much enthusiasm, and she threw her bolt with such force it sent every other one flying—something we found hysterical until several of them careened towards the edge of the deck.

Nati and I reacted first: we gasped, lunging for the scattered bolts. But they were too far away. Five of them plunged off the side of the ship.

We gaped at each other. The girls behind us stopped laughing abruptly.

A roar from Shaena cut through the silence, and she left her post at the helm to storm over to us.

"I knew you were going to do something stupid!" she yelled. "I should've stopped you ages ago!"

"It was an accident, Shae," said Holly. "We obviously didn't mean to chuck weapons into the water."

"Well you have to be pretty dumb to play a game that risks losing our ammo! Where's Mannoh?"

She looked around wildly, eyes bulging.

"Relax!" I said, working hard to keep from shouting back. "We have an entire hull full of ammo. We have bigger issues if five bolts is going to make or break us."

"It could!"

"Well we can't get 'em back now," said Fern, shooting a nasty glare at Shaena. "So simmer down a bit."

"I . . . I'm so sorry," said Eyrin, her voice high. I thought I could see her eyes brimming with tears.

"It's not your fault," I said, gripping her shoulder. "It was all of us. Don't worry about it."

Shaena glanced around, and I knew she was hoping Dani would come help yell at us. But Dani was on dinner duty. So Shaena inclined her head, then whirled around and strode back to the helm.

I checked the position of the sun. We'd been playing all afternoon.

The game had been bittersweet, and the first time I'd been able to forget the sense of impending doom hanging over us like a blanket of chain armour.

My anxiety returned like a tidal wave as the sun approached the horizon.

After dinner, I found Linoya on her back with her feet in the air, heels resting on the main mast. She examined an herb closely, like each tiny flower held the answer to a secret.

I wasn't sure if she knew I'd approached, but then she said slowly, "Shouldn't we have seen a mermaid by now?"

She popped the herb in her mouth.

I sat beside her. "Maybe. I'm not sure how close we are to the Arc."

"But they live everywhere."

"Right."

She held out a hand to me, offering me some herbs.

"No, thanks," I said. "I'm not seasick."

"Neither am I."

She spoke in a drawl, eyes abnormally narrow. "Texas was right," she said. "I'm useless. I should be standing by, ready to kill demons. Just trying to chill the nerves."

"Take them if you need them," I said. "I don't care."

We sat in silence, Linoya popping herbs in her mouth at regular intervals.

"I don't like that they're waiting until we brush their nest," she said. She was surprisingly coherent, considering how dim she looked. "They're smarter than Anyo gives 'em credit for."

My stomach churned. I dropped my eyes to the sleek crossbow laid across my lap.

"But we have better weapons."

She gave me a lopsided smile. "What d'you think will matter in the end? Weapons or numbers?"

"Weapons," I said, trying to put a victorious edge to my voice.

Linoya just squinted at me and laughed, short and deep.

A shout came from the helm, and I turned to see Shaena jumping up and down. Dani stood beside her, a smug look on her pointed face.

"The Arc!" said Shaena, flapping her arms. "I see it!"

I leapt to my feet. In the distance, a mountainous chunk of land was just visible through a coating of fog. I knew I wasn't imagining the clouds billowing from the islands: Anyo had told us the Aleutian mountain range was full of active volcanoes.

My breath halted in my throat, and I caught Annith's eye across the deck. She'd thrown her hands over her mouth.

I made my way to the ship's nose. I hadn't noticed until that moment, but the days spent in the empty, endless sea had been pulling at my nerves. The snow-covered hills and billowing peaks evoked a sense of comfort that solid ground was near. At the same time, terror bubbled in my stomach. We were officially within range of the demons' nest.

The silence grew as heavy as the fog cocooning the islands.

"Think anyone still lives there?" said Blacktail. She leaned against the railing beside me.

"I was wondering the same."

"Bet they fled to mainland Alaska."

I shook my head. "I wouldn't leave Eriana Kwai. Would you?"

She squinted ahead. "No. Guess not."

"The demons are a lot closer to them," I said. "Do you think they Massacre too?"

"I doubt it. If they did, the rest of Alaska would help. And if they were helping, we'd know it. We'd be better off."

The waves lapped against the ship, and I peeled my eyes away from the ghostly volcanoes to watch them. Maybe if we were more important on Eriana Kwai—if we were officially a part of North America, or if we had something more valuable to trade than fish—we'd be getting outside help.

"Maybe the Aleut people died," said Blacktail hesitantly. "Because of the mermaids."

"Nah." I thought of what the US would do if hundreds of their own people died because of the sea demons. "I think we'd know it if they'd all died, too."

"True."

I dropped my hands from the railing and turned to her. The wind swept my sticky hair into my eyes. "What, then? They live on the islands, still, but don't need to Massacre?"

Our gazes locked. I couldn't help but feel like we were missing something.

"Hop to it, ladies," shouted Dani, making me jump. I turned. Shaena, Texas, and Akirra were already patrolling the starboard railing, scanning the water as if hoping to be the first to shoot a mermaid in the head.

Mannoh scowled at Dani, then told everyone with even more volume that we should take our positions and be on careful guard.

I ran my hand along my crossbow, the iron smooth beneath my palm. "I'll take the port side." I started towards the main deck.

"Meela."

I kept moving. "I know I'm supposed to take the starboard, but Dani's toadies are over there and no one's—"

"Meela," said Blacktail again, and this time I caught the desperation in her voice.

I stopped and turned around.

Her eyes were the widest I'd ever seen them. Her mouth was open, lips strained tight with horror.

I whirled around, muscles reacting before I had time to think.

A long-fingered hand worked its way up the railing beside me like an oversized spider; the black hair of a young woman followed. Her eyes were large and bright, emerald green, and curiously scanning their surroundings.

Beads of seawater dripped from her sleek hair and down her chest. Her other hand came up to rest playfully beneath her chin.

She smiled.

CHAPTER ELEVEN

Blood and Flesh-eaters

I stood rooted to the deck, mere steps away from her, unable to do anything except stare.

Her bottom half wasn't visible. If we didn't know any better, we could have mistaken her for a young woman. But we did know better. We knew from the waist down she was mutated—a demon.

"*Hanu aii*," she said. Her high voice rolled as smoothly as the waves.

The overlarge eyes found mine, unnaturally vivid, a flare I couldn't look away from. She motioned me forwards with long, white fingers. A soft noise came from the base of her throat, almost like purring.

I stepped back. She was trying to hypnotise me.

She dropped her hand, seeming to realise her seduction wasn't working. Her eyes hardened, and she looked around as though suddenly aware of the rest of the crew.

Nobody said anything; we only stared at this benign creature. She was just a girl our age, and vastly more beautiful than any of us. But from the waist down . . .

Dani stepped forwards, shoulders squared.

"Stay back!" she yelled to the mermaid, aiming her crossbow.

The mermaid scrutinised Dani, and though her smile fell, not a trace of fear showed in her enormous green eyes.

Dani tightened her grip but didn't fire. The crew seemed to hold its breath. Something felt amiss about sending a bullet through this teenage girl. Was this really what we'd come here to kill?

But then the mermaid's lips curled back, and before my eyes, her teeth changed. They lengthened into points. A gust of wind swept her hair forwards so the jet-black locks billowed around her, and the beautiful young girl looked suddenly feral. She screeched, a high-pitched wail that echoed across the water.

The instant I realised how immobile we'd become, she launched herself over the railing and landed on the deck with a thud I felt in my legs. Movement erupted around us; dozens of hands and faces appeared between the railings on all sides.

I had to admire Dani's reactions: before my muscles even responded, she shot the black-haired mermaid through the heart. The mermaid choked to a halt, crimson blood splattering from her chest. But we'd all been transfixed for too long—were we hypnotised?—and at least fifty mermaids scaled the Bloodhound on all sides.

I stared at Dani's victim. Head bowed, she tried to hold herself up with trembling arms.

An earthquake rumbled the deck. Around me, the mermaids descended on the ship with a dexterity I'd never seen.

But the girl! I turned back to her. She was dead. Her glistening corpse lay face down in a spreading pool of blood.

She isn't a girl.

The proof lay in front of me. I could see the demon's tail.

A smell met my nose, infusing me with panic, bringing forth a memory I'd buried for so long—rotting fish, smoke, seaweed—the smell of a mermaid freshly defiled by iron.

Blacktail reacted beside me. She fired at a mermaid and ran for the main deck, already loading another bolt.

My hand tightened around my crossbow. Did I just witness a murder, or a step towards freedom? That didn't matter now. I forced my eyes away from the pool of blood, cranking the lever and notching a bolt with numb fingers. The other mermaids advanced, and they moved more quickly than I imagined.

One of them thundered onto the deck across from me. I stepped back, hoisting my crossbow to my shoulder. Her eyes locked on me—on my throat. Time slowed. The girl's smooth body transformed before my eyes . . .

And more than ever, without a mask of darkness, I understood why they were called sea demons.

Her eyes were red the whole way through, deeper than blood, without a pupil or the surrounding whites. Her heavy auburn hair fell over her face and shoulders but never covered her diabolic eyes. Her skin was rotten, the colour of seaweed, and even the shape of her ears reminded me of the slimy algae that often washed up on the beach.

She moved across the deck with a jarring stiffness; if I hadn't known she was a mermaid, I would've thought I was witnessing a girl possessed by the devil. She used her arms to drag herself forwards, rigidly shifting her weight, locking her elbows to keep her body upright. With each shift, her bony shoulders seemed to pop out of place. One of her hands clawed the deck—the hand of a fish, webbed with clear skin between the fingers from grooves to knuckles. Her other hand gripped a weapon, a conch shell, and she smashed it into the deck as though the planks of wood were just as much her enemy. The way she advanced was a practiced technique, swift enough to catch a fleeing human.

My lungs contracted frantically; my limbs numbed of all feeling. This was no human. This was the furthest thing from a human.

Shoot it, Meela!

The sound of whizzing bolts, thundering feet, screaming girls, and screeching mermaids pounded in my ears. I leaned my head down to aim. My frozen muscles finally responded as the demon drew near enough to attack. I aligned my sight with her chest, and pulled the trigger.

The bolt shot wide of her heart and pierced her shoulder—enough to fatally wound, but not to instantly kill. Still, she advanced.

Cursing, I pulled another bolt from my quiver. My hands must have been shaking.

Without warning, the demon threw her conch shell at my face with the strength of a cannon fire. I ducked, but felt the tip slice across my scalp. Pain exploded and warmth oozed from the wound. My knees weakened at the feel of my own blood.

Anger shot through me—mostly at myself for wasting so much time. I straightened, jammed the bolt against the shaft, and paused for a millisecond to aim.

Before I even finished pulling the trigger, I knew I had her. The bolt hit her dead in the throat. Her mouth opened like she was trying to scream, but no sound came out. I gasped, turning away as the blood spilled from her like a geyser.

My muscles had awoken, vibrating with adrenaline. Blood pulsed into my limbs and forced away the queasiness that had taken hold.

Another demon lunged at me from the side. I spun and fired without hesitating. It hit her in the heart and she collapsed. But already the next demon was upon me, nearly wrapping her slimy fingers around my ankle. I shot her through the top of the head. Blood splattered into my eyes.

Blinded, I stumbled backwards, reaching into my quiver for another bolt. But no other mermaids came. Screams and hissing crossbows filled the air. I wiped my face on my sleeve and scanned the corpse-laden deck.

Dani was at the fore mast in the thick of the action. She stood on the boom, firing downwards, battling four mermaids at once. Rocks and blow darts peppered her. Some knocked her off-balance and darts stuck into her arms, but she was quick. She reloaded smoothly and without pause, firing at each of her attackers in turn. She pulled darts from her skin only to launch them back at the mermaids.

More approached but three other girls took them out in sequence. Beside them, Linoya roared at the demons, swinging her crossbow and egging them to come get her. Beside her, Nora shot them down with lightning-fast reactions.

At the edge of the deck, Eyrin had dropped her crossbow. A brown-haired mermaid swung a jagged spear—once a harpoon, perhaps, but ravaged by the sea and covered in sharp barnacles. Twice, the spear caught Eyrin in the arm, and bloody gashes spilled open.

I ran forwards, but before I could raise my weapon something whizzed past my nose and I turned in time to see a demon rushing towards me with a fistful of short spears. She hurled another with blinding speed. I ducked, keeping my sight aligned, and pulled the trigger. The bolt hit her in the stomach before she could throw another spear. She made a wet coughing sound and buckled over.

I turned back to Eyrin. Her assailant raised an arm to strike again. I didn't have time to get there. I rooted my feet on the swaying deck. My bow steadied as I exhaled. I fired.

The bolt buried in the mermaid's ribcage. She fell to the side, dead instantly. Eyrin scrambled backwards.

Another mermaid had been waiting. She launched herself at Eyrin with a barnacle-covered rock in her hand and knocked them both to the deck. I slammed another bolt against the shaft. Eyrin shrieked. She tried to push the mermaid off but the mermaid had her pinned.

I aimed—but the mermaid's arm was a blur. She smashed the rock into Eyrin's temple. I screamed and let the bolt loose too soon. It shot wide, skimming the mermaid's tangled mess of hair. She flinched but didn't look.

Eyrin went limp. I loaded my crossbow with a violently shaking hand. The mermaid gripped Eyrin's head with a webbed hand and brought the other back, and met Eyrin's skull with another blow. I fired. The bolt sliced through the mermaid's tail as she continued to bludgeon Eyrin's limp body.

The mermaid fell off but still held onto Eyrin's hair. She struggled to pull herself upright.

"Eyrin!"

I sprinted towards them. She wasn't moving. She couldn't be . . . she was just unconscious. I had to take her away from the demon.

The mermaid looked at me, still clenching the bloodied rock in one hand and Eyrin's hair in the other. Her red eyes gleamed. For a moment they faded into white—into human eyes—but then she smiled and her jagged teeth grew back, and she lunged at Eyrin like a striking cobra.

I froze, as though the air had turned to ice. My brain and my eyes disconnected—what I saw couldn't be real. Nature couldn't function this way. The monster I stared at, this half-formed human, couldn't be ripping flesh off Eyrin's body like a mountain lion on a deer. The chunks she swallowed whole couldn't be pieces of flesh. The blood— she was covered. It stained her sallow flesh red.

This wasn't happening.

I reloaded and aimed at the feasting demon, but before I could fire, a change beneath my feet threw me sideways. I landed hard on my hip, the crossbow flying out of my hands.

The deck tilted, sending loose items sliding towards the water; I lunged for the bow, desperate not to lose my weapon. It crashed into the railing and leaned dangerously against it, threatening to fall through.

Above, the great fore mast tilted towards the water as the ship careened. I should have been panicking but I still felt numb, the vision of Eyrin's bloody corpse burned into my eyes, blinding me to everything else.

As the ship continued to lean, I lost control of my limbs and was suddenly face down on the deck, head smacking hard into a post. Still, I kept an eye on my crossbow. The tip of the black handle rested feebly against a railing, the ocean thrashing beneath it. I brought my knees up and pushed myself closer.

Whatever had been making the ship tilt, it released. I swiped for my crossbow and my fingers closed around it as we rocked back the other way. The deck levelled. I scrambled to get my feet under me.

Blacktail appeared beside me, her bloodstained hands void of a weapon. She crouched, bracing herself. The entire ship shuddered. It lifted on its side again, this time tilting the other way. Something other than the waves was at play.

The ship lurched and I nearly went down again, but I leapt forwards and grabbed the railing. Blacktail did the same.

Below our slipping feet, the mainsail drew dangerously close to the water. The deck was nearly vertical.

"They've cornered a whale," said Blacktail.

Her eyes were enormous, her breathing fast and panicky. She had a white-knuckled grip on the railing.

Between fits of swinging my legs to get a hold on something, I managed to choke out, "What d'you mean?"

"I saw a few of them. They're using harpoons. They cornered a whale against the keel. They jab at it, so it has nowhere to go but further into the ship."

Below us, the masts drew almost parallel with the water. A swarm of demons clung to them like leeches, trying to weigh them down.

"They'll capsize us!"

The saw-whet owl flag was half-submerged. The mermaids hung off it, tearing at it with their teeth and webbed fingers. The rope holding it to the mast seemed as feeble as a thread. Then, like a shrivelled maple leaf in autumn, it plucked loose and fell into the water, taking several cackling mermaids with it.

"Meela," said Blacktail. She was staring up at her hands. "I'm slipping."

Her voice was so calm, she might as well have been commenting on the direction of the wind.

I looked down, trying to find something for us to rest our feet on.

"Let go," I said. "Try and land on those crates." I nodded to the other side of the deck.

"I'll break my legs!"

But she didn't need to worry, because the whale must have escaped, and the Bloodhound crashed back down to the sea. My stomach lurched at the free-fall.

We slammed into the water and a solid wave pounded down on us. I held onto the railing with all my strength to keep from getting washed away. My crossbow pushed painfully into my arms as the deluge swirled around us. My ears knew nothing but the hollow, rushing sound of a current.

The water swirled endlessly over us. My lungs begged for air, the muscles in my hands and arms trembled, and I wondered if the demons had capsized us after all. But then the hollow underwater sound shifted, deafening me with a noise like a rushing river.

I welcomed an enormous gulp of air into my lungs.

The ship rocked violently, threatening to overturn with each tilt.

Beside me, the railing was vacant. Blacktail was gone.

I cried out, searching across the way for her body. But I couldn't see her. So many corpses littered the water it was as though we'd taken a wrong turn at the River Styx. I scanned the bodies frantically.

A head emerged from the red water, staring at the rocking ship. The demon's eyes had faded to normal, her skin ivory white. Her gaze found mine, but when I reached for my crossbow, she submerged once more.

The screams and firing crossbows had been silenced.

Panting with fear, I glanced around. My legs shook too badly for me to stand up. My hands still clamped the railing. I couldn't pry them away.

I tried to yell for Annith but my voice stuck in my throat.

"Meela," said a voice close to my ear.

I started. Blacktail hung on the other side of the railing, clinging to the same one I was.

"Help me over," she said, her arms visibly trembling. "My feet touch the water when the boat rocks."

I scrambled to my knees and pulled myself to my feet, using the railing as support. I leaned over it and grabbed her under the arms.

"Have you got a foothold on something?" I said. My voice was weak and quiet.

"A bit."

"Next time it rocks up, push with your legs."

She grunted. The Bloodhound swayed, and her legs touched the water, and as it rocked back up I pulled as hard as I could. I heard her legs scrambling to push on anything they could find, and then I wrapped my arms around her waist and hauled her aboard.

We collapsed onto the deck, gasping. Both of us shook worse than ever—probably from the cold, as well.

I hugged her tightly when she landed, feeling a surge of gratitude that she was alive.

"What happened?" she said breathlessly. "Where'd they go?"

I glanced around the empty ship. "I think they retreated for now. We were slaughtering them."

My eyes fell onto Blondie and Kade, who showed bloodied signs of having been in a struggle on the far end of the deck.

"There's Annith," said Blacktail, and I whirled around to see her and Linoya coming from the helm. I struggled to my feet to meet her.

"You're okay!" I said, though she appeared miserable and shaken.

Her eyes raked my scalp. "You're not."

I lifted my hand, suddenly remembering a demon had sliced it open. It felt like it was on fire. Blood covered my clothes, probably most of my face. I didn't know how much of that blood was my own.

"Annith," said Kade, her voice high. "We need stitches here."

We all turned to see Zarra stumbling forwards with a hand over the entire right side of her face. Blood cascaded down her cheek and between her fingers, and I had to drop my gaze because my head suddenly felt like it drained of fluid.

"I'll get the first aid kit," said Annith, dashing to the cabin.

I took a mental inventory of the girls standing before me.

Sixteen. Only sixteen of us remained, including me.

"Where's Shaani?" said Fern.

A dark silence fell over us. I couldn't look at Fern.

After a moment I said, "Eyrin's gone."

Every eye fell on me. I stared down at my bloody clothes.

"I saw it," I said, my voice barely audible.

After a few seconds, Holly said, "Nati, too."

"Mannoh. Mannoh got pulled in."

Nora said it, but after a shocked silence, the entire crew turned towards Shaena.

Shaena stepped back, her eyes huge and white behind her blood-covered face. The training master had chosen an order of captaining for us, should anything happen to Mannoh. After Mannoh was Shaena. After Shaena, Linoya. After Linoya, me. After me, Dani. And so on. I'd taken dark reassurance in the thought that as long as I was still alive, Dani could never be my captain.

Nobody said anything for a long time. We'd lost four warriors that day, including our captain. The first battle, and already our numbers were cut by one fifth.

"Clean up the ship," said Shaena, her voice dull and tired. "See Annith if you're hurt."

Annith returned and sat down with the first aid kit. I looked away when she pulled out a needle and silk thread.

"Who else is hurt?" she said. Her voice was high and shaky, and I could tell she was trying to keep busy so she wouldn't break down.

I wished I felt confident enough to reassure her. My mind was still trying to process the fatalities.

Annith spent at least a couple of hours patching everyone up. We took turns changing clothes and cleaning the deck—though the surge of water had washed off most of the blood and bodies.

"We did well, though," said Annith once she'd finished with my scalp.

I raised my eyebrows.

"I mean, we killed a lot of demons," she said. "If we keep going at this rate, I think we might be able to cut the population down enough—"

"If we keep going at this rate," I said, "we're all going to be dead by the fifth battle. We have to do a better job looking out for each other."

Annith frowned. "You know what Anyo said. It's survival of the fittest. The ones who aren't cut out for this get picked off in the first battle."

I stood. "Eyrin wasn't weak. None of these girls are weak."

"I never said they were."

I ran my fingers over the stitches on my scalp. The feel of them made me queasy. "I'm going to reload."

I descended into the hull. We kept the ammo safely behind iron bars, which I fought to unlock with shaking hands. My eyes brimmed with tears, but I forced them back, afraid I wouldn't be able to stop once I started.

What kind of hellish mission were we on? Was this really what the Massacres had been like for more than a quarter century? Did Eriana Kwai knowingly send their eighteen-year-old boys out to face this, year after year?

This wasn't like shooting a target, or a rabbit, or even a full-grown buck. This wasn't the simple task of harnessing an invasive species, like we were a team of biologists on an expedition. This was the most gruesome combination imaginable: an attack by the most nightmarish demons the devil could summon . . . yet shooting them was like shooting humans, normal teenage girls. Those mermaids looked like any one of us when their appearances faded back to normal.

I couldn't let their human facade faze me. That was what the demons wanted. The human image was just that: an image. Inside, they were as hideous as their rotten-looking skin, and they deserved to die.

They're the reason your people are starving, I thought. *They're the reason you don't have a brother. They came all the way to your homeland to make your people suffer. They kill children and lure sailors and . . .*

My quiver was full. I realised I was still trying to jam bolts into it.

They eat humans.

I put everything down and breathed deeply, closing my eyes and willing myself to stop trembling.

I needed to get outside again. Standing in the darkening hull did nothing to calm me. I tried to call the training master's voice to mind, telling me to turn off my emotions. But I couldn't. My emotions rampaged around my insides like they'd been shot from a cannon.

How many demons were there? After we killed five hundred and four like my father had, would we find our victory?

I stared numbly around as I emerged from the hull. The deck was already stained red, and deep crevices in the wood aged the Bloodhound by years. This was our brand new ship. The men and women of Eriana Kwai had spent an entire year building it for us, sawing and hammering a dream of peace and prosperity.

As I took in the battered girls around me, pushing past their exhaustion to clean and repair this dream, pride surged through me. Twenty—now sixteen—girls on a brigantine ship had become Eriana Kwai's only hope.

Annith stepped up beside me and put an arm around my shoulders.

She was right. We did well. We must have killed a hundred demons already.

"For Eriana Kwai," I said, slinging my crossbow across my chest.

Annith patted her own crossbow and took a deep breath. "For Eriana Kwai."

Thinking of my people made it easier to force that black tar to melt over my heart. I could almost feel it dripping, coating my insides with thick vengeance on behalf of my fallen comrades.

Five hundred and four demons weren't enough. For them, and for all the people who depended on me back home, I would slay every single one.

CHAPTER TWELVE

Pirate Democracy

By the time we cleaned off the deck and jammed the holes with tar, the sun had long dipped beyond the horizon.

That smell still hung in the air—the stench of freshly slaughtered mermaids. Or maybe the wind and sea had already taken the smell away from us as swiftly as it had the bloody evidence. Maybe it was stuck in my nose, a reminder of all I'd just witnessed.

In the galley, we had rice and carrots for dinner, and Dani had managed to catch two fish in the net that we split between all of us.

Before we started eating, I stood and raised my mug.

"To Eyrin," I said, "inventor of Morbles and one of the nicest girls I knew."

My toast was met with a dim chorus of "Eyrin," and then silence as everyone took a sip.

I was about to toast the other girls, but then Blondie stood.

"To Shaani and Nati," she said, "my lacrosse buddies. Both of them were kind, thoughtful, and always made time for family. Inspirations to us all."

"And our captain," said Zarra, her speech thick through her fat lip.

My eyes watered as I looked at her face, which bore a gruesome line of stitches from temple to chin.

"Mannoh saved my rabbit once when we were kids," she said. "We weren't even friends, but she did it anyway. Got herself all scratched up in the bush chasing it down for me."

We toasted to each of them. A lump formed in my throat that seemed to block it entirely, because I couldn't eat. I knew I had to keep my strength, but I barely managed to get the few bites of fish down.

"I'll make sure to have a big breakfast," I said to Annith when she tried to force-feed me a spoonful of rice.

She dropped it and hugged me tightly, whispering, "I'm sorry you had to see it."

Only a few of us choked down our food. Most girls couldn't eat, seasickness lingering from the rocking boat earlier, so they abandoned the table and went to take some herbs instead. Other girls looked equally sick, but for an entirely different reason. A few—Fern, Linoya, Sage, and Dani—ate as much as they could. Dani seemed determined to gorge to keep up her strength, but the foggy, distant look in Linoya's eyes suggested she was just experiencing the hungry side-effects of seasickness herbs.

I scraped my rice back into the pot—we never wasted food, even if it had been on our plates already—then climbed the stairs to the main deck. The sky had become pitch black in that time, the clouds not offering even a tiny star to light the way. A single lantern cast its weak glow near the cabin door.

As much as I wanted to sit on the edge of the ship with my legs dangling over the side, that wasn't an option. Instead, I sat in the middle of the deck and leaned against the main mast, gazing into the darkness. I ran my fingers over the wound on my scalp, willing it to heal.

Footsteps stopped beside me and I looked up to see the shadow of a narrow figure, ears poking out from a high ponytail.

Blacktail considered me silently for a minute, then sat down.

"They didn't tell us anything about them using whales."

I nodded. I'd been thinking about that too. After all our training, we were still unprepared for what the battles were really like.

"It must be a pretty new strategy," I said. "We just didn't know about it because there haven't been any returning warriors."

She picked at a splinter in the deck by her leg. "The way they fight. It's so . . ."

"Predatory?"

"Yeah. They warned us the mermaids moved fast. Didn't imagine it'd be like this."

"We'd be dead in seconds if we were out here without weapons. If we were an ordinary fishing boat."

"Think they knew we're a battleship?"

"If they didn't before, they do now," I said, watching her push a long splinter back into the deck as though trying to put it back together.

"We need a way to keep us aboard. Next time, if they use the whale."

I'd been thinking about it a little. We couldn't tie ourselves to the boat though. I suggested the only answer I'd come up with. "We need to stop them from using a whale in the first place."

She stared at me.

"Kill the whale." Even as I said it I felt guilty, because the whale was no more than an innocent bystander.

Blacktail thought for a moment. "We don't have the weapons to kill a whale. We're only equipped for mermaids."

"What if we aimed for the mermaids cornering it?"

"Won't work if they're underwater. They're too small and fast." She paused. "Bet we won't even be able to see them."

"What if we used a fishing net?" I said. "Launch it at them with crossbows and get them tangled."

"They'd cut through it."

"Not before the whale got away."

She didn't say anything for a while. Then, "Could work. Better than letting the whale pummel us."

"We just have to use the nets sparingly. We've only got five."

"Let's bring it up. We'll try it next time." She stood and put a hand on my shoulder.

"'Night, Meela."

"'Night."

I watched her descend into the cabin, leaving the deck nearly empty. I could only see Nora's shadow standing at the bow facing the ocean, and Dani over at the fishing net, hoisting it from the water to check it. Something was in there, and she pulled it out and tossed it in the barrel. Then she dropped to her hands and knees and began vigorously scrubbing the deck with a wire brush.

She must have been tired. We all were. Though something about the way she moved was compulsive, like she had no choice but to keep scrubbing.

I stood, deciding I should get to bed too.

Some girls still shuffled around the cabin when I entered. Annith sat on her bed cross-legged, staring down at her hands. I realised she was twirling her promise ring around her finger, and I averted my eyes, feeling like I'd intruded on something personal.

I crashed into bed without looking at anyone else. I felt homesick and wished I could curl up next to my mother.

A spider was active in the window by my face, spinning a web in vain hope of a meal. I reached up and squished it. A creature so fragile didn't belong at sea.

Even in the cabin, the temperature was uncomfortably cold. We were that much closer to the polar region while we floated by the Aleutian Arc. I pulled my thick quilt over my head and waited for it to remove the chill from my bones, staring into the blackness until everyone's shuffling faded to light snoring. Nora came down the stairs shortly after and climbed into the bed above mine. I listened to her toss around for several minutes before she stilled and her breathing steadied.

It felt like a very long time before my eyelids grew heavy.

I was one of the first girls up in the morning. Dani's bed was the only empty one, but she must have gone to sleep at some point because her blankets were askew.

By the time the rest of us had gotten dressed and eaten breakfast, Dani was already sweating from cleaning the deck and was sitting on a barrel like she'd been waiting for hours.

"All right, girls," she said, jumping to her feet once we all made it up the stairs. She crossed her arms and stood tall, feet spread. "Shaena and I have been talking, and we've decided something."

The rest of us glanced at each other.

Shaena stepped beside Dani. "As captain of the Bloodhound, I hereby promote Dani to be captain in my place."

A moment passed when nobody said anything.

"You can't do that, Shae," I said. "We need to stick with the order set by Anyo."

An approving murmur passed over the girls around me.

"The captain gets the final word," she said. "I think Dani will make a better—"

Fern spoke up. "Dani, did you threaten Shaena or something?"

"Shaena can make her own decisions," said Dani, "and if you don't obey your captain, that constitutes mutiny. Shaena has the sense to know what's best for this crew."

"We're close to the demons' nest now," said Shaena. "I'm sure of it. We need a leader who's top-notch in combat or we're all going to get slaughtered."

Nora raised her hand, like a kid in school. "Anyo said—"

"Anyo isn't here," said Dani. "The training master's job is done now."

"But he—"

"The success of the Massacre is up to us," said Dani loudly, "and I won't let us fail because of some random order the training master chose based on parentage."

"The order might not make sense to everyone, but it can't be changed," I said, trying not to erupt at the idea of Dani being my captain. "If Shaena steps down, fine. But Linoya is the rightful captain."

Dani glowered at me, then tossed her hair and addressed everyone else. "Who wants the top combat student as their captain?"

She raised her hand, and so did Shaena, Texas, and Akirra. Hesitantly, and without meeting anyone's eyes, so did Kade and Holly.

Dani looked between them, then fixed her glare on me. "If anyone else wants to survive this Massacre, you know where to find us. We'll be discussing strategy."

She motioned for them to follow, and the group descended into the cabin.

After a moment of silence, Linoya said, "Does this mean Shaena stepped down?"

All faces turned to gape at her. She just laughed.

"All right. Guess that gives us two captains," she said. She slung her weapon across her chest and made for the helm. "Let her have her fan club. As captain of the Bloodhound, I command you not to worry."

We decided it was time to float parallel to the Aleutian Islands, knowing we must be near the merpeople's nest. This was our time to kill as many as possible.

But the day passed, and we hadn't seen so much as a salmon float by.

I stood at the starboard railing, watching the Aleutian volcanoes billow silently in the distance. Tiny, under-nourished snowflakes blew around us, not sticking to anything, but floating in front of our eyes and reminding us how cold we were.

"Where *are* they?" yelled Texas, looking frustrated enough to start firing random bolts into the water.

"They'll come," said Dani. She was sitting on a barrel overlooking the main deck, holding her crossbow like a king might hold a staff.

"The rats are scared because we butchered them," said Shaena with a devilish grin. She rested a hand against her quiver, which was bursting full of iron.

Across from me, Nora eyed Dani's group with a sour expression. Their hostility had stretched beyond just mermaids, and they'd gotten snappy. Anyone who ventured near was bound to get yelled at for something stupid. At one point, Annith got hollered at for walking too loudly, as if the mermaids would hear her footsteps and get frightened away.

"It's a good thing if the demons don't want to fight us, isn't it?" Sage whispered to Zarra as they watched the patrolling girls. "It means they're giving up?"

I kept my eyes on my compass—I'd been finding the bobbing arrow therapeutic—but said quietly, "Or it means they're creating a plan."

I felt their gazes on me, and looked up. They'd been chewing on herbs for hours and their eyelids looked heavy.

"You really think they're smarter than Anyo let on?" said Zarra. The combination of the herbs and the still-fresh laceration across her cheek made her hard to understand.

"Yes," I said. "I think they're as smart as people."

They were quiet for a minute, then Sage said, "Maybe we don't need to massacre them to win. Just figure out a way to outsmart them. Use logic."

"Maybe. But I think some of us have different goals than others."

They stared at me again.

"Take Dani," I said, nodding to Her Royal Highness on top of the barrel of fruit. "She just wants to prove herself as a warrior by killing as many mermaids as possible."

"Well, that's obvious," said Zarra. "I thought she was gonna stab someone for real in combat class."

"I just want to get home alive," said Sage. "I wish we didn't need to be here." She glanced over her shoulder as if someone might be listening. "Is that bad?"

"Of course not," I said, though in truth I wasn't sure.

"I want the demons to be scared to come anywhere near our island," said Zarra. "If that means I need to be here slaughtering them, then I'll slaughter as many as I need to."

Sage gawked at her. "You're so brave, Zarra."

Zarra laughed, her smile lopsided, and threw a dried flower in Sage's face. Sage smiled dimly.

"What about you, Meela?" said Zarra.

"I want Eriana Kwai to be free again," I said. "I don't like being here, but I want the sea demons to . . . I mean, for everything they've done to us, I want . . ."

Revenge. I wanted revenge.

"You want them to leave us alone," said Zarra.

I grimaced. "Yeah."

"At least you're not just here because you've got an appetite to kill," said Sage.

We watched Akirra and Shaena practice stabbing each other at the helm. We needed to find more mermaids, very soon.

CHAPTER THIRTEEN

Kyaano

The sun had not yet risen when the violently rocking ship startled me awake. I bolted upright, my dream-addled brain filled with images of mermaids. Wind screamed through the cracks in the door and I peeked out my tiny oval window. Huge waves thrashed against the ship.

Around me, the other girls had also awakened from the storm, some already rushing about the cabin. I dressed quickly and clambered up the stairs behind Annith. Nobody spoke, whether because of grogginess, nausea, or—more likely—fear.

Nora burst through the door at us, drenched and panicked. She and Chadri had been staying awake. She stepped back when she saw us all rushing up the stairs. "Good—we need help."

The crashing and groaning was deafening as the ship careened across the waves, the wind pushing us forwards at blinding speed. The gusts wrapped around me like an icy blanket, suffocating me so I had to bury my mouth and nose inside my jacket to breathe. Rain and waves soaked me from all sides; at my feet, it flooded across the deck in torrents.

Through the dense rain and mist, I saw Shaena already taking over Chadri's post at the helm, pulling the wheel with all her weight to keep us on course. Just like we were taught, she steered us into the waves so we tackled them head-on, rather than allow them to toss us sideways. Still, the ship thundered across the water, making each crest over a wave feel like we were slamming onto rock-hard ground.

I squinted up at the sails. They flogged and strained against the mast with a force that could make them burst.

The girls around me scrambled to tie down anything loose. I wondered how much had already washed away in the rivers swirling over the deck.

The sails were going to break if we didn't do something. Already, Shaena fought more than was safe, trying to control the wheel with too much force acting against her.

I yelled at the top of my lungs, my voice raspy. "Reef the sails!"

Closest to me, Annith, Akirra, and Linoya looked over, and all I could see were the whites of their eyes. I nodded and they jumped into action without question. Annith and I grabbed the mainsail line.

I glanced at Shaena to make sure she heard me. Though dawn surely approached, the dense clouds trapped us in their gloom and I could barely see her through the rain. A tall figure appeared beside her—Texas—and she waved a hand to show they'd heard. Together they struggled to keep the ship angled into the wind. It rocked wildly beneath us; several times it knocked me off my feet and I had to use the mast to steady myself.

Annith and I eased the halyard and pulled on the reefing line, bringing the sail down halfway. My palms burned against the sliding, grimy ropes—but to let go would be to seriously hurt Annith.

Only after Annith and I spent several exhausting minutes jumping into the air, using all our weight against each rope, did we manage to secure them. Bitterly, I realised this was where the male sailors would've had more success. The extra pounds of muscle they had over every one of us girls would be crucial for controlling the ship in a storm.

Annith and I collapsed to our knees, panting, and glanced around. The foresail looked successfully shortened too. The ship still rocked dangerously, but we'd slowed down enough that I no longer felt like I would be launched overboard any moment.

I was about to put a hand in the air to let Shaena know we were done when Linoya's voice cut faintly through the howling wind. "I can't get this one secured!"

I looked again to see her small body at the base of the sail, battling with the reefing line. I leapt to my feet. Had she been trying to do it herself? Where were the other girls to help? I dashed over and leaned into the rope while she secured the end.

"Got it?" I said, my arms trembling.

She let go and braced herself on her hands and knees. "Thanks."

I helped her to her feet. Even with the sails shortened, the ship still crashed over the waves, and we had to hold onto the mast as we took a moment to catch our breath.

"Where'd Akirra go?" I shouted over the clamour of the storm. "I thought she was helping."

Linoya wiped a hand over her dripping face. "Dani told her to go get the fishing nets before we lost them."

"You should've made her stay," I said. "You can't reef a sail by yourself."

We both panted voraciously. Linoya's hands must have burned as badly as mine—but the wind still howled, and our work to keep the Bloodhound intact wasn't done.

I was about to turn around when Linoya lurched forwards, falling into me. I caught her in my arms and stumbled back, collapsing sideways.

"What—"

She screamed, a long, agonised wail. I pulled her off me in time to see a flash of scarlet hair duck down beside the ship.

"No," I said breathlessly. Linoya flailed an arm behind her, reaching for something.

"Get it out!" she shrieked. "Get it out of me!"

A jagged spear, calcified seaweed the length of my hand, protruded from the small of her back. I stifled a gasp so I wouldn't frighten her more.

"Lie down," I said, pushing her into the deck. She complied, though seemed to be struggling involuntarily, like her muscles were trying to attack but her brain wouldn't let them.

I grabbed the spear with both hands, and before I could think about it, I pulled. It came out roughly, and Linoya let out a deafening scream that sounded like she was gargling her own blood.

"You're okay, you're okay," I said repeatedly, and I threw the spear to the side. It skidded across the slippery deck.

I pulled a dagger from my belt and used it to slice away her shirt, revealing the gushing hole.

Annith appeared. She pushed me aside. I fell off Linoya and landed hard on the deck.

"Stop the blood!" I yelled. I scrambled to my feet and tried to calm myself by putting my hands over my mouth and nose. What a stupid thing to say. Of course she was going to try to stop the blood.

"Go take care of that mermaid," shouted Annith, not taking her eyes off the wound.

I looked up. The other girls sprinted towards us with their crossbows. Some already stood at the ship's perimeter, firing into the water. I cursed myself, realising my blind moment of trying to pull the spear from Linoya's back could have cost me my life if nobody had been around to keep the other mermaids down. I could've been the next easy target.

I was at my crossbow in two steps. I'd left it sitting against the base of the foresail. The grips were slippery, and I wiped my hands uselessly on my pants as I dashed to the railing.

"Come back and fight, coward!" I yelled, leaning over the water and scanning the thrashing waves for a glimpse of scarlet hair. "This bolt has your name on it!"

Something cracked against my temple, and I turned to see a barnacled stone the size of my fist bounce off the railing.

The blur of a dark-haired mermaid thundered onto the deck. Fighting dizziness, I spun and fired, but the ship crested a wave and tossed me sideways, and I missed her narrowly.

She hurled another stone; it collided with the end of my crossbow and bounced to the side. My crossbow smashed into my nose and I felt warm blood start to flow.

The mermaid slammed her webbed hands into the deck, dragging herself towards me.

Blinking away the tears blurring my vision, I reloaded and fired again. She was close enough that my eyesight didn't need to be accurate: the bolt pierced her sternum.

The mermaid fell into me, dead by the time her hand reached my neck. Her grip slid off me and she landed on the reddened deck at my feet. I turned towards the water and loaded another bolt without glancing back at her. The blood pouring from my nose would have to wait. I could feel its warmth running over my lips and down my neck, but to take a hand off my crossbow could be lethal.

I gritted my teeth at the sight below. Four mermaids scaled up the side. Two others waited, half submerged. Still, I couldn't see the scarlet-haired demon who'd impaled Linoya—but she wouldn't get away from me.

I fired at the first demon and got her square in the chest. She hit the water before she'd finished screaming. I reloaded and fired twice more, hitting my targets in quick succession. The fourth one let go and fell back into the waves before I could pull the trigger.

Blondie shouted from the main deck. "They're aboard! Watch your backs!"

I hesitated for a fraction of a second, and in the time I glanced sideways, the scene below emptied. Only a lost sea spear floated in the deep red water, rising and falling in the violent swells. I spared a half second to take my hand off my crossbow and sweep the salty blood and water from my face.

Something scraped across the deck behind me. I whirled around, ready to fire. A mermaid propelled herself forwards with her arms, strides away from me. A conch shell was locked in her webbed fingers. She had scarlet hair.

My lip curled. Vengeance overcame me as I stared at the hand that'd gored my crewmate minutes ago. I fired, but failed to balance myself against the motion of the ship. The iron bolt shot too far left and pierced her shoulder. She fell back. I reached for another bolt, furious at myself for missing. But at that moment the ship hit an enormous wave and we lurched skywards. I fell, losing my hold on the crossbow.

No sooner had the heels of my hands hit the deck than the mermaid's icy fingers closed around my wrist. She pulled, bringing me flat on my stomach. Her thick hair covered most of her face, drenched and tangled from the wind, but her blood-red eyes glinted through the mats.

I cried out, straining to pull my arm away while my other hand searched frantically for my crossbow. Her grip was impossible, like no natural strength would be able to pull me away from her.

The mermaid's breath was raspy as she struggled to work past the bolt still protruding from her shoulder. She raised her other arm that held the conch shell. The sharp edge of the conch faced downwards, lined up with my wrist.

I shrieked, straining wildly against her steel grip.

She was going to amputate my hand.

My free hand made contact with something sliding loose on the deck. I clamped down on it and swung it without hesitation. At the same moment, the mermaid brought her arm down on my wrist. My crossbow smashed into her head with a sickening crack, and the impact jolted her enough that the conch only caught the side of my arm.

Blood poured from the gash, my head whirling as the skin gaped open. I jumped up, fighting to keep my balance. I had no time to load my crossbow—the mermaid had regained her composure. She glared up at me, her rotten-looking face contorted.

The ship crested another wave and I stumbled forwards, but kept my eye on my target. We hurled into each other, and I slammed my crossbow again into the mermaid's skull.

Her cold, slippery arms locked around me and we fell sideways. She made a screeching, hissing noise like an angry wildcat and tried to roll me onto my back so she could pin me. But she seemed loose, dizzied, and I pushed her arms off me and thrust my knee hard into her stomach. She didn't flinch, already reaching down, grasping my throat.

For the third time, I brought my crossbow as hard as I could across the mermaid's skull. I heard the crack as it smashed into her, and she toppled sideways. Her arms splayed open, her body limp. The conch shell rolled out of sight.

I gripped my wounded arm, holding the skin together to stifle the flow of blood. My muscles trembled from pain and shock. I barely noticed Holly smack into me as she sprinted across the deck—maybe to the aid of whoever was screaming for help.

Already a scraping sound came from behind me. I gasped and turned, feeling a surge of vulnerability. My iron bolts were low; many of them had scattered when I fell.

A mermaid fixed her red eyes on me from the other side of the railing. She clamped her elbows over it to hold her in place as she aimed a blow dart at my head.

I ducked before she could fire, notching a bolt while trying to align my crossbow with her chest.

Abruptly, I stopped.

The mermaid's eyes widened. She froze, like she'd been petrified into a statue.

She lowered the blow dart almost imperceptibly, but then took aim again, her brow furrowed. For a moment, the red drained from her eyes, leaving behind two sapphire blue irises.

I stood panting, unable to move. Her skin was rotten seaweed, ears long and bulbous, hands slimy and webbed . . . but I was staring at her hair, which was blonde and coppery, and her deep blue eyes that bore into me beneath the fading gleam of crimson.

Everything inside me erupted. Hatred poured through me like venom. But I couldn't move. My hands gripped the trigger, steady as ever, but I couldn't pull it.

Despite every feeling pulsing through me, despite every cell in my body screaming for vengeance, my arms acted of their own accord. They lowered the crossbow.

The mermaid's hand twitched, but she kept the blow dart at her lips.

Someone behind me yelled my name.

Crimson bled through the mermaid's eyes again. She lowered the blow dart and her lips curled into a sneer. The wind carried her whisper in my direction.

"Kyaano."

She lifted her elbows, and let herself drop.

My legs responded before my brain did; I ran to the railing, where a head of coppery blonde hair sank into the black water.

Only a ripple in the waves took her place.

Someone stumbled up beside me. Dani. She aimed frantically at the water, though the gesture was useless. The mermaid was gone.

Dani turned to me, eyes wide and manic. I gaped back, recognising accusation in her glare. She'd seen me hesitate.

I had no time to make an excuse. She spotted something behind me and bolted towards it.

I turned back to the water, breathing fast, but nothing stirred among the choppy waves.

Kyaano.

The word was unmistakable. Untranslatable into other languages, it was one only the people of Eriana Kwai could understand completely. Equally an accusation of weakness, and equally meaning, "I dare you." A sea demon couldn't possibly know that word.

My quiver was light. I needed bolts.

Down in the hull, anger bubbled in my chest as I slammed bolts into my tool belt by the fistful. I shouldn't have hesitated. What a cowardly thing to do.

That mermaid was my enemy. Just because she looked familiar didn't mean she was familiar. She'd become a monster, with instinct to sink her teeth into my flesh.

The gash on my arm burned, gushing blood, and I pulled off my sock to use as a bandage. I cinched it tight with my teeth, grunting at the pain.

That demon was the reason my people were suffering. Once already, years ago, she'd nearly succeeded in having me killed.

My throat clenched.

Why had I hesitated? My blood boiled at the sight of her. She'd nearly taken my life—and she could have easily been one of the demons to snatch those children off the beach. She needed to pay for her crimes against my people.

No, my reaction was normal. I hadn't expected to see a face I recognised. Of course I stalled. It didn't mean I thought twice about killing her. I'd just been surprised— surprised she was alive.

Her time had come. She'd swum away freely once before, but now I had to kill her. I had to kill Lysithea.

Something smashed at the top of the stairs and I whirled around, hitching my crossbow to my shoulder.

A spear whizzed by me and stuck into the floor at the back of the hull. Another thump on the stairs.

I stepped behind the barrels and crates stacked against the wall, ducking down.

A thump. A noise like a cackling dolphin.

A strong-jawed mermaid with deep crimson eyes descended into the hull, a stair at a time, scanning the room with each thump. She opened her mouth and another high-pitched noise came out. A second demon responded, right behind her.

The first one held a blow dart to her lips so she could blast a needle-sharp spear faster than I could aim. A conch shell hung from a slimy rope around her waist.

I held my breath, crouching as still as I could so they wouldn't see me. I tried to straighten my crossbow and take aim, but the distance between the wall and the barrels was too narrow. The butt of my crossbow scraped against the wall, and the first mermaid snapped her head around, blow dart ready. I ducked, not sure if she saw me.

She voiced another sound and thumped to the bottom of the stairs.

I leaned around the barrel and watched them pull themselves across the floor. What were they doing down here? They crossed the room, and my heart sank: I'd left the door of the iron enclosure wide open.

The first mermaid stood guard while the second slid into the enclosure. Slender, with a seaweed bandana holding the hair away from her eyes, she was able to manoeuvre through the iron-hooped barrels with precision. I couldn't see well, but I caught a glimpse of her carefully positioning her webbed hands to push the barrel across the floor.

Bile jumped up my throat when I saw her face. Blood dripped over her chin, deep red and running in streams down her neck and chest. She'd killed one of my crew. She'd feasted on human flesh. Who was it?

The dark mermaid dragged herself to the wall, where a small window would provide access to the sea.

They were going to dump the iron bolts out the window.

Suppressing a bubble of panic, I glanced to the wall beside the door, where several extra crossbows hung fresh and unused. They could get those next. I had to stop them.

The dark mermaid put down her blow dart and picked up the conch shell at her waist. I gripped the trigger. This was my chance. Her reactions were faster than mine, so I'd have to shoot without aiming properly.

In one motion, I stood and fired. The bolt crashed through the conch and stuck into the wood behind it, just missing the window. The shell shattered, and both mermaids screeched and turned to face me. Where the whites of their eyes had been draining in the absence of threat, they burst crimson again, throbbing like pulsing hearts and echoing the frantic pounding in my ribcage.

The dark mermaid reached for her blow dart, but she didn't get there in time. Leaning over the barrels, I immediately shot another bolt. It sank into the mermaid's throat and she fell back with a hollow gagging sound.

I was too slow for the second mermaid. She'd removed her bandana and used it to grab an iron bolt from the barrel in front of her. Before I could flinch, the bolt whizzed across the room and drove into my arm.

Gasping, I staggered back. I plucked it from my skin, numbly shocked at how deep it penetrated.

Every sound was amplified in the quiet belly of the ship. Beneath my own rapid breathing, I heard a menacing rumbling coming from the mermaid's throat—and I swore I heard a gurgling noise coming from the casualty behind her.

The mermaid glanced at her fallen comrade with her mouth stretched open. Blood stained her fangs. She roared. I raised my crossbow and pulled the trigger as she flung herself at me, a second bolt held strong beneath the seaweed in her hand. But I'd beaten her to the attack. Like the other demon, she made a suffocating sound as my bolt made contact. She faltered. I reloaded and shot her again. This time she fell back and landed in the same pool of blood still gushing from the other mermaid's throat.

They both shuddered. I could still hear an odd gurgling sound as they took their last breaths.

The air roared through my lungs. The place where the bolt had penetrated my arm seared, like it'd been white-hot before it hit me.

I became aware of the thundering deck above, still teeming with mermaids. I leaned my good arm on the barrel in front of me and jumped over it, landing in the shallow pool of blood. Without another glance at my victims, I leapt up the stairs two at a time.

Adrenaline coursed through me, numbing the pain and replacing fear with vengeance. I wanted only to kill, to massacre, to find Lysithea and finally end her, because ending her would end the desire for revenge that'd boiled in me for so many years.

A mermaid waited for me at the top of the stairs, but she hesitated when she saw me emerging instead of her accomplices. I barely looked at her as I shot an iron bolt through her chest. I was already scanning the deck behind her, hunting for Lysithea.

I wanted to be the one to kill her. She had to look me in the eye as she died, and rue the moment she'd decided to treat me like a game.

The deck around me was a state of turmoil. Blood trickled across the planks. The mainsail flapped loose and bore a gash the length of an arm. And though the downpour had eased, the wind still howled.

Someone screeched beside me. "Akirra!"

I turned to see Shaena on her knees. Blood and something black—maybe tar—coated her face and chestnut hair, so all I could see were the terrified whites of her eyes. Her chest heaved, and it, too, was covered in a splatter of blood that dripped down her body. Whatever she'd done, it must have just happened. She scrambled over a dead mermaid on her hands and knees, reaching desperately for another body—a human body.

"No," I breathed, and started towards Akirra's limp figure. Her eyes were wide open, staring unseeingly at the sky.

A sudden blast of air came from the water beside us, drenching me in a salty spray. My stomach sank.

"Whale!" I screamed. Several of my crewmates turned to me in horror.

The ship groaned, and the starboard side rose. I lunged for the railing to try and wrap my arms around it, but it rose higher, higher, until I lost my footing and landed on my hip, sliding down towards the icy water.

A mermaid shot past me, gliding down the angled deck. I heard a childlike laugh as I hit the lower railing, and it angered me—I tried to get my crossbow around so I could shoot her in the spine. But then the ship lurched.

My stomach flopped as the whale ducked under us and the ship careened the other way, dropping into the trough of a wave and sending an arctic waterfall over the deck.

I held my breath as the wave washed over us. Before I could surface, the boat rocked again. Did they find an entire pod of whales, or were they forcing one back and forth along the keel? I braced myself, crouched on my hands and knees, but still slid helplessly across the deck, scrambling to get a hold of something.

The fishing nets, I thought. *I need to find my crew. We need to launch the fishing nets.*

But even as I thought it, I knew it was no use. We'd never get to the nets with this five-ton animal tossing us around like fish in a frying pan.

The salty spray filled my lungs, choking me. I wiped my eyes and rolled onto my front, wrapping my arms around my crossbow, determined not to lose it. A frantic impulse to stand up overcame me. For all I knew, a mermaid rested beside me, waiting until she had the satisfaction of my seeing her before she struck a fatal blow.

The thought brought me to my feet whether I was ready or not, and I fell into the main mast, trying to balance myself against the rocking ship.

Crack. The boat lifted and I wrapped my arms around the mast, still gripping my crossbow. I wanted to be sick, but my stomach had clenched into a boulder.

Something smashed across my lower legs, bringing me down so my limbs sprawled across the slippery deck. My crossbow was ripped away from my hands.

"No!" I screamed, my voice rough.

Before I could roll over to try and take it back, my assailant had an icy grip on both my wrists. She sat on my stomach, the weight of her body leaving me unable to move. Her eyes blazed.

Lysithea.

Her teeth were long and needle-sharp, her skin a rotten mixture of green and grey, and her ears had sprouted long like pieces of bulbous seaweed. Despite it all, it was unmistakably her. She lifted a hand off one of mine and gripped my throat. For a moment I was too horrified by the feel of her webbed fingers to fight back.

"Pathetic," she said, baring her teeth. "They broke you down, after all."

Her voice rolled like a purring cat, deeper than when we were kids—but underneath, it was still the same, still that odd accent that turned everything into a song.

"I should've known you'd give into that human instinct to destroy everything," she said. "How does it feel? Do you feel powerful now that you're slaughtering every last member of my family?"

I tried to speak. She was choking me. My face felt pressured, like the blood was building and leaving my skull ready to pop. Buried nightmares pushed forwards, and I tried frantically to pry her wrist off with my free hand, unable to stop myself from panicking. I hoped she didn't see fear. I hoped she saw only anger in my bulging eyes.

"What'll it be, now that you've got me here? Are you ready to impale me properly this time?" she said, tightening her slimy grip.

In a last attempt at getting oxygen to my brain, I reached down and found an open pouch on my tool belt. I pulled out the first weapon I laid hands on.

Lysi screeched and drew her hand away when she saw the dagger. I rolled over, knocking her off my stomach, casting about for my crossbow. It was lying steps away from us against the main mast. My eyes locked onto it like magnets. I got to my hands and knees and scurried forwards, but already she was upon me.

I whirled around with the dagger outstretched. It made contact with her cheek—but it wasn't the iron dagger. The serrated blade slid across her skin like dull plastic, not even leaving a mark. She caught my wrist and threw me onto my back. I roared in frustration as she pinned me down, her fingers clamped on my wrists so tightly I couldn't even ball my hands into fists. The dagger fell from my grip and skidded across the deck.

"I've spent my whole life poor and starving because of you!" I shouted. "You're a traitor and a murderer!"

Her scarlet eyes widened, giving me the impression they were going to pop from her head. "My family is in the middle of being massacred! You see all the blood around you? That's your doing! You're killing my family!"

"I'm only taking back the lives you demons stole."

Her lips curled back from her pointed teeth as she glared at me, and I couldn't understand how I'd ever been foolish enough to believe she was part human.

The ship rose again, higher until we began to slide. The top of my head crashed against the mast, and still she didn't give me room to budge.

"Listen to you," she said. "You never used the word *demon* before."

"That was before I knew what you really are."

"And what am I? A monster because I have a tail? Because I live underwater? The Meela I knew would never pin someone as an enemy because—"

"Because you have teeth made for ripping into my flesh! You're a demon. Even your eyes thirst for blood."

I remembered the feeling of terror when she'd first shown me her crimson eyes.

She scoffed. "I knew I shouldn't have shown you. You're too fragile."

"Fragile? You think I'm fragile?"

The ship released, and my stomach flopped as we plummeted. Another icy waterfall engulfed us, and when I opened my eyes, we were hanging off the side of the ship, both of us holding onto a railing to keep from falling into the water. I fumbled for a better grip, not knowing where my crossbow was anymore. I shot a horrified glance at Lysi, knowing how easily she could kill me. But her expression was passive, save for her scarlet eyes.

"Yes. You trust too quickly and are easy to manipulate. I bet within the first week of that training program they had you reciting verses about how all demons deserve to die."

"You made it easy for me to hate you," I said, thrashing to try and get a foothold. "You set me up to become another victim."

"I didn't set you up!"

"I—what?"

"You're the one who ran for help when you got scared."

"I never ran for help!"

"So this scar magically appeared?"

I glanced down.

"A permanent reminder of the traitor I once called a friend," she said. "Iron never heals."

I gasped when I saw it. It looked like someone had dragged a molten spike down her waist. From ribcage to hip, the iron bolt had left a gash, scorched red and as clear as if it'd just happened. At the bottom was a black hole: the point of impact, like the bolt had burned a path as it grazed her side, then buried into her skin once it reached her hip bone.

Our eyes met, and suddenly I remembered the day I lost her as clearly as if it were being played out before my eyes. I remembered the terror on her face as my father aimed to kill.

Why was she calling me a traitor? I wasn't the one who betrayed our friendship.

I struggled to readjust my cramping fingers. They were slipping from the post alarmingly fast so I had to keep scrambling to get a better grip.

"Lysi." Her name felt strange on my tongue. "I never told my father."

She broke our gaze. The ship was silent. I watched her pull herself up effortlessly and peer across the deck. When she came back down, a hint of white and blue bloomed in her eyes.

"Get up," she said, sounding angry. Something solid pressed against my feet, pushing me upwards.

"Stop it," I said firmly. "I don't want your help."

I pushed the balls of my feet against the hull and tried to climb it, knowing I must look pathetic.

Lysi made a noise of disapproval. "Don't be stupid."

And before realising what'd happened, I was putting my hands in front of me to stop my face from hitting the deck.

I heard a splash as I crumpled in a heap, and—as quickly as she'd come—Lysi was gone.

CHAPTER FOURTEEN

Captain Dani

A cold hand closed around my arm the moment I collapsed on the deck, but I couldn't gather the strength to pull away.

I moaned weakly.

"Meela," said Annith, "it's me. Get up."

I glanced sideways, overcome with relief at the sight of her human legs.

"We aren't sure if they're really gone," she said, pulling me awkwardly to my feet. "Dani has an idea, though."

I walked beside her, taking in the state of the ship around me. Everything was as destroyed as the last time, if not worse, and again my eyes found the huge gash in the mainsail. The boat still rocked, sending overturned barrels rolling, but the wind had eased off.

In the centre of the deck, Dani was yelling herself hoarse.

"Don't get too comfy, girls! We're over the nest now. They'll be back."

"I bet they're trying to find a new whale," I said.

Annith said nothing, but her grip around my arm tightened.

The girls spread out, forming a circle with no more than an arm's width between themselves. Dani turned to Annith and me.

"Nice of you to join us," she said. Her eyes blazed, manic and bloodshot.

Before I could spit out the nasty words on my tongue, she added bossily, "Stand in a circle and face the water. We're going to use a new tactic next time they attack, and it'll be sure to take out every sea rat that tries to climb aboard."

"That's hardly a new tactic!" I said. "It's the same thing we're supposed to do in night battles."

"If it works at night," said Dani, "it'll work during the day."

I looked at Annith in protest, but she just nodded once.

"Some of us need tending to first," she said, and leaned around Dani to scan the other girls in the circle. I saw a few bloody faces and clothes, and Linoya—I remembered Linoya's spear wound with a jolt of panic—she was nowhere to be seen.

Dani scanned me up and down, and wrinkled her nose like I smelled particularly bad.

"Fine," she said. "Take the girls down one at a time to fix them. Start with her. She looks like hell."

She nodded at me, her pointed face puckered in disgust. Nothing but a scratch on Dani's cheek threatened to stain her clothes with her own blood. I glanced down at myself and realised how much blood I'd lost. Pain flooded back to me in both arms, and something resembling splattered paint down my front reminded me that my nose had been bleeding. I reached a hand up, confirming it'd stopped.

"Where's—"

"Linoya's in the cabin," said Annith. "She's not doing so well. It's not fatal, but she lost a ton of blood and I think the spear might've damaged her spine. She keeps saying her legs are tingling. She can't move them too well."

I bit my lip, lost for words. The taste of blood met my tongue.

"Akirra's gone," whispered Annith. "And Chadri."

I concentrated on stepping down one stair at a time.

"Anyone else in rough condition?" I said.

"Nothing horrible."

Two more girls were dead. I felt too numb to cry.

In the cabin, we sat on my bed while Annith fixed up the puncture in my arm from the bolt, and the gash from the conch shell. She had blood all over her skin and clothes, and a tear in her jacket that revealed a clean patch of gauze over her ribs. The ring on her finger looked tarnished. I was pretty sure it was just covered in dried blood.

Linoya slept soundlessly a few beds over, and I wondered aloud more than once if we should check to make sure she was alive.

"She's fine," whispered Annith. "If you stop panicking for like, one second, you can actually hear her breathing."

Something scraped across the deck above us, and we both stared at the ceiling. When nothing further happened, I went to wash the blood off my face before changing into a clean jacket and cargo pants. Even my dry clothes felt cold and uncomfortable.

"Go get Sage next," said Annith, handing me a hair elastic so I could pull the soaking wet locks off my face. "She looked beaten up."

Light-headed, I climbed back to the deck and called Sage over. Blood covered her face and hair, and she limped heavily as she walked.

In the middle of the circle of girls, a barrel of ammo sat open next to the main mast. So that had been what they were dragging. Beside it rested three extra crossbows. The wooden mast had chunks missing from the base, as though someone with brute strength had taken an axe to it.

I made a mental note to keep the demons away from the masts.

"What's the plan with the circle?" I said as I took up one of the crossbows and stood next to Blacktail.

She looked at me with a fat lip and dried blood on her chin. "Don't let your guard down, and shoot like hell."

"Are we standing here until they come back?"

"'Til we know they've retreated for sure."

It seemed like a decent plan, though I hated admitting it to myself. Blacktail looked sour about following Dani's orders, too.

Most of us had come to recognise Linoya as the rightful captain—but what would happen now that she was injured? Would she step down? I was the next girl in line. It would be me fighting against Dani's attempted coup.

Blacktail and I were among those elected to stand guard while others cleaned the blood and bodies off the deck. Zarra stood in the centre on the boom, tied to the mast and working feverishly to sew the torn sail back together.

Facing away from the crew, I took a private moment to let my thoughts shift back to Lysi. Why did she help me get back onto the ship? Was she trying to delude me into trusting her again?

I gripped my crossbow tighter.

I'd just started to accept that the mermaids weren't coming back when Nora screamed, and the unmistakable sound of an iron bolt whizzed through the air behind me. I whirled around to see a dark-haired mermaid collapse onto the deck, then realised I'd just turned my back to the open water and spun back around with my crossbow ready.

A mermaid was climbing over the railing, but Blacktail shot her down instantly. As she fell back into the water, three more mermaids threw themselves aboard. Before I could even aim, Blacktail shot again at the one in front of me, Holly took down the one beside that, and Dani jumped forwards to thrust her iron dagger into the last mermaid's stomach. She gave a firm twist, and the mermaid collapsed with a strangled grunt. From behind us came one last sound of a crossbow firing, and then the air was silent.

I looked down at my hands, white-knuckled around my crossbow. Why were my reactions so slow?

For a moment we all stood there, gaping. Dani wiped the bloody dagger on her pants, but held onto it. The bloodbath was over in seconds, and no more mermaids tried to climb aboard. Perhaps these ones had been meant to give a signal . . . or perhaps the others saw what'd happened.

"Was that it?" said Holly, lowering her crossbow a fraction.

The only sound came from the waves slapping against the hull.

I scanned the dead mermaids, and when I realised I was searching for a head of coppery blonde hair, I became furious at myself.

"Come on," I said to no one in particular. "Let's get these bodies off the deck."

Together, a few of us pushed the mermaids into the water. I averted my eyes from their lifeless faces, the skin of which had faded back to a human complexion in death.

"We knew they'd come back," boasted Texas. She looked at Dani with sick admiration that made me roll my eyes.

"What do we do, then?" said Zarra. "Stay in this circle twenty-four hours a day?"

Dani straightened, narrowing her eyes at the horizon. The weather was clearing in the distance. She rested the tip of her index finger on the point of her dagger. "We'll be all right for now."

Nobody said anything.

After a minute, Dani faced us. She nodded firmly. "We slaughtered them today. While they're picking themselves up, let's regroup and make a plan."

"We shouldn't let our guard down," I said. "You don't know for sure they've backed off."

"They have."

"How do you know?"

She turned to me, her eyes as wide and manic as ever. "Intuition, studying patterns ... I'm starting to learn how these demons think."

"You don't know any better than the rest of us," I said, exasperated. The way her crew ogled her made my blood curdle—like she was some chosen, troubled hero who knew all the secrets of the volcanoes looming beside us.

"I share what I know with my crew," she said. "Not that I'd ever want someone as pathetic as you on it. But just know that anyone who joins me has a better chance of surviving."

In the corner of my eye, Texas stood up taller.

"I'd rather have my guts eaten than be one of your puppets," I said.

Annith put a hand on my shoulder, but I shrugged it off.

"A few of us should stay here for a bit," I said. "Just in case."

Dani laughed coldly and flipped her dagger over before sliding it back in her belt. She started towards the galley.

"Fare you well, my dove!" she sang in a high, falsely sweet voice.

Before disappearing into the hull, she glanced back and smiled at my expression.

"Shaena," she said, and out of nowhere Shaena appeared at her heels. "Help me make dinner. I love the way you do the salmon."

They vanished, leaving the rest of us staring at the empty doorway.

"Crazy bitch," I said under my breath. Annith frowned, but behind her Blacktail's eyes gleamed in amusement.

We didn't encounter any other mermaids that day, and it irked me that Dani's crew would trust her that much more for being right. She'd been lucky. But luck wouldn't always be on her side.

At dinner, nobody had the energy for conversation. Everyone bowed their heads, focused on their plates and nothing else. I kept my own head down and ate in silence.

"What are we going to do about the whales?" I said after I'd finished, and a few girls looked up at me as though surprised there were other people in the galley.

When no one spoke, I said, "The plan we had with . . . with Linoya's group . . . was to target the mermaids who were cornering the whale, and—"

"My crew," said Dani, "is working on a plan for this."

I stared at her. Annith shifted beside me. I felt her give me a sidelong glance.

"Want to share with the rest of us?"

"If you want in on the plan," said Texas coldly, "then join our crew."

"We *are* in the same crew!"

"Don't you think your almighty plan has a better chance of working if everyone's in on it?" said Fern, scowling at Dani.

"No, I don't!" Dani jumped to her feet. "I'm asking for a little cooperation here, and if all of you are still hell-bent on being rebels then you deserve to be eaten!"

"Don't get your undies twisted," said Zarra.

Dani's jaw tightened. She glowered at the side of Zarra's scarred face.

"If anyone wants to join us, we'll be meeting at the helm. If not, maybe you can find a way to make yourselves useful."

She jerked her head, and Texas, Shaena, Kade, and Holly ascended the stairs with her to the main deck. When Blondie stood, too, the rest of us gawked at her. She said nothing, but averted her eyes and hurried after them.

Fern stared after her for a long time, looking crestfallen. I realised Blondie had been the last of Fern's closest friends who was still alive and not in league with Dani.

After a few moments, the rest of us rose and crossed over to the cabin to put on our nightgowns.

No matter what Dani or her crew said, I would never put myself under Dani's command. Never in my life had I trusted her, and I wasn't about to start.

Not even when an explosion of laughter came from above deck, and a few of the girls around me looked up at the ceiling, and Annith whispered, "I wonder what they do every time they meet," did I have the faintest urge to find out.

"They're doing that because they want us to wonder," I said. "They're trying to make you want to join their cult."

Annith said nothing, but she kept her eyes open as she lay in bed, staring at the ceiling.

Long before the sun was ready to rise, Shaena shook me awake so I could take my turn at the helm. I hadn't been sleeping well and my muscles ached, but I rolled out of bed wide-awake. I pulled my parka on over my nightgown, slung my crossbow across my chest, and left the cabin barefoot.

The sky was so void of clouds, I could see every star and planet with startling clarity. The dark side of the moon overtop its glowing crescent was like a half-closed eyelid, peeking open at me as though wondering why I was up at this hour.

I leaned against the helm and faced the water. The sea was calm enough that I could leave the ropes in place over the wheel, letting the ship float with the breeze.

The wispy white trail of the Spirit Path crossed above me, flowing between the more vivid stars that flecked the sky. I wondered if my brother was up there, watching me slay my way to the same fate.

Somewhere not too far away, a whale surfaced to breathe. And then another. I listened to the air blowing from their lungs, a noise that rang through the still night.

In some other life, it might have been a peaceful sound. I waited, still as a fawn, until the blows faded into the distance.

One at a time, I focused on the stars, forcing my thoughts to be simple and meditative. I listened to the steady beat of the waves passing under us while the ship rocked smoothly. I wondered if animals appreciated the beauty of the stars on a night like this, or if my feeling of awe was a human emotion.

I became aware of a presence suddenly, but it didn't startle me. I squinted at the side of the ship, where a dark shape had appeared and remained, motionless.

The presence should've alarmed me. I should've reached for my crossbow. Any other girl would have. Instead, I dropped my shoulders.

We stared at each other, neither of us moving.

"Lysi," I said, finally.

The shape sunk down a bit, but didn't vanish.

"Why are you here?" I said, and my voice was less accusatory than I intended.

Still, she said nothing.

After another minute of silence, I started to get angry. "Are you working up the guts to finish me off yourself, rather than send someone else to do it?"

The shape became taller, and she said quietly, "I never sent her to kill you."

"You just set up the rock tower and told her when I'd be there?"

"No," said Lysi.

I ground my teeth together. Part of me always wondered how much of our friendship—if any—had been real.

"Were you sent to befriend me?"

"No," she said firmly.

"Were you sent—"

"Nobody knew about us until Panopea."

"The one who . . . the one on the beach?"

She made a small noise.

"Who was she?"

"My cousin."

I bit my lip, then sat on the deck. A few seconds passed before Lysi apparently realised I was giving her a chance to speak. She crossed her arms on the deck to better hold herself up.

"Panopea noticed I went out, heading in the same direction nearly every day, towards Eriana Kwai," she said. "I guess I wasn't as secretive as I thought I was. She followed me one day when I went to meet you, and she saw me leave the water to go into the tide pool."

"What did she care?"

"We hated each other. She always used to get me in trouble. On my way back from seeing you that day, she shoved me inside this broken barrel lying on the ocean floor, not far out from where we met. She wouldn't let me out until I told her what I was doing."

"So you told her about us, just like that?"

"No!" said Lysi, sounding desperate. "But she kept me in there for so long . . . I had to surface to breathe. Besides, I had to say something, or she'd tell my parents. She never would've understood, so . . . so I said I was trying to trick you into the water."

The waves lapped serenely against the ship. Motionless, I stared at Lysi through the darkness. "Did she believe you?"

I knew the answer. The mermaid had told me that my friendship with Lysi wasn't real. Had Lysi just told her this to protect me?

"Yes," said Lysi. "She was horrible. She loved the idea of making a game out of your life. But she must have kept a watch, and when she saw my burn she grabbed me again. She told me to kill you and prove I had no attachment. I wouldn't do it. So she said she'd do it herself, because you were a danger to all of us.

"I tried to fight her. I really did. She was so much stronger than me."

"So," I said, "you set up the rock tower and let her come attack me."

"I didn't know Panopea caught onto our pattern with the rock towers! I only set it up so I could see you. Then she told my parents about you, and they wouldn't let me out of their sight no matter what I said or did. And I knew the rock tower was still set up, and I hoped and wished you wouldn't see it."

"But I did."

I squinted at the black deck beneath my legs. All the things Panopea had said could've been her repeating a lie meant to protect me.

"You still don't trust me," said Lysi after I'd been quiet for a while.

"How do I know you're not making this up?"

"Do you really think I'd be here if I wasn't desperate to make you understand?"

After another minute, I said sceptically, "But you taught her to speak Eriana."

"I didn't think I had a choice."

"Why not?"

"She threatened to tell my parents about you, Mee! I knew they'd kill me if they found out!"

"But they did find out, in the end. Panopea told them anyway."

"I know. I should have just dealt with my punishment and gotten it over with. I didn't know everything would get so out of hand. I didn't know she would . . ."

I studied her face in the moonlight. No matter how furious I was, something about looking her in the eyes made me soften.

"But why did she want to learn it?"

"She wanted to teach it to . . . to King Adaro."

I raised my eyebrows, remembering her talking about him when we were kids. "Why would Adaro want to learn Eriana?"

"He wants to learn all human languages. I think he's fluent in Spanish and Japanese so far."

"And now Eriana, thanks to Panopea."

"No."

"Why n—"

"Don't," said Lysi. "Just leave it."

I stared at her. "She never got the chance?"

Lysi buried her face in her hands and made a muffled sound.

"I . . . I killed her? With the iron?"

She shook her head. After a long hesitation she said, "She killed herself. She couldn't bear to live with the scars on her face."

"She killed herself because of me?" I said breathlessly. "I was a murderer at ten years old?"

"You didn't kill her, Mee. Mermaids are vain . . . she didn't need to end her life because of that. You were only defending yourself."

"I guess so." My voice sounded detached.

"I didn't teach anyone but her."

I dropped my eyes again to the deck.

"Tell me why mermaids are attacking Eriana Kwai," I demanded. I wanted all of the truth from her now, and if she really was being honest, and she really did want me to believe her, she'd give it to me.

"Adaro wants control of the seas," she said. "He wants humans out of the water so he can build—"

"Utopia," I said.

"Right." She paused. I felt her eyes on me.

"Of course I remember."

She gave a half-smile.

"But why Eriana Kwai?" I said.

"Well, he wants to rule everywhere. He's working on an underwater domination too. He's got the Pacific, but no one lived here before him, so that was his from the moment he crossed over the Ice Channel. He's fighting merpeople colonies at the other end to take the—um—I don't know what you call that other big ocean."

"The Atlantic?"

"No, the other one."

"The Southern?"

"No."

"Black Sea."

"No, it's really warm."

"Mediterranean."

"Which one is—"

"Hudson Bay!"

"No, that's not even wa—"

"Arctic!"

"Mee! I said it's warm!"

We burst out laughing, Lysi's perfect smile and overlarge eyes glistening in the moonlight.

"What about the Indian Ocean?" I said. "That one's huge. I think it's the warmest."

"Maybe that's it. Anyway, that's where all our men are right now. Fighting those colonies of merpeople to the death for it."

"So he trains mermen to fight below-surface and the mermaids to fight above-surface?"

She shrugged. "It worked until you girls showed up."

I grimaced. "So what's next? After he takes those oceans?"

"He takes the Atlantic."

"That's where your family came from—where the Atlantic Queen rules."

"Right. That's Medusa's ocean," she said, her voice bitter, "and I'm sure Adaro is going to have a hard time—"

"*Medusa?*" I said, astounded. "Turn-you-to-stone Medusa still lives in the Atlantic?"

Lysi laughed again, leaning her head against a railing in mock exasperation.

"Not the original Medusa! Honestly!"

"Oh."

"Queen Medusa is a descendant of the original, though."

"Does she—"

"Have snakes for hair? No. Sorry to disappoint."

We fell silent, holding each other's gaze. I bit my tongue, feeling a twinge of guilt for letting her talk to me for so long. The sky was lightening. Lysi's eyes seemed to shine—and I felt a long-forgotten comfort staring into them.

I looked away.

Despite the part of me that wanted to trust her, Lysithea was still a mermaid, and I a human. Last time I let myself trust her, I'd nearly been killed.

Besides, it didn't make sense that Adaro was sending his warriors to attack Eriana Kwai when the people of the Aleutian Islands had no apparent struggles. Why us?

"I should get back," said Lysi, her voice sounding odd, like she knew what I'd been thinking.

"Right." I dropped my hands, realising I'd been rubbing my forehead.

I still didn't look at her as I stood. Hearing her story only left me agitated and confused.

"Goodbye, Lysi."

"Bye, Mee."

She let herself fall into the sea with a gentle splash. I turned around and took my post at the helm, not glancing back.

CHAPTER FIFTEEN

Annith's Allegiance

I rubbed my hands down my face and wiped them on my pants, clearing off the warm blood that'd splattered across my front. The mermaid fell forwards, so close that her golden hair landed on my foot. I leapt back, wrinkling my nose.

We'd stood in our defensive circle again after breakfast, and sometime around noon found ourselves surrounded by mermaids.

We were well-armed and prepared, our reactions sharp, our iron finding its way easily into the flesh of every mermaid who threw herself at us.

At least thirty demons lay immobile on the deck, and no more attempted to climb aboard.

Shaena whooped, thrusting her crossbow in the air. "No demon can beat us!"

I reached into my coat and pulled out a clean corner of my shirt before the blood dripped into my eyes.

Beside me, Sage extracted two iron bolts from a mermaid's ribcage. I looked away when she rolled the mermaid over—exposing the blank, lifeless face—and dumped the body into the water.

"What'd I tell you?" said Dani to nobody in particular. "'We should be prepared today!' Didn't I?"

I rolled my eyes and began refilling my quiver, keeping my gaze averted from the mermaid corpses. Dani had been relentless in her quest to prove she had some sort of psychic mermaid-reading powers.

As I stuffed my belt full of iron, I couldn't stop myself from wondering whether that golden-haired mermaid was related to Lysi, or whether any of the mermaids we'd just killed were friends or family of hers.

I felt Annith watching me, but I avoided her eyes.

We began alternating in two-hour shifts, standing guard in the circle. This gave us a chance to rest our legs, escape the icy slush falling from the sky, and grab a drink of water while the other half of the crew kept watch.

By late afternoon I found myself standing by the railing anyway, even though it was my turn to rest. We floated as close as we'd ever get to the Aleutian Islands, and I watched one of the volcanoes billow smoke into the patchy sky.

Part of me wondered about Lysi, and what'd happened in her life since we were kids. Was she trained to kill, like I was? Did Adaro conscript her into his army?

I wanted to know more about this merman king and his quest to take over the oceans. My old curiosity about life underwater prodded at my subconscious, and I wanted Lysi to come back so she could tell me about it.

You just want to talk to her, said a voice in my head, *like when you were kids and you were weak and naïve.*

Back when just being with her made me feel better.

Could I trust her? Was she as pure and honest as I once thought?

The mainsail flapped noisily above me. I squinted at it, deciding it needed tightening. I grabbed the thick, salt-encrusted rope and leaned against it until I was out of breath, and when I was satisfied it was taught, I wrapped it securely around the cleat.

That was when I noticed Annith standing at the helm behind Shaena, facing the water. She gripped her crossbow tightly, as though ready to aim and fire any second.

I coiled the excess rope slowly, watching her. She resembled a soldier standing guard, but it wasn't her turn to be on duty.

I walked towards her, glancing around in confusion. "Why are you standing like that?"

She kept her gaze forwards, her features stony.

"I'm on helm watch with Shaena."

"What's helm—"

Realisation hit me like a tidal wave. "Oh, Annith, don't tell me you joined her."

"Some people might find her impossible to get along with," said Annith, "but her captaining skills—"

"She sleeps with her crossbow!"

"She's prepared!"

My mouth hung open. At the other side of the deck, Dani sat against the wall by the entrance to the galley. It was the most secure place on the ship if someone wanted to make sure no one was going to sneak up on her. Dani's crossbow rested on her lap while she ran her iron dagger rhythmically along a sharpening stone. The rest of her body was a statue as she stared straight ahead at the horizon.

"I know Linoya's down right now," I said calmly, peeling my eyes back to Annith, "but let me talk to her. You're making a mistake letting Dani be your leader."

"She knows what she's doing, Meela."

"Who else joined? Who did you talk to?"

"Nora."

I ran through a mental list of everyone Dani had managed to recruit. Besides Dani's original toadies, Shaena and Texas, she now had Annith, Nora, Blondie, Holly, and Kade in her cult.

Shaena whistled a tune and made a point of shifting her eyes everywhere except at Annith and me. I ignored her.

"You all trust Dani?" I said.

"I trust she knows how to fight," said Annith, "and I trust she wants to get out of this alive."

"We all want to get out of this alive," I said through gritted teeth.

"This ship needs a plan for survival, and Dani's the only captain who's been able to give us one."

"I wouldn't say Mannoh or Linoya had much of a chance!"

Annith opened her mouth to argue, seemed to realise I was right, and closed it again.

There was no way our crew would ever mutually agree upon a captain. That was why Anyo had assigned an order.

"I'm going to talk to Linoya," I said. "If she steps down, that makes me captain."

Shaena stopped whistling and turned, a charming smile fixed to her face. "Captain to whom, exactly?"

I bit my tongue. Why was nobody following the protocol that'd been drilled into us for five years?

Annith opened her mouth, glanced sideways at Shaena, then looked back at the water without a word.

Stealing Annith back from Dani would be declaring open warfare. Team Dani gets the port side of the Bloodhound; Team Meela, the starboard. But Annith was giving me no reason to think she'd choose me over Dani. What quality did Dani have that Annith admired so much? Was she that willing to sever our friendship?

I stomped away, trying to ignore a pang of betrayal.

Besides, weren't any of them concerned that Dani cared more about herself than anyone else? I couldn't have been the only one to notice that bloodthirsty gleam in her eyes.

In the cabin, I stopped short at what I saw: a thin frame in the darkness, bending over Linoya's bed.

"Dani?"

She straightened, but my eyes hadn't adjusted to the dim light and I couldn't read her expression.

"What are you doing?" I said.

"Just checking on your captain. Making sure she's comfortable."

I walked forwards. Something about her smooth voice curdled in my stomach. "Let her rest."

"Don't worry, I am," said Dani. "She's out cold."

I stepped into the narrow gap between her and Linoya. Dani's face became visible. I returned the sneer.

"Get away from her."

She stepped back, raising a hand in salute. "Aye aye."

I glanced beside Linoya's head, where her closed trunk had been upturned to create a makeshift nightstand. The top was littered with random contents from her tool belt—water flask, vial of kohl, lip balm—and some herbs.

"Later," said Dani, in a tone dripping with false camaraderie.

She strode from the room with a bounce in her step that made me want to hurl the water flask at her head. I waited until the door slammed at the top of the stairs before sitting.

"Linoya," I said, unable to hide the urgency in my voice.

She didn't stir.

"Linoya." I touched her shoulder this time, shaking her gently. When she still didn't move, I leaned over and let my ear graze her mouth and nose. Her breath tickled my cheek.

Relieved, I looked back to the trunk and hesitantly reached for the water flask. I sniffed its contents, even dumped a little in my hand, but it was only water.

"What did she do to you?" I whispered, pushing a greasy lock of hair from her eyelid.

For the next hour, I stayed with Linoya in the empty cabin, shaking her every few minutes. But the rightful captain of the Bloodhound did not wake.

The demons attacked in an ongoing swarm over the next few days. We had little time to eat, rest, or think, but conditions were in our favour and we killed more mermaids than any of us could count.

Anyone but Texas.

"Seven hundred! I swear that was our seven-hundredth!" she yelled as the sun set on the fourth day. "Let's see them hit us with a whale now we're over their nest. Whales will be steering far and wide of this place."

We stood guard for an hour longer before deciding the demons must have been regrouping. I massaged my upper arm, permanently sore from holding up my crossbow and cranking the lever to notch bolts.

Shaena skipped from her place in the circle and paraded around the ship, thrusting her weapon in the air like she was leading a marching band.

"Who owns this ocean?" she yelled.

Around me, Dani's crew bellowed. "We own this ocean!"

"Who's getting slaughtered?"

"They're getting slaughtered!"

"We won't back down, we'll beat them down!"

"In their own blood they will drown!"

Only Fern, Blacktail, Zarra, Sage, and I remained in the outskirts of Dani's crew. Everyone else, including Annith, roared the words like a bunch of feral hunters.

With a final cry, Shaena kicked a dead mermaid hard in the face, then stood on top of her like an explorer claiming new territory. The gesture was met with raucous cheers.

Annith's small face twisted into an ugly expression. I turned away, unable to recognise her.

I took the next shift standing guard in the circle, watching Annith as she left to help Shaena and Blondie with something at the bow of the ship. They pulled around heavy barrels and pointed out past the bowsprit, making angles with their arms.

At the stern, Texas and Kade were also in mumbled conversation. They had wrapped fishing nets around more barrels on both sides of the deck. I shifted on my feet, uncomfortable with having the crew so disunited.

"Has anyone been able to talk to Linoya?" whispered Zarra beside me.

"Fat difference it'll make now," said Fern, who stood on Zarra's other side. "Dani's got too many lackeys. The original structure's demolished."

I think Dani is keeping her sedated, I wanted to say, but even in my head it sounded ridiculous. We didn't even have sedatives.

I glanced at Holly, who stood to my other side, and lowered my voice. "We can't just let Dani take over the ship."

I didn't want to be the one to bring up the idea of taking over Linoya's position, but the thought of letting everyone fall under Dani's control was worse.

"Would either of you object if I took over as captain?" I said.

They fell quiet for a minute, then Fern said, "No. I'd be in your crew."

"Me, too," said Zarra.

Beside me, Holly repositioned her crossbow, but her eyes were cast towards the water when I chanced a look. I leaned closer to the other girls. "Then a crew we'll be. I . . . I'll talk to Linoya the next chance I get."

My turn for a break came as the sun crept towards the horizon after dinner. Most of the other girls who'd been in the circle with me headed straight below deck to warm up.

"Go check out the net they set up," I said to Fern. "Try and figure out what it is. I'll take the helm for a bit."

Ropes held the wheel in place over the calm waves. I left them there and faced the water, needing a minute alone.

To Fern and Zarra, I was captain now. I knew Blacktail and Sage wouldn't have a problem with it either. Despite them, I felt abandoned. I found myself wishing I could talk to Annith. I needed my best friend.

Would anyone in Dani's crew join me? Would Dani let them, even if they wanted to?

My main concern was to keep everyone working together on a common goal: to massacre demons. We'd studied military command in training. Discord in a crew could be fatal. As much as I wanted to dismantle Dani's crew, to take back the girls she'd stolen from the captains before me, my focus had to be on the Massacre and not on Dani. I had to remember who the real enemy was.

I wasn't sure how long I'd been leaning against the helm, but I must have fallen into a trance. When a hand appeared over the railing, mine were an alarming distance away from my crossbow.

I started into alertness and grabbed for the weapon across my chest, twisting out of the mermaid's line of fire so she couldn't impale me.

She poked her head up and made no move to attack. Her eyes weren't even red. They were sapphire blue.

"Lysi!" I said, struggling to keep my adrenaline-charged voice at a whisper. "You scared me half to death!"

"Sorry," she said, pursing her lips to hide a smile. "You sure looked like a maniac trying to get your crossbow in time."

I ducked behind the helm, trying to hide my own smirk as I strapped my weapon across my chest again. "Maybe I was just testing how fast I could ready my weapon."

She tilted her head. "Well, it would've made for a decent scrap, if I was going to attack you."

I poked my head around the helm to check on the girls. Nobody seemed to have seen my struggle. Fern must have felt my gaze; she looked straight at me and lifted a hand in a small wave. I returned it nonchalantly before pulling back.

"I can leave if you want me to," said Lysi, ducking a little.

"No," I said quickly. "It's okay. Stay."

I didn't know why I said it. I didn't want to trust her, especially after what she'd said about my trusting too easily.

Her eyes smiled, just as they had before I'd left her the last time.

"I've been wanting to come see you again," she said, propping her porcelain arms on the edge of the deck. "But . . . well . . ."

Her eyes swept over me, fixing on each place I'd been beaten and cut open, and then her brow knitted as she stared at the last stripe of sunlight across the water.

Her face still had the youthful glow I remembered, though it had grown leaner and more defined.

The deck creaked as we rocked over the waves, and I glanced over my shoulder impulsively.

"Don't worry," said Lysi. "I'll be able to hear someone coming before you will."

She tucked a golden lock behind her ear as though to prove she was listening. I leaned against the helm. "All right."

"So you got sent to warrior training, too?" She was studying my crossbow.

I nodded. "Five years of it. I never got to finish school. Neither did Annith."

"Annith! Your best friend, right? How's she doing?"

By her tone, I knew she wasn't asking in the light, conversational sense.

"Oh, you know," I said, not sure if I should go into the whole situation with Dani. "Still boy-crazy. She's pretty serious about a guy back home."

"Do you have anyone back home?" said Lysi.

For some reason, I shook my head. Then I caught myself and sighed.

"His name's Tanuu."

She looked at me for a long time before the corner of her mouth twisted up. "Oh?"

"Before I left, he told me he loves me and wants to marry me, and . . . I don't even like kissing him, never mind having kids with him," I blurted.

Lysi burst out laughing, stifling it by ducking her head over the side of the deck. "Why are you going out with him, then?"

I shrugged, flustered, but at the same time relieved by her reaction.

"Wait—is this the boy who always tried to give you dandelions?"

I groaned and put my head in my hands. Lysi burst with laughter all over again. It took her longer to surface this time.

"He's a good friend," I said. "But I don't love him like he does me."

"There's nothing wrong with going out with somebody for fun," said Lysi. "Sometimes it's nice to have some kind of . . . you know."

I raised an eyebrow. "Some kind of what?"

"Action," she said.

"Right." I flushed, embarrassed and trying to suppress a fit of giggles. "Well, yes."

She pressed her lips together.

At the back of my mind, a voice was yelling at me, telling me this conversation shouldn't be happening, telling me to make Lysi leave.

Instead, I grinned. "Do you have a boyfriend?"

She stalled and glanced sideways. "No . . ."

"But you have in the past?"

She nodded. I couldn't suppress the giggle.

"What happened?"

"Don't change the subject," she said. "What happened with you and Tanuu before you left? Did you tell him you loved him, too, and . . ."

"No!"

". . . share a sweet, teary goodbye, and . . ."

"No, I—"

". . . blow him kisses and wave a handkerchief as you sailed into the sunset?"

"No!" I said, but I laughed as she put on a romantic expression and batted her long eyelashes.

"Things were weird between us when I left. I feel terrible about it in case I never see him again."

"Don't say that," said Lysi, abruptly serious. "You'll go home alive. I'll make sure of it."

"That's a big promise to keep."

"I'm not losing you again."

My heart swelled at her words, and all I could do was stare. Did she really mean that? Was I stupid to think she wanted things to go back to the way they used to be?

Was I stupid for letting myself want that, too?

She broke our gaze to trace her finger over a crack in the deck.

"Tell me about your boyfriend," I said.

Her mouth twisted but she kept looking down. "We went out for almost two years."

"Then?"

"Then I broke it off."

"Why?"

She said nothing, still tracing her finger along the deck.

"Come on," I said. "You wouldn't shut up a second ago! What's his story?"

"His name's Kayton."

"Whoa, don't reveal too much," I said sarcastically.

Lysi laughed. "Well—he was a human once."

My mouth dropped open. "You changed him?"

"No," she said quickly, "it wasn't me. Another mermaid did it. But she did it without thinking. She didn't really love him."

"Bummer for him," I said.

"Oh, he's all right with it, if you know what I mean. He's gone out with a lot more mermaids than just me and the one who turned him."

I inclined my head. Maybe this Kayton guy saw the mishap as one enormous blessing. The thought made me smirk.

"Are there a lot of mermen turned from humans?"

"Not too many, but I know a few."

The idea of fishermen transforming into sea demons both thrilled and terrified me.

She went quiet again, so I said, "And? Why did you dump him?"

"I found out I wasn't the only mermaid he was going out with."

I stared at her. The words took a minute to sink in. "But . . ."

"Don't make that big-eyed seal face," she said. "I'm fine. I wasn't really into him anyway."

She smiled, but I couldn't return it. How could anyone cheat on Lysi?

"Lysi, I'm sorry," I said. "I shouldn't have pressed—"

"Oh, Mee," she said, flicking a spray of water at my face. "Stop it. I'm fine."

Her honest smile made me believe her, but I still wanted to throw my arms around her in a hug.

"Maybe I'm the one who trusts too easily," she said.

I opened my mouth, but Lysi looked over my shoulder and her eyes widened. A pink tinge bled through her eyes, and then I blinked, and she was gone.

I stared at the place where she'd been, and a second later heard footsteps behind me.

"Your turn," said a voice. I turned to see Annith's feet.

"I'm going to get a warmer jacket," I said, standing. A chill crept over me as the sky blackened.

I couldn't meet Annith's eyes as I strode past her, afraid of what I'd see.

"You can have that spot for *helm watch*, or whatever," I said.

I'd been trying not to let it bother me, but I could tell Annith wasn't always comfortable with the duties Dani gave her. She was wary of heights, yet the night before, I'd seen her scaling the main mast. I tried to remind her she was a free person who didn't have to follow Dani's orders. Annith argued that being a part of Dani's crew was what she wanted, and she was willing to overcome her fears if it meant staying on the crew.

I pulled my arms from my sleeves as I descended into the cabin, trying to push the issue from my mind. There was nothing I could do about it.

At the bottom, Holly and Shaena were in whispered conversation. They fell into abrupt silence when I entered. I ignored them and pulled my trunk from under the beds.

"So she wakes up and there's blood on her pillow and sheets, right," whispered Holly.

"You think she was hurt and didn't tell anyone?" whispered Shaena.

"No, I think she scratches herself in her sleep. I see her doing it sometimes."

She pointed across the way to her own bed. They both looked at it, and then down at Dani's bed as though a dying person lay under the mussed up sheets.

"She's putting herself under too much stress," said Holly.

"I know."

"So what do we do?"

"Nothing we can do. Just don't put any more strain on her."

"She's being so weird. Have you talked to her lately?"

"No. Have you?"

"No. She said she didn't want to talk to anyone."

"It's been, like, four days."

I pulled out my jacket and snapped my trunk closed, and the two of them paused again as I crossed in front of them to check on Linoya.

She still wouldn't wake, even when I shook her lightly. Her chest barely rose and fell.

Shaena and Holly couldn't have been the only other girls to think Dani wasn't doing so well. There was a wild desperation in the girl's eyes that'd never been there before.

Maybe I couldn't control what the other girls did, and maybe it wasn't a good idea to openly oppose Dani, but I could at least keep a close watch on her.

After all, the main responsibility of captain of the Bloodhound was the safety of the crew. Dani's crew was still my crew—and I had the nagging feeling safety wasn't Dani's top priority.

CHAPTER SIXTEEN

The Unknown Plan

By the middle of May, the Bloodhound was in a sorry state.

Fern squinted up at the torn sails and sighed. "How's this thing still moving?"

"I think she's just bobbing with the waves, at this point," I said grimly, jabbing a needle through the canvas with aching fingers.

I'd been stitching for close to an hour, and still the mainsail was a gigantic piece of Swiss cheese.

My stomach growled noisily, and I tried to ignore the pains shooting up my chest like fireworks. While Annith and Nora made dinner, I mended the ship with Texas, Fern, and Shaena—patching holes with tar, sewing up the sails, cleaning debris, taking a mop to the blood-sodden deck. I'd offered to repair the sails because I had a hard time keeping myself from lingering hopefully near the railings when I tried to do anything else.

I was torn between wanting Lysi to come back and wanting her to stay away. What if one of the girls saw her?

Could I live with myself if she got hurt again because of me?

Footsteps approached and stopped behind me. I finished my row of stitches before turning.

"I need to talk to you," said Holly shortly.

She jerked her head, motioning that we should step away from everyone.

I glanced around; nobody was listening to us, anyway. Fern had gone back to fixing the galley door, which a mermaid had ripped off its hinges the last time we were attacked. Everyone had been too preoccupied with the other mermaids to see her sneak over, and then the entire door had flown across the deck at us.

I humoured Holly and stepped aside.

"You told Dani," she said with a less-than-friendly expression.

I sighed and looked past her. "I don't know what you're talking about."

"You told her what I said the other night, about her scratching herself and being weird. You were the only other person in the room besides Shaena, and Linoya was asleep."

I blinked. I'd all but forgotten about their conversation. "You think I tattled?"

"How else would Dani know what I said? I trusted you'd mind your own business!"

"Maybe you need to talk to Shaena, because I tend not to share all the random conversations I hear."

"Shaena would never do that to me."

"Do you honestly think," I said stiffly, "I care enough about Dani to go telling her the stuff I overhear about her?"

Holly said nothing.

"Exactly," I said. "So go talk to Shaena if you're concerned. It sounds to me like your problem is coming from within your cult."

She stared at me passively for a moment before saying, "I heard you're captain now."

"Yes."

"Maybe you were trying to make me leave Dani's crew."

Her tone had become much less hostile.

"If anyone wants to leave Dani's crew," I said, choosing my words carefully, "they can make that decision on their own."

A shout from Dani cut across the deck, and Holly jumped.

"Look what I caught!"

Whatever it was, it emitted an ear-splitting shriek before Dani had finished talking. I squinted at it, some kind of fish she held away from her body at arm's length.

My jaw dropped. She was holding the tail of a tiny mermaid. The toddler wailed and thrashed in Dani's grip, trying to claw at her arm, but she didn't have the strength to pull her body around and grab Dani's wrist.

Dani laughed, watching the little body struggle at the end of her bony arm.

"Throw it back in—make it shut up," yelled Texas, turning back to her blood-soaked mop.

Dani ignored her and rummaged in her tool belt, still keeping the toddler carefully away from her body.

I stepped closer. "What are you looking for? Just throw it back in."

She narrowed her eyes at me. "This thing is going to grow up to kill your own kids one day. You want me to release it?"

"It's just a baby! It doesn't even have red eyes or fangs yet!"

Her bloodshot eyes gleamed. "It's not a *baby*, it's a sea rat, and it's going to eat my arm if I don't get rid of it soon."

I reached out. "Give it to me. I'll get rid of it."

Dani pulled away, and the baby mermaid's head cracked against the railing. She screamed even louder.

"Oops."

I clenched my teeth. "Dani, give me the mermaid."

She stepped back, sneering at me. Sweat shone on her face from the effort of holding up the flailing toddler.

Her hand closed around something in her tool belt. She pulled out her iron dagger.

I lunged forwards. "Dani, no!"

She was too quick. The knife sliced across the child's throat and the bright red blood poured freely from her upside-down body, flooding onto the deck like a waterfall.

"NO!"

I grabbed for the toddler, but Dani blocked me with her hand, still clutching the dagger.

"One less demon contaminating our waters."

She shoved her other fist into my chest, and the tiny mermaid slapped against my front. Blood poured down my legs.

"Now," said Dani, "you can get rid of it."

I stared into her empty eyes, reflecting nothing but a callousness that turned her irises a dead shade of beige. The way she looked at me, I could have sworn she'd left her soul back on Eriana Kwai. There was no human left in this girl.

"Your morals may have sunk to the bottom of the ocean," I said, taking hold of the baby's tail, "but someday, your sense of remorse will find you, and you'll realise you've failed to honour humanity."

Annith stepped through the doorway to the galley. "Dinner!"

She balked when she saw Dani and me standing nose-to-nose with the dripping corpse hanging between us.

"Great," said Dani, sliding the bloody dagger into her tool belt. "I'm starved!"

Without looking at it, I threw the light, cold body over the side of the ship. The deed was done and I couldn't stand to hold it any longer.

Feeling everyone gawking, I turned and strode down to the cabin, peeling off my soaked clothes. My hands were shaking. I could smell the blood.

"Disgusting," I said, throwing my shirt and pants on the floor and digging through my trunk.

None of the other girls had tried to stop her. Was a mermaid nothing but a target to them, even if only an innocent child?

I scrubbed the blood from my hands—though I swore they hadn't come truly clean in two weeks—then stomped back up the stairs and across to the galley, avoiding the eyes of the girls still on duty.

The table was silent when I sat down. I stared at my plate, willing my gag reflex to calm down so I could have a bite of something. Moments ago I'd been ravenous.

"Let's have a roast with our next kill," said Shaena after a minute, sweeping a finger across her already-empty plate to pick up any remaining grease.

A few girls chuckled.

"Like a pig roast?" said Nora.

"Wonder what mermaid tastes like," said Texas, peeling apart a chunk of fish with calloused fingers.

"Bet it's gross," said Nora. "Like fish mixed with chicken."

"Or human," said Fern grimly. "Fish mixed with human."

"Wonder what human tastes like," said Texas, and there was a brief moment of silence before she, Shaena, and Nora burst into laughter.

I stood, leaving my plate untouched.

"I'm going for some air," I said. Feeling their gazes, I added, "Seasick."

I climbed the stairs two at a time and went straight for the railing. My breathing was fast; I needed to calm down. I leaned over the side and looked down at the water, feeling like I might be ill.

What was wrong with these girls?

Or was it me? Was something wrong with me? I should have been better at numbing my emotions. I should have cared less about killing.

A coppery blonde head poked out of the water below me and I straightened up. Lysi's eyes met mine, wide and pleading. She nodded towards the helm.

I glanced behind me at the girls on duty, a couple them watching me with concern.

"Feeling okay, Meela?" said Sage.

"All right," I said. "Just need to walk a bit. Seasick."

She nodded sympathetically, and I strolled along the railing as though idle.

When I got to the helm I sat down casually, masking myself from the girls in the circle.

Lysi poked her head up, still looking desperate.

"What?" I whispered.

"I need to . . ."

"What?"

"What's wrong?"

"It's just . . . the girls," I said, knowing how vague I must sound.

"What'd they do?" said Lysi. "Need me to kick someone's ass?"

I smiled a little in spite of myself, but shook my head. "You remember me telling you about Dani?"

Lysi groaned. "Oh, no . . . she's here?"

Without pausing for breath, I launched into everything about Dani and her crew, and how Annith had joined them, and how Dani's behaviour was getting weirder and yet everyone still trusted her, and how they were killing without thinking and making brutal comments about what a mermaid would taste like.

"They're just so sick," I whispered, my voice breaking into high-pitched hysteria. "They're disgusting. They're losing what it is to be . . . to be . . ."

"Hey," said Lysi, reaching out a hand to calm my flailing arms. "Stop. Calm down."

Something in her expression made me relax. I rubbed my hands across my face and mumbled, "I don't want to do this anymore."

Cool fingers closed around my wrists, and Lysi gently pulled my hands from my face. She'd lifted herself up so she sat on the deck in front of me, her face so close to mine I could feel her breath.

"I know," she whispered. "I wish this whole war would end."

Her breath was sweet, like herbs or fruit, or how I would imagine the colour green would smell. I recalled what my father had said so many years ago, about how even a mermaid's scent is appealing.

"Mee?"

I blinked, realising I'd gone quiet. "What did you come here to say?"

Lysi hesitated. She dropped my hands.

Her words flooded out, like she wanted to say them before she changed her mind. "I wanted to warn you they've been directing a pod of whales this way. They're going to push one into your ship before morning."

My eyes widened, and I peered around her as though expecting to see the whales coming towards us.

"Tonight?"

Lysi nodded.

I opened my mouth, and it was a moment before I could get any words out. "Why are you telling me this?"

"I thought I made it clear I want you to stay alive. I owe it to you."

"You don't owe me anything."

My eyes dropped to the scar on her waist. I felt guilty for staring, but I couldn't look away.

I could hardly believe my father had left this mark on her forever—a tattooed reminder that she and I were enemies, and a reminder of what my people did to mermaids.

I felt Lysi's eyes on me, but I kept studying where the iron had burned her skin. It was like the black nucleus of a comet, heading a red tail from her ribcage to the top of her hipbone. Jagged lines stretched out from the point of impact, like cracked porcelain.

I lifted my hand automatically to feel the laceration, but caught myself. I met Lysi's gaze.

"Do you mind?"

She shook her head.

I placed my fingers over the shattered skin. When she didn't flinch, I moved them inwards to the black hole above her hipbone. Her icy skin became warmer, but not in a pleasant sense.

I could only manage a whisper. "Does it hurt?"

She gave a small shrug. "Sometimes it still burns."

I got to the edge of the black hole and stopped. The skin felt hot, like something freshly cooked. My throat tightened as I tried to imagine what it must have felt like, to have this burning gash every day of my life. I opened my hand and placed my palm over it.

Lysi's eyes were still fixed on me, and I looked up. Her expression had changed; she stared at me curiously now. Seconds ticked by where we only held each other's gaze, and something passed between us that I couldn't quite understand.

I took my hand away from her skin and dropped my eyes. "I should go take my place in the circle. It'll be my turn soon."

"Meela." She caught my wrist, gently, before I stood. "Come back here tomorrow night."

I nodded once. The following night was far away, and first I had to get through whatever was ahead of me.

I turned away so I wouldn't have to watch her leave. The splash she made dropping into the water blended with the waves.

Whales were coming. How was I supposed to tell the girls I knew we were going to be attacked? They accepted

Dani's speculations about when the attacks would happen, but I didn't want them wondering about my sanity, too.

"I just saw a whale spout on the horizon," I said loudly as we positioned ourselves in the circle. "Let's be prepared, just in case."

The sky had darkened, leaving us in the dim glow of a not-quite-full moon. The whites of Fern's eyes glinted as she scanned the water. Beside her, Holly glanced nervously to Shaena and Annith, who stood taller and looked around with haughty expressions.

"Blacktail, Sage, do you mind staying up for a bit so we have all hands?" I said.

"No," said Dani, suddenly right next to me. "We need to stick with the shifts we had planned. They need to sleep for these first six hours."

"There's a whale nearby," I said, turning so we were face-to-face. "We can't have half of us asleep and risk an ambush."

Dani's skin was clammy, her cheeks gaunt. The darkest part of her was the thick layer of kohl around her eyes, which she never removed so it was hard to tell where the old makeup ended and the dark circles under her eyes began.

"We're always at risk of an ambush," she said. "And half of us need to sleep so we're strong enough to fight when the time comes."

I wondered how Dani was strong enough to do anything, given the amount of weight she'd lost.

The girls around us were as silent as shadows. I bit my tongue, remembering my promise to myself that I wouldn't tear the crew apart even further.

Then Sage spoke, her voice quiet. "I'm part of Meela's crew. I'm going to stay up."

I looked from her to Blacktail. Blacktail nodded.

Dani's fists clenched. She trembled, glaring at me.

"My crew, stick with the plan," she yelled, and a fleck of spit hit my cheek. She stormed into the cabin, leaving Texas, Kade, and Nora to follow in her wake.

"When the whale comes, hit the deck before you try to kill any demons," I said to the girls around me. "You won't be much use if you fall overboard. An attack will likely happen before dawn, so this circle will be more valuable than ever. Remember our night battle tactics. Keep your backs to the rest of us, and fire at every approaching shadow. We'll be safe from our own bolts as long as none of us breaks from the circle."

Without another word, everyone took position. Sage placed a few lanterns in the centre and lit them. They flickered in a ghostly way that made me think it would've been less eerie not to have any light.

Time crept. I kept my ears tuned for whale spouts as we bobbed over the high swells. Each time we hit a rough wave, my heart jumped into my throat.

I hoped the girls below deck weren't falling into too deep a slumber. Under the pretence of warming my feet, I stomped noisily every so often, hoping the sound would keep them awake.

The moon started to make its way back towards the horizon, but I still hadn't done so much as relax my grip on my crossbow when Blondie suddenly cursed. I whirled around, hearing an intake of breath as we all raised our weapons.

In the moonlight's path over the shallow waves, the water flattened. Something black and glossy flipped up, pushing white swells in all directions.

The whale was on a straightaway to our ship, moving so quickly there was no need to wonder whether something was chasing it.

"Get down!" I yelled. We flung ourselves onto the deck, the ship trembling as if we'd smashed into a reef. Everything groaned, and for a fleeting, terrifying moment, I thought the Bloodhound might crumble beneath us.

At once, a thunder of mermaids landed around me. I staggered to my feet and hitched my crossbow to my shoulder, seeing only shadows and glints of flesh. Every lantern clattered to the deck, their flames snuffed so only the moonlight was left to guide us. But I didn't need my sight. We'd prepared for this. My ears and intuition would guide me as they'd done many times in training.

The figures swarmed us, obscuring the stars, their shadows blacker than the sky behind them. I spread my feet wide and crouched to brace myself against the rocking ship. Keeping my footing would be more important than ever.

A shadow pulled itself forwards, and I sensed it with every part of me: seeing her outline, feeling her presence, hearing her claws and a blunt weapon slamming violently into the wood.

I fired. I couldn't see the bolt but I knew its path. It missed the shadow's head completely.

I stared at the black sky where the bolt had gone, dropping my crossbow a fraction. I must have been rusty. We hadn't had a night attack yet.

Another shuddering crack against the hull. I steadied myself, jammed a bolt against the shaft, aimed again—and hesitated.

The mermaid was close enough for me to see her glistening skin in the moonlight. Still, my fingers wouldn't move.

A stride away from me, a bolt met her chest and she collapsed.

"What the hell, Meela?" shouted Holly from beside me. I heard her notch another bolt.

I pretended not to hear her and hitched my crossbow again, aiming at the next mermaid. I could see a wild nest of hair on top of her head, tied in place with a slimy rope. But behind the veil of darkness, she had Lysi's face. My hands shook too much to fire.

It's not Lysi! I told myself. *Shoot it!*

The cabin door burst open. The rest of the girls' footsteps stampeded out.

I blinked away the vision of Lysi and, before I could think about it, fired.

Dani was screaming something. Holly disappeared from beside me.

The mermaid got away. My bolt would have hit her; it would have pierced straight through that thick, wild head of hair, but she'd thrown herself into the water during the time I wasted with my finger frozen over the trigger.

Numb with the realisation of it, I loaded another bolt and stared at the empty, black place where she'd disappeared. Dani was still shouting.

"Let down the drag on the port side!"

The drag? What was *the drag?*

The shadows of Holly, Shaena, and Annith gathered at the stern. They strained to push a fishing net full of barrels over the railing and off the side of the ship.

"What are they doing?" I yelled. "One of us could shoot them! They need to stay in the circle!"

Sage spared a glance at them. "For the whale! To turn us out of its path."

Behind her, the glistening whites of Kade's eyes caught mine. I saw desperation.

"Hold onto something," she shouted, and then the ship lurched.

Thrown off my feet, I yanked a dagger from my tool belt and slammed it into the wooden planks, stopping myself from sliding. Sage rolled into me.

The barrels were acting like an anchor. The weighted fishing nets turned the ship away from the whale so sharply, it'd given the whale a clear escape from the keel.

"They should've told the rest of us," I said. "We would've gone flying if Kade hadn't . . ."

Sage scrambled to disentangle herself from me as the ship careened in a circle.

Kade was nowhere near.

"Kade!"

A bloodcurdling scream came from somewhere beyond our broken circle. I turned to see shadows approaching Sage and me. The blackness blinded me to what was happening, but beneath all the other sounds was a long, slow scraping noise. Kade was being dragged off the ship.

"No!" My eyes fell on a pair of shadows, silver-lined in the moonlight, struggling at the end of the ship. What held Kade by the ankle had a wild mess of hair tied up with rope. She was the demon who'd gotten away from me.

Sage and I advanced, abandoning what was left of our defensive circle. I fired at the shape closest to me and heard the bolt make contact. I reloaded and fired again, keeping my focus on the struggling pair at the end of the ship. Kade's abductor masked herself behind the other demons. I couldn't get a clear shot.

A series of hollow thuds punctuated the sound of Kade screeching as each dead mermaid collapsed onto the deck. More advanced, and Kade was being hauled through the railing now. There were too many. We weren't fast enough.

"Get those last ones!" I yelled. I hoped Sage had a good enough shot.

I sprinted through a gap in the shadows and lunged for Kade, landing hard on my stomach. Her outstretched hands were there. My fingers locked around her wrists. The mermaid didn't seem to notice the extra weight, because she continued to drag us both over the edge.

"Don't let her take me," said Kade, clawing at the slippery deck. Splinters peeled up, flaking under her nails.

I kept a bone-crushing grip on her hands, refusing to let go. I kicked my feet wildly, trying to lock them around something to stop us from sliding.

But the mermaid still pulled, until Kade hung off the side with me clinging desperately to her. The glistening waves sprayed my face, like the frothy swells were trying to wrap their fingers around Kade's legs.

I screamed for someone to help us, but the effort took away from what I needed to keep holding on. I couldn't loosen my grip. Not to scream, not to reach for my crossbow. She'd be pulled under before I could blink.

"Meela," said Kade, pleading.

Her eyes were clear in the moonlight. We held each other's gaze, and I saw in the way she looked at me that she knew this was it. She was going to be dragged in. She was going to die.

The mermaid beneath her blended with the water, though I could see her black hair flowing among the debris. Her dark, glossy eyes were all but indistinguishable.

My entire upper body hung over the side. I bent my knee to hold myself between two railings, but the mermaid's strength was unimaginable. One more tug and I'd be pulled in with both of them. But I couldn't let go. I couldn't give up on Kade.

A wave swelled into Kade, drenching her whole body and sending an icy shower across my face.

Kade's breathless words blended with the wind. But I knew what she said.

"Tell them I love them."

The waves clasped their frigid hands around us as the ship rocked downwards, and my legs slipped dangerously. Kade seemed to take this as the final threshold. She released her fingers from around my wrists.

I screamed, tightening my grip so my knuckles popped, but her slippery fingers pulled through my own.

I watched her shadow fall, seeing it before I felt it in my empty fists.

The last part of her I saw was a pair of emerald green eyes: the only glimmer of brightness in the black water. Then they faded. And she was gone forever at the hands of a mermaid.

CHAPTER SEVENTEEN

Dance of the Flickering Light

Standing over my bed, I folded a dry shirt for the sixth time and laid it flat in my trunk. I'd flattened and re-folded everything several times, unable to go back upstairs.

Outside my window, the sun had already begun to set, returning the water to pitch-blackness. A dizziness fogged my head, which blended with the rocking of the ship, leaving me unsure how rough the waves were beneath us. Their hollow sloshing had become nothing but white noise, drowning me in silence.

Kade was dead, taken by the very mermaid I had failed to kill. She was dead and it was my fault.

The reason gnawed me from the inside out. If I hadn't been talking to Lysi, thinking of Lysi, I wouldn't have hesitated.

I needed to stay a warrior. I couldn't be loyal to both Lysi and my people.

Someone's footsteps clicked on the stairs, but I didn't turn. Instead, I pulled out all my socks and began re-balling them, lining them up perfectly before turning them over on themselves.

"You need to join our crew, Meela," said Annith.

My entire body tightened and I stayed facing away from her. "Absolutely not."

"She got us away from the whale with her plan."

"I know."

"So you admit she knows what she's doing."

I narrowed my eyes at the tiny window in front of me. "She has some good plans, but I'd sooner jump ship than call her my captain."

"Why?"

"I don't trust her, Annith!"

"She might be your only chance at staying alive."

I rounded on her. "You think I can't stay alive if I don't join your cult?"

"I just don't think," she said, and I could tell she was fighting to stop her voice from shaking, "that you're taking this all very seriously."

I drew myself up taller, not breaking eye contact. "Not taking this seriously? You don't see me making jokes about eating mermaids, or keeping all my plans a dramatic secret so—"

"Not like that. I mean you hesitate too much. You still don't like to kill. I see it on your face."

My stomach felt like it'd reached its boiling point, but I didn't know what to say. Could she not read the regret in my eyes?

I know! I wanted to shout. *I know I screwed up!*

I needed to bring the training master's lessons to the front of my mind again. I needed to force that black tar over my heart and kill every mermaid I laid eyes on. The survival of my crew and my own skin depended on it.

I glowered at Annith. She had no business telling me this. Besides, the Annith I knew would never have accused me of being too compassionate.

"Did Dani send you here to tell me this? Are you her personal slave now?"

Annith crossed her arms haughtily. "She's the captain. As captain—"

"Don't you have any pride left?" I said, my voice growing heated. "Since when do you let someone else make your decisions, especially that psychotic—"

"Since she proved she can keep me alive."

Never in my life had I wanted to slap Annith, but at that moment I was prepared to use any means possible to knock the sense back into her.

She uncrossed her arms, revealing her clenched fists. I stared at the sharp, white knuckles—a sight I'd rarely seen on Annith.

The stairs creaked beside us and Dani appeared. Drawn to an argument like a shark to blood.

"What's going on, girls?" she said with mocking lightness. She dropped her pointed chin, eyes fixed wickedly on the two of us. Her face looked worn, sunken, her hair more un-groomed than I'd ever seen it.

"Just talking," said Annith, straightening up with an important look on her face that made me want to slap her even more.

"So mind your own business," I said, feeling my upper lip curl.

Annith shot me a glare.

"Ooh," said Dani, gleefully. "An argument between the two best friends in the whole world. Isn't this fun?"

She leaned against the wall, clearly with no intention of going anywhere.

"Dani," I said, my voice growing louder by the second, "if you don't get out right now—"

"She's right, you know," said Dani.

I closed my mouth, teeth snapping together.

Dani picked at her worn-down fingernails as she spoke. "You've got no guts to properly kill a mermaid. I've known it since we started training. If you don't harden up soon, you'll end up like the other pathetic *captains* before you: mermaid lunch, or lying useless with a big hole in your back."

My breaths grew heavy as more than a decade of hatred for Dani bubbled up inside me. My fingers throbbed in my tightly balled fists.

"It must run in your blood," said Dani. "You won't be the first in your family who's too inept to fight."

I lunged at her.

Annith must have known it was coming because she grabbed both my arms. Dani seemed torn between backing off and attacking, and she made a funny lurch that ended in a half-crouch.

I yanked myself free from Annith's grip, and her full weight landed on my back. She let out a long, high-pitched scream, hitting me over the head with one hand and waving the other in Dani's direction to keep us apart.

Dani came at me with her fists up. I punched her hard in the stomach. Annith, still screaming and hitting me on the head, kicked her feet at Dani and used her free hand to grab her around the throat.

A roar came from somewhere behind us.

"STOP!"

The three of us froze: Annith glued to my back, one of her hands in the middle of cracking me on the head and one around Dani's throat; Dani buckled over and reaching out to claw me in the face; and me with one hand on Annith's wrist to stop her from hitting me, the other winding up to punch Dani again in the stomach.

We all turned to gape at Blacktail, shocked that someone besides the unconscious Linoya had been in the room this whole time. She emerged from the dark end of the cabin.

"*What - are - you - doing?*" I'd never seen Blacktail get angry, and the tendons in her neck bulged. "Meela, Annith, you've been best friends since the beginning of time. Shut up, accept each other's decisions, and get on with it."

The stairs creaked on the other side of us, and Shaena, Fern, Nora, and Blondie peeked in.

"Dani"—Blacktail eyed her with an air of revulsion— "save it for the battlefield. I think we'd all appreciate you directing your venom at the enemy."

I dropped my hands, and so did Dani. Annith's legs unclamped from my sides and she slid to the floor.

Dani shot a sour glance at Blacktail before marching up the stairs, parting the girls with ease.

I avoided everyone's gaze as I turned around and closed my trunk.

Blacktail shooed everyone up the stairs and followed in their wake, leaving Annith and me alone. I exhaled slowly and faced her again.

"I appreciate your concern for me," I said, and I tried to sound earnest but my voice ended up in a monotone. "I really don't want to join your crew."

Annith nodded once, her jaw tight. I pushed past her and climbed the stairs.

My limbs vibrated, like they were still ready to deliver a swift blow to somebody's cheek. After more than a decade of antagonizing me, Dani always knew exactly what to say to make me snap. And why didn't Annith defend our dead crewmates? My dead brother? She'd deserted me. I couldn't even trust her to take my side any more.

I hadn't lost my temper like that in a long time. The training master had made sure of it. I recalled the main goal he'd drilled into my brain for five years: *control your emotions.* Somehow, though, that had leaked out my ears in the panic of real battle these last two weeks.

The stars twinkled in the cloudless sky, and I remembered my promise to meet Lysi that night. I breathed deeply as I strode to the helm. Shaena was there steering, despite the smooth water and dead breeze. She must have been putting off going to bed.

I hovered by the railing, pretending to scan the waves for threats. Finally, any remaining girls trickled below deck and Shaena followed, apparently deciding she'd stalled long enough. Only six girls stayed up, taking their places in a circle on the main deck.

After a few more minutes, I slipped behind the helm, sat down, and waited for Lysi.

A flicker of green in the black sky made me look up. A glowing curtain stretched above me, flapping softly beneath the stars. My throat tightened as I watched it dance.

I thought of Kade ... and Eyrin, Shaani, Nati, Mannoh, Akirra, and Chadri. And I wondered if Nilus was watching over me. When I'd been a kid and he was still alive, he and I would sit under the lights and he'd tell me our grandparents were up there. It was hard to believe I could still miss him this much after so many years.

"Makes you feel calm, doesn't it?"

Lysi poked her head up in front of me.

At the sight of her, I couldn't help pressing my lips into a half-smile. "Serene. Yes."

"Serene." She repeated the word to herself a few times, adding it to her vocabulary.

"Makes me think of all the girls we've lost," I said.

"We say it's the pathway the spirits travel through." She pointed towards a long, dim stretch of the emerald curtain. "See how the lights hang down like seaweed? They're passing beyond it to a better place."

"Eriana legend says it's the spirits dancing," I said. I could almost see Kade's bright green eyes as she jumped through the sky, finally free.

My eyes welled with tears and I looked down. Lysi was watching me sadly.

"What happens?" I whispered. "When a mermaid takes one of us into the ocean? Does she eat us?"

Lysi's porcelain face seemed to whiten even more. "She usually kills, yes. The way she does it depends on the mermaid."

I tried not to let my imagination run away with me, but my heart skipped a beat at the possibilities that flashed across my mind.

"She won't always kill, though," said Lysi, barely audible. "Sometimes she'll change her victim."

"Into a mermaid?"

She nodded. "A merman, usually."

"How does she decide which victims to change?"

"Selfishly. If a mermaid falls in love with a sailor, she'll do it to be with him. It's frowned upon."

"Like what happened—"

"—to Kayton, yes."

We fell silent, and again I turned my face up to the curtain of lights. I was betraying my crewmates' souls by talking to Lysi. I was betraying my people.

"You can't come here anymore," I said.

She looked at me sharply. I kept my eyes skywards, because they'd brimmed with tears and I was afraid they'd fall if I looked down.

"I can't have you in my life if I'm going to fight for my people," I said.

When she didn't respond, I met her eyes. Her expression was cold.

"You don't have to choose," she said.

"Yes, I do. I can't fight knowing at any moment, you might end up one of the corpses on the deck."

I shook my head violently, like it would dislodge the vision.

A stupid urge overcame me, and the words flooded out. "Stop coming to battles. You don't have to risk your life."

She opened and closed her mouth. "I—no! You're fighting for your people. Why should I stop fighting for mine?"

"I have no choice. I'm stuck on this ship. You have a choice. I want you to choose to stay alive."

"Mee, we're on opposite sides of a war. You're asking me to surrender."

"It's not about the war. I'm asking you to save your own life!"

But I knew I was wrong as I said it. It was about the war. Everything was about the war. Her life and mine, her culture and mine, were dedicated to it.

She reached out and locked my hand in her icy fingers. "Let's not talk about this."

I held her gaze, breathing hard to push down the bubble of panic.

Lysi pressed her palm against mine and stretched her fingers skywards. I did the same, feeling our hands align perfectly—brown skin against white.

I stood before she could change my decision. I'd never forget Kade's face as she was pulled into the water. Nobody else knew what that felt like, and nobody else could understand it.

"Our paths were never meant to cross."

"I don't care—"

"Do it for your people," I said. "They need your loyalty, and my people need mine."

She went quiet. I had to turn away from her sapphire eyes.

I opened my mouth, trying to dislodge the word *goodbye*.

"You've been here a while," said Annith's voice.

I started. Annith was standing an arm's length from me. I whirled back around without thinking, but Lysi had vanished.

"Yeah, well, I can't sleep," I said, staring at the brightening horizon. I took a breath to calm my heart rate.

"It's your turn."

When I faced her again, her eyebrows were knitted together. I knew that expression. It was the same one she wore whenever she asked me, "What'd you do this time?"

All she said was, "You must be exhausted."

I shrugged. Of course I was exhausted. We all were.

"Is it Kade?"

Hearing Kade's name made my throat tighten, and I felt a burst of fury at Annith for bringing it up so casually.

"I'm fine, all right?" I said, pushing past her.

"I just thought you might need—"

"Well, I don't need or want to relive it," I said. "It was bad enough seeing it once."

I felt Annith watching me as I strode over to take my place in the circle. When I turned around to face the water, I noticed she was squinting beyond the helm—at the very place Lysi had disappeared.

I felt like I'd just fallen asleep when I was awoken by a low, steady rumbling. I stared at the ceiling, perplexed. The noise was rhythmic—not frantic, as if we were being attacked.

Fern sat up and squinted straight ahead, her hair poking in every direction. Her stuffed cat fell on the floor. "Wha'zat?"

I grunted and stood to go investigate. Fern watched me put on my jacket and slouch over to the stairs, then I distinctly heard her flop back down in her bed.

The sun must have risen, but I could hardly tell. Dark clouds had moved in, smothering any rays of light. It wasn't raining, but a downpour was imminent.

Dani and her crew had set up a dozen lanterns in a large circle, which cast a flickering glow across the deck.

Standing between the lanterns, the girls formed a circle around Holly and Dani. They stomped their feet, sending an eerie thunder across the otherwise quiet waters.

I approached Blacktail, Sage, and Zarra, who looked on from beside the cabin door.

Dani had strung iron bolts together with fishing wire and slung them across her chest like a soldier. Her hair was slick and pulled back from her face—which she'd painted all over with kohl. The region around her eyes was black, like rectangular sunglasses. Thin lines sprouted from the rectangle to sweep down her cheeks. She'd also blackened the backs of her hands across the bones, making her appear even more skeletal than she already was.

"Are you aware, Holly," she shouted over the stomping, "of the crimes you have committed against your captain, your crew, and the Bloodhound?"

"Yes," said Holly in a high, loud voice.

"Prove it!"

"I cowered! My crew was fighting, and I cowered."

"Exactly." Dani turned to the rest of her crew. "This type of selfishness ought to be punished, don't you agree?"

The girls in the circle turned their glares on Holly and made hissing noises.

"But the demon cornered me! I had to hide—"

"Quiet!" yelled Dani, and the way her voice carried across the empty water seemed to remind everyone how alone we were, because the circle fell into silence. A few girls glanced over their shoulders. Their stomping faded to a low rumble.

"You cowered, and you will be punished for it," said Dani, more quietly now.

"Yes, Captain," said Holly.

Where I stood, the four of us were stunned into silence. Zarra's jaw had fallen open, stretching the scar across her cheek.

"This is ridiculous," I said.

I stuffed my hands in my pockets and marched towards the circle.

Dani stepped inside the ring, and Holly stood taller.

"How should we punish her?" shouted Dani.

The responses ranged from "lashings" and "keelhauling" all the way down to "double kitchen duty."

"Oh, I like that one," said Dani, pointing a finger at Blondie. "We'll dunk her."

"No you won't," I said, stopping behind Nora.

The stomping faded, and Dani turned with exaggerated slowness, eyeing me over her small, pointed nose like I was a humble servant. So I added snidely, "Sorry to interrupt, oh Queen of the Universe."

Several girls drew a breath. I rolled my eyes.

"You are not *dunking* Holly. She'll get hypothermia. And what if demons are nearby?"

"Last I checked," said Dani, loudly enough to ensure everyone heard. "Holly was not part of your crew. She's part of my crew. Isn't that right, Holly?"

Holly nodded and made a small noise.

"Your crew," I said, even louder, "is nothing but a sorry attempt at mutiny. I don't care if you think you have authority over Holly, but I'm the rightful captain, and I say you aren't dunking her."

Dani's eyes sparked in the flame of the lanterns, and for a moment I wanted to step back. Between the dark kohl painted across her face and the gauntness in her cheeks, she looked ghostly in the flickering light.

She ground her teeth together, then lifted a hand up by her ear and said, "Girls."

I was too shocked to do more than gape as Blondie and Nora grabbed me by the arms.

"Are you serious?" I said, keeping my eyes fixed on Dani and wrenching my arms away.

Dani said nothing, only crossed her arms and watched the girls grab me again. Texas stepped forwards to help, and I found myself being hauled backwards across the deck.

"This is insane," I said, trying to sound calm despite the frustration boiling inside me. "You know we can't afford to weaken our own crewmates!"

None of them looked at me. Texas said, "Subject will remain in exile until otherwise noted."

They dumped me at the top of the stairs leading to the cabin and opened the door.

"Get down there," said Texas through gritted teeth. "We don't have time for your interruptions."

"You're all acting—"

Blondie and Nora stepped closer to me and hissed, and without consciously deciding to, I stepped back. I stood on the top stair, rendering me smaller than the rest of them. I felt like an insect beneath Texas' towering figure.

I stared up at their determined faces, not recognising them behind their maniacal eyes. The door slammed, leaving me in blackness at the top of the stairs.

"Dunk her!" shouted Dani, and roars and stomping erupted again.

I turned and traipsed down the steps. As much as I wanted to get those girls away from Dani, they were all adults. They could make their own decisions.

Still, I hated feeling so powerless.

Fern was snoring, Scarf the cat wrapped safely in her arms again. I sat on my bed and stared across the empty room, coming to the grim conclusion that the members of Dani's crew were losing their minds.

If we really had killed over seven hundred mermaids, surely their attacks must have been close to subsiding, and we could soon go home. Until then, if we physically survived the demons, I could only hope we'd mentally survive Dani.

Above, the stomping grew louder. I scanned the cabin for something to do. In the front bunks, Linoya still lay there, the same as she'd done day after day. I feared to think how her muscles were deteriorating. Not that it mattered. No one said it aloud, but I was sure she'd broken her spine. If we did make it home, she would be in a wheelchair.

"Meela," she said.

I started. "You're awake!"

"Are they ten-pin bowling up there?" There was a note of bewilderment in her slow, drugged voice.

"It's Dani's crew," I said, making my way over.

Linoya cursed under her breath. "She still thinks she's captain?"

"Yes."

I couldn't see her well in the darkness, but the outline of her face looked sunken, her hair sweat-soaked and matted.

"Guess I've been a deadbeat captain down here."

I took one of her cold, clammy hands in mine. "Don't say that. You haven't even . . . It's not your . . ."

Would she know if my suspicions were true—that Dani had been sedating her?

"You've been comatose," I said. "I've tried to wake you."

She dropped her gaze.

"Linoya, you can trust me. Is there anything you want to tell me?"

She waved a hand at the trunk. "It's just the herbs. I've been taking a lot of them. Maybe too many."

I picked one up and studied it closely.

"Wanna hand me some?" she said. "My back's killing me."

I passed her a fistful and watched her eat them. It didn't make sense. The herbs weren't powerful enough to sedate her so deeply.

"But I guess I don't need to feel bad about taking these anymore," she said. "Now that I really do need them. If I wasn't useless enough already . . ."

"You're not useless, Linoya."

She picked at a dried flower. "Sometimes I only pretend to be asleep, just so no one will talk to me."

I smirked. "I'd probably do the same."

"I overhear things."

When I raised my eyebrows, she said, "Oh, it's mostly boring. A lot of talk about being scared."

"Of dying?"

"Dying . . . suffering before dying . . . death coming too quickly . . . being drowned . . . being impaled. Blah, blah."

"I'd want it to happen fast, so I wouldn't know it was coming," I said, and even as the words came out I surprised myself, because I hadn't realised I'd made a decision on the matter.

Linoya grunted. "You wouldn't want the chance to come to terms with it?"

I thought about that for a moment. "If I could come to terms with it, I guess that would be nice. But I don't know if I'm ready for that."

"I've come to terms with it," said Linoya. Her tone was so casual, it took me a moment to absorb what she'd said.

I looked at her sharply. "You've come to terms with dying?"

"I'm aware I might not make it back, Meela."

I squeezed her hand in what I hoped was a reassuring way. "We've killed more mermaids than any of the past Massacres. They're bound to slow down soon, and then we'll head home. You'll make it."

She paused. And then: "I heard you've taken over my duties."

I bit my lip. So she knew I'd replaced her as captain. Was that disapproval in her voice?

"I meant to tell you," I said. "I just—"

"It's fine. I don't care. Just be careful, okay?"

"Of what?"

"Dani. She's not right, that kid."

"That's pretty obvious."

"I've heard you two going at it a few times."

Her tone seemed accusatory, so I said, "Well, she pisses me off."

"Meela, some girls are saying they want out of her crew. They're scared of her."

"Like who?"

She lolled her head to the side so she stared at the dark wall. "Don't know if I should say."

"What about Annith?"

She looked back at me, eyebrows pinched on her sallow face. "It must be hard to have your best friend volunteer as one of Dani's servants."

"She just wants some guidance," I said, trying to convince myself. "She must be scared. Dani's easy to follow."

"Annith never badmouths you. She's doing it 'cause she wants to stay alive. For some dude named Rik."

I smiled. "She's in love."

"She and Nora both," said Linoya, sounding exasperated. "The two of them won't shut up about their *soul mates*."

She made a gagging sound. I laughed.

"It's good they have something to live for," I said. "We all need that. Someone to fight for."

The door burst open at the top of the stairs, making me jump. Linoya was too drugged to have any reaction.

Holly thumped down the stairs, dripping water from her clothes and hair, leaving a small river behind her that began to pool at the base of the steps. I could hear her teeth chattering from across the room.

I jumped up and hopped clumsily over the clothes and open trunks littering the floor.

Fern had woken up, and her jaw dropped as she scrambled out of bed. "What the hell happened?"

"Dani's crew dunked her over the side of the boat," I said, helping Holly remove her icy clothes. She stood trembling with her knees bent and her arms crossed, like she'd been frozen in that position.

"Help me get her out of these," I said to Fern, who jumped into action.

"She should rinse the salt off," she said.

Our shower was lukewarm at best, but it would probably feel hot to someone who'd just been dunked in the Pacific Ocean near freezing point.

Fern and I helped Holly shower and change into dry clothes.

"I th-think I liked it b-better when she ignored m-me," said Holly through chattering teeth, pulling on a thick sweater. Her face had returned to colour a little, but she still shivered violently.

"I bet you're not the only one," I said, turning her around and running a comb through her brittle, salt-faded hair.

"A-all I know is I'm staying c-clear out of her w-way tomorrow."

"Why?" said Fern. "What's tomorrow?"

"She's g-got some big plan to k-kill a bunch of m-mermaids."

Fern and I exchanged a glance.

"What is it?" I said, abandoning pretence.

Holly shrugged. "S-something to do with the fishing nets. T-Texas and Shaena know more than the rest of us."

Fern sighed loudly. "Dani can shove these secret plans up . . . I mean, someone's going to get hurt, don't you think? She can't stay so mysterious all the time."

Out of the darkness, Linoya spoke in her sleepy drawl. "She just wants all the glory for herself."

We fell silent, then Holly said in barely a whisper, "Yeah."

My mind jumped to Lysi. I wished she'd listened to me when I told her to stay away from the battles. Should I try to warn her? I owed this knowledge to her after what she'd told me about the whales. She could take that knowledge back with her, and . . .

And possibly ruin Dani's plan of killing a bunch of mermaids, giving the mermaids an advantage and a chance at killing my crew and me.

Did I really owe Lysi this warning against Dani's fishing nets? Or was it better to keep myself safe?

I finished braiding Holly's hair and fastened the bottom with my own elastic. She turned and smiled at me.

"I think you make a b-better captain," she whispered.

"Thanks," I said, unable to return her smile.

Holly glanced uncomfortably at the foot of the stairs. "D-don't tell her I said that. For both your sake and mine."

CHAPTER EIGHTEEN

Ensnared

Misery washed over us with the frigid rain and dribbled down our backs. A torrential downpour blocked our view of the mountain range, so our compasses were the only indication of which direction we faced. The temperature must have been below freezing because the deck had an icy glaze that made it difficult to walk without slipping.

Texas, Nora, and Blondie were setting up a fishing net at the bow, clearly not for the purpose of catching fish. They pulled it taut between the railing and the fore mast, nowhere near the water.

"There's the big plan," I said to Fern, speaking loudly to get past the pounding rain. I frowned, watching them crank a rope tighter until it was straining and ready to pop closed over someone.

"They've used up all our fishing nets," said Fern, scowling at them as we trimmed the mainsail.

"Want to try telling that to Dani?"

She jerked the line she was holding with a little too much force, saying nothing.

Around the main mast, six girls stood in a circle facing the water. I wasn't sure they should even bother. The ice rain fell so hard it was difficult to see from one end of the ship to the other, never mind oncoming attackers.

A grim feeling pounded into the slippery deck with each heavy raindrop. These conditions that impeded our vision and sent us sliding across the deck would be ideal for a mermaid.

So when Sage screamed, a noise partially drowned by the clamour of the rain, it felt more inevitable than surprising. I only had time for a fleeting glance at Sage—she plucked something long and sharp from her thigh—before I had to dive out of the way of a small boulder hurling through the air. I heard it crater the deck behind me.

Countless blurry outlines of mermaids flung themselves aboard, and I forced that black tar to melt over my heart. I would not hesitate. There was no Lysi on the Massacre—only my life and the lives of my crewmates.

I set my jaw and fired, sending a demon keeling backwards into the water. The demons throwing themselves at me became mere targets. I fired at one after the other, keeping my arms and legs moving.

The mermaids must have been waiting for a downpour like this. They glided through the deluge swirling around our feet, using the icy streams for momentum while we stumbled and slipped as we tried to aim.

Blacktail was rooted at the fore mast, leaning against it for support while she massacred an endless swarm of demons. I slid my way to her and backed into the mast on the other side.

"All right?" she yelled. I heard a demon collapse at her feet.

"Yeah, you?"

Her response was drowned in a loud surge as we crested a wave. A heavy spray crashed over us. I opened my eyes to a golden-haired mermaid skidding towards me with a fistful of darts. I ducked barely in time. A dart whistled past my ear, pinning a chunk of my hair to the mast.

I pulled the trigger, and my iron bolt pierced straight through her. She collapsed—but another demon had been waiting behind her, and she lunged at me before I had time to think.

Her cold hand closed around my throat and brought me to my knees. She wrenched me away from the mast, sharp teeth bared. I thought she was about to rip into my flesh when a loud snap rang through the air and a net enveloped the mermaid, yanking her up and away from me. She shrieked, but still held on, dragging me with her. I clutched her wrist with both my hands, trying to stop myself from being strangled.

An eternity later she seemed to decide I wasn't worth it and let out a wail, clawing frantically at the ropes around her face and neck.

Gasping, I turned to see who'd let the trap loose—but nobody was there. It must have activated on its own when the mermaid crossed a threshold. Still on my knees, I raised my crossbow to finish her off before she could tear through the ropes.

In the time I'd taken to check over my shoulder, the mermaid's skin had faded to olive. She looked at me with her human face, emerald eyes wide with unmistakable pleading . . .

"No!"

Before the tar could melt from my heart, I pulled the trigger. At her last, strangled breath, I turned away.

The ice rain pounded into the deck with such force, I thought it might leave permanent grooves in the wood. I could barely see. The cries of girls and mermaids battering each other rose over the deafening rainfall.

Amid the chaos, a piercing shriek struck the air that went straight up my spine. I'd heard it before, years ago, when a bolt had shot from my father's crossbow.

Lysi.

I jumped to my feet and sprinted towards the stern without thinking. Searching frantically, I blew past Zarra, who fended off three mermaids at once. I ducked to avoid a flying spear, but didn't allow myself time to fire at the mermaid who'd thrown it.

Then I saw her, caught in the trap net on the starboard side.

Annith jumped out from behind the helm, her crossbow aimed at the tangled mess of skin and rope.

"Annith!" I screamed. "Stop!"

She wavered, looking over her shoulder at me, her savage expression clouding with confusion.

I slid towards her through a river of water and blood, not hiding my desperation as I extended my hand.

"Not her," I said, my voice muffled by the rain. "Please, not her."

She opened her mouth but seemed at a loss for words. Her gaze darted between Lysi and me. For a moment she stared at me with a knitted brow, but there was nothing I could say. Seconds of agonizing silence passed between us, and then, the best friend that she was, she lowered her crossbow.

"I'll explain later," I said. "I . . . Zarra needs help by the main mast."

Annith nodded once, the whites of her eyes popping against her tar-smudged skin. She turned and ran across the deck. I lost sight of her in seconds.

I bolted to Lysi and helped her untangle herself. My heart was in my throat. All I could think was that Lysi needed to get off the ship as fast as possible.

"I told you, you should've stayed away!" I said, pulling a steel dagger from my belt with trembling hands. "You could have been—"

"Stop it, Meela! It's not that simple!" She yelled to get past the thundering rain, which, if possible, had grown worse in the last few minutes. Her hair was a mess around her face, full of seaweed and pushed flat by the netting, and her eyes still flamed red.

I glanced over my shoulder, but the rain poured so thickly I could barely see beyond it. All my plans to massacre, all my intentions to forget any feelings about Lysi, washed away. Desperation all but drowned me as I severed the ropes.

The second Lysi was free, she grabbed me by the wrist and pulled me out of sight behind the helm. Her pupils drained to blue as we held each other's gaze. Beads of water rolled down her smooth face and neck.

"I don't know what to do," I whispered. The words were lost in the rain, but she knew what I'd said.

When I looked into Lysi's eyes, I knew exactly what I wanted: to turn the Bloodhound eastwards and go home. I wanted to stop the Massacres, and stop dreading the moment when one of my crew put a bolt through Lysi's chest. Was going home an option? Could I convince the rest of the crew?

Lysi touched a soft, icy hand to my cheek.

"We need to make peace," she said. "This isn't the right war."

I felt my forehead crease as I stared at her. "What do you mean?"

She opened her mouth, but hesitated. "I'll explain later, if you'll meet me. We can stop all of this."

I nodded, placing my hand over hers. Her icy skin was soothing against my own, which felt hot and sticky from the battle.

My pulse quickened as I looked into her eyes, and I felt a sudden, inexplicable urge to go with her into the ocean—to leave the land behind forever and become a mermaid.

I glanced down at her lips. The way to do it was there in front of me. I could get off this ship right now if I wanted to.

She leaned forwards almost imperceptibly. My breath hitched, but I remained still.

The noise of the rain dimmed around us, though I couldn't be sure if it was really the clouds easing off.

Then someone screamed, scattering my thoughts, and I realised how long I'd been sitting motionless.

I jumped up. "What are you doing?"

She recoiled. "What?"

"You're ..." I turned away from her, trying to compose myself by scanning the deck for oncoming attackers. "That mermaid hypnosis. I don't want you using it on me."

She was quiet for a long time, and eventually I had to look at her again. Was that what it felt like to have a mermaid lure you in? Some kind of strange, all-encompassing pull?

"Mee," she said, "you know it doesn't—"

"Just stop it, all right?"

Lysi stared at me for a moment, then leaned over and narrowed her eyes at something beyond my shoulder.

"I have to go," she said.

Before I could respond, she dove headfirst off the deck. I jumped forwards to watch her disappear, but by the time I looked over the edge I only saw thrashing waves and the rings from the falling raindrops.

I swiped a wet arm across my forehead, trying to process what just happened. Was Lysi hypnotizing me without knowing it—or was I being naïve, and whatever that was had been intentional?

Someone roared beside me and I flinched, drawing my crossbow before realising it wasn't directed at me. Dani landed hard on her back. I couldn't see her crossbow anywhere. She scurried backwards on her hands, but even as she did so, a mermaid with wild brunette hair climbed on top of her with a conch shell in her fist. She clubbed Dani repeatedly with it, which Dani tried to block with her meagre arms.

"Drop the net, Shaena!" Even through the hammering rain, her shriek was deafening.

Behind them, Shaena aimed a trembling crossbow at the mermaid's back. "It'll trap both of you! I need to kill her!"

"Shaena," yelled Dani, her voice hoarse, "drop the net now!"

"She'll kill you!"

"*Shaena!*"

But Shaena didn't drop the net. She shot a bolt through the mermaid's spine as she was about to deliver a blow to Dani's head. The mermaid lurched and collapsed on top of her prey.

Behind Shaena, two more mermaids rapidly approached, but she hadn't seen them. I fired without thinking about it, then dove to avoid a barnacled rock. Shaena cried out and shot the last one. She met my eyes, her mouth a gaping oval.

Dani grunted as she pushed the dead mermaid off herself. Her face was red and blotchy, her teeth bared, her entire body trembling. She looked deranged with fury. Shaena turned on her heel and stomped away, leaving Dani to help herself off the deck.

The scene around us quieted. The rain slowed and the screams subsided. I searched the deck, crossbow raised, but not a single demon met my eyes as we crossed the deck. Their ability to appear and disappear so rapidly was eerie, and although every one of us was shivering and covered in goose bumps, we waited a few more silent minutes before declaring them gone.

We filed down to the cabin quickly to change out of our sopping wet clothes—many of which were hardening into ice.

Feeling the cold seep into my bones, I peeled my shirt off before reaching the bottom step and threw it to the floor. I tossed clothing from my trunk until I found the warmest thing I owned—a thick woollen sweater, several sizes too large.

"So what was all that about?"

As my head popped out the top of my sweater, my eyes came to rest on Annith. Her eyebrows were raised and her arms crossed. She was half-dressed in thick sweatpants.

I glanced around meaningfully at the other girls, hoping Annith would get the idea that I didn't want to talk about it right now.

Footsteps thundered down the stairs, anyway, and I heard Dani shouting.

"You ruined the plan, Shaena!"

Shaena spun around, yanking a dry sweater over her head. "That mermaid was going to kill you!"

"I had her!"

"You did not have her—you didn't even have your crossbow! You were unarmed!"

Dani looked more enraged than ever. "How dare you speak ill of your captain," she said, spitting each word.

"I'm not speaking ill of you," yelled Shaena. "I'm just telling you that you would've died if I'd followed the plan."

Dani parted everyone in the cabin as she stomped to her bunk across from Shaena's. The rest of us watched in silence.

Dani threw her crossbow on her bed. "We would've killed all the rats at once if you'd carried out—"

"We killed them all, anyway!"

Dani pulled her ice-encrusted shirt over her head while Shaena stood facing her, fists and teeth clenched in fury.

"If you'd just have a sliver of flexibility—"

Dani rounded on her with a glare so intense that Shaena stepped back. "*Stop - arguing - with - me!*"

Without darkness or a jacket to cover her shoulders, I realised how emaciated Dani had become. Her hipbones and shoulder blades protruded. I could count the vertebrae in her spine. Her waist was thin as plywood when she turned sideways. Barely-healed scratches covered her arms, shoulders, and stomach, and new bruises were already forming.

"Dani," said Texas, taking a confident step towards her. "You need to calm down, all right?"

Dani snapped her rabid eyes onto Texas. "You don't get to tell me what to do!"

Her lips parted to reveal clenched teeth. A vein in her temple throbbed.

"None of you get to tell me what to do!"

She seized her crossbow.

I put my hands out. A few girls stepped back.

"I just think you need to—"

"I don't need to do anything!" she yelled, swinging the weapon so anyone near her jumped back several feet.

"Put the crossbow down," said Shaena firmly, stepping forwards again. The volume of her voice had lowered significantly. "This whole captain thing is clearly putting you in a wrong place."

Dani screeched, her voice filling the cabin. "Shut *up*, Shaena!"

"No! Dani, the crew is over. We want out."

"You can't get out! I say when you can get out!"

Shaena reached for Dani's crossbow but Dani jumped back, notching a bolt and pointing it to the room at large.

All of us screamed at Dani, yelling at her to calm down, to relax, to put down the crossbow. Holly and Nora jumped into the stairwell as if to flee the room.

"No, Dani," yelled Shaena. "You aren't captain anymore!"

"Shut up! Shut up, Shaena!"

She yelled the words with such vigour, her voice broke.

"Dani—"

"I'm your captain!"

Her eyes bulged, and without hesitating, without pausing to aim properly, she pulled the trigger. She shot an iron bolt straight into Shaena's chest.

CHAPTER NINETEEN

Anarchy

Not until the thick, crimson bubble of blood popped in Shaena's gaping mouth did Dani seem to realise what she'd done.

The only muscles in her body that moved were in her fingers. She dropped the crossbow. Her expression contorted into a mirror of Shaena's: mouth gaping, eyes bulging, a mixture of fear and pain.

Shaena made an odd whimpering sound. A trickle of blood rolled down her chin.

The rest of us had scrambled backwards, but then reality dawned and Texas dove to catch Shaena before she fell.

Dani's pupils were enormous. Her hands clenched and unclenched a few times as she stared at Shaena. Nobody approached her.

She turned abruptly and ran up the stairs two at a time.

Several long seconds passed before I realised what I'd just witnessed. I didn't even flinch when it'd happened. After everything I'd experienced in the last three weeks, a kill was just another kill.

Then a cold sweat broke over me, and I could do nothing but stand paralyzed as Annith fumbled for the first aid kit, and as she and Texas screamed at each other to remove the bolt and leave it be and hold her up and lay her flat and . . . Holly pushed past me with a damp rag to wipe the blood from Shaena's chin.

Texas and Annith abruptly stopped yelling, Annith's hands still working feverishly.

Shaena's breathing slowed. It sounded wet and gargly. She had no hope of surviving.

Texas, Annith, and Holly bent over her, murmuring, trying to get her to say something. They swam in my vision, the world melting around me.

I couldn't understand what the girls were saying. But then Texas leaned forwards and her body heaved with sobs as she hugged Shaena. The tangles of Shaena's chestnut hair spread across the floor like a fishing net washed ashore.

My breathing became panicked. This was one death too many. I couldn't watch another crewmate go—especially not at the hands of her best friend. I turned and climbed the stairs, swallowing the sobs that threatened to escape.

I hurried past the blurred figures of three other girls who hovered outside. They shouted something at me but I took no notice as I made for the helm. I crumpled behind it, trembling all over.

I stared out at the grey horizon, breathing deeply. A panicked whimper escaped my lips. Was the warrior mindset so deeply ingrained in Dani that she didn't even think before killing? Was her finger permanently over her trigger, ready to massacre anything in her path?

Some time later, Annith joined me. She placed my crossbow in front of me, which I'd forgotten below deck. Then she sat down and rested her head on my shoulder. She sniffled thickly.

"Did you see the way she killed her?" I said, unable to control the pitch of my voice. "It wasn't even different! It was no different than killing a mermaid!"

"I know," whispered Annith.

"It wasn't different, Annith," I said again. I leaned forwards to rest my head in my hands. My eyes burned.

Neither of us said anything for a long time. We sat with our heads resting on each other, leaning against the abandoned helm, and watched the thick raindrops fall until the sky began to darken. Behind the dense mess of clouds, the sun must have been crossing the horizon.

I spun the tarnished ring on Annith's skinny finger. It looked so old, so fragile.

"We need to go home," I said in barely a whisper. "We're done. The Massacre is over."

She made a small noise that I took to mean she agreed.

"We'll turn home as soon as we deal with Dani," I said, "but only after we figure out what to do about her. We don't know if she'll snap again, and who might be in the way if she does."

Annith looked down, hesitating for a long time before she met my eyes. "Then let's lock her up until we get home."

"Like in a brig?"

She nodded once.

"But we don't have a brig."

"We'll use the hull, where we keep the ammo," she said. "The bars are already in place. We'll move the ammo and put a bed in there or whatever . . . it won't be so bad."

I nodded slowly. The idea of keeping Dani separate from us was reassuring.

Annith set her jaw as she glared at the horizon. Clouds blocked our view of the Aleutian Islands, leaving us to feel, once again, the vast emptiness of the Pacific Ocean.

"We'll need to talk to the rest of your crew," I said. "They need to be okay with the plan, and they should probably be willing to help."

"After what they just witnessed, I doubt they'll be—"

"We need to know for sure. They can't interfere."

To my surprise, she stood. "Okay. I'll go talk to them."

"Right now?"

"Yes. I need to let a couple of them know it's going to be all right. Holly . . . and Nora. They'll be a total mess."

"Do you want me to come?"

"No. It's better if . . . if it comes from within her crew. I should do it."

We stared at each other. The word 'mutiny' came to mind. It made me uneasy. Annith nodded once, then turned away.

A childlike impulse overcame me to make her stay. The idea of being alone was unsettling. I needed the comfort of my friends inside the cabin, not the sight of the endless ocean to remind me of the infinity of death.

I shivered. The waves I stared at might as well have been fog rolling through a graveyard.

But I couldn't bring myself to go in the cabin. Where had they placed Shaena's body? Where was everyone else?

Between me and the infinite horizon, a blonde head popped up.

"I thought she'd never leave!"

I gasped and stumbled to my feet. "No! You can't be here."

Lysi's already-large eyes widened, and she looked past me in confusion.

"Get lost!" I said, holding out my crossbow like a shield.

"What's the matter with you?"

I hadn't had much time to think about Lysi since she disappeared from the tangled net earlier. But subconsciously, I must have been thinking about her, because I felt inexplicably leery of her too-gentle smile, and her too-sweet scent, and her too-pretty face.

"I've seen enough delusional friendships today," I said, still holding out my crossbow like I was trying to shield myself. "It's not going to happen to me. I don't need your manipulation."

"Manipulation! What are you talking about?"

I took a breath. I wasn't making sense. Lysi wasn't going to murder me. She cared about me. But did I care about her only because I was a victim of her mermaid allure?

"You tried to hypnotise me," I said. "I won't live in a delusion. If nothing I feel is even real . . ."

I rubbed a hand across my aching neck.

"Mee!" Her voice dropped, and her eyes pleaded with mine. "It doesn't work on females. Think about it. Has any other mermaid been able to hypnotise you?"

I opened my mouth to retort, but no words came. I felt the sensation that a block of ice had dropped into my stomach. She was right.

"Then why am I . . ." I didn't know what to say. Why was I *what?* What was I feeling?

I tried again. "When you come close to me, or when I look at you . . . I wonder if that's the feeling they warn you about. When a mermaid is about to lure you in."

I risked glancing up at her. Her expression was unreadable.

"What kind of feeling is it?" she said.

I squinted at my bare feet, which had grown numb with the cold. But a long time passed, and I found I couldn't put the feeling into words I wanted to say aloud.

"Mee, anything you're feeling is real. I promise."

I looked at her. First it was easy to be angry, to glare at her accusingly, like she'd set out to trick me. But the longer I held her gaze, the harder it became to pretend I hated her.

"I don't want you to be mad at me," she said, her voice thick with restrained tears, "because you're the only thing keeping me going, and I don't want to be out here fighting and killing people, and I don't want one of my family members to murder you. I can't lose you because of this. This whole war isn't right. It shouldn't be happening."

"No," I said, my voice softening. "It's going to be all right, Lysi. We're going home. We'll all be safe in a few days."

Two thick tears oozed from Lysi's eyes, and she covered her face.

I dropped my crossbow with a hollow clunk and stepped closer. "What's wrong?"

She had trouble getting the words out. "Adaro says you girls shouldn't have made it this far, and he wants you dead. Letting your ship return home isn't an option. He's so angry, I . . . I don't think his army has much left. He's pulling in more troops—he's even graduating the trainees early."

I froze, my hands on her shoulders. Such a range of emotions passed through me, I didn't know what to think. It was good for my people that we'd made it this far and killed so many mermaids. But Lysi—we'd murdered a horrific number of her friends and family members. Adaro was angry. What did that mean? Did we have cause to be even more afraid for our lives, or was Adaro's threat as empty as his presence in the battles?

"When will they get here?"

"A few days, maybe."

"We could be home by then. They might not get here in time."

She lifted one shoulder in a feeble shrug, looking unconvinced.

"I'm not afraid of him," I said. It was hard to be afraid of Adaro when I had never seen him. As far as I was concerned, he was a coward who never showed his face on the battlefront.

She stared at me, pulling her hands away from her face. The whites of her eyes and pale skin were distinct against the darkening sky. I sat down, still holding her shoulders.

"Look," I said. "I've been scared every moment of every day since we left. Really, I've been scared since the day I found out I was going into training. But that fear has become a part of me now. You and I have both made it this far, haven't we?"

She nodded once, still teary.

"This whole Massacre—everything—it's all out of hand. We're going to try and lock Dani up until we can get home. She . . . she killed someone."

"One of your own?" said Lysi, breathless.

I felt my face contort all over again. "I knew she was . . . but I didn't think . . . even she wouldn't . . ."

"Are you . . ." she said, then stalled. "Of course you aren't okay."

"No," I said. But somehow, I always felt better in Lysi's presence.

I became conscious of my hands resting on her shoulders and quickly dropped them, flushing. But Lysi reached out and slid a hand around the back of my neck. A shiver ran down my spine that might not have been related to the falling temperature.

"When I'm home, we can meet on the beach," I whispered, "like when we were kids."

The thought of home, of the beach, of a careless afternoon with Lysi, all seemed so distant. I might as well have been describing a fairy tale.

Lysi's gaze flickered to my lips. "Come with me."

I stared at her sapphire eyes. My brain stalled as I processed what she meant.

"Let's leave this behind," she said. "I can change you—we can live together. Maybe escape to a better place."

"I can't, Lysi. I can't abandon them all. I need to stay with my crew and keep them safe."

I thought of Annith, Blacktail, Fern, Holly, Sage . . . and Tanuu, and my parents back home. It pained me how much I missed them. Fleeing was never an option. I needed to fight for them.

Lysi bit her lip and rested her forehead against mine, agony in her eyes. I opened my mouth to speak but couldn't get the words out.

She put her other hand around the back of my neck, holding me in place. "What?"

I ran my hand up her waist, feeling her smooth, icy skin beneath my warm palm. "Lysi, I don't want to lose you again."

"So don't."

I wouldn't. I realised then how much I needed her. She kept me sane amid so much fear. I had to keep her in my life.

"Explain what you meant," I said, pulling back to study her expression. *"This isn't the right war."*

She hesitated, and when she spoke her voice sounded strange, like she was trying to stop it from shaking. "I mean we shouldn't be fighting each other. Humans and merpeople shouldn't be enemies."

"Right," I said. But she already knew I agreed on that front.

"The thing is, coexisting was never a problem before. Mermaids have always lived in the Atlantic, and we always kept to ourselves, except for the odd time when a ship came too close to a city."

"So you're saying the problem only started when you migrated to the Pacific."

She nodded. "Haven't you wondered why?"

"You explained it to me," I said. "It's because Adaro wants control of . . ."

Her eyes widened, like she wanted me to understand something she couldn't say aloud.

"Adaro," I said. "He's the only reason for the attacks."

Her eyebrows pulled down at the corners, but she remained silent. I thought for a moment, listening to the creaking ship and the swishing waves.

"The Atlantic Queen never wanted control of the seas the way Adaro does," I said. "That's why humans and mermaids coexisted when you all lived in the Atlantic. Do other mermaids even want to attack humans?"

"Not many."

"But they have to."

She nodded once. Of course it made sense. Why would Lysi be here if she didn't have to be? She wasn't interested in killing.

"So Adaro is forming an army," I said. "When you say we shouldn't be fighting each other, you mean we should be trying to stop—What's wrong?"

She combed her trembling fingers through her hair. "Nothing. It's just that he wouldn't . . . I mean, he . . ."

I stared at her. "What would happen if you resisted him?"

Her face paled, and almost inaudibly, she said, "You're right. We should be fighting Adaro, not each other. And I would be dead if someone heard me say that."

Everything made sense. Adaro was a tyrant. He forced mermaids to attack humans, to fight his battles, so he could have control of the seas.

"He won't let us leave," whispered Lysi. "Anyone who tries to return to the Atlantic is killed."

My stomach churned. This war—the one between humans and mermaids—would get us nowhere.

"He'll keep going until humans are out of the seas forever," she said.

"And humans won't rest until we gain the seas back."

"So the war will keep going until . . ."

I gazed across the black water, a chill penetrating my bones. "Until one species annihilates the other."

Adaro would never stop attacking my people until we surrendered to his demands—but the Massacres would keep happening, because my people needed the sea. And what about the other nations? We weren't the only ones dependent on the ocean.

The Massacre wasn't the right answer. It was a bloody, dirty strip of cotton over a gaping laceration.

Until humans submitted to Adaro and retreated to the land, Adaro would keep sending mermaids to fight. Mermaids just like Lysi, innocent ones who had no desire to kill, who just wanted to live in peace as they'd done when they lived in the Atlantic.

As far as I was concerned, we had one option: we had to overthrow Adaro.

"We need to stop the problem at its root," I said, breathless.

"We can do it, the two of us."

"This would end the Massacres."

We stared at each other. I could tell Lysi's mind was spinning as fast as mine. This was the answer.

"First you need to survive your own Massacre, Mee. Don't let his army catch you." She took my hand, squeezing it hard. "Sail home as fast as you can."

Zarra, Blacktail, Fern, and I waited in the cabin in a thick silence. What if Annith hadn't been able to convince the rest of them? What if she'd been persecuted for even suggesting a mutiny? I wondered if I should've insisted on going with her. I'd hardly thought about it before I let her go alone to suggest to Dani's battle-trained followers that they betray her.

The minutes ticked by, and finally the door creaked open at the top of the stairs. I snapped my head up to see Annith supporting Sage as she limped down the steps. A thick, bloodstained bandage covered Sage's thigh. Behind them came Holly, Blondie, and Nora.

Only one person was missing.

"Texas is with Dani," said Annith. "We haven't talked to her yet."

I looked at each of the girls in turn. "And the rest of you?"

"We're in," said Holly.

"For Shaena," said Blondie.

Zarra, Blacktail, Fern, and I let out a collective sigh of relief.

"I nominate one of you to convince Texas," said Fern.

Zarra grimaced, twisting the scar on her face. "We'll work on her later."

She, Fern, and Blacktail stood to go stand guard, taking the place of the girls who'd just come down.

"So what's the plan?" said Holly, dropping onto the bunk beside me. "How are we going to get her into the brig?"

"That's what we need to figure out," I said. I glanced at Annith, who was wringing her hands.

"I just have one concern," said Nora, her face stony.

"All right," said Annith with a tone of forced liveliness.

"What's going to happen in the battles once Dani is locked in the brig? She's our best fighter."

A few seconds of silence passed. There was no denying that Dani was the best warrior of all of us. It pained me to admit it.

"That's the choice we have to make," I said. "Do we want to lose Dani to the brig and possibly have a harder time in battles? Or keep Dani with us and . . ."

"Never sleep again," said Holly.

Annith grimaced.

"I'd rather keep Dani safely away from us," I said. "Just because she's not there in battle doesn't mean we'll lose. We're all trained for this. We're all warriors."

"Definitely," said Annith. "I think we're better off with Dani in the brig."

Besides, I thought, *Dani won't approve of us turning for home—and we need to sail home as fast as we can if we want to avoid Adaro's entire army.*

Nora nodded. "You're right. This needs to happen."

"Well, it won't be easy to catch her off-guard," said Sage. "She's too suspicious already."

"And by suspicious, you mean totally insane," said Blondie. "I swear, she never properly goes to sleep. Sneaking up on her would be like sneaking up on a mountain lion."

"A paranoid one that hasn't slept in a week," said Holly. "And has rabies."

"We could ambush her," said Nora.

"Oh, that sounds great," said Blondie, rolling her eyes. "Ambush the nutcase who's got a loaded weapon on her at all times."

"She has to put down her crossbow at some point, doesn't she? We'll ambush her then."

"What, when she's on the toilet?"

"We could trick her into putting it down," said Sage.

Nora shook her head vigorously. "Her reflexes are too fast. I bet she could pick up her crossbow again quicker than any of us can think."

"What if we tranquilised her?" said Sage.

"With what?" said Blondie. "All we've got are those seasickness herbs."

"We'd have to slip a ton of it in her food to properly tranq her," said Nora.

"We could do it, I bet," said Holly.

Blondie put her hand up, looking exasperated. "Hello? Didn't we just establish she's ridiculously suspicious? Do you really think she'd accept some random plate of food that has a bunch of weird stuff mashed into it?"

"She wouldn't notice," said Sage.

"Girls," said Annith loudly. She looked as stunned as I felt at their keenness.

They fell silent.

"You know the kohl we've been putting around our eyes?" she said. "Do you realise what it's made of?"

We all stared at her.

"They get the colour from grinding up Ravendust leaves. Ingesting just a little bit will knock you out for like an hour."

Everyone's jaw fell open at once.

"What else is in it?" said Holly, breathless. "Anything poisonous?"

"Nothing serious. Dani's been using it to . . . to keep Linoya settled since she hurt her spine."

I stood, fists clenched. We collectively looked over at Linoya's bed, where she lay, soundless.

Keep Linoya settled. The idea sounded tender, thoughtful, like Dani only wanted to ease Linoya's pain. Fury curdled in my stomach—but I didn't want to blame Annith for Dani's crimes.

"Who else knows this stuff is a sedative?" I said.

Annith didn't meet my eyes. "Just Dani," she whispered.

"Why didn't you tell us before?" said Nora.

"I . . . She didn't want me to."

Annith looked close to tears.

We fell quiet. The ship creaked softly around us.

"Is that what we'll do, then?" I looked around at each of the girls. Nobody protested.

"How do we feed it to her?" whispered Holly, glancing at the staircase. "We've never brought the meals out on plates—it's always been *help yourself*. She'll get suspicious."

"We'll rub it into the fish," I said, pacing the room. "Just . . . don't eat it. Eat everything else first."

Nora nodded. "I like that. It'll work."

"What do we do about Texas?" I said.

"I'll talk to her," said Blondie, straightening up. "She'll listen to me."

"It's settled then," said Sage, rising from the bunk. She looked like she was preparing to go fight.

The others rose, too.

"Tomorrow at dinner, we take down Dani," I said. "And then we're going home."

CHAPTER TWENTY

Blackened Feast

The following night, Blacktail and I were in charge of making dinner. A vial of kohl waited in my tool belt, heavy as a boulder.

Blacktail turned off the fryer where a slab of whitefish lay greasy and scorched. It smelled delectable, even if mixed with char and smoke.

"I had to sear it," she said. "The black powder would stand out."

I popped the lid off the vial. "Good call."

Her stomach growled as I smeared the powder into the fish.

"Shame it has to go to waste," she whispered. "It still looks delicious."

"Well, here," I said, pointing to the end of the tail. "I haven't touched that part yet. Eat it. The tail's the best anyway."

She hesitated, then brought the spatula down on it and sliced off a piece as big as she dared. "Want some?"

I opened my mouth—my hands were still busy—and she popped a bit in.

I rolled the fish over my tongue, savouring it. "Gub ibea," I said, trying to cool it off by sucking in air through my teeth. "Ib's yummy eben burnt."

She chuckled and took some for herself.

By the time we finished sharing the measly bit of tail, I'd rubbed the entire vial of kohl into both sides of the fish. The powder blended nicely with the charred surface.

"Ready?" I said, taking a breath.

Blacktail picked up the rice and sliced apples. A few seconds passed when we just stared at each other. She resembled a deer more than ever, eyes wide and alert, face solemn, frame thin and upright. I nodded firmly, and together we plastered smiles on our faces and strode from the galley.

Dani, Texas, Holly, and Annith waited at the table. The other girls were on duty and would take their turn eating after we finished. After Dani was safely locked in the brig. A couple of those girls would be removing the ammo from our makeshift brig at that very moment. Another would be turning the Bloodhound eastwards, starting our journey home.

"The fish is a little overdone," said Blacktail cheerily. "But charred meat is a delicacy on the mainland, right?"

Annith and Texas forced a laugh. Holly looked paralyzed, like a rabbit about to be eaten. Dani glared at the blackened fish as we placed the dishes in the centre of the table, but said nothing.

The ship rocked steadily, creaking against the rolling waves as we passed the food around. I thought I could feel the ship turning—or maybe I was imagining it.

The candles flickered in the dim hull, the clouds outside offering little natural light through the tiny windows. Nobody said a word. We took our portions with such forced casualness, my heart thumped with fear that Dani would pick up on it.

As we began to eat, I watched Dani from under my lashes. She ate all her rice first, one slow bite at a time. Had she always taken this long chewing?

I slowed my own pace, afraid I'd be done everything else and then she'd wonder why I hadn't touched my fish. She placed her fork down gently, picked up her cup, and took a long drink of water.

Under the pretence of grabbing more rice, I glanced up at the other girls. They looked on edge, also eating with unnatural slowness. Holly's face was clammy, her eyes huge, like she was about to have a breakdown.

Still, we were dead silent. The only sound was the ship creaking around us. I wanted to say something casual—start a conversation—but not a single topic came to mind.

Dani put down her cup and made a pointed satisfied sound. Then, piece-by-piece, she started on her apple slices.

My rice and fish were cold. My apple slices were brown. While Dani focused on her plate, I mashed up my fish to try and make it look like I'd eaten some.

Dani brought her last bite of apple to her lips, then froze. The ship groaned as we crested a wave. She put down the apple and reached beside her, and I nearly jumped to my feet before realising she was only taking out her compass.

She stared at the needle for several long seconds, her brow pulled down.

"Aren't you going to try the fish, Dani?" said Texas, forcing lightness in her voice.

Dani snapped her head up and fixed her narrow eyes on Texas' plate, which had some of everything left. It was unusual for any of us to leave food on our plates. And here all of us had taken our time as though we were fine diners in a French restaurant.

The rice, apples, and morsel of charred fish in my stomach suddenly felt unsettled.

"Why haven't you eaten your fish?" said Dani with the same tone of forced lightness.

"I have," said Texas, pointing to a chunk out of the side that I was sure she'd buried under her rice.

Dani's eyes widened.

"You haven't!" She looked frantically around, then jumped up. "None of you have! You guys put something in the fish!"

"No!" said Holly. "We didn't!"

She jumped up too, but I wasn't sure what she intended to do. Dani was breathing fast, looking outraged.

Holly stared into Dani's bloodshot eyes for only a second before she said, "Look, I'll show you," and scooped a forkful of cold fish from her plate and put it in her mouth. I had to force myself not to react.

She chewed slowly, evidently hoping Dani would believe her before it came time to swallow. There was a moment where she tried to store the food in her cheek, but she seemed to realise that was too obvious.

At long last, she swallowed. The entire table seemed to draw breath.

"See?" she said quickly. "It's fine. Now you can have some."

I glanced at Dani, naïvely hoping, for Holly's sake, she'd believe Holly in the next ten seconds. But already

Holly's eyelids drooped. She seized the edge of the table and swayed dangerously.

"I . . . I'm just . . . tired . . ."

I jumped up without thinking as Holly's eyes rolled back. Her hands slipped from the table. Blacktail lunged for her before she fell.

Dani screamed.

"You *back-stabbing*—you *two-faced*—you—you think as your captain, I wouldn't be suspicious?" She leapt back from the table, pointing at us. "You think you're the first crew in the world to attempt mutiny? You've all been jealous since I was elected. I was right not to trust any of you!"

It was barely noticeable, but Dani's hand moved a fraction towards her crossbow, which she'd rested against the bench. And without thinking about it, without considering whether she intended to use it, I flung myself at her.

She screamed as we toppled to the floor. Adrenaline burst through me, every cell in my body desperate to pin her down. I could not let her go. I saw and felt only flailing arms and legs, and then she attacked my face with her ragged fingernails, forcing my eyes closed.

The girls around me must have been too shocked to do anything, because I found myself in solitary battle with Dani's teeth and claws. She kicked and thrashed beneath me, all the while shrieking and giving everything she had to scratching and biting any part of my skin she could reach.

I pinned both her wrists and opened my eyes, but then she kicked upwards and twisted, throwing me sideways. I automatically let go of her wrists to brace myself with my hands, but my legs stayed in a vice around her. Instinctive tactics came back to me from when I was a kid, and I locked my feet together at her stomach to stop her from scrambling away.

Annith appeared beside me. I wrapped a fist around Dani's hair and yanked her back down so I could sit on her. Annith had to use both hands to pull one of Dani's away from my face. She slammed it into the floor and held it there. Blacktail seized the other arm.

I gasped for air, winded from the struggle. No longer expending all my effort keeping my eyes from being clawed out, I spared a breath to screech for more help.

"Texas!"

She hesitated only for a second before jumping behind me to sit on Dani's thighs. I rolled off and caught one of Dani's thrashing legs, wrapping both my arms around her calf to keep her from knocking me in the chin.

"Grab the other leg," I said, panting. Texas did so, copying the way I held it.

"We - have to - do it now," I said, fighting to keep Dani's knee away from my nose.

Conscious or not, we had to get her in the brig. I couldn't imagine life with Dani still loose aboard the Bloodhound when the rest of the crew had attempted to drug her. What would her revenge be? Who would be her next target?

Together, the four of us lifted the roaring, flailing Dani and started up the stairs.

Her teeth were bared, eyes blazing through the sweaty web of hair across her face. She looked completely deranged.

"You don't know what you're doing! You need me!" she shrieked, voice breaking.

She screamed and kicked against us with such ferocity, even with one of us on each of her limbs we had trouble carrying her. Several times, one of us tripped on the stairs and fell to our knees—but we all knew that no matter what, we couldn't let go.

"You'll die without me! Put me down!"

Dani's breathing was so furious, so enraged, I couldn't tell anymore if she was panting or sobbing. She didn't stop screaming the entire way across the deck—where the other girls watched in mute horror as Dani roared for them to help her—and all the way down the steps into the hull.

She must have been hurting herself as much as the rest of us. My face stung mercilessly and moist cuts oozed across it, and every few seconds her knee cracked into my face or ribs.

Her thrashing became so violent it must have taken us a full minute to get her through the narrow door of the brig, by which time we were all struggling for breath and glistening with sweat.

"We - won't be able to - put her down - and - get out of here," said Annith, fighting to keep Dani from sliding through her grip.

"What do - we do?" said Blacktail.

I gaped at the space around us. Annith was right. In the second I spent hesitating, Dani thrashed wildly, and all four of us gasped as she slipped through our arms and crashed to the floor.

She thrashed again and her foot pounded against my stomach. I fell back. Blacktail was the only one who still had a hold of her. She grabbed Dani's shoulders and kept her from rolling over as I threw myself on top of her. But then Dani's fist seized my ponytail. Fleetingly, I saw her grab onto

Blacktail's hair too before my head was wrenched to the floor. Spots erupted in my vision as my skull hit the floorboards. Blacktail moaned beside me.

A second later, Dani screamed in pain as Annith's nails dug into her bony wrists, prying her grip away from our hair.

Thumping sounded behind us and Nora leapt down the stairs, a vial of kohl clenched in her fist. "Give her this!"

"How?" I said, the word coming out as a grunt as I wrapped my arms around Dani's waist. My head felt like it'd been pushed into a blender, my vision blurry with tears.

Nora jumped in the middle of our scrap. She unceremoniously grabbed Dani by the jaw and squeezed until it forced her teeth open. The scream Dani let loose must have carried all the way to the Aleutian Islands.

Nora dumped the entire contents of the vial on Dani's face.

Texas swore. "You'll kill her, you idiot!"

"She isn't going to swallow all of it!" Nora yelled back.

Sure enough, all of it ended up on the floor or in a wad of spit that Dani gracelessly ejected from her mouth.

Only a pinch was needed, though. We held on for several agonizing seconds while the Ravendust and Dani's adrenaline seemed to be contending. Her struggles weakened. Her screams faded to panicked sobs.

I blinked a few times to soak up the tears that'd sprung when my head hit the floor.

Dani shuddered. Her eyelids flickered. And with one last raspy cough, she passed out.

None of us moved. For several seconds, we stared at her immobile body.

With a trembling hand, Annith brushed the sweaty nest of hair from Dani's eyes and opened one of the lids to check if she'd really lost consciousness.

"Looks real," she said after a moment.

We slowly relaxed our hold, keeping our eyes on Dani's unconscious face. Even comatose, she made me uneasy. Her features were skeletal, like she'd been wasting away, and her skin—once perfect, smooth, and youthful— was chapped and scratched everywhere.

"Still," I said, wiping an arm across my sweaty forehead, "don't turn your back on her as we're leaving."

Blacktail pointed to the tool belt around Dani's hips. "The daggers should go."

I winced. "Right."

We removed the tool belt—iron dagger still morbidly stained with the blood of an infant mermaid—and ran our hands along her coat and pants to check for more weapons. We found a knife in the inside pocket of her coat, an expensive one made in Switzerland that she'd clearly brought from home. Her father had probably given it to her.

"Keep it somewhere safe for her," said Texas, watching Dani with an expression of pity.

I narrowed my eyes, irritated at Texas' stupidity. "She murdered—"

"I know!" She shot me her nastiest glare before bending down to pick up Dani's limp body. She placed her on the bed we'd set up in the corner and laid the blanket across her. "She'll be cold. Dani's still a human being."

I found it difficult to accept the words "Dani" and "human being" in the same sentence, but I kept my mouth shut.

"Can we go, then?" I said.

Texas nodded once. We backed out of the brig, locking it behind us with its thin iron key.

We'd been victorious, but somehow we couldn't bring ourselves to smile at each other. I stared at the unconscious Dani, lying crumpled on the bed. It was hard to believe what that frail, tiny figure was capable of.

"She'll be sore when she wakes up," said Texas. "That bed's so hard."

"We'll all be sore," said Blacktail.

As far as I was concerned, Dani could get up and make herself comfortable when she woke up. I wasn't about to go in there and fluff her pillows.

"She'll be fine for a few hours," said Annith.

We stared at the unconscious form for a moment longer. For anyone else on the planet, I might have felt pity. But for Dani, I only felt relief that she was locked up on the other side of the bars.

We all turned away at the same time, like the sight became too unsettling for us to contemplate any longer.

"All right," said Texas. "Now that's done with . . ."

I took a single step towards the stairs before she pushed a hand into my chest and stopped me.

I looked down at her hand, raising my eyebrows.

"It's time to address the other danger to this crew," she said, her expression darkening.

I stepped back, too shocked to say anything.

"You've been in a secret alliance, Meela, have you not?"

"I . . . what?" I said, and though I sounded defiant, my insides flipped over.

"Drop the innocent act. You're plotting with the enemy and we all know it."

I turned my gaze to Annith, whose eyes had widened and sprung with tears. She was the only one who knew anything existed between Lysi and me. She'd been the only one there when I stopped her from shooting Lysi in that fishing net.

"Prove it," I said, not taking my eyes off Annith.

Texas said nothing. I turned my gaze to her and said in a low voice, "You're going on nothing but a morsel of gossip, no doubt planted by a girl who's eager to prove some kind of pathetic loyalty."

She stepped closer, reminding me of her tremendous height.

"If you want to talk about pathetic loyalty," she said, her hand still on my chest, "we can bring it up next time you visit with the sea rats."

"You've got nothing on me," I said. My voice was steady and confident. "So until you gain a better sense of who is and is not a traitor, I suggest you avoid pinning false accusations on your crewmates."

She opened her mouth to argue, but I cut her off. "Dani's crew is officially dispersed, Texas. So yes—we *are* crewmates."

I wanted to leave, but somehow that would feel like fleeing—like I was being weak, and admitting Texas was right. So I stayed put.

"If her loyalty wasn't with us," said Blacktail, "we'd know it. We're nearly home and Meela's still fighting, isn't she?"

Texas looked at Blacktail as though she'd never noticed her before.

"We'll find out soon enough, won't we?" said Nora, crossing her arms.

Texas spun on her heel and marched up the stairs. With a final warning glare at me, Nora turned and followed.

"Thanks, Blacktail," I said in a low voice, but I didn't pause before pushing by Annith to climb the stairs.

Annith just watched me pass. Her silence was the worst part. She would've defended me if she wasn't also suspicious—or if she hadn't been the one to rat me out. What did she hope to gain, anyway? Was approval from the crew more important than our friendship?

"What happened, Meela?" said Fern as I stalked past. She looked clammy and distraught, and I imagined it must have been alarming to see the lot of us drag a screeching Dani past them minutes ago.

"She's out cold," I said, not stopping on my way to the cabin. "So's Holly. Someone should go check on her."

I had a feeling she was also asking why Texas and Nora had just stomped by angrily, but I didn't want to explain. The two of them stood at the helm, their eyes following me across the deck.

I ran down the stairs, not wanting to talk to or see anyone. When I reached the bottom, I grabbed my hair in my fists and breathed deeply. The quiet, empty room did little to ease my racing pulse.

The girls would never understand if I tried to tell them Lysi could be trusted. Maybe that was why I'd found it so easy to defend myself; I could truthfully say I was not plotting with the enemy, because Lysi was not our enemy. More than ever, I understood who our real enemy was.

But the girls would never believe that. I had to be careful. I didn't know what they'd do if they saw me with Lysi—shoot her? Capture and torture her? I didn't want to find out.

My face still burned from Dani's nails, and I crossed to our grimy bathroom mirror to examine my wounds. Long cuts stretched from my forehead to my throat. I bent over the sink, palming water over my face to clear the blood.

Sail home as fast as you can, I thought, remembering Lysi's words. Well, we were on our way. I hoped the Bloodhound was fast enough.

Beneath Annith's bed, the first aid kit was alarmingly bare. It was as big as a drink cooler and stocked full when we started, and since then we'd used up almost everything inside. What were we supposed to dress wounds with? I couldn't remember—probably because I'd spent most of that class trying to distract myself from puking. I dug around for something that might be labelled 'for cuts'.

"I brought your crossbow," said a voice from behind me.

I tensed, Annith's voice sending boiling anger through my chest.

"Do you want help?" she said.

"No," I said through gritted teeth.

"Is it for your face?"

"I said I don't need help!"

My fuse had reached its end with her, and I couldn't even reason with myself to keep my anger down. She'd betrayed our friendship and turned the entire crew on me. How could she even look at me after that?

"What's your problem?" she said.

I rounded on her, fists clenched. I glanced at the stairwell to make sure no one was listening, and it took all my effort to keep my voice at a whisper. "You told them, Annith! I trusted you!"

She stared at me like I'd sprouted an extra head. "I didn't say anything!"

"Where did they get the idea, then? What made them think I was about to betray everyone?"

"Maybe they noticed you disappearing all the time! The ship's not that big. It's easy to spy on people."

"You're telling me nobody tipped them off? Nobody happened to mention I stopped you from killing—"

"You won't explain to me what happened, Meela! All I know is you didn't want me to kill one of the demons or whatever. I don't know why, or what it means, or what you've been doing!"

"So you automatically assume I must be plotting something?"

"What are we supposed to think when one of our crew suddenly shows compassion for the thing we were sent here to kill?"

"Annith, even if I tried to explain, no one would understand—"

I broke off, listening to something happening above us. Annith looked up, too. There was an abnormal amount of thumping on the deck. Then came a hailstorm of smashing sounds from outside the hull. Someone screamed.

The mermaids were back. And only half of our crew was left to fight.

CHAPTER TWENTY-ONE

Into the Deep

Annith cursed and snatched up her crossbow. We started up the stairs two at a time, but then I stopped, the balls of my feet balancing on the edges of two steps.

"You keep going," I said, and leapt back down.

"What—"

"Go!"

She hesitated for a moment longer before I heard the door crash open. The sounds of battle flooded down the stairwell, and I heard the hiss of a bolt leaving her crossbow. The door slammed.

I dashed to the end of the hull, where Linoya lay in her bed.

She was awake, sitting up. The whites of her eyes glinted in the dim light. I dropped my crossbow onto her lap. "You might need this."

Not that I intended to freak her out, but we were direly short on warriors and might not be able to keep demons from getting below deck.

"Don't go out there unarmed!" she said, thrusting it back at me.

I pulled my iron dagger from my tool belt. "I have this. I'll sprint across to grab a new crossbow. It'll be fine."

Before she could say anything more, I threw myself up the stairs and burst through the door. Annith was still near the entrance. She fired and took out a mermaid that had Sage pinned to the deck. My eyes locked onto another mermaid just beyond that. The body she hunched over was bloodied and limp.

"No," I said, but before I could identify the victim, something crashed into me, throwing me backwards into the cabin.

My shoulders and head hit the stairs and my feet came up. I lost all sense of direction, knowing only pain as I toppled down the steps, crashing into the walls on either side. After what felt like an eternity, I lay sprawled on the floor, empty-handed, gasping and coughing violently as I tried to suck air back into my lungs.

Dizzy, I raised myself on my hands as something wet dripped into my eyes. My head was bleeding.

Something thumped down the steps after me.

Still coughing, too faint to stand, I scurried backwards on my hands, trying to put distance between myself and the stairs. My dagger was nowhere to be seen.

The mermaid hit the bottom. Two more followed close behind.

Above our heads, the stampede still ran, punctuated by screams and yelps of pain. The hailstorm crashed around me; it sounded like the mermaids were breaking holes in the hull.

They can't be, I thought, my head whirling. *The hull is flecked with iron. It would be suicide.*

The first mermaid dragged herself towards me, glistening eyes fixed to my throat and a slimy harpoon in her teeth. Her shoulders popped as she moved.

Iron. I needed iron. My back collided with the wall, and the mermaid reached up to take her weapon in a web-fingered fist.

I was about to scream when a bolt sliced through her neck from the side and sent her toppling. Her eyes drained in an instant, and I stared at the empty brown irises of an olive-skinned girl.

I turned to see Linoya sitting up with my crossbow braced on her shoulder. But her move was fatal.

In one motion, the other two mermaids turned and hurled their spears at her. A sickening noise met my ears as the spears made contact. Linoya let out an agonised, gargling scream, and the crossbow clattered to the floor. The mermaids turned back to face me.

I pulled myself to my feet, preparing to lunge for the fallen crossbow. One of the demons snatched the harpoon from her fallen comrade and swiped it at me. I leapt to avoid it, but she swung it again and the shaft caught my shins. I cried out at the impact. My feet swung out from under me and I landed hard on my shoulder. The harpoon shattered into a dozen pieces.

I rolled onto my hands and knees and scrambled for the crossbow. Not a sound came from Linoya's bed. I moaned, knowing I could do nothing to help her.

One of the mermaids grabbed me by the ankle and pulled me backwards before I could grab the weapon. The disturbing coolness of her hand seeped through my pant leg.

I swung a fist around to attack her, but my arms were like jelly against her inhuman strength. She watched me, her lips curling.

If I could just get a hold of a weapon ... anything made of iron. I tried to locate the dead mermaid who still had a bolt in her neck. The other mermaid pulled herself over to the spears they'd cast at Linoya.

As the demon dragged me back, my eyes landed on a dark shape on the floor next to us. With a gasp, I flung a hand over the iron dagger and twisted around.

The blade sliced across the mermaid's chest and she let out a deafening scream. I jumped clumsily to my feet, brandishing the dagger. Blood poured from the gash but I barely spared a glance as I leapt for the staircase.

I almost crawled up the steps in my haste, catching myself with my hands. A spear whizzed past my head and struck the stairwell, and a second later the remaining mermaid grabbed my leg before I could make it out of the cabin. I fell forwards, smashing my chin into the deck.

My attempt to swing the dagger at her was easily blocked, now that she knew I had it. She grabbed onto my wrist and smashed my arm down. The dagger clattered out of my fingers. I thrashed and screamed with everything I had, trying to kick and punch and bite her, but she seized me by the ankle and dragged me across the deck.

Realising where we were headed, I clawed at the wood, screaming, still kicking ferociously.

The unyielding certainty in the mermaid's stone grip, in the way she dragged me like a doll towards the icy black ocean, made me realise I'd never get out of this on my own. I took a deep breath—nails digging into the wooden planks, legs thrashing against the mermaid's grip—and shrieked for help. My heartbeat was so quick and every part of me so frantic, I swore I heard the sound echo off the empty water.

"Help! Please, someone!"

Faster the mermaid dragged me, and soon I was at the edge of the deck, the icy depths behind us. I screamed again.

The deck was a blur of moving feet and thrashing tails. Loose weapons rolled and slid across the planks. Bright red blood splattered the wood in places. But there were fewer mermaids in combat than usual, because at least two dozen scaled the masts, slashing holes in our sails. Cracks still echoed from outside the hull. They were breaking the wood, despite the chunks of iron that burst out and seared them raw with each gash.

This was a suicide attack. Adaro must have ordered them to destroy our ship no matter what the cost. Were they trying to sink us, or slow us down to give the rest of his troops time to get here?

My assailant stopped abruptly, her eyes focused on something to her right. A loose dagger lay there, glistening in the sunlight. Pointed, double-edged. For stabbing, but not for mermaids.

She glanced back at me, something forming behind her bared teeth and narrowed eyes.

"No!" I kicked harder than ever, screaming for help.

The mermaid seized the dagger in her webbed fist, and no matter how much I thrashed, I couldn't break loose. Holding me in place with one hand, she drew the other back, aligning the blade with my stomach. I gave one more, desperate twist as the dagger came down full-force. The blade missed my stomach—and drove deep into my thigh.

I could count each millisecond as I watched the blade disappear into my skin, as I watched it open a gash all the way down like a gutted fish. At first I felt nothing. Then the pain exploded in my thigh as though she'd buried a grenade beneath the skin. My brain disconnected from my body; I could only hear myself scream, and watch the blood cascade from my leg.

Black splotches erupted in my vision. I thought I might throw up, only my stomach was too tight to heave.

The mermaid raised her arm, aiming again for her original target. I told myself to twist away, to protect my soft stomach, but my muscles were paralyzed.

Then she flinched, as though a bolt had nearly hit her. Whatever it was, it reminded her to keep moving. She turned and hauled me between the railings, keeping a hold on the dagger.

My vision was still spotted, my brain unable to think, but my body was desperate for survival. I found myself clinging to the railing in a last attempt at keeping myself aboard the Bloodhound.

I cried out again for help, but the sound came as a sob, barely audible, stifled by the pain of the gaping hole in my leg.

Nobody came to my rescue. I heard the scuffling sounds of fighting, but my vision was too blotchy to make out whether the blood-covered bodies were people or mermaids. Maybe, at last, we were so outnumbered we could no longer put up a fight against this wasps' nest of sea demons.

Something told me I was going to die at the hands of this mermaid. I, a warrior of Eriana Kwai, had always been destined to meet the end of my life out here. Death might even be welcome—it would ease the blinding pain shooting through every nerve in my body, and the exhaustion begging me to close my eyes and never wake up.

What would this mermaid do after pulling me into the water? Would she wait until I died to start feasting on my body, or would she tear into my flesh while I was still alive?

My strength was laughable next to hers. My attempts to stop her must have felt like a bump in the deck. But I still gripped the railing with white knuckles until she wrenched my fingers away, leaving me clawing at the edge of the deck.

We couldn't go down now. Not when we were so close to home. Not when we'd put a bigger dent than ever in Adaro's army. Not when, finally, I understood what we needed to do to gain back our freedom.

Only I understood too late. I'd always been right to trust Lysi. Trusting her—working with her to take down Adaro—might have been the only way my people could find peace.

The cloudy sky blurred, and I only saw the dark outline of the Bloodhound's railing against it—and my wet hand slipping away.

"Meela!" Annith's panicked voice cut through the wind tunnel that'd closed around my ears.

Two hands closed around my wrists. Annith was screaming. Her blood-splattered face appeared through the spots in my vision. The collar of her jacket was mangled. Her hands were void of weapons.

Her fingers locked tight around mine, and I clutched their humanly warmth.

"Hold onto me, Meela!"

I closed my fingers with new determination, focusing on Annith's hazel eyes with numb shock. The spots in my vision seemed to recede, like my body was giving me every remaining bit of strength, knowing that to pass out would be the end.

"Annith ..." I tried to speak, but choked on the words.

"I've got you. Don't let go. Help, someone!"

She turned her head to scream at the deck behind her. If someone could just lean over with a crossbow and shoot the mermaid . . .

"Annith," I said. "I'm not ready."

We were both sliding now; Annith's arms hung over the edge, one on either side of a railing. It would have been a good anchor, if only this mermaid wasn't capable of putting a dent in the railing with her fist if she wanted to.

I knew she had to let go. She wouldn't be able to hold on, or she'd get dragged in with me.

The demon beneath me made a funny cackling sound, like she found our struggle entertaining.

Our slippery hands were prying apart. I heard Annith's panicked breathing as we stared desperately at each other, and it felt unmistakably like we were sharing a silent goodbye.

Something hard pressed into my hand, digging through the skin and muscle, pushing at the bone.

Annith's ring. The ring promising her a lifetime of happiness when she got home.

Comprehension dawned on me like a bucket of seawater. I understood why Kade had let go.

I couldn't drag Annith in the water with me. She'd tried to save me, but the effort was futile—and this was my death, not hers. My time might have come, but Annith still had a future to live out. I had to let go.

The muscles in my fingers relaxed.

Annith screamed, and her fingers closed tighter around mine. "No!"

But we were falling, and Annith needed to stay alive. I opened my hands, and I let her go, ready to be engulfed by the sea.

Something rammed hard into Annith. It pulled her backwards onto the deck with such speed, I barely had time to process her disappearance. I slipped into the frigid water, but the burning cold only lasted a moment, because something dove over my head and threw me upwards, and the stony fingers no longer clasped my legs.

I tumbled over the railing and onto the deck, retching as the gaping flesh on my leg pulled more painfully than ever.

Beside me, two mermaids slammed into each other. A red-eyed, seaweed-skinned Lysi grabbed my assailant by the throat and pushed her away with enough strength to send the mermaid toppling onto her back. She righted herself quickly, screeching. They charged each other with a sound like two rams colliding, each looking like she was attempting to snap the other's neck. Lysi pushed the other mermaid back so hard she skidded halfway across the bloody deck.

Again the mermaid charged Lysi, and again they slammed into each other with a resounding crack. But once more, they gripped each other's throats for only a moment before Lysi threw her back.

The other mermaid collapsed on the deck with a roar of frustration. She tried once more, but her attack was feeble—and at last she cowered. She bared her pointed teeth and made a low hissing sound at Lysi, all the while slinking back towards the railing.

My breathing came out in sobs. I thought I might throw up, or pass out.

Lysi shuffled backwards to where I lay, and bent over me protectively until the other mermaid disappeared over the side of the ship. Then she looked down at me, her chest heaving. Her skin faded back to normal, though her eyes and teeth remained predatory.

She studied my bloody, twisted leg, then scanned the rest of my body before ending on my face.

"Did she break your leg?" she said quietly, still panting.

I gaped at her, unable to form words.

Around us, the ship had fallen silent. A moment passed when Lysi and I stared at each other, and I saw comprehension dawn on her face as my heartbeat ground to a halt. Everyone had seen. Everyone—mermaids and humans—they all knew.

I felt dozens of shocked gazes as the surrounding warriors tried to comprehend what had just happened. We were traitors, both of us. There was no way to try and make excuses now.

At once, three mermaids lunged at us and grabbed Lysi by the arms, hauling her backwards. They dragged her across the deck, shrieking and struggling, leaving me screaming for them to stop.

They disappeared into the water. I knew screaming after her was only digging me deeper into this rut—but too much damage had already been done. I found myself gasping, trying desperately not to vomit as I stared at the place where they'd disappeared.

A high-pitched cackle sounded behind me, and the rest of the mermaids vanished.

Annith bent over me in the next second.

"Your leg," she said.

I didn't look down at it. I couldn't.

"It hurts," I said.

"I know."

She yelled for a tourniquet. Even the thought of a tourniquet made me dizzy. I might have fainted, because next I found myself being carried into the hull by several pairs of hands.

What happened to Lysi? What were the other mermaids doing to her? I choked back an onset of tears that had nothing to do with my leg.

"Give her this."

Someone forced a bitter powder into my mouth and told me to swallow.

That was when my stomach began to heave. The last thing I remembered was leaning over to vomit. Everything went black.

CHAPTER TWENTY-TWO

The Brig

I awoke more than once to a searing pain in my thigh, like someone had lit my bones on fire. Each time, I slammed a hand onto the upturned trunk beside my bed, groped for something to ease the pain, and washed down some powder with dirty water before blacking out again.

I wasn't sure how much time passed before I came fully awake. I stared at the bunk above mine, trying to envision the stabbing pains in my leg dissolving into thin air—something my mother used to tell me when I was a kid and scratched my knees playing Demon Tag.

The trick didn't work in the slightest on a laceration this big.

Light shone dimly through the window by my head, so I knew it was daytime. The stench of tar met my nose, along with a strange odour that reminded me of having the flu. The room was quiet, apart from my laboured breaths.

Then, a whisper: "Quick, she's waking up. Get her legs."

"Linoya?" My voice sounded like a toad.

I was met with silence, at first.

"Linoya's dead," said the voice. "So is Zarra."

Texas' face appeared in front of mine. She crossed her arms and glared down at me. "Yet, the traitor lives."

I tried to sit up, sending a wave of pain into my leg that made me gasp. Blondie and Nora stood at my feet, hands outstretched to grab my legs.

"Looks like Nora wasn't just trying to—what did you say? Prove some pathetic loyalty?" said Texas.

I spluttered, trying to think of a defence.

Footsteps thundered down the stairs, and Annith appeared beside the girls, frantic.

"Wait," I said. "Nora?"

Nora squared her shoulders. "I was the one who saw you with that blonde rat. I knew it was just a matter of time before you slipped up and proved it to everyone."

"I thought . . ." I said, looking past them to Annith.

Annith's eyes brimmed with tears.

"You thought what?" said Texas. "You'd be able to weasel out of this?"

She nodded to Nora and Blondie.

I raised my fists. "Stay away from me. Anyone steps nearer and I'm not afraid to clobber them."

She laughed coldly. "I bet you aren't."

"Stay back!" My voice broke with panic.

Texas, Nora, and Blondie jumped on me at once, and I swung my fists without restraint. I made contact with a couple of skulls, but in no time they were carrying me up the stairs, Texas and Nora at my arms and Blondie at my legs. Annith shrieked behind them, but whatever fight she put up had no effect.

Stabbing pains shot up my leg and spots bloomed in my vision with each step they took. Any struggling brought me closer to heaving, but I thrashed anyway.

"Listen to me!" I yelled, abandoning pretence. "We're not going to fix anything with the Massacres. We need to work with the mermaids if we want freedom."

"Maybe you'd rather go live with the demons," said Texas. "We'll happily toss you in. Just say the word."

"No, Texas!" A rare note of fury shot through Annith's voice.

"Relax, bucktooth. We'll just put her in the brig with Dani."

I screamed, pulling harder against them and kicking my good leg, which connected with Blondie's shin.

"You can't put me in there! She'll kill me!"

"That's not our problem. We've only got one brig, and you're both a danger to the rest of us."

I caught a fleeting glimpse of the girls standing guard in the circle as we passed them. Blacktail stepped uncertainly towards us, before a still-screaming Annith blocked my view.

We thumped clumsily down the stairs, and by then my struggling became nothing more than feeble, exhausted writhing.

"Hold her legs still, you idiot!" shouted Texas.

Blondie made a pathetic whimpering sound. "She keeps kicking me!"

"Maybe I should help her with the legs," said Nora, grunting as I swung my hand up and cuffed her in the face.

"Leave it," said Texas. "She's only got one good leg anyw—"

I twisted my body and sent her tripping down the next step; her shoulder and the side of her face stopped her from falling when they smacked into the wall.

"Stop being so weak, Nora!" she shouted. "Hold her up properly!"

"It's not my fault, Blondie keeps pulling!"

The three of them bickered the whole way down, and I did everything I could to keep smashing them into the walls.

As we reached the bottom step, Dani stood up from her bed. Dishevelled as ever, her hair a pillow of frizz rather than its usual silky mane, she sauntered to the front of her enclosure with a nasty gleam in her eye.

"Nora, don't let go," said Texas. "Blondie, drop her legs and open the door."

"I can't without her kicking me!"

"Shut up and do it!"

Dani licked her cracked lips, her malicious eyes still fixed on me.

"Would you look what the hounds dragged in," she said, and the words came out in such a low purr, I wasn't sure anyone but me heard them over the yelling.

I kicked out as Blondie let me go, confirming her fear as I cracked her hard in the shin. She squealed like a pig.

"Ready, Nora?" said Texas.

"Wait, I—"

Annith jumped in front of us, blocking Dani's glare. She slammed her back against the bars and roared more loudly than I thought was possible from her soft-spoken mouth.

"Texas, *no!*"

Everyone shut up and gawked at her. Her eyes were wide and manic, her hair stuck to her clammy face, and her nostrils flared. I'd never in my life seen Annith look this deranged.

"You are not putting Meela in the brig with Dani," she said through gritted teeth. "Given the way Meela and Dani feel about each other, and what we all know Dani is capable of, I don't think I need to elaborate."

Dani chuckled darkly. "Oh, she'll be—"

"*Shut up, Dani!*" yelled Annith, and to my surprise, Dani shut up.

Annith paused to take a few breaths. Nobody spoke.

"We'll compromise," she said, stepping closer to us. "I know you're too thick-skulled to leave Meela in her bed— even if that's where she should be, given her state."

"So leave her down here, just not with Dani," said Blacktail. Her boots clicked down the stairs behind us. Her eyes flicked to me briefly, and they were full of confusion and some kind of mixture of distrust and pity. "Doesn't matter what she did—you're not stuffing her in with someone who . . ."

She clenched her jaw, seemingly unable to finish the sentence. She stepped between the brig and me, next to Annith. Neither of them would meet my eye.

I kept my mouth shut, feeling like anything I said would only make this worse for myself.

Texas towered over Annith and Blacktail, looking like she was nowhere near backing down. "If we don't lock her up, she's going to keep sneaking around and making plans with her demon friend. So move aside, or you'll both be next."

"She's not going anywhere if you leave her out of the brig!" said Annith. "She can't even get up the stairs on her own."

"You're outnumbered," said Nora, but her voice wavered.

Annith pointed at the stairs. "Go up and ask the other girls for their opinions! I bet none of them want Meela shoved in the brig with that mental-case, either."

"Ouch," said Dani. "That is no way to speak to your—"

"*I said shut up!*"

Texas, Nora, and Blondie exchanged a glance. They loosened their grip on me and I slid to the floor, which turned out to be ankle-deep in water. Murky with tar, it sloshed across the hull as the ship bobbed through the waves.

For a moment, I thought they were giving up, but then Texas brought a fist back and swung hard at Annith's face. I shouted, but Annith was quick. She ducked under Texas' arm and ran into her stomach like a charging bull; Texas grunted at the impact, then they both splashed into the greasy water.

"Stuff her in," shouted Texas between punches.

Annith screamed, punching Texas everywhere she could, but Texas had both height and width on Annith and soon Annith was pinned down in the water. It splashed over her face and she coughed as some of it swelled into her mouth.

I was shocked into silence, having never seen Annith like this. Then reality hit me and I pulled myself through the sludge, screaming at Texas to get off her.

Nora and Blondie picked me up by the arms and dragged me backwards. I roared, thrashing against them with everything I had.

"Get off! She could drown! Blacktail, help her!"

Blacktail had been standing back, seeming uncertain, but when she saw Texas' full weight on Annith's tiny body, something snapped, and she jumped on Texas' back.

Nora and Blondie still hauled me backwards. I glanced over my shoulder. They'd opened the door to the brig.

"No!" I yelled. "Dani's going to esc—"

Dani was already lunging for freedom. Where she planned on going, I had no idea—but we couldn't let her loose on the ship with access to crossbows and daggers.

She hadn't made it any further than the door when she smacked into Fern, who'd come running down the stairs with Sage and Holly, startled looks on their faces. Dani flew backwards into the brig and landed on the floor with a splash.

Shrieking, Holly and Sage jumped into the fray between Texas, Annith, and now Blacktail, and all I saw was a scuffle of arms and legs and soaking wet clothes.

As much as I kicked and flailed, Nora and Blondie didn't let me go. They dropped me on a bed while Fern shoved Dani back onto hers at the opposite end, each of them panting and yelling at the other. After a moment, Dani fell back, and Fern took the opportunity to flee.

I jumped from my bed and limped towards the door, but Fern leapt out and slammed it shut, sealing me inside with Dani.

I grabbed the bars, pulling as though the lock would shake open if I rattled it hard enough.

"You can't leave me in here," I shouted. Beads of sweat and water dripped down my face.

On the other side of the bars, the scrap on the floor had broken up, the girls holding Annith and Texas apart. Everyone was panting and dripping in grimy water, but the shouting had stopped.

"You're outnumbered, Annith," said Texas. "Nobody else wants that traitor sleeping in the cabin with us."

Annith struggled against Blondie and Nora, who held her in place. "You're being such a—"

"We're almost home," said Blacktail, watching Annith with her eyebrows pulled down. "She'll be okay."

Annith looked between Blacktail and Texas, then to the rest of the girls, and deflated. She seemed to realise at the same time I did that nobody else trusted me. They really did think I was in allegiance with the enemy.

"She doesn't have any weapons, right?" said Holly, barely audible. "Dani, I mean. She can't hurt Meela."

"Of course not," said Nora, face puckered like she'd just swallowed sour milk. "We don't want her dead. We just want her away from us—and away from the ocean."

I dropped my gaze to the bed they'd placed me on, and it came to my attention that they'd already set this up for me. When did this happen? How long ago did they decide they'd shove me in here?

The girls pulled Annith and Texas up the stairs. Nobody looked back.

The last one up, Sage shot a quick, terrified glance at Dani, who stared back with the type of unblinking, passive expression generally seen on dolls. The door banged closed behind them.

In the silence, I kept my eyes on the staircase, holding myself up on my elbows. Dani didn't say a word. The ship creaked around us and the water sloshed across the bottom of the hull.

I struggled to peel off my wet clothes, unwilling to let myself fester in murky seawater.

The mermaids had done serious damage in their last attack. The Bloodhound felt sluggish. How long had I been unconscious? Had the others managed to patch up all the holes?

My mind jumped to Lysi. Was she being punished? Did the other mermaids take her to Adaro? I dreaded what he might do to her.

Adaro's troops were sure to catch up to us now. And I was in a cage.

"So, what are you in for?" said Dani, breaking up my thoughts.

I glanced at her. Her cracked lips turned upwards. She hadn't moved from where Fern shoved her back on the bed. The only light in the room, a dim, flickering wall fixture, cast a yellow glow over her face.

I ignored her, staring out the window at the patchy clouds.

"Come on," she said. "If we're going to be prison mates—"

"Oh, shut up."

Holding my tongue was never my strength, and I hated listening to that fake, pouty voice of hers.

"I knew you could talk," she said. "So, why are you down here?"

I rolled my eyes. "Please. Like you don't know."

"I don't. I've been a little *incommunicado*, if you didn't notice."

"Nobody talked to you about it before we shoved you in here?"

Her jaw tightened. I wondered if Dani's crew was less trusting of her than I'd assumed.

"I . . . tried to take over your crew as captain," I said.

Dani might have been locked safely away from weapons for now, but we'd be home eventually, and she would be free again, and I didn't want to consider what would happen to me if she knew the truth. I thought of Holly, and the way she'd come trembling down the stairs after being accused of hesitating. But that was merely Dani's idea of punishment. I wondered how the people of Eriana Kwai would feel if they knew the warrior they'd invested years of time, money, and hope into decided she wanted to help the mermaids rather than kill them.

Dani let out a short laugh. "You're a bad liar, Metlaa Gaela."

I stared at her, trying to match the way she didn't blink. But my eyes got tired and I turned my head so she couldn't see them watering.

"Look what I found," she said, standing up and pulling something from under her pillow.

"I'm sincerely hoping it's your humanity."

She held up a tube about the length of my finger. A blow dart.

"It was wedged between my cot and the wall," she said airily, studying it from all angles. "I figure one of the demons dropped it and it rolled away. Still has something inside."

I automatically tensed up, but restrained myself from pulling further away from her.

"Put it down, Dani," I said, trying to sound exasperated.

She smiled wryly and looked at my fists, which had clenched around my sheets. I let go and crossed my arms.

"I think we should try it out," she said.

"Sure! Maybe you should try inhaling it."

I stole a glance at the floor behind me. Despite the pain it was sure to cause, I considered launching myself off the bed and hiding behind it.

"Or maybe I'll wait," said Dani, still sneering. "I'll do it when you're asleep. More peaceful that way, don't you think?"

Unable to stop myself, I grabbed my pillow and held it between us like a shield. "Would you just put it down?"

She laughed, a high, disconnected sound that made me queasy. "You're fun."

"You think this is fun, you psycho bitch? You like tormenting other people?"

"It's been boring down here."

"Don't blame it on the cage," I said. "You've always taken joy in others' misery."

"If that's what it looks like to you."

Still holding my pillow, I eyed her white-knuckled fist, gripped tight around the blow dart.

Dani began pacing. I followed her with my eyes, hardly allowing myself to blink as she moved in and out of the dim glow of the light fixture. Her clothes hung off her body like rags, partly because they were so dirty and worn, and partly because she was little more than a skin-draped skeleton.

She paced for a long time, all the while playing with the blow dart in her skinny fingers. I listened to her feet slosh rhythmically through the giant puddle. Her lips moved, like she was arguing with herself.

Not wanting to bring her attention back to me, I kept as motionless as I could. I still wasn't wearing any clothes, and I'd started to shiver, but I was hesitant to wriggle around to get my blanket over me. I didn't want to distract her from her trance. After what must have been an hour, I even wondered if she forgot about me.

By that time, my skin was like ice, and I couldn't bear it any longer. I reached behind me and cautiously pulled the blanket over my trembling shoulders.

Dani stopped and turned towards me, hands on her hips.

"You must have done something really terrible."

When I didn't say anything, she grinned.

"You're predictable, Meela. You've always been predictable."

"Don't pretend you know me," I said, disgusted at the idea of Dani understanding me.

"You think you've got it so figured out," she said, "what's right and what's wrong. You're determined to do the right thing even if nobody else thinks it's the right thing. Even if you're wrong."

I looped her words in my mind, trying to make sense of them. She licked her cracked lips.

"Paired with your sympathy for those undeserving savages . . . you're reckless."

"What's your point?"

"I heard you yelling up there. You want to stop the Massacres. You want to make peace with the demons rather than annihilate them."

Something in my expression made her lips turn upwards.

"You could've been the best, Meela. You're a born warrior. You shoot like me—your hand, the way you move it over the trigger, feeling its curves. Like it has a pulse, like you need to pull it while its heart beats strongest. Your shot could be dead-on, every time."

The acid in my empty stomach curdled at the way Dani caressed an invisible crossbow.

"So why am I not the best?" I said. "If I'm such a natural killer, according to you."

"Because you *chose* not to be. You chose to be weak, to let your soft conscience get in the way."

She raised a fist and stared at something invisible hanging from it, as though reminiscing about the tiny form she'd slaughtered days ago.

"Don't talk to me about conscience, Dani."

She dropped her fist. "Why? Because you're too pig-headed to admit I'm the best? I'm the model warrior, Meela. I know what comes first—what my purpose is—and I won't let weakness get in the way."

"Model warrior? You're out of control! You shot an iron bolt through—"

With a speed I'd only seen in mermaids, Dani spun to face me and lifted the blow dart to her lips. I gasped and ducked behind my pillow. But Dani only gave a low, cold laugh.

"Don't piss me off, Meela."

I didn't say anything else, and Dani lowered the blow dart.

"You pitied one of the demons, didn't you? That's why you're down here. She was dying in front of your idealistic eyes. And rather than shoot her in the face . . ." She pointed the blow dart at the wall, closing a bloodshot eye as though aiming at an invisible target. "You saved her."

"You're wrong."

No, that wasn't why I'd been stuffed in the brig. So why did my blood feel cold all of a sudden? Why did it feel like she'd struck another bull's-eye in the middle of my chest?

"Why are you so trusting?" she said, eyeing me like she could smell my dread. "You'll bleed yourself out for anyone. And now you've bled yourself out for a sea rat."

"You don't know anything about mermaids," I said. "You can't hope to understand them because you'd sooner stab someone in the back than trust them."

"So you admit it, then?"

"I admit to being more human than you. I admit I'll never be your sick version of a warrior."

"How touching."

"Whatever noble qualities you think you have, I'd sooner die than become anything like you. An admirable warrior doesn't murder her—"

"Stop it!" she shouted, making me jump. She stepped forwards so her clammy face became more visible in the dim light. "I didn't mean to do it! I didn't mean to kill her!"

I opened and closed my mouth, tightening my grip on the pillow.

"Well, you did," I said, feeling as reckless as she had accused me of being. "Shaena's dead, and it's because of your determination to be a *model warrior.* When you ditched all compassion at the bottom of the ocean, you lost with it the ability to tell the difference between your targets."

Her face contorted, reminding me of the day she'd murdered Shaena. She looked like someone had run her stomach through with a dagger, and yet her brow furrowed, as if offended I'd brought up the subject.

"You don't think I regret killing my best friend?"

"Was she your best friend, Dani? Or just another of your followers?"

"She meant something to me!"

"If she meant something to you, you would've fought to the death for her, not shot a bolt through her heart!"

"I said *stop!*"

She clapped her hands over her ears, still holding the blow dart between her fingers.

Her chest heaved, and she stood for a long time with her skull locked in a vice between her hands.

"You really think the path you chose is something we should all strive for?" I said, certain she could hear me when her eyes found mine.

She dropped her hands, fists clenched. "Shaena's accident was a nasty side effect of the ultimate goal. In the end it's all going to be worth it. Once I get home, and my father knows how many demons—"

She squinted at her submerged feet, then abruptly resumed pacing through the water, as though our conversation had never happened.

I said nothing more. She was a lost cause if she thought Shaena's death was an accident—a sacrifice, even, for the overall Massacre.

If being the perfect warrior meant ridding myself of all compassion, and not caring who or what I harmed, then I decided I didn't care if I was the worst warrior in the world.

After what felt like an hour, Dani sat on her cot and leaned against the wall, staring blankly across the darkening hull. I stayed facing her, perfectly still and painfully uncomfortable, flashes of pain shooting through my leg.

The night passed slowly and we didn't say another word to each other. Dani's bony fingers looked like they'd need to be shattered with a chisel in order to pry them away from the blow dart. Her expression never changed. I wondered if she'd fallen asleep with her eyes open.

I watched the waves roll by through the small window over her head, vaguely surprised when the sky began to lighten. I'd stayed awake all night.

When the door at the top of the stairs opened, Dani abruptly shoved the blow dart under her pillow and folded her hands in her lap, feigning innocence like a misbehaved child.

Holly descended carrying two plates. Keeping an arm's length away from the brig, she held one out to Dani, whose unblinking gaze made the plate rattle in Holly's hand.

When my turn came, she took a hesitant step forwards, offering me the plate with downcast eyes.

I wanted to scream, "Don't leave me!" and hold her by the pant leg so she'd stay in the hull with me. Should I tell her about the weapon under Dani's pillow? Would she care?

"Holly, can you get Annith—" I said, but she mumbled something unintelligible about fish bones and before I could say, "Wait!" she had fled back up the stairs.

After a minute of staring after her, I looked down at my plate. Cabbage. There was no steam coming off of it, which led me to believe it'd been dumped straight from a jar and unheated.

I wasn't hungry, anyway.

Dani was eerily silent. I glanced over. She'd fallen asleep, finally, slumped over on the bed, plate tipping sideways off her lap. I supposed even insane people had to get shut-eye, eventually.

Annith came down the stairs shortly thereafter carrying some clothes, an enormous stack of gauze, and a tensor bandage. She opened the brig quietly, keeping her eyes on Dani, and stuck her arm through the bars to lock it behind her. She sat at the foot of my bed.

"I should replace the bandage you have on," she said, keeping her eyes on the covers. Her cheek was almost black with bruising, a bloody patch of gauze taped across the whole left side of her neck.

"Annith—"

"We slipped some Ravendust in her breakfast," she said, still not lifting her eyes. "She won't be able to bother you. We're almost home, anyway."

I looked at Dani, and suddenly it made sense. My heart swelled for the frail, battle-worn girl sitting in front of me. And the other girls . . . maybe a glimmer of trust was still there.

"Annith," I said again. "I'm really sorry. I thought you—"

"I would never have told the others about that mermaid. Even if I don't understand what happened, or why you wanted to save her, I still wouldn't betray you."

"But why didn't you defend me? When Texas accused me the first time?"

"I didn't know what to say! I . . . I was afraid I'd say the wrong thing if I tried to defend you. Make it worse."

I kept my eyes averted from my leg as she gingerly laid fresh gauze over it.

"You're my best friend, Meela. I'd never want to hurt you." Her whole body shook as she broke into tears. "W-we're almost home," she said, hardly understandable beneath her trembling voice. "We're s-so close. They w-won't have enough time to attack us again. You'll be in proper hospital c-care soon."

I reached out and squeezed her hand, which she somehow kept steady as she worked.

"This isn't r-right. I'm s-sorry you're down here."

"Stop. Please."

She inhaled deeply and held in the next sob.

"You're my best friend too, Annith. I'm sorry for getting mad at you for joining Dani's crew. You—"

"But you were right about her!" she said squeakily. "You tried to tell me and I totally—"

"Listen," I said. "We're all scared. You joined her crew like everyone else because you wanted guidance. I understand. Let's forget it now, all right?"

She nodded once and sniffled loudly. We were quiet as she finished wrapping my leg and helped me get dressed.

Her promise that we'd be home soon did nothing to calm me. In fact, it made me more nervous, because nobody but me realised Adaro's entire army was on its way. We were close to home, but we weren't finished yet.

"Annith, I need to tell you—"

"We can't forget this," she said. She plucked the copper badge off my dirty clothes. The saw-whet owl glowered up at me, blue-green in colour after weeks of being sprayed by salt water.

She leaned forwards and pinned it to my chest.

"The other girls will come around. You're brave, Meela. You deserve to wear this proudly."

"You don't think I'm a traitor?" I whispered, studying her freckled face.

"Not a traitor. A warrior who stands up for what she believes in." She held out her crossbow. "Hide it. It's best if you have one, just in case."

I stared at its worn grips and frayed sinew. "But—"

"I'll grab another one. No one will notice. It's fine."

She stuffed it beneath my pillow. I smiled grimly and opened my arms. "Thanks."

She leaned forwards and we hugged each other for a long time.

"There's something you need to know," I said seriously. "We aren't done. If we're attacked again, you need to let me and Dani help—"

Something smashed against the hull, making us both jump.

We looked at each other. The sound came again, like someone was bashing a stone into the hull. Above deck, Sage let out a bloodcurdling scream.

Annith cursed and leapt to her feet.

"Here," I yelled, pulling the crossbow from under my pillow. I thrust it at her, but she didn't take it.

"You might need it," she said, and hurtled up the stairs, leaving me screaming after her.

"You need to take it! Please!"

I couldn't forget what'd happened to me when I ran up the stairs without a crossbow. A second without a weapon aboard this ship could be suicide.

"At least let me out to fight," I shouted.

"You'll be safer locked behind iron!"

At the top of the stairs, the door slammed.

"*Annith!*"

But she didn't come back. She left me, panicked, in the dead-silent hull.

The ship shuddered and I grabbed my bed. Dani fell sideways on her cot but didn't stir.

The number of mermaids crashing above and around me was inconceivable. The ship shuddered and rocked, and so many screams filled the air it was like the roar of an enormous crowd.

Annith, Blacktail, Holly, Fern, Sage, Texas, Blondie, and Nora.

Only eight girls remained above deck to battle. And that number of mermaids swarming us could only mean one thing: this was Adaro's last, desperate attempt to slaughter the Massacre warriors of Eriana Kwai.

CHAPTER TWENTY-THREE

Brig to Brine

Listening to the battle above my head was worse than being in the heart of it. On all sides, I heard only the roaring mob and the thundering hailstorm of attackers. Twice, I swore I heard the gurgling sound of someone being impaled.

I was at the brig door, my arm through the bars and an iron bolt in my hand. I couldn't bear to sit still while my crewmates screamed above me, so I'd limped across the floor to pick at the lock with the end of the bolt. I'd never picked a lock before, but I was sure I could figure it out. Tanuu used to talk about pushing the pins on the inside.

Minutes passed. Valuable time, wasted. Frustration pulled at my nerves for every second I spent stuck behind the bars, unable to help my crew fight. Only eight girls were up there, facing who-knew-how-many mermaids.

The bolt was too thick. I hurled it at my bed; it bounced off the side and splashed onto the floor. I needed something thinner. I ran my hands over my hips where my tool belt should have been, feeling naked without it.

Dani was still lying unconscious on her bed. That blow dart would be under her pillow.

Balancing myself with the iron bars, I limped over. The Ravendust meant she wouldn't waken, but I still held my breath and took extra care as I lifted her pillow. I couldn't hear her shallow breathing over the clamour around me, though her ribcage rose and fell beneath her bloodstained coat. She'd slumped over and I thankfully couldn't see her face.

The blow dart lay against the sheets like an innocent toy. I turned it upright, shaking its contents into my hand. A needle-like piece of calcified seaweed slid out. The tip was sharp enough to break skin at the lightest touch.

Something heavy smashed into the deck above my head. I started and looked up. Somebody screamed, but I couldn't tell who it was.

With the calcified seaweed clutched in my fist, I limped back to the brig door. I jammed it inside the lock. The seaweed gave me such precision, I poked around for mere seconds when –

Pop.

I froze. I'd done it. That was the sound of the lock opening; I was sure of it.

But then the door to the hull crashed open, and the sound of the battle flooded down the stairs. Holly was yelling. The thumping sound that came next could only mean one thing.

I abandoned the piece of seaweed in the lock and dove for my bed, where my crossbow lay on the pillow. I tipped off-balance as I seized it and landed on the floor with a splash. The greasy puddle did nothing to soften the impact.

A spear punctured the back wall. I cranked the lever and my stomach flopped. I'd lost the bolt. I'd thrown my only one. Our remaining ammo—and I only saw one unopened barrel left—was on the other side of the iron bars.

I glanced to the opposite end of the brig, where Dani lay unconscious. Without thinking about it, I swiped the blanket from my cot and lunged for her. I threw it over her body, hiding her from view, just as a mermaid propelled herself down the stairs without restraint.

The mermaid hit the bottom and straightened up with alarming speed. One webbed hand clenched a fistful of spears the length of my arm. A seaweed bandana encircled her head, holding her dark brown hair away from her blazing eyes. Her glare locked on me as I scrambled backwards on my hands. After a moment of apparent surprise, her lips curled back in a snarl.

I scanned the floor around my bed frantically. Where did the bolt land? I couldn't see beneath the layer of grimy water.

The mermaid was at the brig door, then. She studied each bar, hunting for a way past the iron.

Not taking my eyes off the demon's webbed hands, I wrapped my fist around a leg of my bed and threw it on its side like a shield between us. My pillow fell into the water and cold swells splashed over my lap.

Something thundered on the stairs again. Screams and roars and whizzing bolts flooded through the open door. I looked up to see more demons joining us. The one with the bandana glanced over her shoulder and cackled at the others. When they saw me, they sneered. They studied the brig, trying to find a way in.

Cursing, I ducked down and groped blindly for my only bolt. *You can still take them,* I thought. But I didn't know how I'd be able to kill several demons with one bolt.

Why hadn't they thrown something through the bars? They all had weapons. I couldn't believe their stupidity.

The mermaids stopped cackling. I snapped my head up. They were studying the lock I'd picked. One of them—a head shorter than the rest and probably no older than thirteen—pointed at it. They considered it, purring to each other.

Don't push on it, I thought desperately. My hands still swept frantically through the puddle.

The mermaid with the bandana curled her lips back, red eyes meeting mine. She gently leaned one of her long spears against the lock.

The door swung open.

Iron. Just find iron. Anything to throw at them.

Abandoning the hunt for my bolt, I raised my crossbow and smashed it down on one of the bed legs. A screw popped. I put my feet on the underside of the bed and wrenched the leg, biting my tongue at the pain in my thigh. The iron leg snapped off and my bed scooted forwards through the water.

I jammed the bed leg into my crossbow where the bolt should go. It fit awkwardly, but already the mermaid with the bandana entered the brig. Rolling onto my knees, I flung the bow upwards with my finger on the trigger.

The mermaid slammed her hands against the mattress, knocking the bed into me. I toppled backwards and hit the floor, but I kept my crossbow aimed at her torso and fired. The bed leg struck her in the stomach and sent her flying.

She spluttered, her flesh sizzling as she hit the bars of the brig behind her.

I crawled to the other side of the bed and smashed a second leg, just as a hand wrapped around my hair and jerked my head sideways. My scream echoed through the hull. I swiped the crossbow over my head to dislodge the mermaid's grip.

She let go before it made contact, and I heaved myself backwards through the water. Something hard knocked against my wrist. My fingers closed over it. *The bolt.* I rolled over and jammed it into my crossbow.

The mermaid came at me again and I fired. The bolt pierced her heart, killing her instantly. But another mermaid was already entering the brig behind her. She swung a piece of splintered wood, knocking my bed aside.

Drenched and grimy, I swiped my crossbow wildly in front of me, keeping her at bay as I scrambled to my feet. I needed to get that other bed leg.

The mermaid stabbed the wood splinter at my legs and I leapt back against the wall, grunting at the pain. Behind her, another demon gripped a spear, waiting.

Something was wrong. Something wasn't right in the way these mermaids fought. The mermaid slashed her weapon downwards to disarm me rather than thrusting it forwards to kill me. The wood splinter hit my wrist and I gasped, but held tight to the crossbow.

The way the light flickered across the grimy water caught my eye; I glanced up to the burnt-down candle by my head.

I spun and brought the end of my crossbow down, smashing the iron fixture loose from the wall. It cracked away and I wrenched it off, a piece of wood still nailed to it.

The mermaid struck me across the knees with her spear. Pain shot up my legs and I hit the ground, the sconce still clutched in my fist. I launched it at her head. She screeched and ducked, but not before the iron swiped her across the cheek.

Using the chance, I dove to my overturned bed, grabbed the loosened leg, and stuffed it against the crossbow's sinew, my finger already pulling at the trigger. A rock hit me in the stomach and I fell back, winded. The sinew snapped and the bed leg buried itself in the ceiling.

I stared numbly at the end of my broken weapon. Three demons closed in on me, and more waited outside the brig, watching us tensely. How many were there?

The mermaid with the wood splinter smashed my wrist again, and this time my crossbow hit the wall and splashed to the floor. Gasping for breath, I lunged for it. My fingers closed around the stock just as the demon tried to shove it away with her spear. She hissed and jumped back, reacting before I could swing it at her.

There were too many of them. They seemed to fill the hull—I counted six demons, all with harpoons and spears and blow darts. One held her burned cheek where I'd swiped it. Two more lay dead.

My heart seemed to grind to a halt as I realised my head could easily be skewered by any one of these demons before my next breath.

But it wasn't. They didn't kill me. The sudden thought occurred to me that they wanted to capture me alive.

Wheezing, I glanced around frantically for an escape. They wouldn't have me. Maybe they wanted me alive so they could torture me.

I kept my crossbow wielded, challenging them to come closer. They hissed, but held their distance. Dani still lay opposite me, unnoticed under my blanket. My eyes darted over the walls and landed on the window out of which I'd gazed all night. It was small, but the menu aboard the Bloodhound hadn't exactly helped me keep weight on. Beyond it, the sea thrashed, perilous as ever.

I leapt to my feet and slammed the end of my crossbow into the window. The glass shattered dully, the sound masked by the battle around us.

The mermaids shrieked. Cold fingers wrapped around my arm. I roared and swung my crossbow, and the fingers fell away.

I reached for the windowsill but realised I wouldn't get through as long as I was holding my crossbow. So I turned and hurled it at the mermaids. They jumped back, screeching. I thought maybe the iron hit one of them but I didn't pause to watch. I locked my fingers on the sill, put my foot on my bed, and pushed myself up.

My legs swung wildly as I squeezed through the tiny hole. I pushed my feet against the wall, scrambling upwards. Shards of glass sliced into my skin—but the ocean spray hit my face, and the fresh sea air felt blissful in my lungs, and the sensation masked all the pain in my body.

Cold, hard arms wrapped around my knees and I cried out, refusing to let go of the ledge. I pulled and kicked, using the demon's bony shoulder to push myself further through the hole. I ignored how the glass opened long tears in my shirt, how it dragged clean, stinging cuts all the way down my arms. My shoulders were almost through. I could fit, if I just . . .

I stomped against her shoulder again, pushing my ribcage past the threshold. Waves hammered against the ship, drenching my face and hair, and I welcomed them.

But more hands wrapped around my legs. They pulled me back. I clawed at the outside of the ship, screaming and kicking wildly. My foot smashed into something soft, but not one hand let go.

They pulled me away from the sounds of battle above deck. I slipped backwards through the window. Still, I screamed and clawed at the rough, broken hull of the Bloodhound. My fingers locked into any grooves I could find, but my strength was nothing next to the demons.

Glass sliced my arms open, stinging like venom. And then I was back in the hull, smelling tar and blood and burnt flesh, and my nails were all that held me to the ledge. I screamed for help, not even sure who I was screaming to.

My fingers gave way and I fell hard on my hands. My neck snapped back as I hit the floor, top-heavy with the mermaids still holding my ankles. The greasy water engulfed my face and I instinctively thrashed around to right myself.

My feet came down a moment later. I rolled over and sat up, gasping.

I couldn't see; the murky water had gotten in my eyes. Blurry shapes moved in front of me, and I spluttered as I tried to stand. Something pushed me back down. The shape nearest to me became clearer. The mermaid I'd scorched on the cheek held her spear over my chest, the tip pushed against my soaking wet shirt.

Again they could run me through with a dozen weapons before I blinked. But again, they didn't. They held their weapons steady.

Then a scream filled the hull that made the blood leave my face in a cold, dizzying rush.

"*Meela!*"

Lysi's bloodcurdling cry seemed to come from all directions—through the broken window, or from somewhere above deck—and the mermaids surrounding me erupted in a chorus of cackling sounds.

I expected them to be alarmed. I expected—hoped, maybe—they'd want to go help their comrade.

They sneered at me.

"What are you doing to her?" I yelled, my voice high with panic.

The mermaids stopped cackling, and I caught a glimmer of satisfaction behind their blazing eyes.

The tiny mermaid opened her mouth, revealing long, predatory teeth. "You . . . want to see her."

Her accent was heavy and her speech broken, but I understood what she said.

"You speak Eriana?" I said, breathing hard. "Where's Lysi?"

"Adaro," she said, her voice a purr.

"Adaro? He's here?"

She stared at me, her expression unreadable.

"You came here to take me to him," I said, suddenly understanding why they wouldn't kill me.

The small mermaid sneered, then made a high sound to the others before turning back to the stairs.

They swarmed me, and I let them. A pair of icy arms wrapped around my ankles, and another around my arms.

If Adaro was here I had to try and negotiate peace, or this attack was going to leave the Bloodhound at the bottom of the ocean.

We left Dani lying undiscovered, untouched, on her bed.

An excruciating pain surged back to my attention as the demons carried me up the stairs. I must have ripped the stitches in my leg.

We burst from the hull and into a buzzing swarm. I expected to see a battle still raging, but all I saw were demons.

Where was my crew? I strained to see through the horde surrounding me. Were they dead? Had they been pulled into the water? I wanted to scream to them, but I was too dumbstruck to make any noise.

Dark clouds swirled over our heads, the cold wind cutting into my bones. The metallic smell of blood penetrated my nose, nauseating me as it mixed with seawater and fish.

Lysi was silent, though her scream still resonated. What were they doing to her?

Someone shouted not far from us, and the mermaid holding my arms ducked to avoid a flying bolt.

My surrounding guards screeched, turning to face their attacker.

Fern's hysterical voice cut through the noise of the hissing mermaids. "Don't shoot! Meela's in there!"

"Fern!" I shouted, finding my voice.

My view of the deck opened up, and the sight brought a cry to my lips.

Texas, Holly, and Fern had backed into the opposite stairwell, their faces bloody, crossbows aimed to block the demons from coming any further. They panted hard, and when they caught my eye, I saw mixed terror and bewilderment.

Two human bodies lay in front of them, sprawled among a sheet of dead mermaids.

"No!" I thrashed against the mermaids holding me, until something rock-hard smashed into my skull.

"Be still," said the small mermaid, baring her jagged teeth.

I blinked away dizziness as they carried me to the railing, tearing me further away from my crew. Whose bodies were those? Where was Annith?

From the water below, Lysi screamed. I heard a frenzy of splashing.

"Meela! I tried to stop—"

Her voice was interrupted by gurgling: someone had pushed her underwater.

I tried to squirm away from the mermaids' slimy grips, but the small one pressed a hand against my throat until I stopped moving.

Lysi's voice came again. "They want to bring you to Adaro and—let go of me!—he wants to talk to you—"

I jerked my head away from the mermaid's grip. "Why?"

Around me, the fighting had stopped, leaving the deck in unnerving silence. A low growling sound came from the mermaids behind us. They stayed cautiously back from the girls in the stairwell.

"It's my f—" Again, the water swallowed her words.

"Because of us?" I yelled, but she didn't answer.

The reality of the battle stung my eyes as I took in the army around me, remembering what Lysi had said about Adaro pulling trainees early. There were dozens of mermaids like the ones we'd always fought, but also young ones, tiny ones whose skin had barely transformed and whose teeth could barely snarl. Children. Many of them were seared from the iron-flecked ship they'd been ordered to destroy.

The thought of the two human bodies on the deck constricted my lungs until I was left gasping.

"I'll go in," I said to the small mermaid. "Please stop. Don't kill my crew."

From across the deck, Holly shouted before I'd finished the sentence. "Meela, no!"

I turned my gaze to see the mermaid closest to the stairwell collapse in her own blood. Before anyone knew what'd happened, Holly made a desperate lunge towards my surrounding guard. I watched in mute horror as she aimed her crossbow at the demon holding my legs.

I wanted to scream for Holly to stop, but already a bolt met the mermaid's chest with a sickening squelch.

She retched and fell forwards, letting go of my ankles. The horde around me erupted in a frenzy. The mermaid by my head lifted an arm, a harpoon gripped in her webbed fist.

"Don't!" I screamed.

The mermaid's blood-red eyes burned into Holly. Her arm moved in a blur.

Holly lurched as the harpoon drove through her stomach.

She collapsed on her knees, and my senses numbed. I was paralyzed. A demon closed in on her. I only caught a fleeting glimpse of the demon's webbed fingers wrapping around Holly's neck, and then the mermaids spun me roughly around so I faced the water.

I vaguely realised I was standing on my own, trembling, and they'd let go of my limbs.

"More die next," said the small one in her high, purring voice. The sound seemed to come at me through a tunnel.

Before I could think about it, I put my hands on the railing and pulled myself up.

I thought I heard someone yell for me to stop, but I couldn't be sure. It didn't matter, anyway, because nothing was going to stop me. Nobody else was going to die on this Massacre.

I didn't look back at my crew, cornered in the stairwell with nowhere to flee. Without hesitating, I pushed myself over the railing and fell headfirst into the black water.

CHAPTER TWENTY-FOUR

Adaro's Request

I had no time to suck in a breath of air before the ocean swallowed me in its freezing mouth. The water burned and my lungs deflated, like someone had stabbed a dagger through my ribs. I kept my eyes closed, knowing I would only see blackness if I opened them.

I paddled blindly until a hand closed around my arm and dragged me forwards. Which direction was it? My lungs begged for the surface, already exhausted. I wouldn't last long.

I forced my eyes open. The faintly bright sky beckoned me from overhead, and the mermaid pulled me towards it. I was too desperate to care that we also angled away from the Bloodhound.

We broke the surface and my arms thrashed, trying to keep me afloat as I gasped life back into my lungs. More mermaids splashed into the water behind us and surfaced on all sides. I glanced at the one pulling me and saw a charred blister across her cheek. I felt no remorse for leaving it there.

Her seaweed face was puckered with hatred, and she didn't look at me as we glided smoothly through the waves.

My eyes burned, and brine scraped my throat as I wheezed each breath. We stopped far from the Bloodhound. Even if my crew wasn't cornered, they'd never be able to shoot the mermaids surrounding me.

I fixed my gaze ahead, because seeing the Bloodhound floating so far away only made my chest tighten until I thought I might suffocate. Fifty mermaids must have surrounded me—but my eyes locked on a group of them a few arms' lengths away.

Only her face and coppery hair were above the surface. The water around her thrashed like the waves in a storm. She panted, struggling in vain against four mermaids holding her in place by her arms and hair. Her eyes burned scarlet.

But the struggle was the only sound between here and the ship. Every demon was silent, as though waiting for something.

"Lysi—"

The mermaid at my arm screeched and dunked my head before I had time to draw breath.

I emerged with a mouthful of saltwater, coughing and spitting. Humiliation somehow registered, and I didn't look at her as I wiped a trembling arm across my lips. I didn't try to speak again.

The silence became absolute, like even the waves were afraid to interrupt. Lysi stopped struggling.

In the middle of the circle, something rose from the water.

A crown emerged first—all black, opaque, with half a dozen sharp prongs tapering towards the sky. It blended with the matted charcoal hair that surfaced with it, as if one grew out of the other.

I looked beneath it and found myself staring into the lurid, seaweed-coloured face of a merman.

Adaro.

His overlarge eyes, the deepest shade of burgundy, blazed more menacingly than those of the mermaids around him. He had a hard chin and a straight, square jaw; his ungroomed hair, tangled in seaweed, ended somewhere below the water. From beneath the locks sprouted a pair of long, bulbous ears.

Even in their predatory state, the mermaids resembled humans—but I couldn't say the same for Adaro. He was a reptile in the way his nose blended with his cheekbones, in how his skin rippled like scales, in his lipless mouth. A crocodile—and possibly more terrifying. His yellowed teeth were bared, his face so inhuman I couldn't discern his expression.

His webbed fingers emerged from the water and commanded us forwards. The hand on my arm tightened, and we drifted to him as though carried by the swells. Between the bone-chilling temperature of the water and the sight of the creature in front of me, my entire body trembled, each breath a gasp.

The mermaids at least gave the impression—however misleading—that a human could overcome them in a battle of strength. Nowhere in Adaro's build did he leave room for such deceit. He held himself high in the water, exposing his torso as though to emphasise that it tripled the size of mine. His arms alone were twice as thick as my legs.

We stopped close enough that he could have reached out and drowned me.

He must have said something to Lysi, because she turned and purred something in response. She breathed hard, her eyes seeming to flicker between crimson and blue, like she was caught between states. The other mermaids still held her tightly, one on each arm, one squeezing her shoulder, one with a fist in her hair.

"Meela," said Adaro. "We have much to discuss. Make yourself comfortable."

A moment passed before I realised he'd spoken to me in my own language, and another passed before I was able to process his words. He spoke with the same fluency as Lysi, though his voice was more of a growl than a purr.

I glanced at Lysi. She froze, gaping at Adaro, the shock on her face mirroring my own. When she felt my gaze, her eyes met mine—blue, now—and I saw all the regret, and apology, and tenderness in the world.

"She can't help you," said Adaro, not turning his reptilian face away from mine. "Though she may prove useful."

I battled with the waves to stay afloat, my muscles tiring. The mermaid holding me did nothing to help me stay above water.

"Our unique situation has been brought to my attention," said Adaro, "and I think we both stand to benefit from an arrangement."

"I agree," I said, forcing the sound from my gaping mouth. "But first tell your army to stop attacking my ship."

"Now, Meela, don't get ahead of yourself," said Adaro, tilting his head so his black crown pointed at the horizon. "I want an agreement before I do anything rash. Like you, I go to great lengths to protect those who are dear to me."

A wave splashed into my face and I gasped. The salt burned my nostrils.

"So let's make an agreement," I said. "You stop attacking my people; we stop sending our warriors out to your Utopia."

I spoke quickly, desperate to get the swarm of demons away from the crew I'd left behind.

Adaro's yellowed fangs became more visible, like he might have been smiling. "I'm afraid I can't do that."

"Then we'll keep massacring your army. Based on this pathetic last-ditch effort, it's only a matter of time before we win."

I had little reason to sound so confident—but he had to know my people would never surrender.

His rotten face grew tight and stony. "If I am not mistaken, this *last-ditch effort* is about to sink your ship."

I turned to watch the Bloodhound dissolve into a veil of fog. In the distance, I could still see demons clinging to the hull like leeches.

"Look at me!" said Adaro.

To spite him, I kept my eyes on the Bloodhound a second longer before turning slowly.

His expression darkened. "Your island has something I need, Meela. And you will give it to me."

I clenched my chattering teeth, processing his words.

Adaro needed something. As helpless as I felt—surrounded by demons and with one of my legs shooting pain into my abdomen at every kick—I wondered if I'd be able to bargain for my people's freedom.

I kept my voice low and challenging. "What do you need?"

"Give me Eriana."

A wave crashed over my head and submerged me. I kicked my good leg until I broke through, seething.

"You want me to give you our island?"

"Not the island. I'm speaking of your ancestor."

"Eriana is a goddess," I said, and I was surprised at the amount of venom I felt at this merman—this ugly, self-righteous sea rat—for trying to tell me about my own home.

He drew himself even taller in the water, dark hair clinging to his neck and chest. "Goddess, mortal, the details are irrelevant. Eriana discovered your island. She had a pet—though legend says it was more than a pet. It was like a spirit, a connection, fully under her control. With its unmatched power and inability to be slain, she used it to keep unwelcome visitors away from her island."

I shook my head, more to myself than at Adaro. I was a native of Eriana Kwai and I'd never heard this legend before. Wherever he'd gotten this story, it was untrue.

"Though the pet was invincible," he said, "Eriana was doomed to meet her end. Before she died, she locked it away so it would never be found. It still lies beneath the island, bound to its master and host to her soul."

I looked again towards the Bloodhound, which had become nothing but a foggy outline in the distance. I couldn't see the leeches climbing up the side anymore. Were they still fighting? How much longer would my crew last?

"There's nothing beneath the island but rock and soil," I said. "Your legend is just a story among sea rats."

Before I turned back to Adaro, I could suddenly no longer breathe. I was underwater, an icy hand holding me down like an anchor.

My lungs were about to give up when the mermaid finally released me and I emerged, gasping. Adaro's voice came from somewhere beyond my rasping breaths, a slow and menacing hiss.

"*Look – at – me.*"

I wiped my eyes and glared up at his reptilian face. My anger overpowered any fear, and all I felt was hatred. This merman had no objections about making others suffer.

"The Host of Eriana is real," he said. "I assure you, merpeople legend is much more informed than human legend."

I stared into his dark, burgundy eyes, knowing he wouldn't be fighting so hard for this Host of Eriana if he didn't wholly believe it existed.

"You need to free the Host and give it to me," he said.

"Provided it exists, why would you want it?"

"That is not your concern."

My teeth clattered violently; I swore my blood must have been turning to ice. I glanced to Lysi, my only comfort in what felt like an arctic tomb. Her eyes softened when our gazes locked.

I turned back to Adaro before he could attempt to have me drowned again.

"I'm not giving you anything without the promise that you'll leave my people alone," I said.

He laughed, a high, barking sound. "Look around. You think you have the power to negotiate with me?"

"Yes. I do."

"Then I'll kill you here and now."

"So do it," I said, and the realisation hit me as the words left my mouth. "It's what I came here for. To die fighting for my people's freedom."

As I fought against the high swells, the brine leaving me parched, the temperature forcing my muscles into convulsions, I wondered how noble a death it would be to succumb to drowning after spending weeks in battle.

Adaro revealed his fangs. "What about the life of our dear Lysithea?"

One of the mermaids reached up and ran her fingers through Lysi's hair, sneering at me. She made a fist in the coppery locks and pulled enough for me to see a flicker of pain on Lysi's face.

My heart sank, and I bit my tongue to stop myself from reacting.

"You can kill me, too," said Lysi. "Give her your promise, or you can kill both of us."

Adaro hissed at her, but said nothing. Lysi's surrounding guard drifted closer, like attack dogs waiting for a command. A lump rose in my throat. Her eyes flamed red again as she boldly faced the merman floating close enough to strangle her. I caught her eye and wished she could read my thoughts. She didn't have to do that for me. My people didn't need to matter to her.

"No one else needs to die," I said, struggling to keep my voice steady behind my chattering teeth. "Give me your word that you'll leave my people alone, and I'll do it."

Adaro thought for a minute, bobbing in the frigid waves like a piece of stiff, gnarled driftwood.

He turned and said something to Lysi. She purred back, her voice rolling and song-like next to his low growl.

Lysi looked to me uncertainly, then back to Adaro. She ducked beneath the water.

"Where are you going?" I said, but Lysi had already vanished. The mermaids surrounding her didn't follow.

"Where's she going?" I said loudly.

Adaro stared at me with emptiness in his gleaming eyes. "To tell my army to stop destroying your means of getting home. You won't be able to fulfill your end of our arrangement if you're dead."

"So—" I choked on a frothy swell. "So you'll leave my people alone?"

"Give me Eriana's Host, and my army will stop attacking your beaches."

"What about the rest of the ocean? Leave our ships alone too."

"No. The water is mine, not yours."

"Stop sinking our ships or I'm not doing it," I said.

Adaro's face hardened. "This is my final offer. Take it, or I will kill both you and Lysithea, here and now."

I glared at him, knowing I'd reached the end of my power to negotiate.

My legs were tiring. My muscles must have been hard, like meat kept in the freezer. My mouth felt scratched from the seawater I kept spitting out.

"What is the Host? How do I free it?"

"Now you think too much of me," said Adaro. "I'm a humble merman with nothing more than an incomplete story."

"What if I can't do it?"

"You are a descendant of Eriana, are you not?"

"By legend, I guess."

"Then you will be able to do it."

What did that mean? The Host needed to be freed by a native of Eriana Kwai? How was I supposed to find it if I'd never heard of it?

"But what if I can't figure out how to—"

"The sooner you do this, the better it will be for your people," he said, snapping. "I will not be so merciful should I find another of your iron-laced battleships floating over my city."

"You can—"

"Further," he said, "I will be keeping Lysithea under close watch until you succeed. Perhaps the thought of never seeing her again will motivate you."

"No!" I shouted. "I'll do it! You don't need to keep her hostage!"

Wasn't the threat of causing my people suffering enough?

I watched Adaro's hard face break into a grin. I had no doubt I was the best opportunity he'd come across in years.

"You'll give me Eriana's Host," he said, running a webbed finger along his crown.

My mind whirled. Whatever the Host was, Adaro needed it desperately. So desperately, he was willing to do whatever it took to make me get it for him.

"It's yours," I said.

Of course I'd do it. I could lose Lysi forever and let those I loved suffer—or I could find and hand over Eriana's Host. Finding the Host was my answer. This was how to gain my people's freedom back.

Lysi resurfaced next to Adaro. She looked so small next to him, like he could crush her with his hands. I had the absurd urge to try and protect her from him.

Adaro squinted in the direction of the Bloodhound, where it had disappeared into the blanket of fog. He seemed not to care that it'd sailed out of sight.

"Good. Take her back," he said, waving a webbed hand at the mermaids surrounding us. "Lysithea goes first so the humans hold their fire."

Lysi shot forwards and threw herself against me in a tight hug, keeping my head safely above water. I tried to hug her back, but my limbs felt like solid ice. I rested my head against her tangled hair, trying to clamp my jaw shut so my teeth would stop chattering in her ear. I didn't want to let her feel how hard I was shivering.

She must have sensed how much pain I was in, because she pulled back with a hint of urgency. "Let's go."

"Meela," said Adaro, his voice low and menacing, "If you try anything—if you so much as think about going back on your word—my troops will invade your beaches until every one of your people has perished."

I nodded once. If there was one absolute certainty in all this, it was that Adaro would never stop attacking my people until he won.

Lysi spun her back to me and wrapped my arms around her neck. I tried my best to hold tightly but my muscles were failing, so she held me in place by my forearms.

We were moving then, so fast I could feel the current pulling my legs back. The other mermaids trailed behind us.

Saltwater kept splashing into my mouth by the cupful, and I no longer had the strength to spit it out. The cold had become unbearable.

Lysi seemed tormented that she couldn't keep me warm. She rubbed my forearms, which was useless for warmth but made me feel better knowing she was there.

"You're blue, Mee," she said a few times, sounding panicked. "Keep moving your legs. Keep moving. You're blue."

I heard her strained breathing as she tightened her grip on my arms, holding me against her back.

"This is my fault," she said. "If he didn't know about us, he'd never have come looking for you, and he wouldn't be making you do this."

"N-no," I said. "I n-need to do this. For my people. For you. We c-can . . ."

I couldn't speak anymore. It was as though my lungs had frozen, making it too painful.

She pushed forwards harder, panting, and somehow she kept talking the entire time—telling me to kick my legs, to move my fingers and toes, to keep my eyes open. But I could no longer feel my legs, and my teeth chattered so fiercely I could barely hear her voice.

My eyelids drooped heavily. I wanted to fall asleep. The cold was like a bed of nails wrapping my body. My veins felt swollen.

Rain began to fall, and the droplets felt mild—warm, even—compared to the sea.

The clouds moved quickly overhead. Lysi's voice became a soothing hum. Sleep would come soon, and I was all right with it.

"We're here," said a distant voice.

Though I couldn't feel, I knew my knees touched something, and I tried to balance them on whatever it was. My legs wouldn't cooperate. Somehow, Lysi dragged me onto the Bloodhound, and I could hear her panting hard.

"Keep your eyes open, Mee," she said, over and over. I focused on her voice so I wouldn't succumb to the cold.

I rolled my head to the side and my eyes focused on Lysi. She was crying. One of her hands brushed my face.

"Look at me," she said. "Keep your eyes open. Move your fingers, Mee."

I could vaguely feel her hand, but the numbness had all but engulfed me.

"He won't let me stay," she said, her voice thick. "But someone's coming."

They were. I could hear them. Footsteps pounded up from the cabin. How many? Who had survived?

Lysi pressed her lips to my cheek.

"This isn't goodbye," she whispered. "I won't let him keep me away. Whatever it takes."

Something grazed my ankle.

"No!" shouted Lysi, and she hugged me tighter as something pulled her away from me.

Our hands locked together. We held on desperately as she slid further away, screaming.

I couldn't lose her. Not when I finally had her back. Not when I finally understood everything.

Three mermaids closed their webbed hands around Lysi's tail. They pulled her through the railing.

I wanted to scream at them, to dive after them with a crossbow, to hurl an iron dagger through their chests. Anything to make them stop. But my muscles failed.

"Mee," said Lysi.

I sealed the image of her sapphire eyes in my mind, determined to never forget them.

"We can't let him win."

"No," I said, and the sound was barely audible through my frozen lips. "I'm not losing you again."

She disappeared. The hollow wind and crashing waves left no evidence that she had been there.

The rain washed over me—a warm shower—and I let myself lie there like a corpse drifted ashore.

A high voice shouted right in front of me. "Meela!"

More footsteps thundered up, and someone draped a blanket over me. A hand closed around mine, searing hot.

I pried my gaze away from where Lysi had vanished, and a pair of hazel eyes bloomed into my vision.

The eyes flitted towards the ocean, then back to me. Her mouth gaped, like she was struggling not to ask a million questions at once.

Despite everything, my lips cracked into a smile.

"Annith."

CHAPTER TWENTY-FIVE

Gaawhist

I stood with Annith at the bow of the Bloodhound, watching the cliffs and shores of Eriana Kwai bloom into existence before us. The fog had thinned, and a rare glimpse of sun reflected brightly off the water.

Above our heads, we'd strung the Homecoming light to the main mast, and it flashed with bold rhythm.

One, two, one-two-three.

Did the lighthouse see us coming? Would our people be at the docks, awaiting our return?

The Bloodhound bobbed through the waves with less ferocity than when we'd left an eternity ago. The hull was flooded, the bottom bunks and all our belongings submerged. Given another day at sea, our loyal ship would have sunk.

Dani had regained consciousness—though her eyelids drooped and she looked ready to vomit—and she stood at the helm with both hands tied to the wheel. Blacktail and Fern flanked her, ensuring she stayed on her feet and fulfilled her captain's duties until the last second of the

Massacre. Fern's stuffed tabby was zipped safely inside her jacket, his dirty face poking out like a baby in a carrier. Every so often, Fern or Blacktail would jab Dani in the back to make sure she stayed alert.

Nora and Sage had been the bodies. Seven warriors had survived. Seven, out of twenty girls who'd been sent to fight for Eriana Kwai. Annith, Blacktail, Fern, Texas, Blondie, Dani, and me.

"I never realised the sea demons were so much like people," said Annith. She'd been staring at me with a dazed expression since I finished telling her about Lysi.

I pressed my lips together in a half-smile, feeling a surge of gratitude that Annith had listened with such understanding. Not once did she question why I'd befriended Lysi in the first place, or why I'd let her come back.

I pulled my blanket tighter around my shoulders, dropping my gaze to the railing in front of me. A spider ran across it, surely flooded out of a cozy home it'd found in someone's bunk. I fleetingly wondered how it managed to survive everything.

"Unbelievable," said Annith. "So you really think this King Adaro came here just to make a bargain with you?"

"This war is bigger than we know," I said. "He's building an army and looking for weapons."

"Is he trying to conquer below water too?"

"Everywhere. Once his army's big enough, I have no doubt he'll keep expanding."

Annith exhaled slowly, squinting at the approaching shore.

"Our Massacre was more successful than ever," she said. "We can totally stop him if we keep training girls—"

I shook my head. "We don't know how fast his army's growing. Besides, we need to protect the future girls of Eriana Kwai. We can't send them out to face this."

She bit her lip. "You're right."

"The Massacre isn't just about us. It's never been that small. We have to stop the problem at its root."

Annith turned and leaned against the railing. Her salt-encrusted hair thrashed across her freckled face.

"Meela, I don't like what Adaro wants you to do. You don't know what Eriana's Host is, or what it's capable of. Setting it loose could leave us worse-off."

"He wouldn't want the Host freed if it couldn't be controlled," I said.

"You think you can control it?"

"I'm going to find out how."

A seagull flew over our heads, greeting us with its cries. The land was close enough now that we could see the abandoned beachfront homes. I thought I could smell the familiar earth—but perhaps I imagined it.

"The way Adaro talked about it, it was like he needed some kind of power," I said. "He needs a native of Eriana Kwai to free it—which means I'm going to have control before he does."

"But if Adaro wants the Host, it's obviously a deadly weapon!"

"You think Adaro will stop trying to get it? If I refuse to do this, do you really think he'll give up?"

Annith opened her mouth, but no sound came out. She gave a feeble shrug.

"Exactly," I said. "He won't stop trying. He won't stop attacking us."

And the Massacres would live on, and our people would continue to starve, and children would continue to get snatched off the beach, and . . .

"The Aleut people," I said abruptly, facing her.

"What?"

"This is why they still live in the Arc. This is why they never had to flee. Annith, this is why Adaro targeted our people—why mermaids have been attacking us on land. He wanted us off the island."

Her eyes widened. "You think the Host was his target from the beginning?"

"I'm sure of it. Adaro knew he'd never be able to find it if our people were waiting there to shoot him. So he decided to kill all of us, or scare us off the island."

"Until a better option came along."

"Right. He's making one of the people of Eriana Kwai do it for him."

Annith slumped. "So to stop him from attacking us, our only choice is to hand over the Host."

I turned back to the water, feeling my lips curl into a snarl. "You're missing the point. I said I'd free her, but I never said I'd hand her over."

"So what are you going to do?"

"I'll find and free Eriana's Host. But it's mine."

I wouldn't let Adaro win. To give him the Host of Eriana would be to hand over a part of my people's history. To betray them.

I clenched my fists around the battered railing. "I'll free the Host, and wait for Adaro to show up with Lysi. And then I'm going to kill him."

The waves glistened as we approached Eriana Kwai. Beyond the water, I could see every tree, every rock, the windows in the lighthouse, the roots sprouting from the cliffs overlooking the sea.

Gaawhist, I thought. *Home, sweet home.*

"You'll help me?" I said, not taking my eyes away from the beautiful island before us.

Annith put an arm around my shoulders.

"For Eriana Kwai," she said. "We'll make sure this Massacre was the last."

"For Eriana Kwai."

And for Lysi, I thought.

I ran my hand along the chipped railing, as though saying thanks to the ruined ship beneath us.

I would see Lysi again soon. It was my only option. I refused to let Adaro take her from me forever.

My people came into view. The enormous crowd had gathered near the shore, and more still flocked to the spectator's hill. Tears sprung into my eyes. My parents would be in there waiting for me.

The toll of the Homecoming bell carried across the water, signalling our return.

My legs moved, though my brain didn't control them. The world felt distant and blurry. I barely noticed the men jump onto the dock to help us moor, and the gangplank extend to form a bridge between my crew and my people.

I didn't use the gangplank. I leapt over the railing and landed easily on the wooden dock. Nothing mattered but the two faces at the shoreline—vacant, shocked, as though not believing who sprinted towards them with tears spilling down her face.

My mother wept as I threw myself against her, and my father had to hold us so I didn't knock her backwards.

"I'm home," I said, over and over.

My body trembled; the steady ground left me nauseated and unbalanced.

My father's strong arms wrapped around both of us, and for the first time in weeks, I felt warm. I inhaled the smell of the earth, of maple and bannock, of wood shavings, and my heart ached with a whole month of homesickness.

I opened my eyes to tears streaking my father's cheeks—and a smile pulling at his lips.

Past his shoulder, a dark face stared at me, stark white teeth jumping out in something between a gawk and a grin.

"Tanuu," I said, choking on the word.

My parents let me go and I threw my arms around Tanuu. I'd survived the Massacre, like he said I would.

The Homecoming bell stopped tolling, the sound giving way to the murmuring crowd around us.

Our return was bittersweet, and I kept my eyes away from the other families. Our Massacre would be called a success, but we'd lost too many lives. Too many warriors had been taken, too many mermaids slaughtered. Our approach was wrong. I needed to stop the future Massacres from happening.

I'd always been right to trust Lysi. And she was right that I didn't have to choose between her and Eriana Kwai. I knew it as much as I felt it: together, we could make peace between humans and merpeople.

I closed my eyes, and Lysi's face swam into my vision. The longer I stayed there in Tanuu's arms, the stronger the image became of Lysi's long, coppery hair, her glistening skin, and her sapphire eyes. I could still feel her cold lips on my cheek.

An unmistakable rush swelled in my chest. I hadn't felt it since I was ten years old on the beach.

Even if freeing Eriana's Host didn't grant freedom for my people—even if it only guaranteed Lysi's return to me—I'd do it anyway. I'd do whatever it took to be with Lysi again.

But why? I thought. *Why would you risk everything? Why not leave her to her fate?*

Adaro had known before I could admit it to myself, and that was why he took her from me. But my heart felt swollen, and I finally *just knew*. It was as obvious as if I'd known it my whole life.

I was in love with a mermaid.

Also by Tiana Warner

Continue Meela and Lysi's journey in book two of the
Mermaids of Eriana Kwai trilogy.

tianawarner.com/books/ice-crypt

An Ice Massacre Graphic Novel

Ice Massacre is now an award-winning comic!
Read it online and learn more at:

mermaidhuntress.com

Note from the author

Thank you for reading Ice Massacre and supporting an indie author. If you enjoyed Meela and Lysi's story, please consider spreading the word and reviewing it online.

To stay up to date with new releases, exciting announcements, and giveaways, please sign up for my newsletter!

tianawarner.com

www.ingramcontent.com/pod-product-compliance
Lightning Source LLC
Chambersburg PA
CBHW021224060726
47590CB00005B/1624